Wedding Wagers

Wedding Wagers

Donna Hatch
Heather B. Moore
Michele Paige Holmes

Copyright © 2019 Mirror Press
Print edition
All rights reserved

No part of this book may be reproduced in any form whatsoever without prior written permission of the publisher, except in the case of brief passages embodied in critical reviews and articles. These novels are works of fiction. The characters, names, incidents, places, and dialog are products of the authors' imaginations and are not to be construed as real.

Interior Design by Cora Johnson
Edited by Cassidy Skousen, Kristy Stewart, Tracy Daley, and Lisa Shepherd
Cover design by Rachael Anderson
Cover Photo Credit: Period Images

Published by Mirror Press, LLC
ISBN: 978-1-947152-78-6

TABLE OF CONTENTS

A Wager on Love by Donna Hatch _____ 1

The Final Wager by Heather B. Moore _____ 127

An Improbable Wager by Michele Paige Holmes _____ 247

Other Timeless Regency Collections

Autumn Masquerade
A Midwinter Ball
Spring in Hyde Park
Summer House Party
A Country Christmas
A Season in London
A Holiday in Bath
A Night in Grosvenor Square
Road to Gretna Green
Wedding Wagers
An Evening at Almack's
A Week in Brighton
To Love a Governess

A Wager on Love

-Donna Hatch-

One

Growing up the son of a duke had provided a few advantages, but being the brother of a duke came with definite challenges—especially if that brother was the famed Duke of Suttenberg, one of the most respected men in England and therefore every season's most eligible bachelor, a paragon. Still, Phillip was nothing if not optimistic. Surely some young lady with discerning taste would view Phillip as every bit as desirable.

Phillip attempted to smile at the young lady twittering about how very pleased she was to meet him, but she never once looked him in the eye. Which was a shame, really, because she missed out on his handsome face and the dimple that so many women found irresistible.

"... hear you are an excellent dancer, Your Grace, and—"

Of course. Phillip should have known. He held up a hand to stop the chatter. "Pardon me, but it seems you have me confused with my brother."

"... and I absolutely adore dancing ... what?" She blinked, looking at him for the first time.

"I am Phillip Partridge, the duke's brother."

Honestly, if one more girl threw herself at Phillip because

she wanted to be part of the Suttenberg ducal family—or because she mistook him for the duke, rather than because of the good looks and charm Phillip possessed in spades—he would put out an eye.

Since he had no desire to start sporting an eye patch—not that he couldn't pull it off with style, but it sounded deuced painful—he managed a polite, curt bow and left before she asked him to introduce her to his so-much-more-eligible brother, the one with the title.

Looking over the heads in the ballroom, he spotted Michael Cavenleigh's blond hair in the crowd. Phillip threaded through scores of ladies scented like flowers, dressed in cream or white silk, and flirting with gentlemen in brocade and superfine who would rather be at a card table.

Upon reaching his friend's side, Phillip jerked his head toward the door. "I believe I'll accept Tristan Barrett's invitation to visit Vauxhall Gardens."

Michael lifted a brow.

"It's fine weather for an outdoor lark." Did he sound desperate?

A corner of Michael's lip twitched. His normally taciturn friend seemed even less talkative than usual tonight, but that smirk revealed his awareness of Phillip's decision to make a strategic retreat.

Phillip tried again. "Barrett desires several gentlemen present—something about making sure there are enough male prospects for all the young ladies he has invited. Care to join me?" Not that Phillip had given the outing much thought until now, mind you.

A small huff that might have been a suppressed laugh escaped Michael's lips. With a glance at the young lady who'd been batting her eyelashes at him, Michael bowed his head. "It seems I am needed elsewhere. Good evening."

Phillip made a note to express his gratitude to his friend. For now, he contented himself with calling for his carriage.

"And where do you think you are going, young man?" His mother stood with all the dignity and authority of a duchess, for obvious reasons, and glared at him, also for obvious reasons.

Phillip inclined his head in a loose bow to the duchess. "Good evening, Mother."

"Don't you 'good evening' me. You promised you'd be attentive tonight." She snapped her fan shut and pointed it at him as though she were a foot taller than him rather than the other way around. How such a diminutive lady could be so commanding remained a mystery.

Phillip put on his most conciliatory smile. "I danced a set." And fended off three girls who implied they'd be wonderful wives to a member of a ducal family—or to the duke himself if he would kindly introduce them—but that did not bear mentioning. "However, I have other invitations this evening, as I am sure you do. Perhaps some of them will be less crowded."

"The Season is in full swing. All of the soirees are crowded." She touched her bandeau as if to assure herself it remained in place. The white feather contrasted with dark hair untouched by gray.

"Some parties are more crowded than others," he said wryly.

His mother looked over Phillip's shoulder at Michael. Her smile always softened for him, especially since he'd lost his fiancée in a tragic accident. "Why, Mr. Cavenleigh. Good evening."

"Your Grace." Michael bowed.

"How are things at your stable?" she asked. "Still breeding champions?"

"Indeed, mum."

"Come for dinner, won't you?"

"Thank you." Michael bowed again.

Phillip jumped back into the conversation, as it were. "Good evening, Mother. I hope you have a pleasant time." Phillip inclined his head again and headed for the door.

"Phillip." His brother's voice stopped him. Hadn't he been across the room a moment ago?

Phillip swung back to greet His Grace, the Duke of Suttenberg, whose ducal poise cracked long enough to smile. Suttenberg's pale shock of hair in front, so starkly contrasting with the rest of his dark hair, seemed lighter than usual—almost white. Of course, everyone thought the unusual birthmark striking and so fitting for the newest in a long line of dukes.

Phillip's matching blond streak served as a glaring reminder that he should be targeted for his connections—not for his dashing good looks, intellect, and charm. All these he possessed in spades, of course.

"Suttenberg." Phillip couldn't help but grin at his brother. It wasn't really Suttenberg's fault he'd been born first and had both the title and the perfectionist instincts to make him superior in every way to a mortal younger brother. Despite common opinion, Suttenberg hadn't always been so perfect. As boys, they'd gotten into their share of scrapes together. Father's untimely death had changed everything.

Phillip never wanted the burden of a title. He sought a girl who actually saw *him* and not merely a fat purse or the means to climb the slippery social ladder. Being the younger brother of a duke, a paragon of perfection, made that difficult. Still, Phillip refused to let his brother's brilliance blind every woman alive. Surely somewhere existed a lady of substance, someone extraordinary, who would see Phillip for the man he was. He would find her, even if it took years, and he would make her his own.

Suttenberg clapped a hand on Phillip's shoulder. "I haven't seen you in a fortnight, little brother."

Phillip shrugged. "We've both been busy. You with Parliament, and I . . ." He jabbed a finger over his shoulder at Michael. "Cavenleigh Stables needed my wisdom moving this year's batch to Tattersall's."

Michael snorted, but Phillip didn't give him the satisfaction of looking at him.

"Ah, yes. I would enjoy looking over your new stock," Suttenberg said to Michael.

"I'd be honored," Michael said. For a man of few words, he usually said everything right.

"Are you leaving so soon?" Suttenberg's gaze returned to Phillip.

"We have young ladies to meet elsewhere," Phillip said. "It's a chore to be so much in demand. Of course, you wouldn't know." He grinned.

Suttenberg huffed a laugh. "I know nothing of demands."

Phillip shook his head mournfully. "You really ought not be such a wastrel, you know. People are starting to talk."

Mirroring Phillip's expression, Suttenberg nodded. "A challenge, to be sure, but I'll make an attempt."

Phillip glanced at Michael, waiting patiently for him by the door to the great hall, and said to his brother, "Good night, Duke."

"Good night, little brother." A grin came with the term of endearment, since they stood at equal height.

Waving over his shoulder, Phillip headed for the great hall. After they retrieved their hats, they went out into the night. Perhaps Vauxhall Gardens would produce an unusual lady of true character and substance who would see him for the man he was, a man who offered more than a powerful family connection.

Two

Meredith Brown stood in the small river park several feet away from the riverbank, clutching her cloak and questioning her sanity. Surely there were better ways to spend the evening than taking a boat across an enormous, dirty, and somewhat dangerous river as the tide came in. The sinking sun offered little warmth, and a chill wind blew off the Thames. Incoming tide rushed through the arches below the nearest bridge and lapped hungrily at the banks, gurgling like some live beast. Little boats filled with passengers bobbed while ferrymen battled against currents, making slow progress toward the far bank.

"Cheer up, Merry."

Meredith jumped. She pressed a hand over her chest and tried to breathe. "Gracious, but you gave me a scare." She frowned at her cousin, Annabel Stafford.

"This will be fun," Annabel said. "They call it Vauxhall Pleasure Gardens for a reason."

"I'm not certain the method of reaching the gardens is safe."

"You can't always play it safe, Merry. Sometimes the best things happen when you take a chance." Annabel tucked a wayward auburn curl back into her bonnet, a stylish creation that sported more flowers than Uncle's garden.

Meredith clamped her mouth shut to avoid voicing the first words that came into her mind about how taking chances is exactly what landed her into her current predicament.

"Look," Annabel said. "Up there. That's Tristan Barrett. Isn't he so handsome?"

Meredith spotted a fashionable gentleman standing on the river's edge, heedless of the churning water. "Oh, indeed."

"His brother is the Earl of Averston—equally handsome, but not terribly social." Annabel lowered her voice. "According to rumor, Mr. Barrett is a bit of a rake, but oh, what a beautiful face." She sighed.

Rumor often bore little truth, as Meredith knew all too well. Still, she'd keep an eye on him if he came near her cousin. Her whole reason for agreeing to her aunt and uncle's sponsorship of her first and only season was to enjoy time with Annabel and help her make a good match with an honorable gentleman who deserved her. At season's end, she would return to her grandmother's house. Perhaps she'd even marry the vicar who had proven himself honest and kind, if somewhat bland. That, at last, might please her parents.

Several more members of their group stepped into small boats and cast off, rocking in the choppy waves.

Annabel gestured. "In the far boat is Mr. Finley—he's the grandson of a viscount—and behind him is Mr. Dixon, the third son of a marquis."

Meredith shrank back. "I don't belong with all these aristocratic people."

"Nonsense." Annabel squeezed her hand. "No one *here* has a title. As landed gentry, we're all technically commoners."

Meredith didn't truly qualify as gentry, notwithstanding her aunt and uncle's sponsorship or her mother's birth.

Behind them, a gentleman laughed. "Nothing to worry about, my dear Miss Harris. Come see for yourself how easily they cross."

Meredith glanced behind her. A pale-faced young woman wearing a purple bonnet stared at the river. Next to her stood a gentleman with a beaver hat and striped cravat. He tugged on the frightened lady's arm to pull her closer to the riverbank.

A gust of wind rose up, tugging at Meredith's bonnet and sending a chill through her. The purple bonnet sailed off the hapless lady's head. The lady let out a cry and reached for her bonnet, but it tumbled in the air like a kite off its strings. Meredith made a grab for it as it swooped over her fingertips. The bonnet landed on the grass several feet behind her.

"My bonnet!" cried the lady, putting her hands on her head as if to protect it from some ill that only befell bare-headed people in public.

"Bad luck, that," said her unhelpful companion.

Either he lacked devotion for the lady or he lacked gentlemanly valor. Meredith ran for the headwear, but the wind kicked it just out of reach. The wind pushed it again, and it bumped through the river park and into the street, where it finally rolled to a stop.

Dodging a carriage one moment and a rider the next, Meredith chased after the purple creation. As if to play with her, the wind pushed it ever farther until it landed against a storefront window displaying buns and bread.

Meredith pounced on the bonnet. "I have you now."

She snatched it up and inspected it. Considering the amount of time it spent bumping on the ground, the ribbons and trimmings all seemed intact, and the brim, though a tad scuffed, retained its shape.

"Spare a coin, miss?" a small voice said. Hanging at the corner of the bakery and a narrow alley stood a ragged little girl. Limp strings of hair hung down her thin shoulders.

Meredith knew better than to go near an alley in this part

of town. Meredith reached into her reticule and pulled out a twopence. "Here you are."

"Tuppence," the girl mouthed, as if offered a king's ransom. The girl wavered, half in the alley and half on the street.

She took a timid step forward on bare feet. Poor thing probably lived in the rookeries. In a rush, the child darted forward, snatched the coin, and rushed around the corner. Meredith would have bought bread for the girl and watched to be sure the child ate. Too often, children handed their coins to their drunk of a father, who spent it on more drink. But a bareheaded lady awaited her bonnet, and no young lady—not even those in disgrace like Meredith—went about London alone, not even into a bakery.

With a firm grip on the wayward bonnet, Meredith returned to the group gathered at the edge of the riverbank.

"Gracious, Merry, you frightened me when you ran out into the street!" Annabel stared with wide eyes. "You might have been hit or trampled."

Meredith smiled at her cousin. "Nothing so exciting." She presented the hat to its owner. "I believe this is yours."

"How can I ever thank you?" The lady accepted her bonnet and inspected it for damage. With a shrug, she put it on and tied it firmly below her chin. Though rather plain, the lady of perhaps sixteen had an open, friendly smile, beautiful teeth, and a certain childlike innocence.

In Meredith's peripheral vision, a gentleman stared at her. She allowed herself only a glance, but oh my, what a sight! As she pinned her gaze downward, the memory of that brief look at him superimposed itself over her vision—the epitome of tall, dark, and handsome. Looking at *her*. Wearing a suit more befitting a ballroom than a garden excursion, he stood a few inches taller than other men nearby. More notably, he had met her gaze boldly, as if he sought to learn all her secrets. No, she'd best not look a second time. She knew better than to trust the attentions of a handsome man.

"Mr. Partridge is looking at you," Annabel whispered. "I declare he is almost as beautiful as Mr. Barrett."

Annabel had it backward, actually, but Meredith didn't contradict.

Pretending to tuck her auburn hair into her hat, Annabel turned slightly toward Meredith so as to make her words even more discreet. "You may recall that his brother is the Duke of Suttenberg—a paragon of a man. Now *that* would be a family to marry into."

Being related to a duke made him completely out of reach, even if she dared risk her heart again. Wryly, Meredith said, "The duke or the brother?"

"Both. You seem to have caught Mr. Partridge's eye. Again."

"He's probably wondering what kind of half-wit charges into the street after someone else's bonnet." Had she made a complete fool of herself? People in London probably didn't do such things. "What do you mean 'again'?"

"He's the one who looked at you more than once at the St. Cyrs' ball last week, if you will recall, although you were never introduced."

She'd met and learned about such a dizzying number of people that she'd failed to remember all of them. Surely, if she'd seen him, she would have remembered.

Annabel tugged on her arm. "We're next." She brightened, her expression almost worshipful, as Tristan Barrett smiled at them and gestured to the boats.

"There is room for only two, plus the ferryman, so you need to pair up." Mr. Barrett gestured to the handsome gentleman who'd been watching her. "Mr. Cavenleigh, will you ride over with Miss Annabel Stafford? And, Mr. Partridge, please ride with Miss Stafford's friend. Miss . . .?" He glanced between Meredith and Annabel.

Annabel made the introductions. "May I introduce Mr. Tristan Barrett? Mr. Barrett, this is my cousin and my dearest friend, Miss Meredith Brown." Annabel gave a melting smile to the handsome Mr. Barrett, who was probably the kind of man best avoided with his too debonair smile and too-handsome-for-his-own-good looks.

"Miss Stafford, have you met Mr. Partridge?" Mr. Barrett asked.

Meredith gripped Annabel's hand without a single glance at the gentleman of whom he spoke. "We are supposed to stay together. I ought not get into a boat with anyone else."

His eyes widened as if unaccustomed to anyone denying him anything, but nodded. "Very well, you two can take this boat then." He handed them in while the ferryman kept the boat steady.

Meredith immediately sank down on the bench as the ferry rocked underneath her, threatening to throw her overboard.

Annabel stepped on board with a ballerina's grace and shot Mr. Barrett a grateful, adoring, smile. "Thank you, Mr. Barrett." She cocked her head at Meredith and asked under her breath. "You don't really have to stay with me exclusively. We're in a public place with a group."

Meredith sent Annabel an apologetic glance. "Forgive me if you're disappointed about not riding in a boat with a handsome gentleman, but . . ." How could she explain her near panic?

"You don't need to apologize, Merry. I understand." Annabel touched her hand.

But she didn't understand, not really. How could she?

"Now you two." Mr. Barrett gestured to the lady with the escaped purple bonnet and her escort.

The lady shrank back. "I . . . I don't . . ." Her gaze focused on the water growing increasingly dark as the sun sank lower.

"Come now, Miss Harris," said the gentleman with her. "It's a short ride to the gardens."

The frightened Miss Harris' breath came in ragged gasps. "But the water is dark and swift, and I hear it's filled with all manner of dangers."

"It's safe here, Miss Harris," her escort responded. "See how many have crossed? The gardens are well worth the little jaunt in the ferry."

Meredith watched the gentleman with renewed suspicion. Was he really trying to help her or lure her to a place where he could carry out his own agenda? If the lady was in some danger from the man, Meredith would rise up and champion her.

Miss Harris chewed her lower lip as if she feared some great ghost ship would appear and destroy them.

The gentleman spoke softly to Miss Harris, and Meredith strained to hear his words. "If you are truly afraid, we don't have to do this. I wouldn't dream of asking you to do something against your wishes."

Meredith let out her breath. Perhaps he was a true gentleman, after all. Still, Meredith would remain close enough to keep an eye on him to be sure that this leopard didn't change his spots the moment he had the lady alone.

"I do want to see the gardens," Miss Harris said. "I've heard so much about them. Only, I'm so afraid of the river."

Poor thing. Meredith had no great desire to get near the polluted river either. Still, she could help assuage the lady's fears. Doing so might also help her manage her own reluctance. When she had become frightened as a child, her governess used to tell her silly stories to distract her, a technique that often worked on adults as well.

Meredith called to the lady. "Have you heard the tale of the foolish woodman and his three wishes?"

The lady turned her attention from the water to Meredith. She hesitated before speaking to her, eyeing her a moment before replying, "Why, no, I don't believe I have."

Too late, Meredith realized she'd just addressed a lady to whom she had not been properly introduced. Add that to her long list of social *faux pas*. Perhaps she should have stayed with Grandmother in Sussex where her parents had banished her. Still, she began her story. "Once upon a time, a woodman went to the forest to fell some timber. As he applied his axe to the trunk of a huge old oak, out jumped a fairy."

Miss Harris let out a gasp, but her color returned to a healthier shade as she focused on Meredith's words.

"The fairy begged him to spare her tree," Meredith continued. "Out of astonishment more so than kindness, the woodman consented."

So distracted by Meredith's story, the now calmer lady hardly noticed when Mr. Barrett and her companion helped her into the boat. She sat and fixed wide eyes on Meredith.

Their ferryman put some distance between them, so Meredith raised her voice. "As a reward, the fairy promised him the fulfilment of three wishes."

Mr. Partridge, the handsome gentleman who had been staring at Meredith, stepped into a boat with a lean, blond gentleman. She spared the stunning dark-haired man only the briefest glance and only the briefest sigh at his beautiful face and how well his shoulders filled out his tailcoat.

"What did he wish for?" the lady with the purple bonnet called.

Meredith smiled. "Whether from natural forgetfulness or

fairy illusion, we do not know, but the woodman quite forgot his encounter with the fey world. That night as he and his wife dozed before a fire, the old fellow waxed hungry. Out loud, he said, 'I wish I had a few links of hog's pudding.' No sooner had the words escaped his lips than several links of the wished-for sausage appeared at the feet of the astounded woodman."

"Mercy me," Miss Harris said.

One of the boats, the one carrying the handsome overdressed gentleman, Mr. Partridge—not that Meredith was keeping track of his whereabouts—and his fair-haired friend bobbed nearby.

"A bit closer, if you please," Mr. Partridge said in a sweet, smooth baritone.

Meredith never trusted a man with a smooth voice. She cleared her throat. "This reminded the woodman of his strange encounter, which he related to his wife. 'You are a fool,' said she, angered at her husband's carelessness in neglecting to make the best of his good luck. Then the wife unthinkingly added, 'I wish they were on the end of your foolish nose!'"

Everyone within earshot chuckled in anticipation of the outcome.

"Come now, get closer." Mr. Partridge whisked an oar out of the ferryman's grasp.

"Oi! Gimme back m'oar!" his ferryman shouted.

With a few powerful strokes, Mr. Partridge brought the little watercraft so close that Meredith feared they would collide.

"Look out!" Meredith pressed her hands to her cheeks.

A large wave rocked the watercrafts, and the bow of the other boat hit the bow of Meredith and Annabel's. Painfully slow, they listed to one side. Meredith made a wild grab for something to hold onto, but as the boat tipped, she plunged into the river.

A Wager on Love

Cold hit her like a blast of winter air. With wildly flailing hands, she grabbed onto the side of the boat before her head went under. She kicked against her skirts. Back home, she'd gone swimming wearing a chemise, not all the layers she presently wore, and barefoot, rather than clad in half boots.

"I'll save you!" A panicked male voice cried from nearby—probably the same idiot who had knocked her out of the boat in the first place.

"I don't need saving," Meredith called. "I have a hold of the boat."

Annabel and the ferryman hauled her on board by her elbows. As she struggled to her seat, she noticed Annabel sitting, dry, except for a few darkened water spots.

"Are you unharmed, Merry?" her cousin gasped.

Meredith attempted to rearrange her wet skirts. "I'm quite well, if a bit damp. How did you manage not to fall in?"

"The ferryman caught hold of me."

A sheepish smile crinkled the craggy face of the ferryman. "My apologies, miss. I couldn't grab you both and keep the boat balanced at the same time."

"I'm so sorry!" said the same male voice that had promised to save her. Mr. Partridge gaped at her, even more handsome up close. And what a stunning shock of blond in the middle of his rich, dark hair visible beneath his hat's brim. What a stupid thing to notice at a time like this.

"I cannot believe I did that," Mr. Partridge gasped. "Please forgive me!"

Her ire toward him for his actions softened at the genuine distress in his expression. But he was still far too handsome and therefore not to be trusted.

"Blamed fool," his ferryman muttered, gripping his oar and glaring at the clumsy gentleman.

"Can I help you in any way?" Mr. Partridge asked Meredith, clearly aghast.

Annabel sniffed. "You've done quite enough, Mr. Partridge."

He flushed. "I was merely trying to get closer—not run into you. I apologize."

Next to him, his friend with sandy hair looked as if he couldn't decide if he were amused or horrified.

Meredith shivered. Her clothing stuck to her, and water sloshed out of the tops of her boots. The whole situation seemed so absurd that she could only do one thing. She laughed.

Annabel stared, then joined in the laughter.

Meredith shivered again. "Well, that was not quite the adventure I imagined."

Her ferryman said, "Back home, miss?"

"Yes, please," Annabel said. "We must get her home and into something dry."

As they rowed back to the shore they had just left behind, Meredith waved to Miss Harris, the lady in the purple bonnet. "Enjoy the gardens!"

Apparently, Meredith would not become the lady's guardian angel as she'd hoped. She must hope the suitor would prove himself honorable or that Miss Harris would see through his façade before he broke her heart.

Miss Harris gave her a disbelieving smile and waved back. She called out something, but they had traveled out of earshot.

Meredith offered a wry smile to Annabel. "Well, that is certainly the most unusual thing that has happened to me since we arrived in London."

"Oh, mercy," Annabel said. "You must be so cold!"

"I am chilled, but fortunately my cloak is wool, so it will keep me from freezing." She glanced back at Mr. Partridge, who sat twisted in his seat next to his friend and stared at her while his disgruntled ferryman rowed them closer to the far shore.

"What in the world got into him, I wonder?" Meredith mused.

"Obviously, he wanted to get close enough for you to notice him."

"He succeeded." She wiped her face with a gloved hand. "Perhaps he wanted to hear my story."

Annabel made a scoffing sound. "I doubt he will ever forget it—or you. Don't worry; I'm certain we'll see him again."

Meredith shrugged. She had no delusions about finding a husband in London. She'd do well to hope for a respectable country gentleman, like her Grandmother's vicar, who could give her a home of her own and the joy of children.

Perhaps such a respectable marriage would earn her parents' forgiveness. In the meantime, she'd do all she could to protect innocent girls from the lies of rakes and fortune hunters.

Three

Even the next day, Michael Cavenleigh was still laughing over Phillip's careless actions that led to the dunking of the intriguing young lady in the Thames.

Phillip slouched in his seat at Michael's bachelor rooms and glared at his friend. He couldn't keep a straight face for long. To be honest, the sight of Michael laughing again after such a long spell of sorrow, even though said laughter came at Phillip's expense, was just too refreshing—and relieving—a sight to behold.

"Enough," Phillip grumbled in mock grumpiness. "I admit, I didn't think that one through, but I had to get closer, and the ferryman wouldn't listen to me."

"You got closer." Michael chuckled again.

"Obviously, I didn't mean to tip her boat or make her fall in. I need to be more clever next time."

"That was clever. I'd wager she'll never forget you." Michael wiped his eyes.

"A step in the right direction. If I could only do something to improve her opinion of me. But first I must find her. I have little to go on beyond her being Annabel Stafford's cousin." Phillip stood and started pacing. Surely someone else would have noticed the lovely lady with hair the color of a rich brandy and in possession of an inherent kindness to all she met. "I need to gain an introduction."

"It hardly signifies." Michael sipped his lemonade, since he'd given up stronger drink years ago.

"How do you figure?"

"She likely won't ever speak to you."

"Of course she will. She didn't seem that upset. She even laughed." Her lovely, musical laugh, colored with a certain ruefulness, sang to him even in his dreams.

Michael's mirth mingled with disgust. "You dumped her into the filthiest river in England. You're both lucky she wasn't struck by a submerged log or something of the like."

"Yes, we were both fortunate, indeed, that it didn't go worse for her. I must find a way to make it up to her. This goes way beyond flowers, obviously. Do you have any ideas?"

"Personal gestures are best," Michael said. "But you don't know her."

"No. I must do some sleuthing. Until then, perhaps I could send both flowers and candy. Even if they aren't her favorites, they will let her know I'm thinking of her and am wholly repentant about it."

Michael nodded thoughtfully. "Her cousin might be an obstacle."

Phillip sank back down in the armchair he'd vacated a moment ago. Her cousin, Miss Stafford, had indeed glared all manner of daggers at Phillip. He clearly fell terribly short of being a paragon like his brother.

Was his inability to be a smooth-talking charmer the reason no one saw Phillip for anything other than a way to marry into the ducal family?

He leaped to his feet again. "I must win them both over— probably her parents, as well, who must not think too kindly of a person who throws their daughter in the river." A formidable task to be sure, but Phillip had never shrunk from a worthwhile challenge.

"Won't matter. She won't give you the time of day."

Phillip straightened his spine. "She will."

Michael choked. "Never. You had your chance. Missed it."

"That will not be my only opportunity." With a reckless bravado, Phillip added, "I will win her love."

"Would you care to bet?" Michael's eyes glittered.

"No. I won't bet on a lady."

Michael shrugged. "She won't have you."

"I will be persuasive."

"You?" Michael laughed.

Phillip gritted his teeth. He'd attracted female company in the past—for reasons other than his status. He could do it again if he really tried. "Yes. She is worth it."

"Worth it? Perhaps. But it's a lost cause."

His dismissive attitude raised the hackles on Phillip's neck. "I will marry her."

Michael choked, coughed, and laughed. "You don't know her."

Phillip struggled against feelings he didn't entirely understand. "I know enough about her to know that I want her. I've never wanted anyone like this."

"I wager anything you name that she won't have you."

With growing ire and a sudden need to prove himself, Phillip stated, "Very well. If I win, you must . . ." He considered. What would be costly to Michael? His horses gave him no small measure of pride. He didn't want to take any of Michael's prize stock, but perhaps something a bit more fun. "You must ride a mule in Hyde Park during the promenade."

Michael frowned. "I'd rather die than ride a mule."

"Are you willing to recant, then?"

"No." Michael jutted out his chin. "I accept your wager." He considered. "If she refuses your proposal, you muck out my stables."

Phillip blanched. He had never done such a thing. It would be backbreaking and smelly and humiliating. And if his family found out he'd done something so far below his standing, they'd take him to task. But he wouldn't have to do it; he would win. He straightened his shoulders. "Done."

"Wedding must be before the end of the Season."

"Agreed." If he couldn't win her by Season's end, he had little chance anyway. Angry for a reason he couldn't quite identify, Phillip stared into the fire, which had died down to a jutting tongue behind the charred log. Silence stretched until finally Phillip glanced at Michael. His friend eyed him silently, that same assessing look he gave to purebreds to determine their worth.

Finally, Phillip barked, "What?"

"Why?"

Phillip blinked. Sometimes determining Michael's meaning required tremendous insightfulness, and he seemed short on supply just then. "Why what?"

"Why *her*? Why so certain? You have never conversed with her. She's pretty, but not beautiful."

Phillip disagreed with Michael's assessment of her beauty but focused on his attempt to answer the question truthfully. "She is different. I've seen her before—at the St. Cyrs' ball last week. She caught my eye right away—like a light shining on her face. She never once made a move toward my brother or me. She didn't even ask for an introduction to my mother, which slyer young ladies sometimes do."

That alone had captured his attention.

Michael toyed with his glass. "Not after your connections, then."

"No. And when I saw her yesterday, I had this sense of recognition, as if she were a long-lost love."

When she chased after Miss Harris's bonnet, so determined to help, and was creatively kind, both to an urchin and to Miss Harris, he'd experienced a pull toward her.

He glanced at Michael, but he wasn't laughing or scoffing, only looking sober and thoughtful. Whether he relived his own attraction to his late fiancée or simply tried to understand, Phillip did not know.

Finally, he added, "She intrigues me like no one else."

Michael nodded. "Then I wish you luck. Or, I would, but I have no desire to ride a mule." His lips twitched.

"I look forward to witnessing the spectacle of you riding a mule in Hyde Park . . . on the day she accepts my marriage proposal." Phillip grinned.

"No." His face a mask of calm, Michael said, "The day after she marries you. Accepting a proposal doesn't allow for a change of mind."

"She isn't a jilt."

"And you know her so well?"

"Yes, I do."

With any luck, he would utter similar words while kneeling at an altar by the end of London's social season.

Four

Standing in the drawing room of her aunt and uncle's London townhouse, Meredith gaped at the flowers and box of candy in Aunt Paulette's hands. "They are from whom?"

"Phillip Partridge." Her aunt narrowed her gaze as if trying to see Meredith better. "His card says rather benignly, 'Kindest regards,' and it is addressed to the family."

If there was a hidden meaning, Meredith missed it. "They are for all of you—not me."

"He's being polite," Aunt Paulette said. "Since you haven't been officially introduced, it would be inappropriate for him to send them to you."

"It's inappropriate anyway," Annabel said. "Brother of a duke or no, he has a lot of nerve sending you flowers and candy as if that atones for knocking you into the water. Why, you might have been injured or drowned or caught your death of cold."

Annabel's protectiveness brought a sting of tears to Meredith's eyes. She'd been her one true friend throughout her entire life, even in her darkest hours.

Aunt Paulette handed the flowers to a maid. "Put these in a vase of water, please." As the maid took the flowers out of the room, Aunt Paulette set the candy on a round Chippendale table. "He's clearly trying to pave the way to a civil reception when he comes to apologize in person. The question is, do we receive him or cut him?"

"We ought not cut him," Meredith said. "He didn't mean any harm, and he apologized the moment it happened—more than once."

"You don't have to be polite to him just because his brother is a duke," Annabel said.

Aunt Paulette added, "People have cut the prince regent."

"I wouldn't be so cruel," Meredith said. "If Mr. Partridge calls, I think we should receive him. But I doubt he will. He really owes me nothing."

Annabel let out a huff. "He couldn't take his eyes off you. He will call if you'll let him. Are you sure you forgive him?"

Meredith nodded. "It was not done with malicious intent, and no harm was done. We will receive him, and be polite, and . . ." She shrugged. "That will be the end of it." Or so she hoped.

"Very well." Aunt Paulette opened the box of candy and held it out to Meredith. "If you have forgiven him, then so shall we."

"I won't." Annabel folded her arms. "Not unless he has a very pretty apology. I know marrying into such an auspicious family would please your parents, Merry, but don't settle for someone who won't make you happy."

Chewing the candy, Meredith picked up a pillow and hugged it. "I'm not so *naïve* as to believe my happiness rests on another or that romantic love is required for a successful match. I will be content with an honorable man, if any still exists, and a home of my own. Perhaps I should go back to Sussex and marry Grandmother's vicar."

"Nonsense," cried Annabel. "A stuffy man like that is not for you."

"At least I would have no delusions about him being in love with me." Meredith hugged the pillow harder and savored the sweet candy in her mouth.

Annabel sat forward. "Don't give up just yet, Merry. You promised to stay with me the whole Season."

"Yes, I did. But since a love match is not in the stars for me, I shall employ my newfound powers of discernment to help others."

A maid entered carrying the tea service and plates of refreshment. After setting the tray on a nearby table, the maid bobbed a curtsey and soundlessly left the room. A second maid arrived with the flowers arranged in a vase and set it on a sideboard table. The flowers smiled from their crystal vase.

"I cannot like your goal of coming between couples, Meredith, but I have to admit, you were quite right about Mr. Wynn." Aunt Paulette inspected the plate of scones and biscuits.

Annabel also leaned forward to select a scone. "And about that peacock trying to woo my friend Charlotte."

Meredith nodded slowly. "I'm only grateful they were spared. And by the way, your handsome Mr. Barrett is not to be trusted either. He strikes me as a rake of the worst kind, just as you said."

Aunt Paulette's hand froze midway to her mouth. "Mr. Tristan Barrett? Oh, yes, indeed, he does have a wild reputation. He might be wealthy and well connected, but no one that rakish will do, Annabel. I hope you know that."

Annabel's expression turned almost sullen. "I know, I know. But he's so . . ."

"By all means, admire him like a piece of fine art, but don't fall for him," Meredith said firmly.

Annabel let out a huff. "But what if gossip has it wrong about him just like it was wrong about you? I mean, you didn't actually do anything truly bad, and if no one had discovered that you had eloped, you wouldn't be considered ruined."

Meredith blanched at the word that had been flung at her, beating her down like a battering ram, almost constantly for years. "I *did* do something wrong: I believed the lies of a handsome face." Twice, but few besides Grandmother knew about the second one. At least she had learned her lesson enough not to attempt an elopement a second time.

Aunt Paulette handed teacups around. "No need to bring up the past. We will focus on the future for you both. Promise me you won't get so jaded that you find faults that aren't there, Meredith."

"I will try, Aunt. And I will try not to be such a failure."

Seven years had failed to completely heal the hurt of lies and betrayal or restore her faith in herself or her trust in gentlemen in general. Nor had it yielded her parents' forgiveness. But if she could protect others from her own folly, she would feel a measure of satisfaction. That would have to be enough.

"Now, now," Aunt Paulette said. "One miscalculation does not mean you are no longer a candidate for a love match. If you are willing to forgive Mr. Partridge for his overzealous attempts to get your attention, you might consider allowing him to court you."

Meredith huffed a laugh. "No one of his status would align himself with someone of my background and the scandal attached to me."

"No one here knows of that," Aunt Paulette said in a soothing voice. "And surely everyone in Loughborough has forgotten all about it."

"Things like that have a way of resurfacing," Meredith said miserably. "Besides, nothing will change the fact that my father is in trade. That disqualifies me from anyone lofty—unless they need my dowry."

"Don't be so sure, my dear cynic. Keep an open mind and an open heart, and you might be surprised what delightful people will come into your life. Now, as far as tonight, our hostess is Lady Daubrey—she's such a dear. She will have a sumptuous dinner. I'm certain all the gentlemen present will be of the very best *ton*."

"Aunt," Meredith interrupted, "if the subject of my dowry comes up at all, could we imply that it's very modest?"

"But my dear, to make an advantageous match—"

"I must avoid fortune hunters, mustn't I?" Meredith interjected.

Aunt Paulette frowned thoughtfully. "Well . . . er . . . yes, but—"

"Would that not be easier to achieve if people believe I don't offer an impressive dowry?"

"Your father might—"

"He might understand, all things considered, don't you think?"

Aunt Paulette's brows creased, and she closed her mouth, frowned, and said nothing for a long moment.

Annabel piped up. "I think she's right, Mama. As her sponsor, you don't have to name a sum, just imply that it's very modest. And really, it's all relative anyway, isn't it?"

"Besides, the last I spoke to Papa," Meredith said as if that had been weeks instead of years ago, "he mentioned reducing my dowry but increasing trust money that would stay in my control even after marriage. For all I know, he's done that."

None of their letters had mentioned such matters. They'd been polite, filled mostly with local events such as marriages and babies born, or the new garden Mama had designed, but no words of forgiveness or an invitation to return home.

Aunt Paulette finally nodded. "I see what you mean. Enough of a dowry so as not to be a true deterrent, but not so much as to attract anyone seeking a way to restore the family coffers."

The tightness that had knotted inside Meredith relaxed enough to allow the first deep breath she'd taken in years.

The butler opened the door and said, "Forgive me, madam, but are you at home to a Mr. Partridge and Mr. Cavenleigh?"

He'd come. Meredith could hardly believe it. She would not allow herself to look too long at his stunning face or she might fall back into her former stupidity and fail to see his true intentions, whatever they may be.

"Show them in," Aunt Paulette said.

The ladies touched up their hair and smoothed their skirts. The butler returned a moment later, followed by two gentlemen. Mr. Partridge entered first, followed by his leaner friend, a sandy-haired gentleman who nearly matched him in height. However, Meredith saw little else of his companion with her attention so focused on Mr. Partridge.

The Master Craftsman had certainly taken his time designing this fine specimen of a man. With beautifully formed features and a mouth perfect for kissing, he seemed to embody her girlish dreams of a prince charming who would carry her off to his castle in the clouds.

He and his friend bowed. Aunt Paulette and Annabel curtsied, reminding Meredith to do so.

"Mrs. Stafford, Miss Stafford, thank you for seeing me."

Meredith had forgotten the musical beauty of Mr. Partridge's voice.

"So kind of you to call, Mr. Partridge, Mr. Cavenleigh," Aunt Paulette said. "May I present my niece, Miss Meredith Brown?"

Mr. Partridge's eyes, the green and blue of a dappled country lake, caressed her face with a contradictory intensity and softness. His blond patch nestled in his dark waves, shining like a beacon. The light in the room emanated from his face, and all else faded away to colorless trivia.

No. Not again. Love was a trite fantasy. She would not be duped again.

"Mr. Partridge," she said coolly. "Thank you for the flowers and candy. I assure you, it was not necessary."

He blinked as if trying to merge her gracious words and frosty tone. "It was not near enough, I assure you. I hope you will forgive me."

"Already forgiven. No need to fret." Her voice still sounded chilly, even to her own ears.

Her aunt cleared her voice. "Won't you both please sit and take a cup of tea?"

Mr. Partridge swung back to speak to Aunt Paulette. "Yes, thank you." He glanced at his silent friend, and they both sat. He addressed Meredith, "I hope you suffered no ill effects from the mishap?"

"Not at all. You can rest easy knowing you owe me nothing. All is forgotten."

His eyes narrowed slightly, and he tilted his head rather like a child trying to determine if an adult had told him the truth or a fanciful tale. It gave him a rather endearingly innocent expression. But she would not be so easily swayed. She had yet to determine his character. Which was foolish, really, since no ducal family member would lower himself to a factory owner's daughter. And that line of thought was even more foolish.

"Truly," she added with a smile. "I harbor no grudge. But thank you so much for taking time out of what is no doubt a busy schedule to call upon us."

A dark brow shot up. "Am I being dismissed?" A curve to one side of his mouth revealed a dimple. Oh heavens, not a dimple!

"I wouldn't presume to do so, Mr. Partridge; only to convey my appreciation of your solicitousness." She had, in truth, been trying to subtly suggest he had no reason to stay. How surprising that he'd called her on it. If only he'd leave before she started to like him! She bowed her head and folded her hands in an attempt to appear demure.

"It is my pleasure," he said.

"Did you enjoy your visit to Vauxhall?" Aunt Paulette addressed both of them.

"Yes, for the most part," Mr. Partridge said in his lovely voice. "But I admit I was so concerned for Miss Brown's well-being that I hardly saw it all. Perhaps we might enjoy it together one day?"

Meredith's palms grew damp. Was he inviting her to spend time with him?

He held up his hands. "I vow not to touch the oars and to leave all the paddling to the ferryman."

Meredith laughed in spite of herself. "I'll hold you to that."

He brightened, and that blasted dimple reappeared. "Then you'll go? We can make a group of it, can't we?" He glanced at his friend.

Mr. Cavenleigh made a gesture that seemed to convey agreement.

"Well," Annabel drew out the word. "I'm not as forgiving as my cousin, Mr. Partridge. If you get even so much as a drop of water on Meredith, I shan't forgive you—ever."

Mr. Partridge held up a hand. "I vow not to cause Miss Brown any further discomfort."

Meredith chewed on her lower lip. An outing with Mr. Partridge was the last thing she ought to have.

"Miss Brown?" he said softly. "What say you? Are we for Vauxhall in the near future?"

Oh, heavens. How to escape this? "I am not certain . . ."

"By all means, Miss Brown, check your social calendar." He stood. "I hope our paths cross again very soon."

Very soon?

He gave her a soft smile that felt ridiculously affectionate. How could she stay strong against the onslaught of his beautiful face and seemingly genuine manner?

Aunt Paulette replied, "I do hope so, Mr. Partridge, Mr. Cavenleigh."

Mr. Cavenleigh inclined his blond head. "Madam." Was he always so quiet?

They bowed and bade a good day. Meredith let out her breath. All the strength in her limbs traveled out on that exhale. She must not lose focus. She came to enjoy time with her cousin, ensure Annabel made a good match with someone deserving of her, and be this Season's guardian of young ladies in danger of falling prey to rakes and fortune hunters. Come summer, she would return to her grandmother and marry a respectable man. Then perhaps her parents would forgive her for her humiliating mistakes. Perhaps she would even forgive herself.

Five

In the foyer of the Staffords' home, Phillip lowered his voice to address the butler as he slipped him enough coins to buy a few pints at an alehouse. "I say, my good man, would you happen to know where the Staffords will be tonight?"

The butler paused, probably considering whether such information made him disloyal. Finally, he said, "I believe they are bound for a dinner party at Lord and Lady Daubrey's this eve."

Perfect. Phillip knew them well enough to enlist them in his scheme.

Outside, Michael shook his head. "Bribing the staff now?"

"I plan to win the hand of the fair maiden—whatever it takes."

"And avoid mucking out my stables."

"I assure you, I'm more motivated by the thought of you on the back of a mule than by avoiding a little time in your stables." He grinned.

They took Phillip's town coach to the Daubreys', where the hostess admitted them even though it wasn't her usual at-home hours.

She hardly kept them waiting a minute before coming to

the front parlor. "Why Mr. Partridge, Mr. Cavenleigh, what a pleasant surprise," the young Lady Daubrey said.

"Always a delight to see you, my lady." Phillip bowed over her hand.

"Oh, pish. When did we get so formal? Do sit and tell me what brings you here today." She smiled.

Phillip adopted a conspiratorial tone. "I have come with a shameless plea for your aid."

"Oh? I can't wait to hear all about it."

Phillip took a breath. "I have met an unforgettable young lady, and I am attempting to be more . . . present in her life."

"Indeed?" Her eyes sparkled.

Phillip mentally congratulated his friend Lord Daubrey, not for the first time, for having the good sense to marry the lady. "I have it on good authority that she is to be included in your dinner party tonight, and . . ." The audacious request lodged in his throat.

She leaned forward and clasped her hands together. "You wish to join us? Well of course you may—you know that. I'm certain one more won't make a difference."

Phillip let out a breath. "You are very perceptive, as usual, my lady—and generous."

"'Tis nothing, and besides, the Tarringtons are uncertain they can attend since her health has been delicate of late."

"I hadn't heard," Phillip said. "Nothing serious, I hope?"

"I am unaware of the exact nature of her condition, alas. I must pay a call on her tomorrow if she does not attend tonight. Shall you join us this eve as well, Mr. Cavenleigh?"

"I am otherwise engaged, my lady," Michael said.

"A pity. Enjoy your evening, then. Mr. Partridge, do come at seven o'clock.'"

"Thank you. I am certain you have preparations to complete, so I will bid you a good day." Phillip stood.

"Do tell who this young lady is who has so completely turned your head." An impish light shone in her face.

"Er..."

"It could be useful you know. I might even arrange to seat her next to you, you know."

A good point. And there seemed little reason to keep it a secret. "Miss Meredith Brown, the Staffords' niece.

"I have not yet had the pleasure of making her acquaintance, but I am most eager to meet her in person now."

Phillip thanked her again, and they took their leave.

Outside as they climbed into the carriage, Phillip let out a breath. "So far, this has been a successful day."

Michael shot him a sideways glance. "Do you plan to continue such methods to pursue this hapless girl until she agrees to marry you?"

"No, I mean to be more direct and traditional in the very near future. But I had to create another opportunity to speak with her."

"Then what?"

"We shall see what this evening brings. If she warms toward me, I will invite her on a carriage ride with me. I may even convince her to allow me to take her to Vauxhall. She was understandably reluctant to do so today, but I vow I will win her over eventually."

"You are obsessed."

"Merely determined."

They crossed the bridge and headed to Tattersalls, where Phillip dropped off Michael to check on some geldings he had up for auction. Phillip headed back to his bachelor rooms to prepare for tonight's dinner. After fussing over his appearance until his valet nearly wept, Phillip agonized over how he might secure Miss Brown's affection. His mother and brother would tell him to be himself. As a younger man, Phillip had suffered no shortage of feminine companionship, but as ladies near his age turned their minds to marriage rather than innocent diversion, so too did they view him through more mercenary eyes.

Would Miss Brown, despite his impressions of her, also set her sights on his family connections and render Phillip, as a man, invisible?

He arrived at the Daubreys' dinner party stylishly late, but not late enough to offend the host and hostess. Upon entering the drawing room, he strode directly to the Daubreys without looking about in search of a certain guest. It wouldn't do to appear overly eager. Egad, he was nervous as a lad anticipating his first kiss.

"So good of you to join us, Partridge," Daubrey intoned, but a gleam in his eye revealed his knowledge of Phillip's purpose.

As they made small talk, Phillip focused on his friends and stiffened his neck to avoid looking for Miss Brown. He would learn soon enough if she had, indeed, joined the party. A footman held out a silver tray with drinks, and Phillip took one but only sipped. He caught himself tapping his fingers on his glass.

Under his breath, Daubrey said, "You seem a tad jittery tonight, ol' boy." His voice betrayed his amusement.

Phillip tried to send him a glare, but it probably came out guilty.

Lady Daubrey came to the rescue. "Mr. Partridge, have you made the acquaintance of my friends the Staffords?"

"Yes, certainly," Phillip said.

"Then you must have met their niece visiting from the north?" She gestured to a point behind him.

Phillip turned. Wearing a simple white evening gown, Miss Meredith Brown stood next to Mrs. Stafford and her daughter, Annabel. How was it possible he'd forgotten how lovely she was? A soft light shone on her face, accentuating the graceful lines of her face and neck. The sweet yet somehow wary expression dared him to discover her thoughts.

Miss Harris, the young lady whose bonnet Miss Brown had rescued, approached her, and they fell into an animated conversation. The liveliness in Miss Brown's eyes, the curve of her cheek, the fluid gestures of her hand, mesmerized him.

"You're staring," Lord Daubrey whispered.

Phillip closed his gaping mouth.

Lady Daubrey giggled softly. "You, my friend, are lovestruck."

A male voice intoned in the perfect blend of authority and boredom, "Dinner is served."

Lady Daubrey tugged his elbow. "Escort her to dinner."

Phillip almost rubbed his hands together. Lord and Lady Daubrey led the way into the dining room. Phillip pulled himself together long enough to approach Miss Brown. Now would be an excellent time to say something witty or suave.

He bowed before her. "Er, dinner . . ." He almost slapped his head.

She blinked. "Why, Mr. Partridge." She looked him directly in the eye, really seeing him in a way that had been notably absent in other ladies of late. She made no move to take his arm . . . which he really ought to have extended.

No one would accuse him of being too charming in her presence. He offered his arm. "If I may?"

"Oh." She shot a panicked glance at her aunt and uncle's retreating backs, then at her cousin on the arm of another gentleman. "You? Are assigned to sit with me?"

He gave her his most disarming smile. "I assure you, since we are far from boats and the river, you are not in danger of taking an unscheduled swim."

She stifled a laugh. "Of course not." Her gaze darted around again. "I didn't realize you were escorting me to dinner."

His confidence cracked, but he fortified his resolve. Somehow, he would win her over. A lady with such a kind and generous heart would surely like him. Wouldn't she? "It's only a meal, Miss Brown, not a lifetime sentence."

A sheepish smile curved her mouth, and she looked him in the eye again. "Never underestimate the power of good food."

"Or charming company?" He gave her his best charming smile.

For a second, the corners of her mouth softened. Almost instantly, that wary expression returned, followed by a mask of coolness. "I am immune to charm."

"Ah. You admit I'm charming, but that you are resistant—or at least, have been thus far."

She almost smiled, he was just sure of it. "Why would a man of your rank escort a lady of mine?"

"Today has been remarkably fortunate for me." He smiled.

Her eyes focused on his dimple, and she pursed her lips, yet the corners of them lifted. Was it possible she was one of those ladies who found his dimple enchanting? He grinned more broadly. He could barely remember the last time someone had noticed. Usually they were too busy noticing his Suttenberg connection.

Archly she said, "Fortunate, how? You haven't knocked anyone into the river today?"

He chuckled under his breath. "Not yet, but the evening is young."

Did her mouth twitch in an effort to suppress her amusement or her annoyance? He'd never found it so difficult to understand a member of the fair sex. Of course, it had never mattered so much.

"Are you going to escort me to dinner or leave me standing here?"

With a gentle voice, he said, "I have, if you will observe, already extended my arm."

As if seeing it for the first time, she put her hand on his arm with a whisper-light touch. Warmth soaked through his forearm and heated a cold place inside his heart. No woman's touch had ever affected him thusly. Her hand trembled. Nervous? Excited?

He led Miss Brown to their assigned places in the dining room and held out a chair for her before taking a seat. "Have you been to London before?"

"Oh, yes, many times, but this is my first Season. I suppose you come frequently?" As she spoke, each motion of her mouth beckoned, *Kiss me.*

He cleared his throat and focused on her words. "I come to London every year to renew acquaintances with friends who come for the Season." With a close watch on her expression, he added, "And my mother wishes me to socialize more in the hopes I might make a match someday."

"You should know, I'm an old maid of nearly three and twenty and have a very modest dowry."

It might be a long shot, but a broken heart could be the cause of her chilliness. If she allowed anyone close, she risked getting hurt. Phillip knew a thing or two about that.

With a gentle smile, he said, "Ladies of three and twenty are hardly old, and your dowry is of little import to me."

She paused as if his easy dismissal had taken the wind out of her sails, as it were. Or perhaps she was thinking up a more convincing deterrent. A uniquely invigorating challenge lay ahead of him.

She moved those luscious lips again. "Yes, I imagine a gentleman of your rank likely has little need of dowry."

"Indeed, although somehow it seems arrogant to admit it." He sent her a self-deprecating smile.

Quickly, she refocused on her plate and wielded her utensils as if fending off an attack. "Then as a gentleman of your rank, you should know my father's hands are sullied by trade. He owns a lace mill in Loughborough."

Her words hit him like a punch. Neither his mother nor his brother would condone a match with a tradesman's daughter. Phillip risked alienating his family if he married so low beneath his class.

He rounded up a playful tone. "Excellent. My mother is excessively fond of lace. I'm sure she could be persuaded to notify her modiste to use lace purchased from his mill."

Bitterly, she said, "His mill was damaged last month in riots. He likely won't be filling any new orders until repairs are completed."

"I'm sorry to hear that." Phillip had read the news with mixed emotions, sympathizing with workers protesting terrible working conditions but also cognizant of the destruction of property and the loss of wages to employees.

"It's much worse for the workers," she added with an earnest tone and expression. "*His* employees were not involved in the riots, but now, due to the choices of others, they are out of work. He's keeping as many on as he can to facilitate cleanup and restoration, but it will take time before he can rehire all of them. Until then, they go hungry."

"I hope he resumes business quickly, then." For her sake, if not for her father's, who sounded like an unusual employer, he wished Mr. Brown well. Apparently, concern for the well-being of others, even the impoverished, was a family trait. Admirable. "None of his employees rioted?"

She set down her utensils, giving him her full attention. "He's fair and adheres to strict safety standards, so injuries are rare. He even provides a school for his employees' children and requires that they attend as part of their employment obligations. He won't allow children to work until after the school day has concluded, and for no more than four hours a day."

He held up his glass in a loose salute. "He is a rare breed of factory owner."

"He is."

He could not mistake the light of pride shining in her eyes. "You must be very close."

The light dimmed. "Not as we once were." She picked up her silverware again and attacked her dinner, but she ate little. A story lay behind that statement, but he didn't dare probe this early in the relationship.

A diversion seemed wise. "Whatever happened to the woodman who found a fairy and was granted three wishes?"

She met his gaze with wide eyes, a lovely shade of blue, unmarred by any other color—no gray or green, just the pure blue of a spring morning sky. "You truly wish to know?"

"Very much."

She shook her head, her brows lowering slightly in confusion. "It's merely a silly story."

"One I have not heard, and you tell it in such a fascinating way that I wish you would complete it."

Pure delight lit her expression and brightened her eyes, and that same animation returned as she slipped into the role of expert storyteller. "As you may remember, his wife was angry with her husband's carelessness in wasting a wish on sausage. Then, she quite unthinkingly added, 'I wish your sausages were on your foolish nose!' As you may have guessed, the wished-for food immediately attached itself to the woodman's nose so tightly that nothing could remove it."

He laughed softly and nodded to encourage her to continue.

"To the dismay of both husband and wife, they were obliged to wish them off, thus making the third wish and at once ending his brilliant expectations."

He grinned. "So, the moral of the story is don't waste your wishes?"

"Or avoid hypocrisy."

He nodded. "An ever more powerful moral."

They conversed more easily after that. Far too soon, dinner ended, and the ladies left for the drawing room so the gentlemen might have their time alone. Phillip waited with growing impatience until they could join the ladies. Normally, he enjoyed the male-only after-dinner discussion, but each minute seemed designed to keep him from the young lady who had captured his attention and even a small part of his heart. Perhaps not so small.

Once the men rejoined the ladies, Phillip went immediately to her. She sat between her aunt and her cousin. Voices and laughter provided the perfect screen to their conversation.

He held out an arm to her. "Miss Brown, would you do me the honor of taking a turn about the room with me?"

Her guarded expression returned, a foil against her aunt's delight and her cousin's cautiously happy expression. At least he seemed to have won over her family.

He lowered his voice and all but whispered, "Please."

She placed her hand in his and allowed him to lead her to the nearest wall. Skirting the edges of the room, they passed behind Miss Harris sitting next to Mr. Morton, the same gentleman who had escorted Miss Harris to Vauxhall. Miss Harris chewed her lip as Mr. Morton leaned forward as if trying to convince her to do something.

Miss Brown gestured to the couple. "Do you know the gentleman conversing with Miss Harris?"

"Mr. Morton? Not well. He seems a decent sort. He's distantly related to the Earl of Averston."

"Is he a libertine?"

"Hardly. He is rather awkward around the ladies, in fact."

"Is he impoverished?"

He gave her a quizzical look. Why the sudden interest in him? From what Phillip knew of ladies and their taste of men, Mr. Morton was not the type to turn heads. "I do not believe so, but as a younger son of a younger son, he probably needs to marry well."

"What do you know about Miss Harris?"

"She's related to the St. Cyrs somehow. Sweet. A bit shy."

"Is she in possession of a large dowry?"

He had to search his memory. "I am not well informed as to the state of everyone's incomes and dowries, but I do not recall hearing anything remarkable about hers." Was it possible she had an interest in Mr. Morton and viewed Miss Harris as competition? But Mr. Morton was all wrong for Miss Brown. Surely she could see that. Finally, he ventured, "Why do you ask?"

"I am looking for possible motives as to his interest in her."

"You do not think she is attractive enough to garner a gentleman's interest unless he is a fortune hunter?"

"I think she is young and innocent—the type of young lady such men are most likely to target. She may not know their true motives until too late." A bitterness touched her voice.

What had happened to Miss Brown? "Do you think I have a hidden motive?"

Her glance revealed her vulnerability. "I am mystified as to why you openly seek me out."

"I wish to become better acquainted."

"I cannot imagine why. I am nobody."

With a reckless courage spurred by his sudden determination to win her heart, he asked, "Do you believe in love at first sight?"

She looked away. "No. Not anymore."

Phillip almost demanded who had broken her heart so he might find and thrash the scoundrel. Instead, he opted for a more playful tone, "How about love at second sight?"

With a small, sad smile, she shook her head.

With the kind of confidence he once wore so easily, he quipped, "I'm willing to let you look at me long enough to change that." He affected a dramatic pose.

A true smile broke through as she met his gaze. Truly, she was beautiful when she smiled. He nearly fell on his knees and begged her to marry him.

Sobering, she tilted her head. "Why, really, are you giving me the time of day?"

"Because you are a remarkable person."

She looked down. "We've met only twice before, and briefly at that."

"They were telling encounters."

She looked at him again, her mouth curving more on one side in an expression that seemed doubtful yet amused. "How so?"

"At the river, you retrieved Miss Harris's bonnet when no one else did, not even the gentleman courting her. This tells me you are thoughtful and caring and aren't overly concerned with society's opinion. Then you gave a coin to an urchin. That tells me you are generous and aware of others in need. But you didn't approach the alley, which suggests you're intelligent enough to stay away from danger."

That day, she'd worn such a gentle, compassionate expression that Phillip had been unable to look away. At the moment, however, her mien retained that wariness he feared had become deeply ingrained. Somehow, he would prove to her he was not of the same ilk as the unworthy man who had hurt her.

He continued to expound on her admirable qualities. "And when Miss Harris grew frightened, you told her a story to keep her distracted, so you're clearly imaginative and quick thinking."

That day, she had been so animated in her role of storyteller that Phillip had wanted to put his head in her lap and listen to her for hours. He'd do it now, if she'd let him.

Now she watched him, carefully, as if seeking reassurance of his truthfulness.

Emboldened by her fixed attention, he said, "When you laughed instead of getting angry or weepy about falling into the Thames, I knew your character is strong and you are capable of finding humor even in mishaps." Wryly, he added, "And you forgave me for causing you to fall in, which speaks volumes about your heart. I prize these qualities."

They continued their slow stroll around the perimeter of the room. "I thank you for your kind interpretation of my actions, but this does not discount the fact that we are not social equals."

Phillip winced. If she were the daughter of a poor country vicar, or a gentleman farmer, their differences in rank would be easier to overcome. Could he convince Suttenberg and Mother to give their blessing?

"Regardless, I wish to become better acquainted with you. And to enjoy your companionship."

Her hand tightened. "If you are looking for a mistress, I am not of that inclination."

He choked. "No, certainly not. I assure you, that is not my intention."

"Then what is your intention?"

With the courage that had spurred him to tackle every new challenge he'd ever thought beyond him, he admitted, quietly, "To determine if you are the one my soul seeks."

She stopped walking and looked into his eyes, all the hard edges in her expression softening until she looked sweet and vulnerable. Had he gotten through to her at all?

Her wariness returned. "Pretty words, but I have learned not to believe such things. Thank you for the turn about the room."

She withdrew her hand and left him standing in the middle of the floor. Alone.

Six

Meredith tried and failed all evening to keep her focus on the game of whist at the Daubreys' party. Mr. Partridge continued to invade her thoughts. Each time she weakened enough to look at him, he met her gaze with puzzled hurt. Her conscience gave her a sharp prod. Yet how could she trust him when he might be no better than the cads who'd lied to her in the past?

When the game ended and the guests stood or sat in groups talking and laughing, Aunt Paulette leaned close and whispered, "He's fascinated with you."

"He should know better," Meredith snapped.

"He's the very best *ton*, niece. Not only does he come from good family, but he has a reputation for being a very decent gentleman."

"All the more reason for him not to be seen with me."

"Meredith," Aunt Paulette chided gently.

"Why on earth should I reach so high as the son of a duke? Not just any ducal family—the Duke of Suttenberg. No one could bear the scrutiny of being aligned with them."

Aunt Paulette nodded sadly. "You would fall under the all-seeing magnifying glass of London's worst social critics."

"If my father's profession didn't bring condemnation on

my head, my past would. Sooner or later, it would be revealed."

"At least enjoy his company while you can. If you are seen with the brother of the Duke of Suttenberg, others will assume you are worthy of notice. This could be used to your advantage."

"I will not use him, just as I will not be used by him—or any man." Speaking of being used by a man, how did Miss Harris fare?

Meredith found her in a circle speaking with other young ladies her age. Mr. Morton approached and tapped Miss Harris's shoulder. They spoke, and he gestured to the balcony. Meredith straightened. Was he trying to lure her outside and take advantage of her?

The young lady shook her head and glanced back at her friends, but Mr. Morton hovered nearby. Time for a rescue.

Meredith walked as quickly as possible to Miss Harris's side. "Good evening, Miss Harris. Are you enjoying yourself?" She glanced at Mr. Morton in clear challenge.

He blinked at her as if uncertain how to proceed now that she had intervened.

Miss Harris, however, greeted her enthusiastically. "I had hoped to speak with you again this eve. Please, do tell me the end of that delightful story." Though Miss Harris would not be classified as pretty, her sweetness gave her a certain appeal.

Meredith smiled. "If you wish. I did not imagine it would be such a popular story." Mr. Partridge had, surprisingly, made the same request, and with such compelling earnestness that she would have found it hard to refuse him anything. Which made him exactly the kind of man she ought to avoid.

Quickly, she completed the tale. Miss Harris laughed over the ending. Still standing awkwardly nearby, her suitor smiled in an attempt to be part of the conversation. Meredith asked him benign questions and shrewdly watched him. Mr. Partridge was right; the gentleman showed no signs of the kind of smooth charm found in *roués*. Still, he might have a hidden agenda. Fortune hunters came in all packages.

An older woman bearing such a strong resemblance that she must surely be Miss Harris's mother gestured. "Come along, Cora dear, our carriage awaits."

Mr. Morton addressed Miss Harris. "Tomorrow, then, Miss Harris?"

Miss Harris nodded. "I look forward to it."

Miss Harris explained to Meredith, "Tomorrow we are viewing the Earl of Tarrington's private art collection. Would you come as well?"

Meredith considered. It would provide another opportunity to observe Mr. Morton and his behavior toward the sweet Miss Harris to determine whether she ought to issue a warning about the young lady's suitor. "That's very kind, but I wouldn't wish to intrude."

"Not at all. It's a small group, but a few more won't make any difference. Perhaps your cousin would join us? Annabel, isn't it?"

Meredith smiled. "Yes. I'm certain she'd be delighted. And of course, we must seek permission from my aunt. Thank you for including us."

As they explained their plan to Annabel, she happily agreed and sought Aunt's permission. The party broke up as guests said goodbyes. Meredith, next to Annabel, followed her aunt and uncle outside.

A male voice, smoother than chocolate, called, "Miss Brown."

Meredith turned. Mr. Partridge strode to her. Her breath stilled. How could she stay strong against him? Not only his handsome face, but his seemingly sincere words tugged at the loose threads of her resolve. One day, it may unravel fully, and she would be once more vulnerable to heartache. Twice was enough; she dared not risk a third.

"May I call upon you tomorrow?" That dimple appeared.

Fortunately, she had the perfect excuse to avoid spending time with forbidden fruit. "I have plans with friends tomorrow."

His gaze darted to Miss Harris and then back to her. "Tarrington's private art collection?"

She managed an articulate, "Er..."

"The very outing to which I had hoped to persuade you to join me." Again, that tempting dimple shone like a lighthouse guiding her to his mouth. How would those lips feel against hers? Ahem! Really, she ought to control her thoughts.

She glanced at Annabel, who smiled. No help from that quarter.

Mr. Partridge took a step nearer. "My friend Michael Cavenleigh and I would be delighted to offer you both a ride in my carriage." His glance included Annabel before he looked to Aunt Paulette. "With your permission, Mrs. Stafford. It's a landau—open and very proper."

Her traitorous aunt, insensitive to Meredith's concerns about Mr. Partridge, nodded with a kindly smile. "Of course you may escort them. I trust you'll take good care of my girls."

"You may count on me, madam." He bowed. "Until tomorrow, then."

No amount of pleading to be let out of tomorrow's outing with Mr. Partridge's tantalizing company succeeded in excusing Meredith from the trip to the private art gallery. Aunt Paulette and even Annabel held firm. Finally, Meredith mutinied the only way she knew how—wearing her oldest frock and pelisse and a plain, unadorned straw hat. Frowning, she descended the stairs, prepared to do battle with her aunt over her apparel, but Aunt Paulette only looked her over and gave her a knowing smile.

Mr. Partridge and Mr. Cavenleigh arrived. Mr. Cavenleigh, as usual, said little, though his expression remained pleasant. Mr. Partridge greeted them all with a wide smile. Did he know the power of his dimple?

As he offered Meredith his arm, he said, "What a pretty picture you make, Miss Brown. How refreshing to see such an elegantly simple ensemble."

She looked down at her faded apricot frockcoat over her plainest cream morning gown. "You're twitting me."

"Not at all. It's nice to see something so unadorned. Most ladies' clothing is buried under mountains of lace and ruffles. Yours is tasteful and a breath of fresh air."

Either he was a quick-thinking smooth talker or an unusual man with simple tastes. As the son of a duke, the likelihood of him being the former seemed great.

Under a gloomy, rain-laden sky, they stepped into the carriage. Mr. Partridge held Meredith steady as she stepped in. She clenched her teeth and put out of her mind the strength and gentleness in his hands. The seats sank under her, soft as a feather bed. Both gentlemen sat across from them, facing backward. Mr. Cavenleigh turned his focus to shops and buildings lining the road.

With a warm smile, Mr. Partridge locked his gaze with Meredith. "Thank you for accompanying us today on such short notice."

"I couldn't refuse." Meredith shot a meaning look at Annabel, but it had no effect on the unrepentant gleam in her cousin's eye.

"We're happy to oblige," Annabel chirped. "I have heard so much about the earl's house and its astonishing art collection. Meredith has quite an eye for art."

"Do you?" Mr. Partridge said, his eyes alight. "Have you a favorite artist?"

Meredith shot another warning look at her cousin, who seemed oblivious. Clearly, Meredith needed to work on her chilling glare. "Er, I'm not a true art aficionado, but I do enjoy Thomas Gainsborough landscapes. I also saw one by a living artist, Christian Amesbury, that caught my eye."

"Ah, yes, Lord Tarrington's youngest son. I've seen his work as well. It's excellent. He did such a lifelike portrait of my mother that I always half expect it to turn its head."

They chatted as they began the short distance to the London home of the Earl of Tarrington in Pall Mall near Green Park. The luxurious conveyance virtually glided over the cobbled streets. They turned a corner and met such heavy traffic that they could not proceed.

Mr. Partridge craned his neck. "I wonder what's amiss."

"It looks like an accident up ahead, sir," the driver commented.

"It does, indeed." Mr. Partridge stood. "Is that the Daubreys' coach?"

Annabel caught her breath. "I do hope not."

Mr. Partridge said, "I'm going to offer assistance." As he stepped out, he shot a concerned look at Meredith. "Forgive me for abandoning you."

Meredith stood. "I'll help."

She followed him down the sides of the street, stepping around groups who had gathered to watch.

He reached back and took her hand. "Stay close. I don't want us to get separated." His hand closed over hers, safe and reassuring. An illusion, surely.

With linked hands, they wound through vehicles, animals, and pedestrians until they reached the accident.

Mr. Partridge let out his breath. "It isn't the Daubreys." Still, he proceeded forward.

A town coach with a missing wheel tilted at a sharp angle nearly touching the ground. The other, a curricle, lay on one side, its axle shattered. Two sets of horses, still in their bridles, bits, and reins, pranced nervously nearby. Someone had thankfully unbuckled their harnesses from the damaged carriages. A coachman held the bridles of each teams' lead horse, speaking in low, soothing tones, a contrast to the shouts of two men gesturing wildly at one another. Both teams danced and shook their heads trying to escape the hands that held them.

Mr. Partridge went to the two shouting men. With his voice turned away from her and the noises of the crowd, his words failed to reach Meredith, but both men instantly turned to him, raising their voices as if trying to plead their case to the newcomer.

Meredith approached the team dancing about most nervously. "There now," she cooed to the lead horse. "All is well."

As she stroked their noses and looked them over for injuries, they settled, their ears swiveling to hear her.

"They ain't hurt," the coachman said. "I checked 'em."

Nodding, Meredith continued to speak to the horses as she rubbed their necks and noses. They ceased prancing and stood quietly, blowing out their breath in snorts.

"Are any of the riders injured?" she asked the driver.

"Nah. Jes angry. Blamed fool in the curricle careened around the corner. I couldn't avoid 'em. Those young bucks with their fancy clothes got no sense a'tall."

The men to whom Mr. Partridge spoke had ceased yelling. With Mr. Partridge as clear leader, gesturing and demonstrating, he and several bystanders lifted the two carriages. They half carried, half dragged them toward the nearest mews. How extraordinary that such a highborn gentleman would help perform a physically demanding task rather than leave it to the working class.

Meredith and the driver with the horses followed the ruined carriages as they limped under human power beneath an arch leading to the mews. They stopped in the mews courtyard. With the blockage cleared, traffic resumed streaming past the arch. Mr. Partridge continued to mediate until the men parted to see to their own carriage and teams.

He turned and smiled. "Forgive me for not attending to you." He brushed the smudges off his tailcoat and cast a rueful glance at his no longer pristine attire. The disheveled appearance lent him a greater charm. That dimple didn't help matters.

Almost against her will, she admitted, "You handled what might have been a dangerous situation."

He shrugged. "I'm happy they didn't come to blows. Shall we find Michael and your cousin?"

Humble too. Was he real? "Yes. I'm certain Annabel will be alarmed at my absence."

"You're close, aren't you?" He held out his arm.

She took his elbow and fought the sense of safety accompanying his touch. "She's a loyal friend."

"Everyone needs such a friend." With head high and walking at a sedate pace, he escorted her as if they were promenading at the park.

"She is not only a friend; I view her almost as a sister. I have none of my own." Why she offered that personal information she could not imagine.

"I have one sister, and she's so painfully shy that I wonder if she'll ever be coaxed out of hiding."

"Poor dear. I have never been shy. She must be lonely."

He glanced at her. "You're very astute. She has confessed to me of her loneliness, but she seems unable to speak when others are present and refuses to attend group gatherings where she might make friends."

"Perhaps she will learn ways to cope. Is she very young?"

"She is not yet sixteen. My mother only managed to coax her to come to one small dinner party to announce that she is out, but has not succeeded to do so a second time. Still, you are probably right."

He stepped in front of her, walking backward. "I know; I shall ask my mother to have a small dinner party and invite you and your family. She would probably like you. I know my sister would. Will you come?"

"To dinner with a duchess? Oh, no, I don't think I could possibly—look out!" She gestured at the lamppost behind him, but her warning came too late.

He backed into the post and let out an *oof*. Frowning, he glanced over his shoulder at the lamppost. "Was that there a moment ago?"

His bewildered indignation tickled her funny bone. She tried to smother her laughter but only laughed harder.

He grinned and finally joined in. "Have I ever told you they called me 'Mr. Suave' when I was in school?"

"Oh, indeed?" she asked skeptically, still chuckling.

"No." He made an exaggeratedly sad expression, which only sent her into peals of laughter.

"Good day, you two," sang out Annabel.

The landau pulled up alongside. Again, Mr. Partridge held her steady, and again a sense of safety and comfort came with his touch. She should not, could not, would not allow herself to fall for him. Despite his growing list of admirable qualities, he had yet to prove he wasn't after her virtue or dowry, despite her attempt to conceal the true amount. Why else would a duke's son give the time of day to the daughter of a mill owner?

Seven

Phillip and his companions reached the impressive home of the Earl of Tarrington while a light rain spattered their clothes. He barely managed to keep his eyes off Miss Brown long enough to step out of the carriage. As a group, they proceeded between large columns to the main door, where they were admitted into the spacious entrance hall. The rest of the group gathered inside, their excited, hushed voices revealing their anticipation of touring the home of the Earl of Tarrington and his art collection.

Miss Brown greeted Miss Harris, and they fell into happy conversation. Phillip drifted nearer, greeting others as he moved, and stood near Miss Brown, but hopefully not so close that she felt smothered by his presence. She had seemed to warm to him after the accident was resolved and laughed easily enough when he'd run into the lamppost. It gave him hope.

"Tell me, Miss Harris." Miss Brown's voice reached him. "Have you met any interesting gentlemen?"

"Do call me Cora," Miss Harris said.

"Only if you will call me Meredith," Miss Brown said.

Meredith. Phillip turned her name over in his mind, imagining gaining her permission to use it.

"I haven't met anyone new, Meredith," Cora Harris said, "but Mr. Morton has been attentive."

"Yes, he does seem to be. Have you known him long?"

"We met a week ago at Lady Hennessy's ball. He has called upon me nearly every day since."

Meredith Brown paused, then asked, "Don't you think that's taking it a bit too quickly?"

Trying not to appear as if he were eavesdropping, Phillip glanced at Miss Brown. She wore a thoughtful, guarded expression he knew well.

Miss Harris nodded. "I admit I'm surprised. As you can imagine, with a face like mine, I've never been considered a great catch. He declared it was love at first sight."

Miss Brown made a scoffing noise. "I have little faith in love at first sight. Besides, there is nothing wrong with your face."

"You are very kind, but I know the truth. At least my teeth are good, which my mother tells me is better than a flawless complexion or large eyes."

"Oh, indeed. I quite envy your teeth."

Another kind remark, considering Miss Brown's teeth were every bit as fine.

Three more gentlemen arrived, including the one Misses Brown and Harris discussed. Mr. Morton looked around. Spotting Miss Harris, he beamed and headed straight to her, leaving his two companions behind nudging each other and grinning.

"Welcome," said an older woman to the group. "I am the head housekeeper at Tarrington House, and I will guide your tour. Follow me, please."

She took them to a gallery upstairs and showed and discussed various portraits, landscapes, fine pottery, porcelain, and other curios inside rooms as ornate as the art they showcased—every bit as grand as the Suttenberg family ancestral home where his mother spent most of her time outside of London. The duchess would be impressed with the Tarringtons' tasteful opulence. Miss Brown made appreciative comments about the art that revealed her interest and knowledge of the subject.

Regardless of the beauty of art and architecture, Phillip mostly watched Miss Brown. She alternated her attention between the art that clearly drew her interest and the couple that concerned her. As she studied each new piece, her face softened, and her eyes drank in the art as if trying to glean wisdom. When she drew her attention to Miss Harris and Mr. Morton, she took on a focused, suspicious air.

Phillip leaned close to speak softly into Miss Brown's ear, but the scent of her perfume scattered his thoughts. Inhaling her softly exotic fragrance, he reached out to touch those little curls next to her ear. He stopped himself. If he hoped to win her trust, moving too fast would have the opposite effect.

Her breath caught as she no doubt felt his nearness. She turned and shot him a wary look.

Under his breath, he said, "You're very concerned about her, aren't you?"

She took a step away from him and fluttered her hands. "About whom?"

"Miss Harris."

She glanced at him, her pupils dilated, and took another step away. Ah, so she was not as unaffected by him as she tried to appear.

In a breathy voice, she replied, "Er, yes. I don't want her to suffer a broken heart."

"Please allow me to offer my assistance. I could make discreet inquiries about Mr. Morton's character, if that suits you?"

She considered. "If you wish."

He edged away from her and approached the two young men who had come in with Mr. Morton. One of them, Mr. Creasey, if memory served, stood near the edge of the group, his head tilted as he stared at a marble statue of a Greek goddess.

"Lifelike proportions," Phillip commented. "The expression of the face and the position of the body are quite remarkable. Out of cold marble, the artist created something almost alive."

Mr. Creasey grinned. "If only I could find a girl so pretty."

"Pretty isn't vital. Your friend Mr. Morton seems to have formed an attachment with Miss Harris."

Mr. Creasey let out a snort. "A pretty dowry can make up for an ugly face, I suppose."

Phillip stiffened at the unflattering way to describe a young lady. Still, he persisted in his goal. "Her dowry is the only thing he likes about her, I presume?"

A shrug came in reply.

"As a friend, doesn't he tell you?"

"Not really."

Which was probably true. Not every male freely discussed his intentions about young ladies with friends the way Phillip did with Michael. "Is he courting anyone else?"

"Presently? No. He tried to court Miss Vivian Charleston—looks and dowry—but she is toying with two others."

A pity. "He dodged a bullet with Miss Charleston," Phillip stated.

"Probably. Beautiful, though," he said wistfully.

Phillip had no interest in shallow women such as Vivian Charleston. He glanced at Miss Brown raptly listening to the housekeeper speaking about a group of paintings of the fox hunt. Miss Brown murmured something to Miss Harris, and they both giggled behind their fans. One day, Meredith Brown would smile and laugh with him the way she did with others.

Phillip returned his focus to his objective. "Was there anyone else?"

"Oh, sure. He always courts girls with big dowries, but they always choose someone else. Unlucky in love, I suppose."

Phillip paused. "He only courts girls with large dowries?"

"He's a third son with a meager income. What else can he do?"

"I see your point." Many gentlemen in his position sought ladies with dowries. It didn't make them mercenaries. Surely some chose carefully and let their hearts guide them to select a bride. "Has he proposed to anyone but Miss Harris?"

Mr. Creasy shrugged. "Two or three, I think. Turned him down."

Phillip winced. That was a condemning bit of news. "He is unlucky in love." So as not to appear to be so single-minded about the reason he had struck up a conversation with Mr. Creasey, Phillip asked, "Are you courting anyone?"

After they chatted about young ladies and parties, Phillip steered the conversation to other interests.

Eventually, Phillip bade farewell to the informative Mr. Creasey and moved back to Miss Brown's side. Upon completing the tour, they thanked the housekeeper and returned to their carriage. The rain had stopped, and even a few rays of sunlight shone as they drove to Gunter's for some ice and then took the ladies home.

As he handed down the ladies from the landau, Phillip said in a low voice, "I have information that may interest you, Miss Brown. May I take you for a carriage ride tomorrow at the park for the promenade?"

She searched his eyes, whether to determine what he had learned by his expression or if he did, indeed, have noteworthy news, he could not guess. That mix of vulnerability and guardedness entered her eyes. It was all he could do not to touch her face.

Finally, inclined her head. "I would be delighted."

He bowed and watched her enter the house with her cousin. A split second before she disappeared inside, she glanced back at him. He smiled, making sure his dimple showed. She hurriedly closed the door. Grinning, he returned to the landau.

"She still doesn't like you," Michael grumbled.

"She's putting up a fence, but I'm getting to her. You'll see. She agreed to go driving with me tomorrow."

"You should toughen up your hands so you can shovel horse manure in my stables without getting blisters. I plan to have a crowd watch, you know."

"You'd best fit a saddle to a mule," Phillip shot back. "You'll be riding one in Hyde Park."

Michael laughed, and Phillip grinned. Wager or no wager, Phillip would win over the lovely and complex Meredith Brown one way or another.

Eight

Meredith paced in the drawing room. She really ought not subject herself to more of Mr. Partridge's tempting companionship. He seemed so genuine, so kind, but she knew all too well how people's true character revealed itself later, after it was too late to spare a broken heart and ruined reputation. On the other hand, she must converse with Mr. Partridge at least once more to learn what he had discovered about Miss Harris's suitor.

The cowardly side of her begged her to send Annabel to question him, thus sparing Meredith from having to see him again, especially in such close proximity as a carriage.

Entering, Annabel smiled at Meredith. "You look so pretty, Merry. Just like a spring morning."

Meredith ran a hand over her favorite lilac pelisse. "I almost wore the old faded one from yesterday, but I didn't want to shame Aunt and Uncle by appearing in such a public place as the promenade at Hyde Park in something so shabby. People might think my guardians aren't providing for me."

"That's wise. I'm surprised you went through with it at the Tarringtons' yesterday."

Aunt Paulette entered the room and stopped short when she saw Meredith. She clasped her hands together. "Praise the Lord; you have finally decided to dress pretty for him."

Meredith almost stomped her feet. "I'm not dressing for *him*, Aunt. I am only going with him today because he has news about Miss Harris's suitor."

Aunt came near and looked her in the eye. "My dear, I understand your hesitation, but I have asked a number of people about him—about his character—and they all assure me he has an excellent reputation. He has never been known to be a libertine or a rake and has no need of dowry. Everyone says he is nearly the paragon his brother is."

"No one knew anything bad about Mr. Todd either," she grumbled.

"No one *knew* Mr. Todd. He was a stranger. Phillip Partridge is well known in London."

Meredith hesitated. "If he is such a paragon, what is he doing with me?"

"He fancies you."

"How can he fancy someone so far outside his class? That doesn't make sense."

"Love doesn't always make sense."

"Love. Ha!" Meredith picked at a loose thread on her glove.

The front door knocker clanged, and Meredith jumped. She sent a panicked look at Annabel. "He's here."

Her cousin put her hands on both of Meredith's arms. "It's only a ride and a conversation. If you choose not to spend another moment with him, that is your right."

Aunt added, "You may certainly refuse him, duke's brother or no."

Meredith nodded and swallowed. As long as she kept a tight rein on her heart, she had nothing to fear.

The butler announced him, and Mr. Partridge entered. A little nervous flutter began in the center of Meredith's chest. Dressed in a plum tailcoat with a gray and white brocade waistcoat and buff breeches, his boots shining like a mirror, he might have stepped out of a fashion magazine. Most men lacked his perfect proportions of height, leanness, and breadth of shoulders. None came close to matching the manly beauty of his face.

He removed his beaver hat, revealing his thick, dark hair with that unusual light streak adorning it. Softly, and with almost-believable affection, he smiled, an action that transformed him into the most handsome man she'd ever seen. Then that dimple appeared, and she momentarily lost control of her heart.

She must not. A highborn gentleman such as Phillip Partridge wanted something from a lowborn lady other than an innocent courtship. She must not forget that. Between his rank, wealth, and stunning good looks, he was accustomed to having whatever he desired.

When he greeted all of them in turn, she curtsied. "Mr. Partridge."

"Miss Brown, how wonderful to see you again. You are as lovely as a picture."

She inclined her head. "How kind of you," she said coolly. At least, she meant it to be cool. Instead, it came out breathy.

Annabel curtsied in greeting. "Have a care with my cousin." The angle of her smile revealed a friendly warning. "She is my dearest friend in all the world."

The smile left his face, replaced by an earnestness that almost pled to be believed. "I vow it, Miss Stafford." He turned to Aunt Paulette to include her. "I vow it."

Either he had perfected his skills as a deceiver, or he spoke with sincerity. Time would reveal his true intentions. Meanwhile, Meredith would proceed with caution. In fact, if she played her hand right, she might catch him in his own game.

He escorted her to his carriage outside. A boy wearing the striped waistcoat of a tiger held the reins of two matched bays, almost as alike in coloring as in size, harnessed to a shining curricle.

Meredith gestured to the horses. "Lovely cattle you have there."

He grinned. "Aren't they beauties? I bought them from Michael Cavenleigh. His family breeds them, you know."

"I didn't realize that."

"Many of the best stock out of Tattersall's are from Cavenleigh Stables." He handed her up, holding her with the right amount of power and gentleness, which might be a sign of his skill as a seducer as well. She would not fall prey to his charms! Still, she could play along; he might reveal his hand sooner. The tiger clambered up to the small seat behind them.

With a light but firm touch, Mr. Partridge guided his team into the streets at an unhurried pace. Years ago, Annabel and Meredith had theorized that the way a man drove spoke much about his character. If that were true, Mr. Partridge was a cautious, conscientious man with the perfect blend of strength and tenderness. Of course, their theory could be flawed.

"Have you been friends with Mr. Cavenleigh long?" she asked, just to make conversation.

"Since Eton. We got into a great deal of mischief together." He chuckled.

"I know what you mean."

"Surely girls don't bond over mischief." He glanced at her and raised a dark brow as if daring her to confess the truth. "Do they?"

"A combination of mischief, playtime, and soul-baring conversations. We take a balanced approach to forging friendships."

"What mischief did you get into?"

She smiled. "When we were children, my cousin Annabel and I used to swim with the boys."

He laughed. "I'm shocked." But he didn't look or sound shocked. "Do you still swim?"

"Yes, but not with boys."

He chuckled. "I'm heartily glad to hear that."

With his attention focused on the road, she allowed herself to look at him, admiring him from head to toe. No, she refused to like him—or trust him—but any woman would be mad not to appreciate his physical perfection like a piece of art. Had it suddenly grown warm? She fanned herself. It didn't help.

They reached Hyde Park and drove under spreading trees. Mr. Partridge glanced at her again, the intense blue-green of his eyes bringing back that little quiver in her chest. He glanced at her pelisse. "That color is pretty on you."

"Thank you." Breathy again, curse her for a simpleton. She must stay focused on her reason for agreeing to go for a drive with him. "You said you had learned something about Cora Harris's suitor?"

"Yes. Perhaps." He frowned. "I'm not certain. Mr. Morton is a younger son of a gentleman, and he is in possession of a respectable income for a bachelor. But like many younger sons, he needs to marry a girl with a decent dowry in order to provide a comfortable living for a family."

"So he does need a dowry."

"Not much more than others of his station. He does not have excessive debts or extravagant tastes."

She considered. It was true that any number of young gentlemen had to seek at least a modest dowry. But she'd made her own inquiries and learned Miss Harris's dowry was sizable enough to attract fortune hunters. Mr. Morton might only be the first.

"What may or may not be troubling," he added, "is that in prior Seasons, he proposed to two other young ladies, both with excessively large dowries."

"So, he does target dowries."

"Possibly. Or he might simply be lucky enough that the ladies who have turned his head happened to possess tempting dowries, but unlucky enough that neither returned his regard."

"I wonder if he told Cora Harris. That may be the most important clue."

"Perhaps. Or he may be embarrassed to admit he'd been refused."

It would be just like a man to defend another man, especially if they both had nefarious intentions.

He turned onto the famous Rotten Row, the place to see and be seen, and kept pace with others' carriages in the promenade. Passersby called out greetings. Some cast flirtatious glances and words. As they passed, the *beau monde* gazed at one another in envy or pride at ensembles, equipages, and horses.

Liveried servants drove carriages bearing family crests in immaculate splendor. Others guided their own carriages in a cavalcade of grandeur found nowhere else.

Next to the handsome and stylish Mr. Partridge, Meredith couldn't help but sit a little taller.

A stunningly handsome young gentleman rolled by in a curricle. An equally beautiful lady sat next to him, wearing a calculating smile.

"Lord Amesbury, Miss Charleston," Mr. Partridge greeted.

"Partridge." Lord Amesbury nodded.

Casting an assessing glance over Meredith, Miss Charleston nodded at them and slid her arm around her companion's in an openly possessive gesture.

"How is your mother?" Mr. Partridge said.

Lord Amesbury paused as a shadow passed over his expression before he quickly schooled it into urbane elegance. "Not much improved."

"I'm so sorry to hear that," Phillip said quietly. True sympathy darkened his eyes, and a little piece of Meredith's heart softened toward him.

"Thank you." Lord Amesbury's mouth tightened. In a clear attempt to change the subject, he said, "May we meet your lovely companion?"

"Of course. I'm very happy to introduce Miss Meredith Brown, the niece of Mr. and Mrs. Stafford. Miss Brown, this is Cole Amesbury, the Viscount Amesbury, and Miss Charleston."

"Charmed, Miss Brown." Lord Amesbury's smile bordered on rakishness, but in a teasing way that failed to raise Meredith's hackles.

Miss Vivian Charleston said with a condescending, overly sweet smile, "Miss Brown."

"I've met the Staffords," Lord Amesbury said to Meredith. "Good people."

"Thank you. I quite agree." Meredith managed a smile and inclined her head. He would not be so kind if he knew her lowly status. Still, she choked out, "A pleasure to meet you both, my lord, Miss Charleston."

After they passed, Mr. Partridge said under his breath, "I thought he had more sense than that."

"What was that?"

"Cole Amesbury. I don't know what spell that vixen has cast on him, but she is poison."

A new kinship arose between them. "Then you understand my concern over Mr. Morton and Miss Harris."

"I suppose I do."

A silver-haired lady nodded to them both with all the condescension of the queen as she approached in her gilded landau. Next to her, an immaculate Dalmatian sat with as much dignity as his mistress. Her coachman wore an old-fashioned flaxen wig and a bunch of lace at his throat. Even his gloves were spotlessly white.

"Mr. Partridge," greeted the lady. "Well, you are turning out all right, aren't you?"

"Your Grace." A smile hovered at the corners of Mr. Partridge's mouth.

Meredith almost choked. This lady was a duchess. Oh, why had she agreed to come on this ride? She didn't belong here among these aristocrats.

The duchess picked up her quizzing glass and aimed it at Meredith. "And who do we have here?"

"May I present Miss Meredith Brown?" He achieved a believable amount of pride in his voice.

The duchess eyed Meredith. "Who are your people?"

Meredith paled. What could she say?

"Miss Brown is related to the Baron of Stapleton," Mr. Partridge supplied.

Meredith almost laughed out loud, but managed to contain herself.

"You have a look about you I like." The duchess nodded in approval. "Take care of our boy, here."

"Yes, Your Grace," Meredith managed.

The duchess passed by, and Meredith let out a breath that took much of her strength with it. "I shouldn't be here where so many people like them will see us together."

Gently, he said, "They are just regular people, Miss Brown."

"They only seem regular to you, Mr. Brother of a Duke. And what's this about the Baron of Stapleton?"

"Don't you know your own genealogy?" Surprise and

amusement lit his voice. "Your mother's great-great uncle is the Baron of Stapleton, isn't he?"

She turned a surprised stare at him. "I didn't know that. You looked up my family tree?"

"I thought it might be useful at some point."

For a reason she could not explain, her ire raised, and she snapped, "Well, it doesn't matter that my mothers' father is a gentleman with distant ties to some baron. My father owns a factory." Then she delivered the killing blow. "His father was a poor factory worker."

He paused. That was it, then. He would likely drop her off and never darken her doorway again.

Benignly, he said, "When associating with aristocracy, it's best to discuss one's most impressive connections."

She let out a sharp, disbelieving laugh. "No amount of exaggeration will place me in your class."

Mildly, but with a firmness she could not mistake, he said, "I would have been proud to introduce you, even if I hadn't found a noble ancestor in your line."

"You are either a liar or a fool." Her voice closed over. Why the lump in her throat? She didn't like him. She didn't trust him. It made no difference that a union between them was impossible. None at all!

His voice took on a hard edge she'd never heard from him. "Miss Brown, despite my feelings for you, I cannot abide you besmirching my honor. I am neither a liar nor a fool, and if you were a man, I would have called you out for that."

His words hit her like a blast of cold water. He was right. She'd insulted him cruelly. No one deserved that. Except her former fiancé, who deserved a dictionary full of unflattering words. But she was beginning to suspect Mr. Phillip Partridge existed on a much higher plane than that scoundrel.

She let out a shaking, emotional breath. "I'm sorry. I

shouldn't have said that. It was unkind and untrue. Please forgive me."

They continued riding in silence, rousing enough to greet passersby, but not speaking to each other. So much for playing a game to try to discover his true motives.

Finally, she glanced at Mr. Partridge. His handsome face had settled into an expressionless mask, and he gripped the reins as if trying to squeeze some moisture out of them. The horses danced nervously. He loosened his grip with a jerking motion.

She moistened her lips. "I don't deserve your forgiveness, but I regret insulting you. I will understand if you wish to discontinue our association." Never seeing him again, never hearing the sound of his voice or basking in the light of his smile, smote her through. But it would be best to do sooner rather than later.

"I am not angry at you," he said finally. "Of course I forgive you." He glanced at her, some kind of desperate longing glimmered in his eyes. "I am angry about ... many things. Our difference in class—my family will not approve of my courting you—but mostly at that cretin who broke your heart."

She reared back. He knew! She clenched her hands to avoid putting them over her face. "H-how do you know?"

"By how guarded and defensive you are. Your suspicion of Mr. Morton. Your protectiveness of Miss Harris."

She clamped her mouth shut.

Achingly soft tones carried true regret. "I'm sorry he hurt you."

Staring straight ahead, she made no sound as he guided the team off the path and turned onto the street. She wrestled with his words, with the meaning behind them. Was it possible she'd been wrong about Phillip Partridge?

Nine

After two days of the kind of drizzle that permeated every surface and even Phillip's spirit, a sunny day with lawn games came as a welcome friend. He arrived at the St. Cyrs' country estate on the outskirts of London with Michael and eagerly looked around for the Staffords and their unforgettable niece.

"You have it bad," Michael said.

"I do, I really do," Phillip unabashedly admitted. "Every moment I spend with her makes me thirsty for more."

Being seen for himself, even if she kept a wary stance as if fearing he'd suddenly turn into a demon, was a unique pleasure. Besides, she liked his dimple. Even better, he'd even caught her admiring his physique.

Phillip made small talk with the host and hostess, Lord and Lady St. Cyr. Then, the inevitable middle-aged mother arrived, towing a girl whose hair was a shower of golden ringlets, probably having her first season.

Lady St. Cyr greeted the mother and daughter and made the introductions to Phillip and Michael.

The young lady—whose name he'd already forgotten—curtsied prettily and said in an overly high voice, "So pleased to meet you, Mr. Partridge." She gave him a blatantly hopeful smile without looking him in the eye.

He bowed. "A pleasure."

The young lady twittered and flirted, but she hardly looked at him. Just another girl who saw through him as if he were invisible, looking only at his heritage.

Out of the corner of his eye, Phillip spotted Meredith Brown. Sun shone on her, making her straw bonnet gold and her pale gown glow with heavenly light. The tightness in his chest eased, and exhilarated energy charged through him.

"Excuse me," he murmured, already moving toward Miss Brown.

Behind him, the girl said in her overly high voice that had turned decidedly condescending, "Who are *those* people?"

Ignoring them, he kept up a steady pace. The moment their gazes met, Miss Brown looked down and fidgeted. As he reached her side, he barely remembered to greet her family before bowing to her. "Miss Brown."

Her hesitant smile contained true warmth, he was sure of it. "Mr. Partridge."

Encouraged, he took a step nearer, close enough that her perfume filled him with more giddiness than his first crush. He'd never felt so alive. "I hear lawn bowls are first on today's agenda. Do you play?"

"I enjoy a game now and then, but I cannot claim to be skilled."

"If you have the right partner, I am certain you can soundly trounce the competition."

"Oh?" She pretended to look about. "Do you have any recommendations?" The playful glint in her eye gave him hope.

He puffed up his chest. "At the risk of sounding self-aggrandizing, I cannot give any higher recommendation than myself."

"I see. Since you come so highly recommended, I should consider you."

"Please say you will partner me?" He held out a hand.

She put her hands on her hips. "Only if you promise a good trouncing."

Theatrically, he laid one hand over his heart, keeping the other extended. "I will make that today's greatest ambition."

"Very well, Mr. Partridge, I accept." She placed her hand in his.

A cheer bubbled up inside him. He tempered it with a smile. He excused himself from her family and escorted her to the bowling green. The afternoon sun toyed with nearby trees and cast dappled shadows on the freshly mowed lawn.

Other couples lined up. The towheaded girl with the high-pitched voice had found a partner probably younger than herself, and Michael teamed up with a demure young lady with lovely eyes.

The host threw the smaller white ball called a kitty onto the green. Thus, the competition began. Each pair took turns throwing their balls to the kitty. Cheers, groans, and jeers followed every toss, and within minutes, the dignified group turned into a group of savages determined to win by any means possible.

The host laughingly accused one of the guests of cheating but got an elbow in the ribs from his wife, who raised her brows. Of lighter heart than Phillip had ever seen her, Miss Brown played vigorously, heckling the opposition with an incisive wit.

The host and his wife won, grinning as they accepted both congratulations and insinuations about their tactics. Merrily, everyone accepted glasses of lemonade served on silver trays.

Miss Brown folded her arms and sent him a playful glare. "You, sir, promised me a good trouncing."

Phillip held up his hands. "We made a valiant effort. Our

problem was we played too honestly. Perhaps next time, we ought to cheat."

She laughed, her eyes alight. Glancing behind him, she gestured. "There's a swing on that tree."

"Do you wish to try it?"

"I would." She looked almost shy about it.

"I'll push you." He held out a hand.

She took it, and they walked hand in hand to an oak so large that three men could not encircle it with clasped hands. From far above Phillip's head hung a rope the size of his wrist attached to a large wrought-iron seat.

Miss Brown sat on the cushioned seat swing and spread her skirts. She glanced back at him, a smile playing with her lips that might be considered flirtatious. Had he finally won her over?

"Ready?" he asked.

"Ready." She held up her feet.

He pushed the seatback, forward and back, forward and back, a little higher each time.

"I've forgotten how much I adore swinging. I haven't done it since I was a child." She leaned back and pumped her legs to keep her momentum.

He watched her contented expression and patted himself on the back for having given that to her. Of course, he couldn't take all the credit; she seemed a different person today. On the lawn, the other guests began a game of shuttlecock, but Phillip had no desire to join them.

She asked, "Do you want a turn?"

He shook his head. "Swing as long as you like."

"I think I could do this all day, but I probably ought to stop."

She held her legs still and allowed the swing's motion to slow. When she had nearly stopped, he stepped in front of her and grasped the ropes. His hand closed over hers, and she looked up at him with a delicate vulnerability. She stood, bringing her mouth within reach. Her eyes dilated, and she moistened her lips. His blood heated. The aching need to kiss her almost drove him to do it. She was finally warming to him. But moving too quickly would only push her away. Besides, they were in full view of the others.

Clearing his throat, he stepped back. "Forgive me."

She watched him with a new expression that he could not name. Curiosity? Approval? Relief? Disappointment? Lud, she was a mystery.

He held out an arm and took several steadying breaths as he escorted her back to the others. Mr. and Mrs. Stafford watched him.

Casually, Mr. Stafford approached him. "Mr. Partridge, may I have a word?" It wasn't exactly a question.

"Yes, sir." Phillip bowed to Miss Brown and followed the older man to another part of the lawn. He clenched and unclenched his hands uneasily. Had her uncle seen that moment when he'd almost kissed her and determined to take him to task?

Finding a shady spot out of earshot of the rest of the party, Mr. Stafford turned to him with lowered eyebrows so bushy they seemed alive. "You have a reputation for being an honorable young man, so I have allowed you to call upon my niece. But now that you are pairing off with her in public, I must ask you: what are your intentions?"

Phillip stared unflinchingly into the older man's eyes. "Sir, I am excessively fond of Miss Brown. It is my intention to court her."

"To what end?"

He chuckled uncomfortably and spread his hands. "Well, customarily a courtship is to learn whether we will suit."

"This is no laughing matter. Are you entertaining the possibility of asking her to marry you despite your differences in station?"

Phillip broke out into a cold sweat. "Yes, sir, I am."

"And your family approves?"

Phillip winced. How quickly he cut to the heart of the matter. "I have not yet made my intentions known to them regarding Miss Brown."

"And if they disapprove of her social standing?"

Phillip squared his shoulders against that disheartening likelihood. "If she will have me, I plan to marry her anyway."

"What if the duke forbids it? If he cuts you off?"

"I have my own income in a trust. He cannot touch it. I could provide a comfortable living for Miss Brown."

The uncle continued to fire questions at him at an alarming pace. "You haven't mentioned her dowry."

"As I said, I don't need a dowry to support a family, sir. Besides, it is my understanding that hers is modest."

"I see." Mr. Stafford considered his words. "I would have preferred that you come to me and ask permission to court her before singling her out publicly."

"Forgive me, sir." Since Meredith was of age, no permission was technically needed, but Phillip appreciated her uncle's protectiveness.

"Just because you were born the son of a duke and are the brother of a paragon does not instantly grant you my approval."

"I understand." Phillip felt like a child of six quaking at the beginning of his first term at Eton when the stern headmaster assured Phillip he would be whipped for any future disobediences just like the other students. He'd been truthful, as Phillip had discovered. "Sir, I have only the tenderest of feelings for your niece and the most honorable of intentions. I believe she is starting to return my regard. May I court her?"

Mr. Stafford cast a piercing look over Phillip. "She is a good girl."

"Yes sir. And a great lady."

Her uncle scratched his mutton chops. "You should know that her heart has been broken. Twice. I will do all in my power to prevent a third occurrence."

Twice? That explained much. "I will as well, sir."

Another long, probing stare came his way. "Very well. You have my permission to court her for as long as she desires. You do not have my permission to marry her. We will cross that bridge if the time comes."

"Yes, sir. Thank you, sir."

Mr. Stafford drew his bushy eyebrows together. "This permission comes with one condition: you must secure your family's blessing."

Phillip deflated. "That may not be possible."

Mr. Stafford nodded. "It is easy now while you are in the first stages of infatuation to think all you need is the girl of your choice and all else will work out in the end. But marrying against the wishes of family creates a rift that often never heals, and that takes a toll, believe me."

Phillip hesitated to ask personal questions, but he took a chance. "Is that what happened when her father and mother married?"

The older man nodded. "Her mother is my wife's youngest sister, Jeanne. When she vowed she would marry the son of a factory worker with plans to own his own factory, we tried to discourage her. Her father even locked Jeanne up to keep her away from that boy. But they were determined. In the end, her father relented to prevent them from simply running off together. Using Jeanne's dowry, my . . ." he stumbled over the words, "brother-in-law started his factory." He shrugged. "They seem happy. But Jeanne's parents never forgave her. They refuse to allow them, or their child"—he jerked his head toward Meredith—"into their home to this day. Meredith has never met her maternal grandparents and likely never will. She does not need that same rejection from her in-laws."

Phillip considered. Would Suttenberg and the duchess be so opposed that they would resort to such measures? He pictured summers, Easter, the Christmas season—even informal dinners—without his family. Having the bride of his choosing by his side might fill that hole, but at what cost? Family tradition ran strong, and the Suttenberg bloodline was a carefully guarded commodity. Generations of great matches had kept the family powerful and prosperous. Phillip would be rocking the proverbial boat by stepping out of traditional guidelines. He risked much. More importantly, he did not wish to subject Meredith to another form of familial denunciation. But he could not imagine giving up Meredith Brown simply because her father owned a factory instead of an estate.

Mr. Stafford watched him silently. Finally, he said, "If marriage is not a likely outcome, I insist you stop pursuing her immediately—before you raise her expectations and subject her to gossip again."

Again? Her heartbreak must have been public, making a difficult situation even worse. He ached for all she'd suffered.

Phillip set his jaw. "I understand, sir, and I agree wholeheartedly. I will do what I can to convince my family to give their blessing. Perhaps if they met her, they would see in her what I see."

Mr. Stafford pursed his lips. "Gain their approval, or you may not call upon her again." He returned to the group.

A Wager on Love

A disheartening condition. Phillip paced and tested the words he might use to convince his family to see Meredith Brown for who she was, not for her family connections or the lack thereof. He would fight for her. She was worth it.

Ten

The day after that magical afternoon Meredith had spent playing lawn games with Phillip Partridge and that unforgettable moment by the swing, Meredith greeted her new friend, Cora Harris. While Aunt Paulette chatted in the parlor with Mrs. Harris, Meredith and Cora linked arms and crossed the street to the small neighborhood park. Enormous shade trees spread a canopy overhead, a haven for twittering birds and scampering squirrels.

Cora described a theatrical production she'd seen the previous night. "I wish you could have been there. There were ever so many members of the *ton* there—grand lords and ladies wearing their finest. Oh, and that scandalous Lord Hennessy with his mistress." She sighed. "I know it's asking much, but I really hope if my future husband takes a mistress that he's at least discreet. I couldn't stand the humiliation if he weren't."

Meredith snorted. "Husbands ought to be faithful, just as they expect fidelity from their wives."

Cora's voice hushed. "If husbands don't find their wives attractive, as mine surely won't, it seems common for them to stray."

"They ought to have self-control regardless of their

wives' attractiveness," Meredith said flatly. "And no more talk about your husband not finding you attractive. You are lovely in many ways."

"At least Mr. Morton seems to think so."

Meredith gathered her courage. "He does *seem* to, but I fear he may not be sincere in his attentions."

"Why do you say that?" Wide, innocent eyes turned to her.

"For one thing, it's common knowledge that you have a substantial dowry. This makes you an automatic target for fortune hunters."

Cora frowned. "My parents have been very open about that since this must be my only Season."

"Why?"

"My younger sister is in love with a boy from our village, and my father has this old-fashioned notion that the elder sister must marry before the younger, so they have determined to try to find me a husband this Season so Sarah can marry this summer." More quietly, she added, "Sarah is pretty."

"Cora, you are pretty in all the ways that matter. And men who fail to see that are fools."

Cora smiled. "You are a dear."

"You may not think so when I tell you what I think I ought." Meredith chewed on her lower lip. She'd done this twice before, but it was no easier now. "Sweeting, I asked about Mr. Morton, and I heard from more than one source that he only courts young ladies who have large dowries."

Cora went very still. "He does"

In a flat voice, Meredith delivered the blow. "He proposed to at least two of them."

Her friend let out a shaking breath.

"He is a known fortune hunter, Cora. You are a means to an end."

Cora's chin trembled. "He told me he loves me."

"I, too, have fallen for that line. Twice. Both turned out to be liars. I know how convincing men can be when they say that."

Cora's eyes filled with tears. "He kissed me last night. It was so . . . pleasant."

Meredith understood that, too. "I'm sorry. I thought you should know." She guided her distraught young friend to a park bench and drew her down to sit.

Cora sniffed. "I have no other prospects. No one else has paid me any attention." Her shoulder shook. "I thought he truly cared. He said he loved me most ardently. Those were his words. Loved me. Ardently." She put a hand over her mouth. A tear leaked out of each eye.

Gently, Meredith said, "It's your choice whether you choose to marry him. Many marry to make a good match, or to please their families, or even because they no longer wish to be a burden to their families and have no other prospects. But I don't want your heart to be broken, thinking he loves you only to discover his true motive later." She handed Cora her handkerchief and held her hand while her friend grieved.

Finally, Cora dried her tears. "Thank you for telling me. That must have been difficult."

"It was." Meredith pushed out a breath. "What will you do now?"

"I'm tempted to tell him I will never see him again, but my family is so happy. Perhaps I ought to discuss it with my parents before I decide."

"That sounds wise." She paused. "If you take my advice, you'd send him packing and seek another. It's early in the Season. You deserve better"

Cora dabbed her eyes. "We ought to return home before Mother worries."

When they returned, Mrs. Harris was saying her goodbyes to Aunt Paulette. "Oh, there you are, Cora." She took a second look at Cora. "Whatever is the matter?"

"I learned that the only reason Mr. Morton is courting me is for my dowry."

"Oh, that." Mrs. Harris waved her hand. "I suspected as much. But that's why you have a dowry, dear. I am confident if he marries you that you will make the best of it."

Meredith snapped her mouth shut and looked downward, lest she glare daggers at Cora's insensitive mother. After they left, Meredith opened her mouth to decry Mrs. Harris, but her aunt beat her to it.

"Many mothers are a great trial."

The statement took Meredith off guard, and she laughed as she removed her hat and gloves. "I suppose. If I am ever blessed with children, I will endeavor not to be."

"You do that." Aunt Paulette kissed her forehead.

A motion outside the bay window caught Meredith's eye. She smiled from the inside out as Mr. Phillip Partridge mounted the front steps. "He's here."

"Mr. Partridge?" her aunt guessed.

"Oh, Aunt. I fear very much that I might be starting to . . . like him." She unbuttoned her pelisse.

"Of course you are. I'm starting to like him."

"But what if he turns out to be exactly like—"

"What if he isn't? What if he is exactly the kind, genuine, caring person he seems?" Aunt Paulette said.

Could her aunt be right?

The door knocker clanged, and Meredith hurried to remove her pelisse and smooth her hair. A moment later, Phillip Partridge entered. Something about his smile felt very private, as if he'd only ever smiled this way for her.

He greeted her aunt, asked about the family, and then turned his full attention to Meredith. "I have a taste for an ice and hoped I might entice you to join me."

Meredith smiled. "An ice sounds lovely."

She put back on her pelisse, hat, and gloves and took his offered arm. Outside, a young tiger sitting in the fold-down seat nodded solemnly at her. Mr. Partridge handed her in and took a seat next to her, his thigh brushing against hers, so warm, but not as warm as the currents zinging through her.

After enjoying an ice at Gunter's, where they laughed over the antics of children playing nearby, he drove to the park and left his curricle and team with the tiger, who held the reins with practiced ease.

Arm in arm, Meredith and Mr. Partridge strolled together as if they had always been this comfortable. They followed the path in to a less-used area of the park where a breeze murmured in the trees and a red squirrel scampered up a trunk.

He pushed out a weighted breath. "Your uncle gave his permission for me to court you on the condition that my family agrees to any possible future union between us."

"Ah. That was the conversation you had with him yesterday." Future union? Was he thinking of marriage?

"It was. I know that feels rather like putting the cart before the horse, since you may decide that we don't suit, but I must honor your uncle's request."

Her heart began an unsteady thumping, half hopeful, half fearful. "What, exactly are you saying?"

"I am not at liberty to ask you to marry me yet." Turning to face her, he enfolded her hands in his and looked into her eyes with clear adoration and hopeful vulnerability. "I love you, Meredith Brown."

She went very still. Nothing about his proposal resembled the others. This one rang of sincerity.

In his beautiful voice, he continued to weave his spell. "I want nothing more than to marry you—if you will have me."

He wanted to marry her—not ask her to be his mistress. He would marry her even though he believed her dowry was small, even though her father came from the working class.

He stepped in so close that his breath warmed her cheek. "My family will not approve unless I proceed carefully with them, but I plan to do all I can to convince them. I'm certain once they meet you, they will see in you what I see."

He deserved to know all about her. Even if it meant he'd change his mind. She had to tell him.

"Mr. Partridge..." She moistened her lips, but her voice all but left her.

"Phillip," he said.

He might regret granting her permission do something so intimate as to use his Christian name. Her knees shook. "You should know that I have been engaged. Twice."

He went still. After a heartbeat, he put his hand on her arm and leaned in closer. "Tell me," he whispered. He brushed his lips over her temple. A thousand little candles lit inside her.

"I..." She grappled for coherent thought. Her confession might change everything. "I thought it was love at first sight. My father refused to allow us to continue courting. He said my suitor was a rake and would make a poor husband, but I was foolish and refused to listen to reason. I thought we were in love. So, we eloped. Or so I thought." Her voice caught.

He went still but didn't step away. Instead, he put his free hand on her other arm.

"My father caught up to us before we'd gotten more than an hour down the road. Later, I learned we were not on our way to Gretna Green after all. He had not planned a marriage—only a seduction." She swallowed through the pain of his betrayal.

He tightened his grip on her arms. At least he hadn't recoiled in revulsion.

"Everyone assumed I'd been ruined and tutted about how fortunate I was not to have had a child." Sickness thickened in her stomach. "Once enough time passed to prove to gossipers that I was not increasing, my parents sent me to live with my paternal grandmother. They said it was to give the scandal a chance to die down, but I knew the truth: they despised me. They could hardly stand to look at me." After all this time, it still cut her all the way through, leaving a ragged, bleeding wound. "Occasionally, they write formal, polite letters, as if I were a distant relative." She let out her breath in a half sob. "I read about my father's mill in the newspaper."

"I'm so sorry," he whispered.

She dragged in a shaking breath. "About a year later, I received a second proposal from a suitor. I thought he was different. He sought permission to marry me from my grandmother, but she suspected his feelings were not genuine, that he was only after my dowry. She offered him money to leave. He snatched the money without a backward glance. I never saw him again."

Silently, he kissed her brow again, taking the sting out of those frauds in her past. But the consequences remained.

Her voice shook. "If anyone in London learns of my scandalous past, it would taint you and your paragon of a brother."

Firmly, he said, "I am not interested in gossip."

"But the Duke of Suttenberg has such a high standard of excellence. And your mother . . . no duchess would want her son embroiled with a lowborn, scandalous woman. Your family—"

"Will need to be won over. But no more now than before you told me." He pulled away and looked her in the eye soberly, earnestly. Then, a faint smile curved his lips. "At the risk of sounding arrogant, the Suttenberg reputation is strong enough to withstand a whisper of gossip from years ago that may or may not have followed you here from up north."

With a wan smile, she teased, "That's the most arrogant thing you've ever said to me."

His smile turned to a grin that showed his dimple. "That's because I'm so confident in my stunning good looks and charm that I need not boast."

A huff of laughter bubbled up inside her. "You are correct on all accounts, of course."

He raised his brows. "Did you just pay me a compliment?"

She pursed her lips, but it collapsed into a rueful smile. "I suppose I did."

"You, my dear, are everything lovely, and I will happily compliment you each time I see you. I look forward to trying to earn another compliment in a few years."

"I'm not sure I'll hand one out that soon."

Laughing, he pulled her into a strong embrace and held her close. "Admit, it; you love my dimple."

"I adore your dimple," she breathed. "And I adore you."

His heart thumped against her, and he pressed his lips into her hair. She sank into him. Her body and soul let out a sigh that at last they'd found their missing parts only supplied by him. If she'd known how wondrous—how healing—it would be to allow Phillip Partridge to hold her, she might have relented sooner. But she hadn't been ready sooner. Now? Now she was ready. Not just ready—starved.

He loosened his grip and pulled his head back enough to look at her. His gaze dropped to her mouth. Her lips tingled, burned, ached. Unbearably slowly, he lowered his head, coming closer, ever closer. An agonizing tightness in her stomach clenched as he moved with all the languid motions of a master torturer. A distressed whimper wrenched out of her. She closed the gap between them, guided to his lips by a magnetic pull. His kiss was sweet and gentle at first but turned to consuming hunger that only fanned her need. Through it, she received his message: he truly loved her.

 Eleven

Phillip cantered his horse on the long, winding drive to the Suttenberg home, Edgeworth House, on the outskirts of London. The Tudor structure with Elizabethan and Georgian additions once reposed in a pastoral area, but as London grew, other homes cropped up nearby. Still, the house and surrounding grounds retained its old-country charm with expansive lawns and spreading shade trees. Sheep grazed on the hills of the estate, and peacocks called as they fanned their glorious tails. The setting sun cast purple shadows on the drive, but Phillip knew the way so well he could have traveled it with his eyes closed.

After dismounting and tossing his reins to a servant, Phillip dashed up the short flight of stairs to the front door.

The butler opened the door before Phillip knocked. "Welcome home, sir."

Phillip handed off his hat and gloves. "Good evening, Barnes. Is the duchess home?"

"Indeed, sir. She is in her bedchamber dressing for dinner, I believe."

"Thank you." It had taken Phillip years to convince the old family butler that he need not announce Phillip to his own mother. Smiling again over that small victory, Phillip strode up the stairs two at a time, unable to contain his nervous energy. Meredith Brown's surprisingly passionate kisses fueled his determination.

No amount of rehearsing had produced the right words to say to his mother. He'd simply have to speak from the heart and hope she would be more receptive than expected.

He knocked at her door. "Mother?"

A pause. "Phillip? Come in."

He pushed open the door and stepped in. Wearing a blue brocade evening gown, she sat at her dressing table while a maid styled her dark hair. Her reflection smiled at him from the mirror.

"This is a surprise. What brings you here, son?"

"Can't a son pay a call to his mother without there being a specific purpose?" He crossed the room and kissed her cheek.

"He could, but he seldom does." Her smile softened her gentle scolding.

He gave her a rueful smile. "I am chastened."

"We shall see. If you are truly chastened, you'll pay me a visit once in a while, just to bask in my wisdom and maternal affection."

He chuckled, his nervousness making it sound choked. "Yes, Mother." He sat in a nearby armchair so he could look her in the eye. "Mother, I know your social calendar is quite full, but I have come to ask you if you will host a small dinner party for some friends of mine."

"Of course. I am not entertaining much this Season, so I'd be happy to throw together one for you. Who would you like to invite?"

"Lord and Lady Daubrey, the Harris family, Michael Cavenleigh, perhaps Cole Amesbury"—the viscount seemed to like Meredith, so that might help Phillip's cause—"and the Staffords."

She nodded. "As you wish. A dinner party that small will be no strain."

"Could you pull it together in a few days?"

"Yes." Shrewdly she watched him from her perch. "What is it that you really want?"

Phillip should have known this would not work as he'd hoped. "I want you to meet the Stafford's niece, Miss Meredith Brown."

"Oh? Oh." A slow smile curved her lips, reminding him of a cat about to enjoy a bowl of cream. "You've found a girl? Oh, Phillip, this is wonderful!" She went still. "Why the dinner party? What is wrong with her?"

He fisted a hand. "There is nothing wrong with her. She is lovely and charming and kind and bright and witty. And I love her."

"Why don't you think I'll approve?"

He ever despaired of her intuition. "Make her acquaintance before you pass judgment. You will like her—I'm sure of it. In fact, Suttenberg will like her. Mother, she's the most—"

"Phillip." With an impatient glance, she waved her hand at the maid. "Leave us."

The woman stepped back, curtsied, and soundlessly left the room.

As his mother opened her mouth, Phillip interjected, "Mother, please, just meet her."

She arose and faced him like an indignant queen. "Who are her parents?"

He stood, his back ramrod straight like a soldier marching to battle. "Her mother is a lady—a daughter of a gentleman and a relative of the Baron of Stapleton."

"And her father?"

He swallowed. He'd rather face that schoolmaster and his switch than confess to his mother. He gathered his courage. "He owns a lace factory in Loughborough."

"No."

He barely managed not to stammer, "I beg your pardon?"

"No, you may not marry her, no matter how beautiful or charming you think she is or how much you fancy yourself in love. You will not water down the bloodline with someone so far beneath us."

Phillip's blood heated. "How can you be such a snob?"

"It is a matter of duty as well as family pride. Our feelings do not matter. We must do right by the family name—generations of Suttenbergs, past and future, rest on our decisions." She took a breath. "You have neither my permission nor my blessing." She took a few steps closer and poked him in the chest. "Do not shame us by continuing to associate with this . . . this . . . factory girl."

"She is a lady in every possible meaning of the term—"

"Not by birth!"

He recoiled.

She softened and put a hand on his shoulder. "Oh, Phillip, you are only four and twenty. You have time. There are plenty of young ladies out there of good breeding who would love to marry you."

Bitterly, he said, "They see only the Suttenberg family. They don't see me."

In soothing tones, she said, "Out there is someone you have not yet met."

"I *have* met her, Mother."

Her face hardened. "My answer is no. I forbid you to see her again. This discussion is over." She turned away and stood with clenched fists and heaving breath.

His anger left him, and in its wake came a searing, aching pain that he would be disavowed by the very people who should love and accept him unconditionally. He would lose them, probably forever. His children would never know his side of the family.

His father would not have approved. No one in his family would condone their union. Grandmama would probably strike him with her cane. The scandal of him marrying a girl of Meredith's birth would taint generations of Suttenbergs. Even his brother, the paragon, would bear the shame of Phillip's marriage to the wrong girl.

He would be selfish to take his little slice of happiness at their expense.

Twelve

Meredith sat in the last row of chairs at the musicale between her cousin Annabel and her friend Cora Harris. Poor Cora. All the light had left her eyes, and she never once smiled. It pained Meredith that she had removed her friend's happiness. Still, it was better that Cora learned of her suitor's intentions before it was too late.

At the end of the performance, Cora excused herself. Meredith stood to mingle with other guests and offer her appreciation to the performers. Across the room, she spotted Michael Cavenleigh. How odd to see him without Phillip. For that matter, it felt every bit as odd not to have Phillip at her side.

Her lips, nay her entire being, still tingled from Phillip's earth-moving kisses. She'd almost begged him to marry her on the spot. But his family would need to be won over. Somehow. And having a long and respectable courtship would please Uncle and, hopefully, her parents before she married Phillip.

Marry Phillip. She smiled. How easily she pictured his face smiling across from her breakfast table, as they rode, as they walked, as they laughed. She longed to snuggle up to his side while his arms encircled her.

A Wager on Love

If only Cora could be so happy. Perhaps Meredith ought to check on her to ensure she was well. She moved toward the door, nodding to Michael Cavenleigh as she passed him.

A gentleman greeted him loudly. "I heard the strangest thing about you, Cavenleigh. You were seen purchasing a mule."

A mule? Why on earth would a breeder of prize-winning stallions buy a mule? Meredith glanced back.

Mr. Cavenleigh's mouth twisted to a grimace. "Who said that?"

"So, it's true, then?" the gentleman laughed. "Why would you do that?"

Riding a mule sounded like the price of a wager typical of two gentlemen bachelors. Poor Mr. Cavenleigh. He really should have known better.

"Excuse me." Mr. Cavenleigh muttered to the still chuckling gentleman as he headed to the door. As he passed Meredith, he gave her a polite nod.

She sent him a sympathetic look and took a guess as to the odd purchase. "Gentlemen's wagers can be a sore trial, can they not?"

He looked startled. "He told you?"

A warning bell rang in Meredith's head. It was probably nothing, but she hadn't spent years developing her suspicious nature to let go of it now. She conjured up a giggle and waved her hand.

"We have few secrets. I don't know all the details, just that your losing involves a mule. I admit, I'm curious. Do elaborate." Phillip had failed to mention the entire wager, but Mr. Cavenleigh could make what he might of her words. "What must Phillip do if he loses?"

"He has to muck out my stables."

She covered her mouth and laughed. "Oh, dear. A

humiliating and difficult task for someone born of a duke. No wonder he didn't tell me." The breadth of how unaffected he seemed by his high station continued to surprise her.

Cavenleigh almost smiled. "As humiliating as a prize stock breeder riding a mule at Hyde Park."

Part sympathetic and part amused, she laughed again. "I see. I almost wish there were a way you could both win to be spared."

He nodded. How odd to converse with Phillip's normally silent friend. Then again, quieter people were often overshadowed by more open, outgoing friends. People like Mr. Cavenleigh, who seemed content to allow their friends to carry conversation, sometimes conversed more when no one else filled that social obligation.

She gave him an encouraging smile in the hopes to get him to continue talking. "When, again, will the outcome be decided?"

"He wanted to make it when you announced your engagement, but I insisted it must be by Season's end, or the day after your wedding, in case you changed your mind."

Everything inside her went still.

He misread her expression. "I didn't know you then—you might have been a jilt. But you aren't flighty."

She put on an amused smile, while deep in her heart, the fear that once again she had been duped by a silver tongue crept out of his hiding place to haunt her.

She'd been the object of a gentleman's bet.

They had wagered about her marrying Phillip.

Had all of Phillip's attention been the result of his desire to give his friend a set down? But marriage seemed extreme. Still, perhaps he'd learned of her dowry despite her attempts and needed the money worse than she supposed. He was a second son, after all, and many families left second sons to fend for themselves by finding gentlemen's employment or marrying well. Perhaps he, too, was lying about wanting marriage and only wanted a dalliance. She should have known it was too good to be true.

Aware of Mr. Cavenleigh's observation, she conjured up a laugh. "That sounds a fitting wager. I doubt he has ever mucked out a stable, and I'm certain you have never sat on less than a prized purebred."

"Indeed. But the wager aside, I do wish you happiness."

At least, that's what she thought he said. The roaring in her ears drowned out most sounds around her. They'd bet on her. With high stakes to their pride.

"Thank you." She swallowed. "We are not engaged to be married, though."

"Of course. Premature."

She managed some sort of reply and took her leave of him. Once again, love had made a fool of her. How could she have been so foolish as to have believed it was real this time?

Home. She must go home. Now, before she lost her composure. Through blurred vision, she sought her aunt and uncle.

Annabel found her instead. "Oh, Merry, you must come. Mr. Morton has cornered Miss Harris." She took Meredith by the hand and towed her to another room.

Cora Harris? In trouble? Meredith cast off her sorrow and focused on protecting her friend. It was all she had left, it seemed.

"Please, listen to me," a male voice said.

In the far corner of a sitting room, Cora Harris stood with her hands upheld. Mr. Morton stood over her, his arms extended.

"I have heard all I need," Cora's voice quivered. "You only desire my dowry, just like those other ladies you courted. You never loved them, and you never loved me."

"That's not true." He stepped closer. "I do love you—more than I ever loved them."

Meredith hurried forward to lend aid to her friend and placed herself between them, facing Mr. Morton like a mother bear protecting her young. "Mr. Morton, the lady is not interested in your lies."

"I am not lying. I love her." He addressed her friend. "Cora, please, I love you!"

Meredith stood taller to protect her friend from doom.

Cora's muffled voice came from behind Meredith. "You only want my dowry. Now go away!"

He raked his fingers through his hair. "All right. I admit that at first, I sought you out only because of your dowry. My aunt cut me out of my inheritance when I refused to marry her half-witted daughter. And I never got the education to have a profession, such as a barrister. I don't have the nerve to enlist in the army. So yes, at first, my only plan was to marry well."

"Then you'd best leave, sir," Meredith said, staring him down. "Your game is over."

He cast a frantic glance at Cora behind her and then looked Meredith in the eye. "Please do not condemn me without allowing me to defend myself." The steady, courageous desperation in his expression gave her pause.

"Very well. State your case." She folded her arms.

"I don't need a dowry to support myself. I need it to care for a wife and children."

At least he was thinking about how he would provide for his family, but he was still a mercenary.

"Shortly after meeting Miss Harris," he continued. "I developed a true attachment to her. I enjoy being with her, and I like who I become in her presence. She makes me want to be a better man. I want to spend all my days with her. And if her dowry did not exist, I would find a way to provide for her—learn some kind of skill. I would marry her even if she were penniless."

Behind Meredith, Cora's breath caught. His earnest expression pled for understanding. But was he truly sincere? Phillip Partridge had seemed genuine too, but it had all been part of a wager, the true purpose of which she had yet to determine.

"Do you mean that?" Cora said.

He stepped to the side and reached for her. "Cora, darling, I mean that with all my heart."

Meredith turned over his words, searching for a hidden agenda. Nothing came to mind. He seemed sincere. She glanced back.

Cora stared at him with tears brightening her eyes and a smile that transformed a plain girl into a beauty. "Oh, John!"

Meredith stepped to the side and allowed them to converse without her in their way.

"I am in earnest, Cora. I will refuse your dowry. Will you agree to an extended betrothal to allow me time to find a means to care for you as you deserve?"

Cora sniffled.

"Please, will you marry me?"

"Yes!" She ran into his arms.

As Meredith strode to Annabel lingering in the doorway, her cousin smiled. "That was brilliantly done."

Meredith shrugged. At least one person had found her true love. If Meredith must be denied that kind of joy, she would become the guardian of young girls to ensure they were never deceived. Someday, she might find and mend the broken pieces of her own heart.

Thirteen

On the ride home, Phillip agonized over his choice. Sever ties to his family and bring social censure upon them, or give up the only girl who'd ever seen—ever loved—him? She hadn't said she did, but her kiss had revealed her heart in a way words could not. One day she would trust him enough to declare her love for him.

Could he disappoint, humiliate, reject his family this way?

Could he give up Meredith Brown?

No. No, he could not, would not give her up. Of course, the condition of Mr. Stafford's permission to court Meredith was to gain his family's permission. He'd failed on that score. He refused to allow that to stop him.

Meredith might have an idea. The very thought of sharing his worries with her and seeking her counsel settled like a healing balm on his troubled heart.

Instead of going home to change, he rode directly to the location of tonight's musicale she would be attending. Wearing riding clothes dirty from the road, he didn't dare enter a home where everyone would be clean and dressed in their evening finery. He couldn't wait. He had to see her. He paced the sidewalk, waiting for her to exit the building.

A Wager on Love

Guests began emerging, and Phillip moved closer to the steps where he would be illuminated by the light spilling out of the fanlight above the door. A few who exited the house recognized and greeted him, and he replied to them as if he always lurked about the streets, dressed for a day in the country.

More and more people emerged, and Phillip grew anxious. Had she already left? Had she decided not to attend after all?

Michael appeared in the doorway and paused midstep as he recognized Phillip. "How was your visit with the duchess?"

"Not as successful as I had hoped."

"You'll prevail." He offered a teasing smile. "Or I'll enjoy watching you muck out my stables."

"I'll enjoy watching you ride a mule," Phillip shot back. "Is she here?"

He glanced back. "I didn't see her leave, but then, I haven't seen her in the last several minutes. Ah, here she comes now." He descended the steps and moved behind Phillip. "You might not want to speak with her now. You smell of horse."

"I know, but I need to see her."

A soft chuckle came in reply.

The Staffords exited, followed by Meredith Brown, who walked with bowed head.

Phillip's heart surged in his chest, and it was all he could do not to rush to her side. "Miss Brown."

She lifted her head. Even silhouetted, her stiffened posture revealed something was terribly wrong. What could have happened? Surely Mr. Stafford hadn't forbidden her to see him after telling Phillip he could court her if he gained his family's approval. What else might have upset her? Had someone snubbed her?

As she passed between the columns flanking the door, he moved to her side. "What has happened?" He reached for her.

With barely a glance, she sidestepped him. His blood chilled.

"I have nothing to say to you, Mr. Partridge," she said, her tone icy.

This couldn't be the woman who had been so warm and willing in his arms only hours ago. "What do you mean?"

"Whatever game you are playing, it is over. I will not be the object of a wager."

"Wager?" The chill in his blood sank into his bones.

Next to him, Michael cursed under his breath.

"High stakes." She folded her arms. "I have heard of so-called gentlemen's wagers, but I never dreamed I'd be the object of one. Did you record it in that infamous betting book at your club?"

"N-no," he stammered. "Of course not."

"As far as I'm concerned, you both deserve to lose."

Aware of a growing crowd around them, including Mr. and Mrs. Stafford, who glared at him, Phillip said, "It's not what you think. Let's discuss this in private."

"There is nothing to discuss. We shall not converse, or even meet, again." She lifted her chin and strode past.

Mr. Stafford stepped up to him nearly nose to nose. "The answer is no."

The Stafford family drove away. Members of the *ton* who had once called themselves friends of his—at least, of his Suttenberg connection—gave him looks ranging from amusement to triumph to pity.

He turned away and grabbed Michael by the arm, walking with long, angry strides. "You told her," he snarled.

"I—"

"Was winning so vital that you sabotaged me? I didn't

know you'd sink so low. I thought, out of everyone, I could trust you. But I was wrong. Everyone is so concerned with appearances, with doing what they think the *beau monde* expects of them, that no one can be a true friend or—heaven forbid—encourage someone to pursue their own definition of happiness!"

After a moment of trotting along to keep up with Phillip, Michael said, "Are you finished?"

"Yes. We are finished here." He pushed Michael's arm away as if it were diseased and crossed the street.

Michael. How could he? His oldest friend. Phillip never would have expected it. He'd lost his oldest friend. He'd lost the only girl he'd ever loved.

He walked and walked, and finally remembered he'd left his horse in the care of a servant at the house where the musicale took place. After retrieving his mount, he rode through the streets until he found himself at the Daubreys' house.

The couple, still dressed in their evening clothes from whatever entertainment they'd attended this eve, greeted him despite the late hour.

"Come in and tell us what has you so blue deviled this, er, morning." The normally stoic Lord Daubrey glanced at the clock. He handed Phillip a glass of something that burned as he swallowed it.

Phillip poured out all his troubles to the silent, sympathetic couple and then sat, exhausted, with head and hands hanging. The clocked ticked in the silent room. Lady Daubrey sniffed and dabbed at her eyes.

Lord Daubrey spoke. "You need to apologize."

Phillip lifted his head. "What?"

"If I've learned anything, it's that when she's upset with me, even if I think I've done nothing wrong, I apologize.

Usually I discover that I *have* done something wrong, and then I can make amends."

Lady Daubrey smiled, still dabbing at her eyes. "He's right. If I'd found out about such a wager, I would be angry and probably suspect you had some other motive for making the wager in the first place."

He should have listened to his first instincts, the ones that shrank at the prospect of betting on a lady.

"Apologize to her," Lady Daubrey said. "Then to Mr. Cavenleigh. You may discover that you have misjudged him as Miss Brown has misjudged you."

Phillip hung his head. They were probably right. In his shock and panic at losing Meredith, he'd probably lashed out prematurely. Unfairly.

"As far as your family," Lady Daubrey said. "I have an idea. Come to dinner in four days' time, and we shall see what we can do for you."

By the time Phillip left his patient friends, the first rays of sun sent a silver shimmer over the horizon, silhouetting London buildings and bridges. After resting a few hours, he wrote a letter, then paid an early visit to Michael.

In his bachelor rooms, Michael eyed him with that urbane elegance he'd perfected as a youth. He raised a brow. "Breakfast?"

Phillip let out a weighted sigh. "Thank you."

Michael uttered a command to a servant and led Phillip to a small round table already set with fruit, coffee, sausages, and bread. Wearing a brocade banyan over his shirt and waistcoat, Michael took a seat and sipped his coffee, still eyeing Phillip.

"I didn't sabotage you," Michael finally said.

Phillip nodded. "I should have known better."

"She seemed to know about it already. Asked me to fill in

details." He paused and a brow lifted faintly, the way it did when he was about to deliver a verbal jab. "What girl wouldn't want to marry into the family of the famous Duke of Suttenberg, wager or no?" He sent Phillip a gently amused expression.

Phillip couldn't make light of it. "I had hoped she might want to marry merely Phillip Partridge. Now..."

"She wouldn't be so hurt if she didn't love you."

Phillip closed his eyes. Michael could be right. If she were only after an advantageous match, she would have shrugged off the wager and agreed to marry him anyway—not that he had ever suspected her of being a social climber. "I vowed I'd never hurt her, but I have."

"Make it right."

"How? She told me she never wants to see me."

"When a woman says that, it means, 'try harder to win me.'"

Phillip nodded slowly, turning over Michael's words. "I don't plan to give up."

When a servant appeared and put a place setting in front of Phillip, Michael gestured to the food. "Eat."

Phillip picked up his silverware. "For the record, I will muck out your stables whether or not she marries me."

"I have already purchased a mule to ride in Hyde Park."

They grinned at each other. His appetite restored, Phillip tucked into the food with a hunger that impressed even his friend. One way or another, Phillip would convince Meredith Brown that he loved her and that they belonged together. Somehow, he would prove to his relations that she deserved to be welcomed into the family.

Fourteen

Meredith Brown lay on her bed staring at the ceiling, more bereft than when her parents had sent her away.

Love would never again make a fool of her. Once she returned to Grandmother's house, she would marry the middle-aged vicar, harboring no silly ideals about love, and simply enjoy being the mistress of her own home. He was a quiet, honorable gentleman. As his wife, Meredith could more easily help parish members avoid making fools of themselves the way she had as an idealistic, naïve girl who believed the pretty words of practiced heartbreakers. Eventually, she would have children of her own to love and guide to adulthood. It would be enough.

Although she had been wrong about Mr. Morton, and it probably would have been best if she had stayed out of their affairs. Instead, she caused them both unnecessary sorrow. She had also been wrong about Phillip Partridge. Now she knew even more about the signs of which to be aware, and she would use the additional knowledge to help others.

If she ever overcame the heartbreak.

She pressed a hand over her chest where the broken pieces of her heart cut her and left her to bleed. The loss and pain of her prior heartbreaks had been child's play compared to the agony knifing through her over and over. Meredith might never breathe again.

Annabel came in and sat on the bed next to her. She put a hand on Meredith's back in a soft gesture of love and friendship and acceptance. For several long moments, she said nothing, just offered wordless sympathy and support.

Finally, she took a breath. "I should warn you, Mama will insist you come to the Daubreys' dinner party tonight."

"I'm not interested in socializing. London has lost its appeal. In fact, I believe I shall return to Grandmother's house as soon as arrangements can be made."

"I cannot imagine how you must feel." Annabel's lower lip puckered. "But don't let him ruin your Season in London."

The door opened, and Aunt Paulette bustled in. "Meredith, you are going to the Daubreys' party, and that is my final word on the matter. When a titled lord and lady invite you to a party, you do not refuse. Other esteemed guests will be there, including one of the most sought-after bachelors, Cole Amesbury, heir to the Earl of Tarrington."

Meredith remembered Lord Amesbury from Hyde Park but entertained no delusions that his rakish smile held any promise for her. Nor did she seek it. Still, she should keep her promise to Annabel and be polite for her family's sake and for the sake of the Daubreys who were kind enough to include her again. Somehow, she'd find the fortitude to survive the evening.

Dully, she said, "Very well, Aunt."

Aunt Paulette paused as if she hadn't quite heard her correctly. "You will come, then?"

"Yes, Aunt, if that is your wish." Warming to the idea, she added, "I might as well enjoy my Season before I return to Grandmother's house." *Enjoy* might be impossible, but she would make a show of living instead of curling up like a shriveled leaf at autumn's end.

"Good girl." Aunt Paulette patted her hand.

After the maid styled Meredith's hair in an unusually elaborate coiffure, per her aunt's instructions, Meredith dressed in her best silk gown, which she had yet to wear, a creation in soft aquamarine silk with a cream and pearl netting. After adding a shawl and gloves, she squared her shoulders and vowed to conceal her torn and bleeding heart.

Downstairs, Aunt Paulette beckoned to Meredith, her eyes alight. "Come with me, please."

"As you wish." Meredith followed behind, unable to muster even the smallest curiosity.

Aunt Paulette opened a door to a sitting room and stepped back, indicating that Meredith should precede her. Two people stood inside. Could it be . . . ?

Dressed every bit as finely as members of the *bon ton*, her parents turned to her. "Oh darling," her mother said. "You are so beautiful!"

Her father gave her a hesitant smile. "My, you've grown up so much."

After all this time, she could hardly believe they had come to see her. She barely acknowledged the door closing behind her, leaving her alone with her parents. Her father seemed leaner, and they both had more gray hair, but little else about them had changed.

Meredith gripped the drawstrings of her reticule. Surprise and wonder and joy mingled with trepidation and even a little resentment. "Why are you here?"

"We wanted to see you," her mother said. "We've missed you so much. We kept hoping you'd say you wanted to come home, but you didn't seem ready."

"Home? You made it clear you were ashamed of me and didn't want to see me again."

Her mother crossed the room to her and put a hand on

Meredith's arm. "Oh, darling, we were never ashamed of you. We sent you to live with your grandmother so you could have a change of scenery and to give gossip a chance to die down."

"That's what you said, but . . ."

"Darling, we could hardly be upset with you for trying to elope as we had."

Tears welled up as the belief that her parents had rejected her returned to wound her again. "But you were angry that I'd been socially ruined."

"Yes, angry with him and disappointed you rejected our warnings. We knew his affection was insincere and that he would not make you happy—although we did not understand the scope of his intentions until later. We never meant to make you feel as if we didn't love you."

Tears ran down Meredith's cheeks. Was it true?

"Oh, my poor lamb. We were angrier with him for lying to you than with you for trusting him."

Meredith shivered in a breath. "Your letters . . . you never said this in any of them. You never said I could come home."

"I didn't want to pressure you into returning too soon."

Meredith put a hand over her mouth as a sob burst out of her.

"Of course we wanted you home. If we'd known . . . I'm sorry!" Her mother, her sweet mama, threw her arms around her and held her close. "We love you, dear one. Always."

Meredith fell against her. The long-absent touch of a mother's embrace healed her hidden wounds.

Papa came closer and put a hand on her back. "Your Mr. Partridge sent us a letter asking us to come. He said you needed us. I can see he was right."

Mr. Partridge had done that? For her?

It didn't matter. Her Mama and Papa were here. They loved her. Enfolded in their arms, she sobbed for all the lost time with her parents. They spent several private moments together, and Meredith reviewed in her mind letters her mother had sent, reexamining them through the lens that they had been trying to help her overcome her heartache and escape the cruelty of gossip. If only she had realized they had been waiting for her to say she was ready to come home while she waited for them to give permission for her to return. She should have known.

A while later, Aunt Paulette knocked and entered. "Are you ready to leave? It's time."

Her parents stood. "We are." Papa sent Meredith a wry smile. "Can you believe it? I've been invited into the hallowed drawing room of a lord and lady."

The Daubreys had invited them too? Meredith smiled. "Obviously they have excellent taste."

Meredith splashed her face and touched up her appearance. At least her eyes were clear and bright, with no lingering puffiness from her tears.

She, her parents, and the Staffords arrived at the Daubreys' house on time. Warm and welcoming as usual, the lord and lady greeted them in the drawing room.

Aunt Paulette looked around. "Are we unfashionably early? We seem to be the first to have arrived."

A decidedly impish expression brightened Lady Daubrey's face. "You are exactly on time. We told each guest a different time so as to have a greater influence over who is seen speaking to whom." She patted Aunt Paulette's arm. "All will be revealed in good time."

The next guest to arrive was the jaw-droppingly handsome viscount, Cole Amesbury. Leaving Aunt, Uncle, Mama, and Papa to converse with Lord Daubrey, Lady Daubrey unabashedly led Lord Amesbury to Meredith and Annabel, drawing them slightly apart so they stood in their own circle.

Lord Amesbury, flirted outrageously with them both, though he didn't seem to take himself too seriously or make the advances of a libertine.

Next Michael Cavenleigh arrived, blinking in confusion, but he, too, was led to join the circle with Lord Amesbury, Annabel, and Meredith.

Meredith greeted Phillip's friend with forced courtesy. "Mr. Cavenleigh."

With a clear apology in his expression, he said, "I regret my thoughtless words caused you distress, Miss Brown."

Lord Amesbury narrowed his eyes at Mr. Cavenleigh and addressed Meredith. "Has this cur offended you, Miss Brown? Shall I call him out?"

She couldn't decide if he were in earnest or merely jesting. "No. Not entirely. Merely informed me of something unpleasant. But it was best I learned of it before I made a mistake."

Quietly, Mr. Cavenleigh said, "It didn't happen the way you think."

Miss Harris arrived and rushed to Meredith. "Oh, Merry, I am ever so grateful to you."

Meredith blinked. "But I was wrong."

"Well, yes, but all along I secretly feared he was only attracted to my money, and if you hadn't exposed him, he might never have discovered his true feelings for me or poured out his heart in such an ardent manner. I no longer worry. We are more in love than ever, and I owe it all to you!" She gave Meredith a quick, tight hug.

Meredith hugged her back. "I'm so relieved. I feared I'd made a muddle of it."

Other lords and ladies arrived, and Meredith smiled at the definition of a "small" dinner party. Out of the corner of her eye, she watched her parents. Lady Daubrey introduced them to each new arrival with the emphasis that they were friends of hers and kin of the Staffords. Her parents mingled with the *crème de la crème* with all the practiced ease of members of the gentry. From across the room, Mama sent Meredith an amused smile.

Mr. Morton arrived and instantly went to Cora, taking her hand to his lips and gazing at her as if she were Helen of Troy. Two newcomers arrived—a dark-haired gentleman who resembled Phillip Partridge and an equally dark-haired lady who carried herself like a queen. Lady Daubrey greeted them and introduced them to Meredith's parents. With curious, friendly expressions, they spoke with one another as well as with her aunt and uncle, who seemed to know the newcomers. After a few moments, she led them to Meredith.

Every bit as handsome up close, the gentleman with a distinctively regal air also had a distinctive blond streak in his hair exactly like Phillip's.

The blood rushed from Meredith's face as quickly as air rushed from her lungs. Heaven help her, this was the famous and powerful Duke of Suttenberg, the paragon, and his intimidating mother.

"Your Graces, I believe you know everyone in this group except one," Lady Daubrey said. "May I present Miss Brown, daughter of the Browns and niece of the Staffords?" She swept a hand over her shoulder in the direction of her parents.

"Miss Brown," Lady Daubrey said, "this is the Duke of Suttenberg and his mother, the duchess."

The duchess, a beautiful, petite lady, cast an appraising glance over her. Her lips formed a faint smile. "Charmed." Despite her size, an aura of power encircled the duchess.

The duke, equal in height to Phillip, studied her with an intensity that made her knees wobble.

Taking herself in hand, Meredith curtsied to them and

somehow managed to do it without falling on her face. All those years with the best governesses money could buy, not to mention her own dear mother, must have come through for her, finally. "Your Graces."

As soon as they learned who she was, they would probably demand she be thrust from their lofty presence.

Cora linked her arm through Meredith's. "Miss Brown is one of my dearest friends, Your Grace."

"How do you find London?" the duchess asked Meredith.

Meredith shored up her courage. "I enjoy it very much and hope to see more of its sights while I'm here."

"What is most memorable so far?" the duke asked in a friendly, yet somehow still aloof, manner.

"Going for an unexpected swim in the Thames is one I'll remember most clearly."

Annabel, Cora, Mr. Morton, and Mr. Cavenleigh, who'd been present for her little tumble off her boat, all laughed. Or choked.

The duke and duchess looked on, mystified. Meredith gestured to Annabel, "We had a minor boating accident as we were ferrying to Vauxhall, which tipped our boat. I fell into the river."

"Good heavens," the duke said.

The duchess raised her brows. "I trust no harm befell you?"

"I'm an excellent swimmer and managed to keep afloat until the ferryman pulled me back on board. I am sorry to say that I have yet to see Vauxhall."

"Perhaps I can change that for you," the Viscount Amesbury said with a playfully rakish grin.

"Only if you promise to leave rowing to the ferryman," Meredith shot back.

A prickling sensation tickled the back of her neck, and

the very feel of the air changed. She turned. Phillip stood in the doorway of the drawing room. Her palms grew sweaty inside her gloves, and she desperately needed a glass of punch. How handsome he was and how dear his face had become.

She turned away. She would not let him use her. Her heart would belong to no one ever again.

He crossed the room with lightning speed. "Mother, Suttenberg," he said as he greeted his family. He nodded to others and inserted himself into the circle next to Meredith. In a tone that suggested intimacy, he said, "Miss Brown."

Memories of his tender, skillful kiss sent heat through her cheeks. She must hold strong against him.

"I see you have met my mother and my brother," he said in his lovely baritone.

"Indeed, I have." Somehow, she had managed to sound almost light. "We were discussing how I have yet to visit Vauxhall Gardens."

"I shall be happy to remedy that for you," Lord Amesbury said with a twinkle in his eye.

Phillip said in a warning voice, "No need. I claim the privilege of seeing to that happy duty."

He turned his full attention to Meredith. A desperate sort of longing shadowed his eyes, and faint blue circles under his eyes suggested a lack of sleep. Did he regret his wager? Or was he merely sorry she'd discovered it? Perhaps he had some other game.

"Miss Brown, I believe it is a bit warm in here, is it not? Please allow me to escort you out to the balcony for a breath of air before dinner."

Meredith clenched her fan tightly enough that it cracked. "I don't think it's overly warm."

"Please." The pleading in his eyes tugged at her. "Come out with me—only for a moment. I wish very much to have a word with you."

Annabel nudged her. "Perhaps just as you allowed Mr. Morton to defend himself, you could allow Mr. Partridge to do the same?"

Cora nodded her head so vigorously that her bandeau slipped a little. Michael Cavenleigh wore a similar look of pleading. Phillip touched her arm, whisper light, his expression grave and heart-wrenchingly vulnerable.

Meredith relented. "Only for a moment."

He held out his arm and waited, desperate, cautious, hurt. Had she hurt him?

She took his arm and accompanied him outside to a balcony. The evening air cooled her heated face. She glanced back to be sure they remained in full view of the room.

He took a breath that seemed to take effort. "First, I am sorry I wagered on you. Second, the wager came as a result of my declaration to Michael that you were the only one for me and that I would marry you one day."

She went still at his unexpected words.

"He said you would never forgive me dumping you into the river. One thing led to another. The wager came as a result. That is all. Two posturing stallions. It has nothing to do with my desire to court you."

She searched his eyes, seeking clues to his honesty.

He put a hand underneath her elbow and gave it a gentle squeeze. "I loved you almost from the moment I saw you. I have been sincere in my affections and love you more each day. If you need more time, I will gladly give it to you—even if it takes years. My love for you will remain constant."

Holding onto her suspicions as if they were her old friends, she asked, "Years? What about your wager?"

He waved away her words. "I'll muck out his stables if I must. That timeline of marrying you before the end of the Season has nothing to do with you and me." He took both of her hands, pressed them together, and enclosed them with his. "Please allow me to court you, to prove to you how much I adore and love you."

She looked down at their hands. Did she dare trust him?

"I would marry you this moment if you would have me, but I'm not asking you to pledge yourself to me just yet. I will give you all the time you need to trust me. Please, *please*, allow me to court you."

He seemed sincere. How could she know for certain? "When did you make this wager?"

"The day after Vauxhall. I think Michael was, in his own way, trying to encourage me to woo you." He waited.

She looked up at him and caught her breath at the cautious hope in his expression.

A lump formed in her throat. She whispered, "I do wish to continue spending time in your company."

He let out a shaking breath. "Then you forgive me?"

She pointed her fan at him. "No more wagers about me."

His shoulders sagged in relief, and he nodded. "I vow it."

A half sob, half laugh broke free. "Yes. What about your mother? And the duke?"

"I am working on a plan to handle them." He tugged on her hand and smiled. "I want so badly to kiss you again, right now, but I'd best not."

"No, not now." Shyly, she suggested, "Perhaps we can sneak away later."

He let out a soft moan. "I can hardly wait."

"Oh, and I want you to meet my parents."

He brightened. "They came? I hadn't heard back."

She smiled tenderly. "You arranged that."

He nodded. "You were so unhappy about the estrangement."

"Thank you. You arranged all this too, didn't you?" She gestured to the party.

"Lady Daubrey was kind enough to arrange it for us."

As they returned to the drawing room, they found Meredith's parents conversing freely with her aunt and uncle, with the Viscount Amesbury, and with the Duke and Duchess of Suttenberg. On Phillip's arm, she approached them.

Phillip's tension was palpable, but he made a valiant attempt to appear casual. He glanced between Mama and Papa and Meredith.

Meredith took the hint. "Mama, Papa, may I present Mr. Phillip Partridge?"

After a quick, proper bow, Papa said, "Ah, yes, Mr. Partridge. Thank you again for your kind letter. It was most welcome."

"If it brought happiness to Miss Brown, then I am happy to have been of service," Phillip said. "Now that you are here, I must take this opportunity to ask if I might formally court your daughter."

Papa glanced at Meredith. She smiled and nodded. He returned his gaze. "I understand you had a similar conversation with her uncle recently."

"Yes, sir." He held his breath.

So did Meredith.

Papa paused. Finally, he said, "He and I discussed you. We determined that you possess the moral character we require of anyone who has an interest in her. You may court her for as long as she desires it—with your family's permission."

"Phillip." The duchess's voice, though soft, had an edge to it.

He turned to her. "Mother, Suttenberg, you may not have been aware that Miss Meredith Brown is the young lady I have been courting and who I deeply love. Now that you have met her and her family, I trust you will give us your blessing."

Phillip's tension spilled over onto Meredith. They waited while two pairs of eyes shrewdly studied her and their linked arms.

Finally, his brother said to Papa, "It is my understanding that you own a lace factory up north?"

Papa said simply, "I own three, in fact."

Meredith leaped into the fray, and her words came spilling out in a torrent. "He is a successful businessman and a fair and honest employer who treats his workers better than most landowners treat their tenants. He is successful through hard work and determination, not because his family inherited land from the crown generations ago."

No one could have mistaken the implication, or the bold, impudent, even disrespectful words. But she couldn't stand their snobbishness another moment.

The duke glanced at her. A faint lifting of his brows came in reply as he studied her. "Familial devotion is an admirable quality." To her papa, he said, "Have you suffered losses to your mills in the recent riots?"

"A few looms were damaged, but we made repairs and are now producing up to standards." He glanced at Phillip. "Her dowry is protected by a trust, if that concerns you."

"And there it will stay for her own use if she agrees to marry me," Phillip said.

Meredith's lingering doubt slipped away. He didn't want a dalliance. He didn't want her dowry. He wanted to marry her. He loved her.

"You mistake my meaning," the duke said to Papa. "I merely asked in the event you needed help getting repairs completed so you could resume production."

"Very kind of you." Keeping eye contact with the duke as if they were equals, Papa said, "Your brother seems a good, honorable man who truly cares for my daughter. I have no objection to their courtship. Do you?"

Meredith had never been prouder of him.

The duke paused, glanced at Phillip, then at Meredith. "I have no objection." Finally, he turned to his mother. "Duchess?"

The stone-faced duchess looked at Phillip in a meaningful way. "Phillip already knows my feelings on the matter."

Phillip went so still he might have been carved of marble.

She continued, "After our last interview, I made some inquiries. It seems there is a touch of scandal attached to her." She addressed Phillip. "Do you know of this?"

Meredith knew her past would come back to haunt her but could hardly believe the duchess would bring this up in front of others.

"I do." Phillip said. "She told me."

"You are still willing to have someone who is ruined?" the duchess demanded.

Meredith flinched.

In a growl, Phillip said. "What is she guilty of? Being young and trusting and falling in love with someone who lied to her? Haven't any of you done that?"

Nearly every eye shifted away, even his mother's.

Phillip drew her closer and put an arm around her. "She is a kind and warm and gracious lady. I love her. I mean to marry her, if she'll have me."

Tears blurred Meredith's vision.

In a softer voice, the duchess said, "It seems you are determined, my son. After meeting Miss Brown and seeing how well received she and her family are, especially by Suttenberg, it seems my concerns are perhaps not as great as I first supposed."

They all waited.

She raised her hand and gave a small wave. "Very well, court her—*all Season*." She emphasized to be sure no one mistook her meaning. "If by the Season's end you still feel you are suited, you may marry with my blessing."

Phillip kissed his mother's hand, then her cheek. Then he kissed Meredith's hand and cheek. She'd get a more proper kiss later even if she had to instigate it. Her joy bubbled up and filled the room with a rainbow of color.

As the smugly pleased host and hostess led them to dinner, Meredith clung onto Phillip's arm, hoping her loving glances and tightened hold revealed what she had not yet spoken. With the last of her doubts gone and their family concerns cleared, Meredith could at last tell him.

After a dinner filled with deliberate brushes of their arms and even a discreet hand holding under the table, they at last stole a moment together.

While the rest of the group concentrated on a game of charades, they ducked into an alcove between columns and behind a large potted plant.

"I love you, Phillip Partridge," she said breathlessly before she lost her nerve.

He let out a smiling breath and closed his eyes. Pulling her into his arms, he said, "I love you, Meredith Brown."

"And Phillip." She pulled back enough to look him in the eye. "I was only *socially* ruined. I vow my virtue is still intact."

He touched her face. "I would not love you any less if it wasn't."

Phillip kissed her with all the love and tenderness and passion of their earlier kiss but with a promise and a bright hope for many more.

Fifteen

Under a bower of summer leaves, Phillip pushed away his wedding breakfast and tucked his bride against his side. "You look beautiful, Mrs. Partridge."

Radiant in her wedding gown, she beamed at him. "You look quite dashing, Mr. Partridge."

Mucking out Michael's stables two weeks ago when the Season officially ended was a small price to pay to keep his promise to their parents that they court the entire Season before becoming engaged. It was a small price to pay to reassure everyone they knew each other well enough to make this mismatch into a marriage. Yes, well worth it. As consolation, Michael vowed he'd still ride a mule through Hyde Park tomorrow. A true friend.

During their courtship, they had even visited Vauxhall together. Twice. Without tipping over their boat.

He kissed her cheek. "Do you believe in love at first sight now?"

"I believe in attraction at first sight and that it can become love later," she said with a conciliatory tone.

"How about love at first sight that grows into a deeper love with time?"

"Very well."

He pulled her to a stand.

With a mischievous, knowing look, she tilted her head to one side coquettishly. "Is it time to go?"

"We've had the obligatory breakfast, the carriage awaits, and our honeymoon is about to begin."

After the well-wishers saw them off, Phillip pulled her close on the seat in the carriage. "I wager our first child will be a boy."

She swatted his arm. "You promised; no more wagers about me."

"It's not directly about you." He grinned and kissed her playfully.

Then he kissed her with purpose. As the coach rolled along to their new life, he poured out his love and commitment to his beloved wife. She returned it and more. Phillip had the one who really *saw* him, who truly knew him, and who loved him with all of her generous heart.

The End

Donna Hatch is the award-winning author of the best-selling Rogue Hearts Series. She discovered her writing passion at the tender age of eight and has been listening to those voices ever since. A sought-after workshop presenter, she juggles her day job, freelance editing, multiple volunteer positions, not to mention her six children (seven, counting her husband), and still manages to make time to write. Yes, writing IS an obsession. A native of Arizona, she and her husband of over twenty years are living proof that there really is a happily ever after.

For sneak peeks, specials, deleted scenes, and more information, visit Donna's website: www.donnahatch.com.

Twitter: @DonnaHatch

The Final Wager

-Heather B. Moore-

One

Lord Victor Roland, Earl of Locken, scowled as two men bumbled into the private room at White's. The card game had finally turned in his favor, and now this interruption. The game was by invitation only, and if these two had made it past Mr. Graham, then there was going to be trouble.

Victor rose to his feet, using his cane to cushion his ankle injury from riding two weeks before. Victor's three companion players rose to their feet at the intrusion as well. "Who let you in here?" he demanded. That was when he recognized one of the men as John Baldwin, Earl of Southill. "Southill?"

The man's blue eyes connected with Victor's. "Locken! The rumors are true. I said I wouldn't believe it until I saw it for myself, didn't I, Ludlow?"

The man with portly cheeks, who was apparently Ludlow, nodded.

"When someone told me that Lord Locken was *the* Captain Sharp who dominated the gambling tables, I didn't believe them," Southill continued. "Because the only Lord Locken I knew barely passed mathematics at Eton."

Victor ignored the insult as he eyed Southill. They'd been at Eton together, yes, but that had been over a decade ago. Southill had changed—not just aged—but he looked as if he'd spent the night on the street. First, he reeked of cheap brandy; second, his cravat was soiled with a dark stain. His deep green vest was out of fashion by at least a couple of years, and the edges of his jacket sleeves were frayed. Had the man fallen on hard times? From Victor's questionable memory, Southill had inherited an earldom upon his father's death.

Southill stuck his hand out, and Victor reluctantly shook it.

"You've grown into your role, my friend," Southill said in a jovial tone. "I remember you as rather short and sort of dim. Always had plenty of spending money, though. Should I be addressing you as Your Grace?"

"Not yet, my man," Victor said, trying to keep his tone conciliatory. "My father might have one foot in the grave, but he is still Duke of Wycliff."

Southill nodded. "Ah, all the best to your family, then."

"And how is your family?" Victor asked. He'd heard of the Earl of Southill's death the year before, but Victor didn't know how rich of an estate was bestowed upon Southill. The man might be getting booted out of this room in about ten seconds.

Southill straightened. "Three months past my year of mourning. And I'm enjoying my new role as the Earl of Southill."

The man's words rankled Victor. If Southill was an earl now, in possession of land and wealth, why did something seem so off about his manner and appearance? Victor folded his arms. "What brings you here tonight?"

Southill grinned. "I'm here to win." He looked over at his friend Ludlow. "Isn't that right?"

Ludlow chuckled. "That's what you did tell me and everyone else in White's."

"Tell him what else I said," Southill prompted.

Ludlow obliged. "Lord Southill has come to beat the best gambler in London."

Victor slowly turned his gaze to Southill. "And why is that?"

Southill's blue eyes widened a fraction. "Let's just say I've lost a few bets, and I aim to earn it all back. And what better way than to win it from the richest gambler in the city?"

"What makes you think I'm the richest gambler?"

"Because rumors are that you never lose and have been dubbed a Captain Sharp," Southill said. "But you haven't played *me* yet."

Victor had more questions, but he'd been issued a challenge, one that he never could turn down. It took him seconds to make up his mind. "One game of *vingt-et-un*," Victor said. "But your friend here has to leave."

Ludlow sputtered; Southill sent the man on his way.

Victor took his seat along with his playing companions, Lord Hudson, Mr. Gilbert, and Lord Duncan. Victor took up the cards and dealt them. Victor might not have been a mathematics expert at Eton, but he was good at reading people. He could spot a bluff instantly and knew all the telltale signs of deception. When someone claimed they had a one or two, Victor instinctively knew if he should double the stakes. That was why he'd only agreed to one game with Southill. Something wasn't right with this man, and if Victor doubled the stakes, he sensed that Southill would be in trouble.

Not that Victor was any sort of saint. But the art of gambling was just that: *an art.* Common sense had to prevail, and that meant rules. And the first rule was to never bet what you didn't have.

Half an hour later, Southill was down one hundred pounds, and Victor was up two hundred and fifty. Nothing surprising there, but Southill looked stunned as Victor collected his winnings.

"It was nice visiting with you, Southill," Victor said.

"Why don't you join your friend Ludlow now? We're about to play another round."

Southill slapped his hands onto the table. "Deal me in."

"I said *one* game."

Southill reached into his jacket pocket and pulled out a stack of bills. "I've got the money, and I want to play. Deal me in."

Victor estimated that Southill gripped at least three hundred pounds in his sweaty hand. It wasn't a small fortune in the grand scheme of things. Hundreds of pounds exchanged hands each night at White's.

"Keep your money," Victor said. "It sounds like you've been on a losing streak, and certainly you have responsibilities at home to take care of. A wife? Maybe a child?"

"Only my sister, but her dowry will keep her husband's hearth plenty warm once she marries." Southill's blue eyes narrowed. "It's not about the money, Locken. It's about beating *you*."

This surprised Victor. "Why *me*? We haven't seen each other for ten years."

Southill laughed. "Of course you would say that. What you did to me ten years ago affected everything—my *entire* future. The fact that you can sit there acting like you've forgotten only makes me more eager to wager against you."

Victor exhaled. "Pranks between schoolboys hardly signify ruining anyone's future."

Southill leaped to his feet. "You almost got me expelled! My father nearly disowned me!"

Victor stared at the man, then he slowly rose. If they'd been nose to nose, Victor would have towered over Southill by a good foot. Fortunately, a table separated the two tempers. "It was a prank, Southill. How was I supposed to know you were really cheating?"

Southill's face darkened a shade. "Don't ever call me a *cheat* again."

Victor curled his hands into fists. Being a gentleman was hard work, hard because the only thing he wanted to do was punch Southill in the face. He and Southill had been about fifteen when Victor had tired of Southill's constant bragging. He excelled in grades and athletics and always had a following of other brats. Victor could hold his own and was of higher station in society, but he kept to himself more than not.

Victor wasn't sure what had possessed him, perhaps it was resentment, but one morning, after hearing Southill once again brag about his test scores in mathematics, Victor had scrawled across the classroom wall four simple words: *Southill is a cheat.*

It was a prank, a *joke*, and as predicted, when the boys all entered the classroom to begin their lessons for the day, there was laughter.

But their headmaster, Beckington, didn't find it amusing because he'd already suspected the perfect grades of Southill weren't without fault. Beckington had ordered a complete search of Southill's room and papers, and sure enough, damning evidence had been found when previous assignments from older students were discovered. Southill had been copying the answers and passing them off as his own.

Until the discovery, Victor had had no idea there had been any truth behind the prank. And now ... Victor understood why Southill stood across from him, his face red, his blue eyes like ice, and his chest heaving.

A man of the gentry might gamble, drink, and womanize to his detriment, but cheating was akin to losing all honor.

Lord Hudson stood. "Enough of this," he commanded. The man was in his fifties, but as a former army colonel, he exuded authority wherever he went. "We are all reasonable men here." He pointed at Southill. "You were guilty of cheating in school, so the failing is upon your head, not the person who exposed it." Then he pointed at Victor. "Let the man play another round, if only to defend whatever honor he's managed to scrape together the past ten years."

Southill's face darkened an even deeper red. "*He* knows? Who else knows?"

Victor refrained from scoffing. "Everyone knows. It's one of the most famous legends at Eton."

Southill seemed to mull that over, then said, "I guess we've all got a reputation for something."

Victor refused to acknowledge that comment. His father had already made him feel guilty enough for being born in the first place. Because of Victor's difficult birth, his mother had lost too much blood. She never recovered, and his father had lost the one person he'd ever cared about in the entire world.

Victor lowered himself into his chair. Guilt was a useless emotion that never led to any good, but it was damned near impossible to get rid of. Guilt had made him miserable for nearly thirty years. Guilt was driving him to propose in the next few weeks to a woman he didn't love in order to fulfill his duties as the future Duke of Wycliff. And guilt riddled Victor's memory of his prank at Eton against Southill.

Guilt guided his next words: "Sit down, Southill. Let's play."

Two

Lady Juliet Baldwin wanted to throw something. *Anything.* A collector had just come to *her home*, claiming that her brother owed a great deal of money to a London tailor. And the Mr. Peregrine something-or-other said he'd sent several notices that had gone unheeded to their London townhouse. Now, he'd had the audacity to make the two-hour carriage ride to Southill Estate to bring the debt notice himself.

Juliet had been receiving quite a bit of mail for her brother over the past few months since their mourning period had ended. She hadn't opened any of the letters, but she'd guessed they were from creditors. Now, Mr. Peregrine had confirmed that her brother was racking up debts and not paying them.

Three months ago, she might have ignored a debt notice. Three months ago, she would have never imagined that her brother would go on a spending spree. Three months ago, she'd thought that losing her last surviving parent was the worst thing that could ever happen to her.

Now she knew better.

Juliet crossed the threadbare rug of the drawing room, picked up an embroidered pillow that had taken her weeks to create, and threw it as hard as she could at the cold hearth. The pillow landed with a soft thump. Hardly satisfactory. She picked up the next pillow—this one created by her mother—and Juliet paused. How had she stooped this low? Throwing pillows in a house that was falling apart?

Her brother, Southill, had promised, *promised*, to see to the remodel her father had started before his long illness that had resulted in his death. Southill had then begged off until the mourning period was over. And Juliet had understood, she truly had, because everything had changed with her father's death. Life was more urgent. Decisions more pressing. Not only did Juliet need to reconcile herself to making a marriage match, but she had to face leaving the home she'd grown up in and loved with all her heart.

Who her husband would be, she did not know. At nineteen, she'd missed two London seasons already due to her father's long illness and then the year of mourning that followed his death. Soon, she'd be on the shelf, but right now she didn't care. Right now, she wanted to strangle her brother.

Juliet set the embroidered pillow down, deciding to treat her mother's needlework with the respect that it deserved. She left the room and made her way to her father's library—well, now her brother's. Not that he was ever home to spend time in it. Regardless, the moment Juliet stepped inside the dim room, she was overwhelmed with memories of her father. His cigar smoke lingered, and she envisioned him sitting in the chair behind the mahogany desk and raising his head when she walked in.

She missed his smile. She missed his rumbling voice and booming laughter. "Papa," she whispered. But no one answered.

She blinked back the threatening tears and straightened her spine. She'd shed a year's worth of tears over her father's death already, and it was time to be strong. She was the lady of the house, and there was a crisis to deal with. Taking out a quill and paper, she began to write to her brother.

Dear John,
This morning, I was greatly surprised when a Mr.—

No. She had to be sterner.

Dear Southill,
It appears you have neglected our finances, and matters have reached a critical nature.

She stared at the words, and despite her resolve, the tears came anyway, dripping onto the paper. She picked up another sheet and began again.

Dear Southill,
You are a careless and cold-hearted man. When I see you again, I will—

The door to the library creaked open, and Juliet looked up, blinking away her angry tears.

The housekeeper, Mrs. Campton, stood there, her hands folded in front of her and worry lines creasing her forehead.

"I hope I'm not interrupting, my lady, but I've used the last of the kitchen money for this week's shopping. And now the egg boy is at the door, asking for payment. I put him off last week, so I don't feel like I can put him off a second week."

Juliet didn't move for a moment. Then she set down the quill and rose to her feet. Stoically, she walked with Mrs. Campton to the back door of the kitchen where young Ernest waited. Juliet reached into the sewn-in pocket of her dress and handed over the required coins. Ernest grinned his gapped-tooth smile, then bobbed into a half bow. "Thank you, m'lady."

Before Juliet could reply, he'd taken off running through

the gardens and out the back gate, his bare feet pounding the damp spring earth.

"When will the master return?" Mrs. Campton asked.

It was the housekeeper's way of asking when they would have funds again. She hadn't been able to make the full salary payments to the household staff, the gardener, and the coachman on quarter day at the end of March. "I am writing to my brother today."

Mrs. Campton bobbed her head. "Very well. Dinner will be ready by six. Would you like it in the dining room?"

"Of course," Juliet said. Though she was the only one inside the house right now, she didn't want to give in to the temptation to take her meals in her bedroom. While her brother was away, she was mistress, and she would keep up the appearance that all was well for as long as she could.

Mrs. Campton returned to the kitchen, and Juliet kept her gaze on the back gardens for a few more moments. They needed to hire an additional gardener for the summer season. Last year, the lands had fallen into disrepair while her brother toured the continent, claiming he wanted to travel to places that their father had enjoyed in his memory.

Juliet had remained behind, so she'd spent the better part of the past year on her own. She'd grown used to eating alone. Tonight would be no different. Juliet kept her chin up as she continued through the house and into the library. It was time for her brother to come home and set things to rights. The mourning period was over, and debts needed to be reconciled.

She had just settled back at the writing desk again, ripped up her first attempts at letter-writing, and begun anew, when someone knocked at the front door. Juliet spilled a drop of ink and quickly blotted it. Mrs. Campton's footsteps echoed across the wooden floors as she made her way to the front of the house.

Juliet rose from the desk and hovered on the threshold of the library, listening to the conversation.

It was a man, and he didn't sound happy.

"If Lord Southill isn't at home, might I speak with Lady Juliet?"

Mrs. Campton murmured something. There was no more reason for Juliet to delay the inevitable. She strode out of the library and into the main hall. Standing in the front entrance was Lord Stratford, their closest neighbor, a viscount, and a widowed man of indeterminable age. His two daughters were grown and married, off living somewhere with their own families.

"Ah, Lady Juliet," Lord Stratford said, his voice rising in pitch as he spotted her. He took off his hat and smoothed the thinning hair on top of his head. His next words were accompanied by rapid blinking, something he did quite often when he spoke. "It is a *pleasure* to find you at home."

His use of the word *pleasure* sent a rash of cold goose pimples across her skin. Juliet had never been bothered much by Lord Stratford's tendency to ogle her—but that was before her father passed and before her brother left. Now, the longer she was left to her own devices, the more it bothered her.

"I'm in the middle of writing my correspondence," she began, but he cut her off.

"This won't take but a moment." He turned to the housekeeper. "Mrs. Campton, won't you bring us a spot of tea in the drawing room?"

Juliet froze. How dare he order Mrs. Campton to bring tea? Lord Stratford used to visit with her father frequently, and they'd talk for hours about the horses that Stratford bred. Since her father's passing, Juliet had avoided him as much as possible.

Perhaps he was a harmless middle-aged man, but she

resented how his gaze frequently rested in the area of her bosom.

Resigned, she led the way to the drawing room.

"Have you been riding lately?" he asked, as he took a seat. "I haven't seen you about."

"I haven't been since the last rainstorm." In truth, she'd sold all their horses but two older mares. Another concession she'd had to make in order to procure more funds. Her brother didn't even know since he hadn't been home to notice. "Have you been riding?" she asked Lord Stratford. She at least had to speak with him until the tea came. After that, she could usher him out.

Rather than answering her question, he said, "How does your brother fare?"

"He is well, I am sure," Juliet said, making her voice falsely cheerful. "I was composing a letter to him when you arrived."

"I hate to bring such a delicate matter to your attention, but I have been expecting payment on a pair of horses he had me send to him four weeks ago." Lord Stratford shifted in his seat and blinked several times. His gaze surveyed her clothing, then returned to her face. "Your brother promised payment within the week, and nothing has come."

Anger flared inside Juliet. Her brother had recently purchased a pair of purebred horses while Juliet had been forced to sell most of what they had? She opened her mouth to reply that she certainly didn't have any information on her brother's financial agreements when Lord Stratford lifted his hand.

"There have been rumors going about the village as well." He cleared his throat. "I think you are grown enough to face the reality of what people are saying about your brother, as much as it pains me to be the bearer of delicate news."

Juliet went very still. "Continue."

"I am only repeating what I have heard, mind you," he said. "Know that I have not spread any of the information. Right here in your drawing room is the first I have spoken of it."

Juliet folded her hands together, clenching her fingers.

"It is rumored that your brother has been frequenting gambling halls over the past year," he said in a slow and careful tone, "and in that time, he's gambled away a good deal of his fortune."

Juliet stared at the man seated across from her. The gray hairs threaded through his sideburns were nearly white now. Why she was noticing such a detail at this time, she did not know. He also breathed loudly, as if he were the one to receive shocking news. And then Juliet realized that it was her breathing she was hearing.

"How much?" she whispered.

Lord Stratford's mouth turned down, and he seemed to be considering whether he should answer her question.

"How much?" Juliet asked in a louder, clearer voice. "How much has he lost?"

Stratford exhaled and blinked before speaking. "I do not know an *exact* number, but he has not paid any creditors in over six months. If I had known, I would have never sent him my horses."

Juliet nodded. "I thank you for bringing this to my attention." She felt as if she'd been hollowed out. She hoped to high heaven Lord Stratford was misinformed, but the emptiness spreading through her told her that he was not far off the mark.

"If there is anything I can do for you," Lord Stratford began.

She lifted her hand. "Say no more. I will write to my brother directly and ask him when he intends to pay for your horses."

"If it won't be too much of a burden."

It was too late to worry about burdens—they were already upon her.

His gaze again dipped, although she was wearing a highly modest dress. "Lady Juliet, for some time I have been wondering if you would be opposed to a match between us."

Her mouth dropped open, but no reply came out. Was he . . . *proposing marriage?* She could not fathom what to say to this man in this moment.

He blinked rapidly as he smiled. "I see that I have startled you. There is no hurry to make a decision, and I would have to speak with your brother in any case. I run a profitable estate, and I will give you a comfortable life." His smile broadened, turning almost greedy. "If we have a son together, then all the better."

Mrs. Campton came into the room, carrying a silver tea tray.

Juliet stood and clasped her trembling fingers. "Lord Stratford was just leaving."

If he was shocked at her rudeness, he didn't show it. Lord Stratford simply stood, bowed before her, then said with a suggestive wink, "I look forward to your reply."

Embarrassment burned through Juliet.

Mrs. Campton stared after Lord Stratford as he left the room, then she looked at Juliet. After a moment, the housekeeper set the tea tray on the low table without another word.

When Mrs. Campton had vacated the room, Juliet crossed to the windows. The clouds were heavy, and sure enough, rain sprinkled the road leading to the house. She needed to finish the letter to her brother right away to make the afternoon post. But right now, she felt numb all over.

She didn't know which angered her more: a marriage proposal from Lord Stratford or the news about her brother's imminent ruin. If she weren't a woman, she would make the trip to London herself to hunt down her brother. As it was, she was well and truly stuck, dependent upon a brother who was apparently gambling every bit of their money away. And Lord Stratford's offer brought her no comfort. She'd rather be a spinster than marry him.

Were those the only choices in her life? Spinsterhood and poverty or marriage to Lord Stratford? The raindrops increased, driving now against the windowpanes. She pressed her hand against the cool pane and felt the cold travel along her arm to her chest until it reached directly into her heart.

Three

"Your money's gone," Victor told Southill in a flat voice. "You need to excuse yourself while you still have a few pounds to hire a carriage to take you home."

They'd been playing for more than three hours, and Victor was leading the night. Southill had won a few hundred pounds in the third round, but now he was reduced to his last ten.

"I've my own c-carriage," Southill slurred after downing another shot of brandy. "I'm the Earl of Southill, you know."

"We know," Hudson muttered.

Southill turned to face the older man. "What did you say?"

Victor leaned forward in his seat. "We're tired of you speaking of your earldom. No one at this table cares, especially when you're lousy at cards and have run out of money before midnight."

Southill's blue eyes focused on Victor. "I have plenty of money, I'll have you know. My carriage outside of White's is b-brand new."

"We don't barter goods in high-stakes games," Hudson cut in.

"Why not?" Southill asked. "I mean, y-you could take my carriage and sell it for nearly what I paid for it. I've only had it two w-weeks."

Victor took the bottle of brandy and poured some into Southill's glass. Maybe if he got drunk enough, he'd pass out and stop his infuriating attempt at bartering.

Southill picked up the glass and sipped. "Maybe y-you're the one who's out of funds. Does the duke keep your purse strings tied?"

Victor wouldn't rise to the insult. He took a sip from his own glass of brandy that he'd been nursing most of the night. Two drinks on gambling nights was his limit. He and alcohol had a checkered past. The last thing Victor wanted to do was end up a drunkard like his father.

"Or maybe the value of my carriage is more than your pea brain can calculate," Southill continued.

Victor clenched the hand resting on the table. He was tired of Southill, and Victor was tempted to take the man for all he was worth just to get rid of him. After Victor was done with him, Southill wouldn't dare show his face in London again.

Victor tapped a long finger on the rim of his glass. "If everyone at the table agrees that your carriage is a worthy barter, then I'll accept the terms. But it's all or nothing." He looked to Hudson, who nodded.

Hudson's agreement was followed by both Mr. Gilbert's and Lord Duncan's.

Southill grinned.

"Looks like you're either the luckiest man in London or unluckiest." Victor dealt a card to each man.

Gilbert took one look at his and said, "One."

"Three," Southill declared.

Duncan said, "Two."

Victor eyed his own card, then dealt one more card to each man.

"Fold," Gilbert said.

"I'm out too," Duncan added.

Victor looked to Southill.

The man was smiling, but it wasn't a friendly smile. Victor noted the streak of panic in Southill's eyes. If Victor lost, then he'd be out a good pile of money, but he would recover. If he won, well he'd just earned himself a brand new carriage. Not too bad for a few hours of gaming.

Southill laid out his cards, revealing two tens.

Victor waited a full thirty seconds before laying his down. Everyone stared at his two cards: an ace and a ten. "Vingt-et-un," he said.

Southill released a hissing breath. "Cur!" he growled, then slammed his palm on the table.

Victor flinched, but he forced himself to stay seated and let the man ride out his emotions.

No one moved as Southill ran his fingers through his hair then clenched fistfuls of it. "Unbelievable. My sister is going to kill me!" He groaned and rubbed his face. Then his gaze settled on Victor. "One more game. Give me a chance to win it back."

Even if Victor liked Southill, giving into him would be akin to cheating. If Southill had nothing to barter, no new game could be played.

"Let this be a lesson, Southill," Victor said. "Go home and get yourself cleaned up. Settle your debts, and never, ever pretend like you can beat me again."

Southill's face flushed. "I have more to barter. All or nothing. You have my carriage now, but I still have my sister's dowry."

Victor barked a laugh. "The sister you just said was going to kill you for gambling away your carriage? What do you think she'd say about you betting her dowry? No one can touch that but her husband."

Southill swallowed, but his gaze remained focused.

"Then marry her. Whoever wins this hand marries my sister and gets her twenty-five thousand. If I win, I get my carriage back, and my sister can marry some other poor sop."

Victor blinked. Southill couldn't be serious. Or if he thought he was serious, then he was drunker than Victor thought.

"You can't wager your sister's hand in marriage *or* her dowry," Victor said in an even voice. "It's illegal, and if there's anything I'm a stickler for, it's keeping the law."

Southill scoffed and finished his brandy. He reached for the bottle and poured his own glass. Drank that one too.

The man could hold his liquor.

"I think you're afraid," Southill said. "I think you've been cheating, and if we get rid of your friends here, we'll see who's the best card player in London."

Victor didn't want to react, but heat spread across his neck.

"Every story I've heard about you is suspicious," Southill continued in a cutting tone. "You strategically lose a little, but you always win big in the end. There's no way someone can be that lucky. Night after night. Week after week."

Victor wrapped his fingers around his brandy glass. "I'm not a cheat. If I were you, I'd leave right now before I call you out."

A smile bloomed on Southill's face. "You're afraid, aren't you? The most eligible bachelor, soon to be duke, in all of England. Yet, you won't marry. What's wrong, Locken? Afraid that putting a baby into your wife will kill her, just like *you* killed your mother?"

Victor hadn't realized he'd shoved the table aside and leaped onto Southill until he'd already driven his fist into the man's nose. Southill toppled backward, taking Victor with him.

Hands grabbed at Victor, pulling him off Southill. It was a good thing too, because Victor wouldn't have been able to stop hitting the man.

Southill cursed in pain, and while Hudson restrained Victor, the other two men helped Southill out of the private room. In the main room beyond, voices of surprise and condemnation reached Victor. There were a few cheers as well as Southill continued his escorted walk all the way out of White's.

Victor only felt numb. His ears were ringing, his hand aching. His shoulder felt strange, and he couldn't quite catch his breath.

"Are you all right?" Hudson asked, but Victor couldn't respond. Not yet.

The other men came back into the room and put the table and chairs to rights. The cards were picked up. Someone cleared away a broken glass, and someone else sopped up the spilled brandy. When the room came back into focus, Victor stepped away from Hudson. "I'm all right."

"Are you sure?"

Victor nodded and scanned the room. It looked how it did before Southill ever entered it. Victor's heart rate slowed, returning to normal. His breathing evened out. Tomorrow, or the next day, he might laugh about this. But for now, he wanted to forget all about it.

"I need a drink," he told Hudson.

"I'll go fetch another bottle," Hudson said.

But before Hudson could leave, a shout went up in the main room.

"He's been hit!" someone yelled.

Men hurried out the front entrance into the dark night. Hudson followed, and Victor made his way reluctantly to the door. Probably some drunkard had stepped in front of a carriage. When he reached the entrance of White's and saw the man everyone was gaping over, his blood chilled.

Victor would recognize the green vest anywhere because he just spent four hours staring at it.

"Is he alive?" someone asked.

"Call for the doctor," another person said.

Victor pushed his way through the crowd and walked up to Southill, who lay prone in the street. "What happened?" Victor ground out.

One of the men said, "He stumbled into the street, holding his nose. That horse reared up and knocked Lord Southill to the ground."

Victor looked to where the man was pointing. The horse looked unharmed, and the carriage unmarred.

"Southill," Victor said, bending down and shaking the man's shoulder. "Wake up."

Southill groaned and turned over to his side, cradling his head. He was already plenty dirty, and he only soiled his clothing more by his movements.

"Call for a doctor," someone said.

"No." Victor held up his hand. "I'll take him home. He needs to sleep off the drink. Call for his carriage."

"Southill doesn't have a carriage," someone blurted.

Victor spun around. "Who said that?"

The portly Ludlow stepped forward. "Southill's carriage was taken yesterday by a creditor," he said in a tremulous voice. "He never delivered payment."

Victor stared at the man. "What is his address? I'll deliver the man in my own curricle."

Ludlow rattled off one of the house numbers at Grosvenor Square. It wasn't far from Victor's own place, and he was surprised that he hadn't run into Southill earlier in the season. With the help of a couple of other men, Victor loaded

Southill into his curricle, and soon they were rattling over the cobblestone streets into the night.

When they slowed in front of Southill's address, Victor was surprised to see no evidence of occupation. He searched his memory and was sure this was the location given him. Exhaling a sigh of frustration, he alighted, walked to the front of the house, and rapped on the door. No candle burned in any of the windows, but perhaps Lord Southill's servants hadn't expected him to return this evening?

No one answered, and Victor didn't hear any shuffle of footsteps coming from inside. He knocked again and called out, "Hello?"

Nothing.

Victor left the front entrance and walked around the house, finding a side door that probably led to the kitchen. He knocked on that door, and in a few moments was gratified when someone from the inside unlocked the door and cracked it open.

An older woman, who had clearly been roused from sleep, blinked up at him. She must be the housekeeper or one of the kitchen maids. Her eyes widened as she took in the whole of Victor, another odd thing. Surely she'd been around gentlemen of the *ton* before.

"Hello, ma'am, I'm Lord Locken, and I have Lord Southill in my curricle," he said. "Your master's taken ill, and I've brought him home. Is there a butler or groomsman who can help me get him to his rooms?"

The woman's mouth gaped, then she tried to shut the door.

Victor shot his hand out to stop her. "Is this not Lord Southill's residence?"

"Was," the woman said in a voice that cracked. "He was booted out this morning. The creditors forced him." She attempted to shut the door again in Victor's face.

He held it firmly open. "Lord Southill needs his bed."

"There's no bed here for a louse like him," the woman continued.

It seemed this woman's high-and-mighty attitude was far above her station.

"Are you his employee?" Victor pressed.

"No longer," she said. "He's paid none of us last quarter, and we stayed on until we could find something else. I've been kept on for the new residents, who will be arriving within the week."

Victor dropped his hand, and the woman seemed to comprehend the frustration in his eyes, because she kept the door open.

His mind raced. He had a drunk man in his curricle—a despicable drunk man. "Where did he take his things?" he finally asked.

"That I don't know," she said with a shrug. "He had few friends that I know of, and no one to put him up. He might have sent them to his home at Southill Estate."

Yes, Southill Estate. If Victor remembered right, the place was at least a two-hour ride from London. Not something to attempt in the dead of night. But . . . what other choice did he have? He could leave Lord Southill on the side of the road, or he could deposit him at an inn, but then the gossips would speculate. So Victor decided to take him home and be done with him for good.

"Thank you, ma'am," Victor said, his mind reluctantly made up. "I apologize for disturbing your rest."

The woman nodded, then slowly eased the door shut. Victor stood outside the closed door for a moment, arguing with himself. He had no responsibility toward Southill. If anything, the man deserved what he'd gotten. He was a cheat, a drunk, and broke as a result. But the knowledge at the back of Victor's mind pushed its way to the forefront. Southill had a sister who could take over the care of her brother. Victor would deliver Southill to his sister and then wash his hands of this whole event.

Victor strode back to his curricle, hoping he could find Southill Estate. He knew the general direction, and the nearly full moon would offer plenty of light. Victor settled into the driver's seat while Lord Southill slept behind him. The man's scent had become rank, and Victor didn't want to guess why. *Two hours,* he told himself. This would all be over in two hours.

He only had to ask for directions once, and by the time he reached Southill Estate, he was so tired, he could have slept sitting up.

Victor turned up the long road leading to Southill Estate according to the directions he'd received. He drew the curricle to a stop and climbed out, stretching his legs. Victor looked toward the towering manor. In the moonlight, the place had an imposing, solid look. A decent estate by the looks of it, but there was something melancholy about the place. Perhaps because its wayward master had bungled up the finances that were meant to care for such a legacy.

Then, Victor noticed signs of renovations in process, although they appeared to have been abandoned. A crumbling gazebo to the left of the house had a few wood braces in place, and a pile of rocks was not too far from where the stone fence that probably surrounded a garden had fallen into disrepair.

Not a glimmer of light appeared in any of the windows. Surely, he'd be waking up the staff; it was nearly two o'clock in the morning. But it couldn't be helped. Victor would haul Lord Southill into the house, then Victor would make the long journey back to London and sleep the morning through. By the next evening, the man would be only a sour memory in Victor's mind.

The Final Wager

Victor strode to the front door and knocked firmly. The sound was much louder in the country than it had been in Grosvenor Square. Just as in London, there was no immediate answer. Victor waited another moment, then knocked again.

A light glowed from the window, which must be the front drawing room. Ah. Someone was awake, and Victor could be done and over with this ordeal in mere minutes.

He waited. And waited.

Then a woman's voice spoke from the other side of the door. "Who are you?"

This he should have expected, but it still gave him pause. Partially because the voice was younger than a housekeeper's should be.

"My name is Lord Victor Roland, and I've brought Lord Southill home."

A gasp was followed by a rapid series of clangs as the door was unlocked and pulled open.

Whoever Victor had expected from the woman who'd questioned him, it wasn't the woman who stood before him, holding a candle. She *was* young. Not yet twenty, if Victor had to guess. Her honey-gold hair spilled over her shoulders, and her eyes shimmered blue in the candle light. She wore a night rail of soft white that was modest, yet gentled over her womanly curves, making Victor swallow hard. The young woman's lips were full and pink and her lashes dark, belying the color of her hair. She was, for lack of a better description, a veritable Venus.

He must still have brandy running through his veins, because no woman's appearance had ever made him speechless, yet here he was. Speechless. The woman was like a living, breathing artist's masterpiece. He told himself it was because he'd expected a housekeeper, or a maid, or a butler, or anyone, but not a well-bred lady.

"Where is he?" she asked.

Victor exhaled. His mind refocused. "He's in my carriage. He's had a bit of an accident."

The woman's hand flew to her mouth. "Is he all right?"

"Yes," Victor was quick to say. "He's merely . . . I am sure he'll be much better once he's slept off his inebriation."

The woman's eyes widened, and then her cheeks flushed a beautiful red. "My brother's *drunk*?"

She was Southill's *sister*? The unmarried sister he'd tried to wager? Victor cleared his throat. "Well, yes—"

The door slammed shut. Before Victor could react, the locks slid into place, and the woman said in a fiery tone, "You can tell him to go to Hades!"

Four

Juliet knew she was being completely unreasonable, but a middle-of-the-night visit from a stranger telling her that her brother had been delivered home as a drunk wastrel had sent her over the edge of reason. If someone were to interrogate her on her true feelings, she could honestly say that at this moment, she hated her brother.

She hated how he'd left her alone at the estate after their father's death. She hated that he'd surrounded himself with friends, drink, women, gambling, and other vices while Juliet had to oversee all he'd left behind.

A soft knock sounded at the door, and Juliet flinched. The man—Lord Victor something—was still there. He was most certainly a member of the peerage, and his name did seem familiar, although she couldn't place it under her current duress. Hopefully he was only a baron and not a viscount or earl, or heaven forbid, a marquis.

"Miss?" he said.

Juliet leaned her forehead against the door and sighed. "Can you take John somewhere else?"

"This *is* Southill Estate, correct?" the man asked.

"Yes."

"I don't think your brother has the funds to pay for a night at the inn," he said.

Of course he didn't, and Juliet's cheeks burned hot to know that this man knew of her family's financial devastation. "Is that why you traveled so late at night?"

The man didn't answer right away, then he said, "Partly."

Juliet wanted all of this to go away. She wanted to be in her bed, sound asleep. But she'd fallen asleep in the drawing room, and that's why she heard the knock on the door. Mrs. Campton slept like the dead, and the butler was gone for a few nights to his ailing father's home.

"What do you mean by *partly*?" she asked.

"Do you think you could open the door so we might have a proper conversation?"

It was true, his voice was quite muffled, and hers must be as well. It would be more practical to open the door and speak with the man face-to-face. She turned the lock and cracked the door open no more than a hand span.

"That's better," the man said, his deep voice rumbling softly.

Now that Juliet was over her original shock, she had a good look at the stranger on her doorstep. He was certainly of the elite class. His dark jacket—perhaps navy or black—was tailored to fit his broad shoulders, and his light brown vest looked to be imported silk. His breeches were also tailored, but Juliet wasn't about to assess their particular fit. The singular glow of the candlelight made it no secret that his boots were of high quality and expertly polished. She was surprised to see that he used a cane, which defied the youth of his voice. When her gaze finally rose to his face, his dark eyes gleamed with amusement, as if he were calling her out for scanning him from head to foot.

His mouth quirked, and Juliet didn't miss the slight dimple on one side of his face. The late hour was also made apparent by the presence of whiskers on his chin and cheeks.

The dark wave of his hair completed the visage and reminded Juliet of a hero in a contraband romance novel she'd once read. She really shouldn't be thinking of him in such terms. He could be married, or even worse, a drunk gambler like her brother. Although . . . his black eyes didn't appear unfocused in the very least.

Juliet realized she was staring at him, and she took a deep breath to refocus her thoughts. "Were you injured?" she asked, gesturing toward his cane, then immediately regretted her question. This man had nothing to recommend him, other than a title, which he could have made up. And the fact that her brother was in his carriage . . . Well, she didn't even know that.

"I was," the man's tone sounded surprised. "I fell off a horse a couple weeks ago. Turned my ankle."

Juliet nodded. So not a war injury or something from a drunken brawl. She swallowed against the dryness of her throat because the man seemed to be doing a thorough exam of her own person, and she was clothed in her night rail. It couldn't be helped, and after tonight, she would never see this man again.

"I don't mean to pressure you," he said, "but I plan to return to London tonight, so I'd like to get your brother situated sooner rather than later."

"Lady Juliet Baldwin," she said. "That's my name. Remind me of your name. I'm afraid I was a bit distraught at waking to someone banging at my door."

"Understood. I'm Lord Victor Roland, Earl of Locken." He gave a brief bow.

Juliet quickly hid her shock—he was an earl, beneath a marquis and a duke. Unless he had yet to inherit a higher title . . .

"Nice to meet you, Lady Juliet Baldwin." His dark eyes

seemed to pierce right through her. "Is there a butler or groomsman who might help me carry your brother to his room?"

She hated to tell Lord Locken that there was no man here to help, and she refused to call upon a neighbor at such an hour. The fewer people who knew about her brother's deplorable condition, the better. "I'm afraid only myself and the housekeeper are currently in residence," she said.

To his credit, Lord Locken didn't look aghast. He simply said, "I can probably manage on my own if you will but lead the way."

"All right," she said. "I need to find a robe first."

It seemed that Lord Locken used great effort to keep his gaze on her face when he stepped back and said, "Very well. I'll try to rouse your brother in the meantime. Perhaps fortune will be upon us, and he will rise on his own."

Juliet nodded and turned from the doorway. She kept ahold of the candle and hurried up the stairs to her bedchamber. She was out of breath by the time she reached her room. Not only was she about to help her drunken brother to his room, but she was about to let the most handsome man she'd ever met into her home. Not that she'd met many men of the *ton*, so as far as she knew, he paled in comparison. Somehow, she doubted it.

She drew on a robe and tied it about her waist. Then she smoothed her hair back and fastened a ribbon to hold the unruliness into place. A lady's maid would be useful right now, but Juliet hadn't had that luxury. She snatched up the candle again and set it on the hallway table near her brother's room. Then she went into his bedchamber and lit another candle.

By the time she returned to the front door, she'd lit several other candles so that Lord Locken would be able to navigate his way throughout the house.

She stepped outside, leaving the door wide open, and walked right into a light drizzle. Of course it would start raining now. There wasn't much else that could happen to make the night worse. She found Lord Locken standing inside the curricle, where her brother must be.

She paused by the pair of bays. Lord Locken must be a wealthy gentleman indeed. The bays were well-bred, beautiful specimens. She stepped around them and moved to the curricle.

Juliet recoiled at the first sight of John. His clothing was rumpled and soiled, and he had a swollen nose, the blood crusted about his mouth and chin. "I thought you said he was uninjured."

"He got into a bit of a scrape with a horse," Lord Locken said. "But he's passed out from the alcohol."

She decided to question him on the fight her brother had gotten into later. For now, they had to somehow transport the man. Lord Locken's cane was propped against the side of the curricle, reminding Juliet of his injury. Mrs. Campton would be useless, so Juliet would have to help carry her brother.

She lifted her night rail enough to step into the curricle. Her brother reeked of alcohol and something more rank. "John," she said, shaking his shoulder. "John, time to wake up."

His head lolled, but his eyes didn't even crack open.

Lord Locken said nothing as Juliet continued trying to wake her brother.

Finally, she turned to face the dark-eyed man. "Tell me how to help you. I don't want you to injure your ankle further."

His brows drew together. "My ankle is of no concern. A small thing like you could hardly carry a full-grown man."

For some reason, his words made her pulse hammer. "I can lift his legs at least, if you hold up his torso."

The man hesitated, then nodded. "That might work. I'll prop him up," Lord Locken said, "and you can go before me and grab his feet."

So she and Lord Locken had to change places, and Juliet brushed against him as they moved. When she climbed out of the curricle, she realized she'd been holding her breath. She wiped at the rain on her face and exhaled. Then she grasped her brother's ankles and walked backward as Lord Locken hefted him until John was out of the curricle. Juliet had really done nothing, but now the real work would begin.

"Ready?" Lord Locken said.

He was hardly breathless, even though his ankle was surely in pain.

Juliet kept her brother's ankles hoisted and propped on her hips as she walked with Lord Locken into the house. He paused when he saw the flight of stairs.

"We could put him in the drawing room on the settee," Juliet suggested.

Lord Locken's gaze connected with her. "He'll be more comfortable in his bed."

"If you think we can make it up the stairs," Juliet said, giving him an out if he should care to have one.

"We'll make it." Lord Locken began to move up the stairs backward.

Juliet couldn't help but notice Lord Locken wincing every couple of steps as he put weight on his injured ankle. She gritted her teeth in commiseration and cursed her brother once again. His actions certainly had far-reaching consequences.

It was nothing short of a miracle that they managed to deposit her brother on his bed without dropping him. She tugged off his boots and then rolled him to the side to work his jacket off one of his arms.

"Let me help," Lord Locken said, moving to her side.

Inside now, she caught a whiff of his decidedly male scent—spice, rain, and the outdoors. She ignored the way her pulse seemed to jump while in close proximity with him, and she started to undo the buttons of her brother's vest.

Together they made quick work of removing John's jacket, his vest and cravat.

Juliet decided to leave his shirt and breeches on.

"I'll roll him if you want to pull the covers out from under him," Lord Locken said.

A practical suggestion. They worked together in silence, the only sound the light snores of her brother and the increasing rain slapping against the bedroom window.

"I'll fetch a glass of water to put by his bedside should he wake," Juliet said, knowing she was making an excuse to leave the room. But with John settled into his bed and Lord Locken's dominating presence, she had to keep moving, keep working.

She paused in the doorway. "Should you care to come to the kitchen, I can brew up some tea to sustain you on your return trip."

Lord Locken's eyes flicked to hers. "Thank you. I'd welcome the refreshment."

Juliet's step felt light as she left the room and went downstairs. The front door was still wide open, and the damp air seeped into the entryway. She should fetch Lord Locken's cane at the very least, and what about his bays?

She hurried out into the weather to fetch the cane, and the wind whipped stinging rain against her skin. Juliet paused by the bays, who were stalwart in their patience as they endured the weather. Neither of them seemed bothered by the wind and rain in the least. She stroked their noses, then went about her task of retrieving Lord Locken's cane. By the time she made it back inside, her hair was quite damp, and Lord Locken was coming down the stairs. His hand had a firm grip on the banister as he took each stair slowly. She shut the door behind her, then headed up the stairs to meet the man halfway.

"You didn't have to do that," he said as he took the cane from her outstretched hand. His gaze surveyed her damp appearance.

"Nonsense." She brushed wet hair from her face. "You've put more strain on your injury." She took a step back from the dark gaze of Lord Locken. She now realized that his eyes were not black, but a dark brown. "Come to the kitchen, and I'll put the tea on."

He looked as if he were about to change his mind. Instead, he nodded and continued down the stairs.

Five

Southill's sister was a temptress of the worst kind, Victor decided. Meaning that she was beautiful and sensual without even knowing it. Her innocence was more attractive to Victor than a woman who knew the art of seduction, and the soft light coming from the few candles in the kitchen only added to the allure. He tried to push such thoughts out of his head as he observed her moving about the room, and it was clear she wasn't too familiar with the workings of a kitchen, but she was trying, and that certainly counted.

"Let me stoke the fire." He moved to her side after she'd tried more than once to get the embers to ignite into flame. He couldn't help notice the scent of rain on her skin and clothing, and he'd never before realized how enticing it smelled.

He added a few bits of kindling to the hot coals and gently blew on them. Moments later, the kindling caught on fire.

"Bravo," Lady Juliet said, clapping her hands together. "You did it."

Victor straightened and smiled down at her. "It's rather simple once you know how to do it."

She blinked her long lashes, and he noticed her blue eyes again, much like her brother's, yet different too. The blue of her eyes was a deeper color, reminding him of a pond on a summer's day. "I'm not as helpless as I might seem." Her lips curved upward. "I've some skills, just not in the kitchen."

He held back the rather suggestive comment that popped into his mind and let her move past him to fill the tea kettle with water.

Once she set that on top of the warming stove, she opened a few cupboards, searching. "Ah, here it is." She turned, holding a plate of butter. Setting it on the table, she again busied herself looking for something else.

Victor leaned back in his chair and folded his arms. He stifled a yawn. He was quite tired, yet content as well.

"Here's the cake Mrs. Campton made yesterday." Lady Juliet carried a plate to the table and set it in front of Victor. "It's still moist."

"Thank you," he said. "I didn't expect to be fed in the middle of the night." He took the fork she'd handed him, then paused. "Are you not eating?"

"Oh, I couldn't possibly eat," she said.

He waited. When she didn't continue, he prompted, "Because . . . ?"

She looked away from him. "I haven't had much of an appetite of late." Standing there, she looked forlorn with her damp hair and delicate features.

"Are you ill?" he asked in a quiet voice.

Her gaze cut back to his. "Oh, no, nothing like that." She exhaled. "Things have not been easy since the passing of my father a year ago. And my brother's follies have compounded my distress."

Of course. Victor should have guessed some of this—what with all the gambling her brother did, and her being practically alone at this big estate. "I'm sorry for your loss."

She blinked and turned away, attending to the tea kettle. Surely, she was not still grieving so deeply? Victor supposed it was possible, especially if she'd been close to her father. Victor wouldn't grieve the passing of his own father, and he supposed that unfortunate attitude might give him something more to feel guilty over, but it was the truth.

"John has taken it hard," Lady Juliet said, her back still turned.

"Yes," Victor said for lack of a better response. Something hung in the air between them—questions he wasn't sure it was his place to ask. "And how are *you* faring?"

Her hands dropped to her sides, and she didn't respond for a moment. "I think you're the first person to ask that."

The tremor in her voice was unmistakable, and he wanted to find a way to comfort her. Was her brother such a cad that he'd neglected his sister's tender feelings?

"What was your father like?" he asked, knowing that the cozy warmth of the kitchen had lulled him into asking more personal questions than he ought.

Lady Juliet looked over at him with her deep blue gaze. "He loved horses," she said with an affectionate smile. She lifted the kettle from the stove, then poured the steaming water into a teapot. "Our neighbor breeds horses, and the two men could talk for hours at a time about them. My father taught me to ride almost before I could walk. He gave me my first pony on my third birthday."

Victor nodded. "I expect you're an excellent horsewoman now."

She lifted one of her shoulders. "I ride as often as I can, when it's not raining of course."

Victor glanced at the dark window that blocked out the rainy night. "What about your mother?"

"She died when I was twelve." Lady Juliet turned to the teapot, but not before Victor saw the fresh sadness in her eyes. She lifted the teapot and poured the tea through a strainer into the two cups she'd set on the sideboard. She delivered one steaming cup to him, then she set a pitcher of milk and a small bowl of crushed sugar on the table.

"I never knew my mother," Victor said when she took a chair across the table from him. It had been years since he'd spoken of his mother to anyone. In fact, he wasn't sure when he last had. Perhaps it had been at Eton when they were all required to write an essay about their family lineage.

"Were you a baby when she died?" Lady Juliet asked, her gaze filled with compassion.

Under ordinary circumstances, Victor would have despised any pity or commiseration. But here, now, he didn't mind the way this woman was looking at him. In fact, it made him feel like they had something in common, since death put everyone on a level playing field. "She died from blood loss after giving birth to me."

Instead of saying how sorry she was, or how horrible of a death, or some other pitying comeback, Lady Juliet said, "Childbirth is a great risk to all women."

Victor took a sip of the steaming tea. The burn felt good in his throat. "Yes, and it has made my decision all that easier." He felt Lady Juliet's gaze on him, so when he looked up, he wasn't surprised to see her curious expression. "I've decided to marry the woman my father has selected. I do not love her. Therefore, if she doesn't survive childbirth, I won't turn into a drunken, pathetic man like my father."

Lady Juliet's lips parted in a soft gasp. "I am sure you don't mean you won't care for your wife, even if it's not a love match."

Victor took another scalding swallow, then winced. He should pour some milk in to cool the temperature, but he refrained. "I mean it with all my heart, Lady Juliet. Taking care of someone is not the same thing as caring *for* them."

She rose to her feet without a word, crossed to where he sat and added a spoonful of sugar to his tea. He watched her movements as she reached for the milk jug and added a small trickle. Then she picked up a spoon and stirred. Finally, she retook her seat and gazed across the table at him with frankness.

"Sometimes when life has dealt us a bitter blow, someone else must add the sweetness back into it," she said in a soft voice, tilting her head toward his teacup as if she'd given him a concrete example. "That's how I envision marriage to be. Whatever challenges we face in life, if we have a partner to face them with, we can find joy."

Victor studied her for a moment, her deep blue eyes, her golden hair barely tamed by the ribbon she'd added to it, the v-opening of her robe that exposed the dip of her night rail so that her delicate collarbones were visible. He picked up the teacup and took another drink. The heat had calmed, and the taste was akin to a pastry. It was, to be honest, sweet and delicious.

"Perhaps you're right, Lady Juliet," Victor said in a slow voice. "I've no doubt that *you'll* enjoy the fruits of such a marriage. As for a man like me, those sorts of opportunities never come knocking."

"What are you? Thirty in age?" she asked. "Surely you can't profess to have the bitterness of a man twice your age."

"I'm nearly thirty, but I have as much right to bitterness as the next man."

"Did you fight in the war?" she pressed.

He was taken aback by her direct question, yet his chuckle didn't seem to bother her. "I'm the only son of the Duke of Wycliff. All I was allowed to do was transport a few private letters."

Her eyes widened a fraction. He probably should have told her sooner who his father was. "You were a spy?" she asked.

"I wouldn't go that far—"

"The eldest sons of dukedoms are valuable to the estate and seen as a commodity," she said. "It's no wonder your father didn't want you to go to war and risk your life."

"That's a pretty thought in your pretty head," Victor said. "My father couldn't care less if I was alive. But his estate solicitor informed me I'd be disinherited if I took up any sort of uniform."

She sipped her tea as if she were considering his statement. "You must love your home, at least," she observed.

Her words had a way of driving straight into his heart and twisting hard. "It's the only thing I'll ever be able to call my own in this life."

Lady Juliet held his gaze, not looking away. "I suppose that's the truth of a man in your position. And I suppose that's why a woman wants to have children, despite the risk to her life. Once I marry, my dowry and possessions become the property of my husband. Only my children will belong to me."

Victor decided not to contradict her words because in truth, a woman's children legally belonged to the father. He was curious about Lady Juliet and her future, especially since her brother had tried to wager away her hand and dowry. "Is a wedding on the horizon for you, Lady Juliet?"

"Oh, no," she said, looking down at her teacup.

Victor didn't miss the flush of her cheeks. "You've been proposed to?"

She hesitated, then gave a short nod.

Victor's curiosity grew. He took another swallow of the sweet concoction she'd made for him and leaned forward, his gaze intent on hers. "Has your brother consented?"

Lady Juliet waved a hand in front of her face as if to ward off a fainting spell. "Goodness, no. It was just today . . . I mean yesterday. But I cannot fathom myself marrying the man."

Victor arched his brows, waiting for more.

The Final Wager

She exhaled and rested her chin on her hand, still avoiding his gaze. "It was surely out of pity. Our age difference is great, and I've lived an isolated life, so I am not very interesting."

Victor bit back a smile. "I think you're very interesting."

Her cheeks stained red, and she rose to her feet, collecting her half-finished teacup. "You're bred to compliment ladies."

He rose as well and blocked her path to the sink. "Horses are bred, not me."

She looked up at him. "I didn't mean—"

"I know what you meant," he said. "But this . . . gentleman . . . who asked for your hand is no fool, and he's not asking you out of pity."

She stared at him as if he were out of his mind, and perhaps he was, because he did something then he knew he'd regret. Eventually. He took the tea things from her hands and set them in the sink, then he turned to find that she hadn't moved at all. He grasped one of her hands and brought it to his lips.

She merely watched him as he pressed a kiss on her smooth skin.

"Lady Juliet, you are a beautiful and enchanting creature," he said in a low voice. "And you are undoubtedly well on your way to breaking a dozen men's hearts."

She laughed.

Victor was at first startled by her outburst, then charmed.

"You, sir, are getting ahead of yourself." She poked a finger against his chest as if they were children teasing each other. "Since my brother has gambled away most of our funds, there will be nothing left for me to have a season. Of course, at nearly twenty years of age, I'm a bit old to debut in London anyway. So I will most likely break only one or two hearts—and they will be very aged hearts—before some poor sop with a crumbling manor house from the north will court me for my dowry."

"From the north, eh?" Victor grinned. "Care to make a wager?"

Her eyes glinted as she laughed again. "I'm no gambler, Lord Locken."

"I beg to differ," he said. "You gamble every time you climb upon a horse. You gambled by opening the door when a stranger knocked upon it."

She tapped a finger to her lips—those pale rose and perfectly shaped lips—and Victor felt a thrill of warmth brush his skin as if she'd touched him instead.

"I suppose you're right," she said. "I *am* a gambler. What will your terms be?"

Ah. He'd caught her. With a slow smile, he said, "That you'll have three marriage proposals by the end of the summer."

Her eyebrows arched. "Only three? I thought you said I would break a dozen hearts."

"That will be true as well, but only three men will have enough courage to propose."

She laughed again. "And how will all this come about?"

"Your brother will throw a house party here," Victor said. "If *I* come, many will follow."

"You have quite a high opinion of yourself," she said in a dry tone, her eyes belying her interest. "And what do I get if you lose?"

"That is for *you* to say, Lady Juliet."

Her smile was soft as she stepped around him, then moved to the other side of the table, putting distance between them. From her position, she surveyed him as if he were a horse up for auction. "All right. If I do not have three proposals by the end of the summer, I get your pair of bays outside."

Victor nearly stopped breathing. "Those horses are purebreds."

Her smile widened. "Are you backing out of our wager, Lord Locken?"

The challenge in her blue eyes was irresistible. He smiled back. "Never."

Six

Juliet had to put distance between herself and Lord Locken immediately. His dark brown eyes missed nothing, and the way he was looking at her now made her feel like she was standing beneath the sun on a hot summer day. There was no sun in this kitchen, though, and she'd just made a wager with a man who had probably won every bet he'd ever made. If the lift of one side of his mouth, the quirk of his dark eyebrows, and the way his shoulders were squared with confidence were anything to go by, this man wasn't used to losing.

The wager was ridiculous, she told herself. Yes, she'd been proposed to by Lord Stratford, but he was a man more than twice her age. And even if her brother did agree to throw a house party and a dozen eligible men attended, that would bring all the ladies as well. And Juliet didn't hold a candle to ladies of the *ton* in either fine manner or appearance.

Lord Locken might have called her beautiful and enchanting, but he was a gentleman of the *ton*, and flirting was all a part of that. She could not fathom two other gentlemen proposing to her. Good thing Lord Locken was the heir to a dukedom and had more money than she could ever dream of, because he was about to lose a pair of very fine bays.

Juliet moved toward the kitchen window and gazed at the streaks of rain pelting it. "Perhaps you should stay until the storm lifts. At least give your horses shelter and food." When she looked over at Lord Locken, he still wore that amused smile.

"You're quite worried about my bays, aren't you?" he asked.

"I always take good care of my horses."

He chuckled. "Very well. I'm assuming I'll be acting as groomsman."

"You assume right," Juliet said. "The stables are on the north side. They'll be warm and dry even in this weather. There's plenty of room since we only have two nags."

Lord Locken nodded. "Thank you. I'll return in a moment." He paused by the doorway and said, "The tea was nice, but do you by chance have anything a little stronger?"

Juliet hid a sigh. Men and their brandy were all the same, it seemed. "There's brandy in the library. I'm afraid none of the bedchambers are prepared for guests, but perhaps you aren't too picky?" *Don't blush,* she commanded herself.

"Don't trouble yourself," he said. "I think propriety demands that I stay downstairs if you are to sleep upstairs."

Yes, he was right. "I will bring you some bedding."

"I don't think I'll be sleeping," he said. "I'll be gone as soon as the weather is passable."

She watched him leave the kitchen, and it was like she could breathe freely again. She hadn't realized how much Lord Locken's presence had affected her, and if she didn't have to see to her brother or their guest, she'd cloister herself in her bedchamber for the remainder of the night.

Juliet heard the front door open and shut, and with Lord Locken completely out of the house now, she decided to write Mrs. Campton a note about their guest. She left it in the center of the kitchen table, then found a clean glass to go with the bottle of brandy in the library. It had been around for many months, since the only person who drank in the household was her brother. She entered the library and lit a few more candles. Noticing her abandoned correspondence to her brother, she crumpled up the half-written letter and put away the ink and quill.

Then she hurried upstairs to check on John. He hadn't moved, and the bruising around his nose had darkened. One of his eyes was quite swollen, and Juliet was sure when her brother awakened, he'd be in plenty of pain. She left her brother to his rest and located a pillow and blanket for Lord Locken, despite his declaration that he wouldn't be sleeping.

By the time she returned to the library, she was surprised to find that he'd already returned and was sitting in a chair that faced the cold hearth. He'd removed his outer jacket and cravat and draped them over the back of the chair opposite him. A half-empty glass of brandy sat on the side table.

"You've returned," Juliet said and crossed to him, holding the blanket and pillow.

But he didn't respond, and when Juliet rounded the chair, she saw that his eyes were closed.

Was he . . . *asleep*?

She wanted to laugh. He'd declared that he wouldn't be sleeping, but here he was, not many moments later, dead to the world.

"Lord Locken?" she whispered, reluctant to disturb him, but she wanted to make sure he was comfortable for the night.

He didn't move, didn't stir.

"Lord Locken?" she said a little louder this time. Still, nothing. She set the pillow on the chair across from him, then draped the blanket over his body, covering him from his torso to his calves. He should have taken his boots off to be more comfortable, but he probably hadn't planned on falling asleep in a chair. Taking off his boots for him wasn't something she dared to do.

She couldn't help but gaze at his sleeping form, the way his long legs stretched out before him, the relaxed state of his capable hands, the dark lashes lying against his cheekbones, and how the whiskers on his face emphasized the chiseled line of his jaw. A piece of his hair had fallen across his forehead, and at this close of a distance, she could smell the rain in his damp hair. She leaned forward, and ever so gently, she moved the lock off his forehead. Her fingertips brushed the warm skin of his forehead. She drew her hand away, primarily because she shouldn't be touching this man and secondarily because her heart was thundering so loudly that there was risk of waking him.

Juliet took a step back so that she wouldn't be tempted to touch him again. He was a beautiful specimen of a man, and that made her more wary. He was about to become engaged, and he probably knew plenty about her brother's financial mess.

His wager was also ridiculous, and she didn't know what had possessed him to make it. Perhaps it was the lateness of hour, and they were both quite out of their senses. Maybe if she won the wager, she could sell the pair of bays and make a dent in her brother's debts. Or she'd sell the bays back to Lord Locken. The thought made her smile. She left the library, and Lord Locken to his rest, then ascended the stairs to her bedchamber.

Juliet made her way to her bedchamber, blew out her candle, and nestled between the cold covers. It was still raining outside, and eventually the sound of the raindrops against her windowpanes lulled her to sleep.

"Juliet!"

She awakened to her brother's voice calling her. For a moment, she couldn't remember how John happened to be home after such a long absence. Then her memories of the events from the night before swiftly returned. She sat up in her bed. The sky outside had lightened to a morning gray, and the rain had stopped, although the clouds were still dark with threat.

Was Lord Locken awake? Was he still there?

Juliet scrambled out of bed and grabbed the robe she'd been wearing the night before. She didn't take time to dress because her brother's voice echoed down the hall once again. Knowing she looked a fright, she hurried out of her bedchamber. If she crossed paths with Lord Locken, well, she couldn't look any more disheveled than she had in the middle of the night when she'd opened the front door to him.

"Coming," Juliet said as she approached her brother's chamber and opened his door.

He was sitting up in bed, and it was obvious that he'd been sick in the wash basin. The stench was like a slap to her senses.

John's blue eyes bugged when he saw her. The bruising on his face had settled into a deep purple now. "How in damnation did I get home?" he growled.

Hello to you, too, brother. Juliet wanted to back out of the room or, at the very least, cover her mouth and nose against the stench, but instead she stood erect inside the doorway. She used a scrap of her remaining patience to reply in a calm voice. "Why, Lord Locken brought you home. He said that you'd been in a bit of a scrape and—"

"*Victor Roland brought me home?*" John nearly shouted.

Juliet's mouth fell open. How dare her brother lash out at her in this way? She'd had nothing to do with the events that brought John to his own bed. "You were . . . incapacitated. He knocked on our door, and then I helped him get you up the stairs."

John shoved his covers aside and swung his legs over the

edge of the bed. The color drained from his face at the effort. "How dare you let that vile man enter *my* home and set foot onto *my* floors? Let alone come into my most private chamber!"

Her face heated. "You weren't exactly in a position to make your opinions clear."

John pushed to his feet, grasping the nearest bedpost to steady himself. "If he *ever* sets foot on my property, I'll be forced to call him out." He swayed as his face reddened with anger. "Never, I mean, *never* speak to Locken again."

"*That* will be quite impossible, Southill," a deep voice drawled behind Juliet.

She spun around to see the man himself. He, of course, wore the same clothing from the night before, but in the light of gray morning, he looked ever the impeccable gentleman.

Lord Locken had somehow tamed his hair and retied his cravat, making himself presentable as if he'd merely appeared for a morning house call. He stepped up to Juliet's side, and his presence seemed to take over by his mere appearance.

But her brother didn't falter. "*You.* I don't know what blasted lies you told my sister, but if you don't get out now, I'll be forced to put a revolver to your heart."

Lord Locken tightened his grip on his cane. "Is that how you should speak in the presence of a lady, Southill?"

John sputtered, his red face growing even redder. "You can't sweet-talk your way out of this."

Lord Locken chuckled. "If I remember right, *you* were the one sweet-talking, or should I say *begging* to join my card game last night at White's."

Juliet inhaled. "*You* were gambling with my brother?" she asked Lord Locken.

Lord Locken's gaze moved to focus on her, and his brown eyes were like amber. She remembered touching his forehead last night, and her breath hitched at the memory.

Before he could reply, her brother blurted, "Locken's a notorious gambler."

Juliet didn't look at her brother because she wanted to read the truth in Lord Locken's eyes. There was no denial there, and a slow wave of disappointment built inside of her. *He's a gentleman of the ton,* she told herself. *That's what they do. Gamble. What did I expect?* Although men who were heirs to a dukedom had the money to finance such habits, unlike her brother. She shoved back the ridiculousness of why she should care about what this man did with his time.

"He's a gambler," John repeated, his voice only growing more agitated, "*and* a rake."

Lord Locken's gaze didn't falter from Juliet's. His lips twitched before he replied to John's accusation. "That last bit was quite unnecessary, Southill."

Juliet had no reply. A gambler and a rake had no business occupying her thoughts, and their conversations from the night before flooded into her mind, making her feel ill with embarrassment.

"Because of this man," John continued, "I've lost our carriage, and . . . I almost lost you."

Juliet snapped her gaze to look at her brother. "What are you talking about?"

His blue eyes widened as if he regretted what he'd confessed, and this alone made Juliet's stomach feel as if she'd swallowed a handful of pebbles.

"Let me explain," Lord Locken said in that deep, smooth voice of his.

A voice she'd once found comforting and trustworthy. But now . . .

"You need to leave, *now*," John said. "My personal affairs are no concern of yours."

Lord Locken didn't move. "Oh, I think they most

definitely concern me, especially when you wagered a carriage in a game that you lost to me, and it turns out the carriage in question was confiscated by creditors."

"How dare you—" John rushed forward.

Juliet didn't know what made her do it, because even with Lord Locken's injury, she had no doubt he could defend himself quite well against her brother, but she stepped in front of Lord Locken.

"Don't you touch him," she told her brother in a voice much stronger then she felt inside. Before her brother could recover his astonishment, she turned to Lord Locken. "I will see to your horses while you break your fast. Thank you for helping my brother, and I'm sorry that he is so ill-tempered. But he is right. It would be better if you left as soon as you are able."

"Ill-tempered?" her brother complained. "Who do you think punched me in the face?"

Juliet looked from her brother to Lord Locken. "Is that true?"

"Your brother needed to be taught a lesson," Lord Locken said simply. "After losing his phantom carriage, he tried to gamble away your hand and your dowry, which is illegal. Even though I didn't know you, I was sure that any sister of Southill's didn't want her future decided in a card game."

Shock jolted through Juliet, and she couldn't even look at her brother. The room had gone dead silent, and that was all the confirmation she needed. She stepped past Lord Locken and left the stench-filled room and returned to her bedchamber. With a numbness, she dressed in her riding habit, then pulled her hair into a severe bun at the nape of her neck.

She would let the men work out their differences, and although Lord Locken seemed to have about one hundred more times honor than her own brother, he was no innocent. He'd been gambling in the first place and had likely seen her brother as easy prey. Juliet was the first one to admit that her brother didn't have a head for games of strategy.

By the time she left her bedchamber, she couldn't hear any conversations coming from the direction of John's room. She walked down the stairs, keeping her chin lifted should she encounter Lord Locken. She didn't know where he'd gone either. Instead of stopping in the kitchen, she left the house and walked to the stables, where she found Lord Locken's bays still in residence. So he hadn't left yet.

She did as she said she would, and she fed and watered the two bays, then brushed down their coats even though it appeared that Lord Locken had done a thorough job the night before. It was then she let the first tears fall. She'd finish her task, then take one of the nags out for a long ride. Because at this moment, the last thing she wanted to do was face her brother and the fact that he'd fallen so low as to wager her future.

Seven

Victor found her in the stables. He leaned against the doorframe and watched her brush down the bays.

"You've been taking care of me ever since I arrived," he said at last. "First bringing me my cane, feeding me, then covering me with a blanket, and now you're playing groomsman."

Lady Juliet spun around. Her cheeks were flushed pink, and her dark blue eyes filled with fire.

Victor straightened from his position, unsure what to expect.

"I am finished with you and your like," she said. "Our wager is finished, and your horses are safe." She brushed a trembling hand over a strand of hair that had come loose from her rather severe coiffure. "My brother has not only disgraced himself, but he has now brought me in the middle of it all. And you, sir, are not what you seem. You let my brother wager more than he had, and then you got into a fight with him."

"I am sorry for allowing him to enter our game of cards in the first place," Victor said. "But I'll never be sorry for teaching him that he cannot wager a woman's fate."

Lady Juliet's fiery gaze seemed to dim, and she looked down and smoothed the waist of her riding skirt. An outfit that she looked very fine in. Whether dressed for bed or dressed for riding, she was a fair woman to gaze upon.

He had no doubt that a house party at Southill Estate would earn her several proposals. Men would be falling at her feet, despite her brother's reputation.

When she looked up, she said, "I've decided to write to my aunt and ask her to take me in."

Victor didn't protest, because what this woman did was truly none of his business. Yet he found he cared what happened to her. "Where does your aunt live?"

"About an hour south from here." Her gaze moved away again, and she looked as if she wanted to be anywhere but here in the stable with him.

He couldn't fully blame her. "Perhaps you should think more upon it before you act in any haste."

She blinked, and he could see she was close to tears. He cursed himself, and even though he could argue a hundred different ways that the tears were caused by her negligent brother, Victor was to blame as well.

"I am tired." She wasn't referring to last night's shortened rest; she was tired of fighting to stay afloat in a sinking estate.

He took a step forward. "Keep our wager, then," he said quietly. When she didn't respond, he added, "Think about it. I spoke with your brother about restoring his reputation by hosting a house party that will bring the elite to this village. You'll have the gentlemen falling at your feet, and within weeks, you'll be engaged."

She exhaled and wiped at a tear that had fallen upon her cheek.

Victor forced his hands to stay at his side. "You can be married by Christmastide and out from under your brother's thumb. His poor decisions will no longer affect you."

Her gaze met his, and the blue of her eyes was like the deepest part of the ocean. "That is one option."

His lips curved. "A better option than hiding yourself away at your aunt's home."

Lady Juliet's eyes flashed again. "I'm not hiding out, I—"

Victor placed a hand on her arm. "I know." She was trembling, and it made him even more disappointed in her brother. Victor knew how it felt to be helpless about one's own fate and be at the mercy of another's decisions. He should have probably left then, bade her farewell and good luck. Instead he brushed his thumb over the moisture along her cheek.

He heard her breath hitch, mimicking the hitch in his chest. "Don't make a rash decision is all I'm suggesting. Take your time. Consider where you want to be a year from now."

She nodded, her eyes luminous as she gazed up at him.

His heart was pounding, and he needed to drop his hand and step back. "Write to me of your decision," he managed to say. Then he did as his good sense commanded and stepped away. "And thank you for preparing my horses."

She said nothing as he led the two bays out of the stables and harnessed them to his curricle. Even though his back was turned toward her, he sensed her watching his every movement.

Once the curricle was ready to go, he climbed in and turned toward the stables. Lady Juliet was nowhere in sight. Had it been his imagination that she'd been watching him? He steered the horses along the drive that led past the Southill manor. Just before he turned away from the house, the front door opened and Southill came out, half dressed.

"Hold up, Roland," he called out.

Victor pulled back on the reins. "Whoa!"

Southill strode to Victor and placed his hands on the edge of the curricle. "I'm going to take you up on your offer," he said in a conciliatory tone, although his eyes were filled with contempt. "You must pay for everything, though."

"I said I would," Victor replied. "My terms are that no one will know of the financial arrangement. Not your sister, not your buffoon friends, *no one.*"

"I give you my word." Southill stretched out his hand, and the two men shook on their agreement. "I'll see you in three weeks, then."

Victor nodded. "See you then." He slapped the reins, and the horses moved forward, pulling him away from Southill Estate—a place that had been full of surprises. He was tempted to wipe the earl's touch from his hand, but instead, Victor focused straight ahead, wondering what he'd gotten himself into.

If it weren't for Lady Juliet Baldwin, he'd have turned around the moment he'd dumped Southill on his doorstep last night. Victor would have washed his hands of the despicable man for good. Yet, now, he felt as if he'd just made a bargain with the devil himself.

He wondered how Lady Juliet would react when her brother told her the news that the house party was indeed happening. Would she already be too far into her plans to move in with her aunt? Victor found that he hoped she would be present at the house party. Forget the wager, he just wanted to see her enjoying herself without the cloud of her brother's actions hanging over her.

Three weeks. It seemed an eternity from now.

By the time he reached London, he was in sore need of a bath and a shave. He pulled up to his London townhome, and Thomas came out immediately to take the curricle around to the stables. Lud, it was nice to have a groomsman again.

And his butler was at the door to greet him and take his coat.

"We're glad to see you safely returned," Fletcher said without inquiring further.

News traveled quickly among household help and servants, so he had no doubt that Fletcher knew he'd carted Southill home.

"I must say that it's good to be home," he told Fletcher. He considered London his home while his father still lived at their Locken Estate. "Can you tell Leeson that I'd like a bath? Oh, and send something up to eat. I'm in a bit of a rush." He was starving, but he couldn't waste any time. He had to get to White's and make light of the situation surrounding Southill. He also had to plant in the minds of the men that Southill's sister was a diamond of the first water.

Then, in two days' time, he'd mention his invitation to an exclusive house party at the Southill Estate. Others would beg him for a reference, and the invitations would then start arriving.

Eight

Juliet stood at her bedchamber window, watching the line of carriages approaching Southill Estate. In a few minutes, members of the *ton* would set foot inside her home, the men and women in their finery and sophistication. They'd be here for two weeks of food, games, hunting, and dancing.

Lord Locken had done it. He'd somehow reconciled with her brother and convinced him to hold a house party. She didn't know how John would afford all of this but could only hope that his new connections would prove fruitful in the long run.

As for herself, she couldn't forget her wager with Lord Locken. He'd mentioned nothing of it in his single letter to her. Yes, he *had* written her a letter, and if society knew about it, it would be considered scandalous since they weren't related. But when her brother had told her of the house party, she'd done as Lord Locken had suggested. She'd spent time going over her options and what she wanted for her future.

Juliet came to the realization that she wanted to fall in love, wanted to marry, wanted a home of her own, wanted children. So . . . she wrote a short note to Lord Locken.

His reply came only a few days later.

Below, the first carriage, laden with two trunks, stopped

in front of the manor, and two women alighted amid a flurry of activity as the hired help that Lord Locken had sent bustled about the women. John welcomed them, fawning over each lady in turn, bowing to kiss their hands, then leading them into the house.

They'd planned for Juliet to enter the drawing room when everyone had arrived. She suspected her brother was scouring for a wife—one with a large dowry—and that might have been why he agreed to Lord Locken's plan.

Now Juliet reached into her bodice and removed the three-times folded letter from Lord Locken. She opened the creased page again, although she had his words memorized.

Dear Lady Juliet,
I received your message with gratitude. I applaud your decision, and I don't believe you will regret it. I look forward to our reunion.
Yours,
—V R

His dark, slanted handwriting complemented his decisive nature. Juliet's gaze dwelt on his signature, *Yours, V R.* His given name was Victor Roland, and ever since she'd received the letter, she'd struggled to think of him as anything other than *Victor*. Something she'd have to put out of her mind so she wouldn't make the error of calling him by his Christian name.

The second carriage came to a stop, and the groomsmen strode over to attend to the next group of guests. The carriage door opened, and out stepped the man who had made all of this happen. Even though Juliet could only see the top of his dark head, she knew instantly it was Lord Locken. He still used his cane. He'd dressed in a light gray jacket with darker breeches, and he wore a vest of a pale yellow. If anything, he was more handsome than Juliet remembered. How that was possible, she didn't know. Perhaps the three weeks had dulled her memory. Moments later, another man climbed out of the carriage. This man was older but looked every bit the refined gentleman.

And then Lord Locken looked up, right at her window, as if he knew she stood there. Her heart nearly stopped. It was impossible to think that he could see her from the driveway. She didn't move, thinking if he *did* see her, maybe he'd think she resembled a bureau situated near the window.

But a smile played on his lips before he turned to the gentleman who'd traveled with him. They issued directions to the groomsmen, although it looked as if they'd traveled much lighter than the women of the previous carriage.

John stepped forward to greet both men, shaking their hands. Even from her position, Juliet noticed the rigidity of her brother's shoulders and stiffness of his posture. Whatever repairs had been made between her brother and Lord Locken, in truth they were both very stubborn men.

Juliet refolded the letter and slipped it into its place on the inside of her bodice. She didn't want to risk the letter being found by the lady's maid Lord Locken had sent to their household. Juliet didn't want to burn it either.

Another carriage rumbled to a stop, and Juliet continued to watch the arriving guests long after Lord Locken had walked with a group of men toward the stables, certainly to check out the horses Lord Stratford had lent them for the occasion. Yes, Lord Stratford was to be a guest at all the activities, and he had yet to renew his sentiments, a fact for which Juliet was deeply grateful, or else she might have to turn him out on his ear.

Marrying the man wouldn't be the end of the world, but

she had let Lord Locken's words go to her head. What if one of these younger men fell in love with her, and she him? What if... her happy ending was about to begin?

Juliet turned away from the window and surveyed her appearance in the mirror. They hadn't funds for new dresses, but she'd had some of her mother's things made over. Today, she wore a pale peach dress befitting the season, and its remade bodice was lower cut than she usually wore, but it followed the height of fashion. Although she was unused to seeing herself presented in such a way, she must act as if she were comfortable in such an outfit when she was surrounded by the others.

By the time the fifth carriage had arrived, Juliet left her bedchamber to join everyone downstairs. The drawing room contained several ladies and a few gentlemen. John was in the front hall, and as soon as he saw her, his smile bloomed as he strode to greet her. "Dear sister, I'd like you to meet my friends from London."

Her brother's wide smile was only a show, this Juliet knew. She returned an equally delighted smile, then turned toward the guests to be introduced to each one.

Lord Locken wasn't among them, and although she didn't know any of the men, their attention was a heady feeling.

"I'd like you to meet Mr. Laurence Talbot," her brother said.

Mr. Talbot's dark green eyes seemed friendly, and his smile quick. "It's a pleasure to meet you at last."

"He owns a whole fleet of ships," her brother continued, clapping the man on the back.

Mr. Talbot chuckled. "Perhaps not a *whole* fleet, but I own my fair share."

"Oh, do you sail on them?" Juliet couldn't help but

wonder what it would be like to marry a man who was a seaman. Would he take her along on adventures?

"Not much anymore," Mr. Talbot said. "You see, my mother has been ailing since my father's death."

"I am sorry." Juliet appraised the man, who obviously cared for his mother. He might not be as handsome as Lord Locken—but who was? A man's dedication to his aging parent was a characteristic to hold in high esteem. "Where is your favorite place to travel?"

"Before you regale her with too many tales," her brother cut in, "I must introduce her to the others."

Mr. Talbot bowed and moved off.

Another gentleman quickly replaced Mr. Talbot, then another, and another, until Juliet's head spun with all the introductions. The women were friendly as well, and Juliet hoped she'd fool them all by acting as if a houseful of guests was a regular occurrence.

"I've heard much about you, Lady Juliet," another man was speaking to her, and she tried to focus.

Her brother introduced him as Lord Owen Brooks. His pale blond hair was tied in an orange ribbon, matching his rather flamboyant jacket. His smile was welcoming as he gazed at her, and she decided she liked him, although he seemed to be young—perhaps only a few years older than herself.

"Lord Brooks has recently returned from a tour of the continent," her brother continued, as if the men were best of friends.

Juliet couldn't help but wonder what type of interactions and business dealings her brother had had with some of these gentlemen.

"You are enchanting, my lady," Lord Brooks said, grasping her hand and bringing it to his lips.

The Final Wager

Rather forward, she thought, but what did she know? She'd have to see if he flirted in such a way with all the women.

More guests arrived, and it seemed the entire house was brimming with people even though only seventeen had been invited. Lord Stratford made eighteen, and with her and her brother, there were twenty in total.

Juliet had much to learn about socializing, and she decided that upon this first day, she'd listen more than she'd contribute. So she moved among the women, welcoming them, asking them where they were from, then letting them carry on the rest of the conversation. The longer she spent among the women, the more comfortable she felt in her low-cut bodice, especially since hers was modest in comparison.

"Southill Estate is so quaint," one of the women cooed. She'd introduced herself as Lady Diana Allen. Her hair was a deep red, and the jewelry at her neck and ears looked to cost more than the entire estate.

"I'm afraid I haven't traveled all that much," Juliet said with a smile. "But I've heard tales of the grand estates."

"Oh, goodness, I could tell you a few stories," Diana continued, and the others around them tittered. "Locken is magnificent."

The woman referred to Lord Locken's home.

"And to think that you will be duchess there one day," another woman said, this one a dark brunette named Lady Penelope Burke.

Diana's cheeks pinked. "Oh, hush, Penelope. He has not yet proposed."

Her friend giggled. "That will change very soon."

Juliet looked from Penelope to Diana. Did they mean . . . ?

"All right, we'll let you in on our secret," Diana said, leaning forward and speaking just above a whisper. "When Lord Locken insisted that I come to this house party, I told him I didn't want to impose."

Penelope leaned closer as well. "And that's when he told her it would be a very important occasion, but her presence was needed to make it so."

Diana clasped her hands together, a pleased smile on her face. "I had to agree after that."

Penelope stifled another giggle. "Everyone knows that he's about to propose. It's all the gossip in London."

Diana smiled. "Our fathers are cousins, and since we've been children, it's been alluded to."

"That might be true," Penelope said. "But you are also in love with him."

Diana's cheeks went even pinker, and Penelope turned her smile upon Juliet. "It's the sweetest story, really—*oh*. There he is now."

Juliet didn't need to turn to know that Lord Locken had entered the room. She heard her brother greet him and Lord Locken's answering reply in that low voice of his. She kept her back to the entrance of the drawing room, feeling that she wasn't ready to face him quite so soon after learning he'd invited his fiancée-to-be to the house party.

Juliet wasn't quite sure why the thought made her feel peevish. She wished Diana and Penelope would continue talking about . . . about *anything* else, but neither of them said a word as they kept their gazes on the man across the room.

"He's coming over here," Penelope said, nudging Diana.

Diana merely smiled and lifted her chin in acknowledgment.

Moments later, Lord Locken stepped up to Juliet's side. She couldn't avoid looking at him now, and when she did, he greeted her with an appraising smile and those dark brown eyes of his not missing a thing. Suddenly, Juliet wondered if she'd tucked away his note far enough into her bodice, because his gaze had dipped low, if only for an instant.

"I hope you are well, Lady Juliet," Lord Locken said, bowing over her hand. He didn't kiss it like he had the last time she'd seen him, but she could hardly hold him to such a familiar greeting. Especially in front of his future wife.

He turned to the other women. "Lady Diana, Lady Penelope, I trust your journey to Southill Estate was pleasant."

"Very pleasant," Diana said, her eyes bright, her cheeks once again pink. "You were correct. The countryside is beautiful this time of year, and this area is charming."

Juliet couldn't blame Diana for blushing around Lord Locken. Juliet was on the verge herself, so it was with a bit of relief when her brother chose that moment to clap his hands together and announce luncheon would be served on the garden terrace.

Diana immediately slipped her hand into the crook of Lord Locken's arm, and it seemed by the time Juliet realized everyone was pairing off, only John was left.

"Sister," he said, extending his arm. "Shall we lead our guests?"

She swallowed and nodded. Then she and John walked through the grand hallway and out onto the garden terrace. Chairs in groups of four were situated around small tables set with linen, china, and silverware. The luncheon had been laid out on a long table, buffet style, and the ladies helped themselves first.

Juliet filled her plate, although she knew she could eat very little of it. Being around Lord Locken again had made her feel fluttery inside. As luck would have it, Juliet ended up at the same table as Diana and Lord Locken, along with the friend Lord Locken had traveled with, Lord Hudson.

Juliet smiled at Lord Hudson as introductions were made. He told her of his estate a day's travel from Southill and of his love for both reading and hunting. She listened attentively, as a dutiful hostess, but in truth, it was hard to fully concentrate on Lord Hudson when Lord Locken was sitting at the same small table. She must get used to his presence. He'd be here for two weeks, after all.

Nine

Victor turned his head as Southill tapped his glass to capture everyone's attention.

"A game of lawn bowling has been set up on the north lawn," Southill said, "and for those who would rather walk through the gardens, you are welcome to the more sedate activity. As for me, I'll be on the lawn."

The guests laughed at Southill's comment. Victor turned back to Diana. "What is your preference?" he asked.

"I think I will go to my room and rest in order to be refreshed for dinner," Diana said with a too bright smile. Her painted lips matched the deep red of her hair. She really was a striking woman and would make a fine duchess. At least that's what his father had told him. Diana touched Victor's arm, something she'd made a habit of late—touching him in small ways—as if she were already laying claim to him. This irked him, but how could he complain? He would soon propose to her.

"You want me to look my best, don't you?" Diana quipped in her cheerful voice.

"Indeed," he said, giving the expected reply. Everything with Diana was expected, planned, dutiful. Everything about her was bright and cheerful, as if only roses bloomed in her life. Just once he'd like to have a conversation with her that moved beyond the latest fashion, who of the *ton* was embroiled in scandal, or which duke or earl was renovating his estate.

"We will miss you on the lawn," Hudson said. Always to the rescue. "Are you sure you won't join us?"

Diana turned her smile upon Hudson, and it seemed more genuine. "Thank you, but I am quite sure."

Hudson nodded. "Very well, then. We shall look forward to seeing you in a few hours."

The men rose as Diana stood. She made her way toward the house, and before Victor could turn to Lady Juliet, who had also shared their lunch table, Hudson had already spoken up.

"What about you, Lady Juliet?" Hudson said. "Do you care to join us on the lawn?"

"I'd love to." Her blue gaze flitted to Victor, then back to Hudson.

When Victor had first caught sight of her in the drawing room upon arriving, he'd known it was her, even though he could only see her back. Her honey-gold hair color was unmistakable, even pinned into an intricate coiffure. Her peach-colored gown made her look like one of the roses from a royal garden. And when he reached the small circle of women she stood in, he had a hard time keeping his gaze on Diana and away from Lady Juliet's sloping shoulders and creamy expanse of skin.

How he'd love to get her alone for a few moments for a private conversation. She'd only written him one letter and had not revealed much. He had many questions, but he had been cautious about corresponding with her through the mail; therefore, he hadn't dared ask her anything that would prompt her to write him again.

Hudson took Lady Juliet's arm, and the three of them began the walk to the north lawn. It appeared as if Victor's money had been put to good use. The estate was in excellent condition, the gazebo rebuilt, the luncheon delicious, and Southill looked half decent in new clothing.

"There's the man I've been wanting to speak to." Southill drew Victor away from the main group walking toward the lawn.

"Hello, Southill," Victor said. "Have you picked out your heiress yet?"

Southill chuckled. "There *are* a few potential women here." He turned his appraising blue gaze upon Victor. "It seems I am in your debt, although I am still unsure of the motivation behind your generosity."

Victor shrugged. "Let's just say I'm willing to give a man a second chance. We go back a long way, and I was thinking we should let bygones be bygones."

"All right, then," Southill said. "I'll take you at your word. In the meantime, after the ladies have retired to their rooms tonight, we'll be commencing in the library for a game of cards."

Victor tried not to show his surprise. Surely, Southill remembered the single rule Victor had set forth—no gambling at the house party. If there was one way for things to get out of control, it was this.

"I'm afraid I've brought some work with me," Victor said. "With all the festivities during the day, I'll be burning the midnight oil as it is."

Southill scoffed. "You know everyone wants to see *you* in action. You're a legend, Victor Roland."

"That may be so, but I'm making some changes."

Southill laughed in disbelief, and a few heads turned in their direction.

Victor gave a polite smile while trying to hide the fact that he was gritting his teeth. He might be an accomplished gambler, but playing against Southill had been what started this all. Not that Victor regretted meeting the lovely Juliet, but it also pained him to watch a woman such as she having to find a husband in a matter of two weeks in order to escape the pending ruin of her own brother.

"You know me," Victor continued, "gambling is always a serious affair. I wouldn't want one of these poor chaps to have his pockets upended by dawn." Victor's smile was as fake as the ones Diana regularly doled out. "Besides, I've promised a special woman I would stop all serious gambling."

Southill's brows shot up. "Do you happen to be speaking of Lady Diana Allen?"

Victor didn't answer, just kept his smile in place. No gentleman could argue against a promise given to a woman. Then Victor called to one of his friends who was behind him. "Catch up, my friend."

Laurence Talbot increased his pace, and once he reached Victor's side, Southill had gone on ahead. "You weren't kidding," Talbot said in a low tone. "The elite of the *ton* is here, and Lady Juliet is enchanting."

Victor swallowed against the sudden dryness of his throat. Talbot had been specifically invited because Victor felt he was a viable husband candidate for Lady Juliet. If that was the case, why did Victor feel the urge to say something critical of Lady Juliet to put off Talbot?

"She has asked genuine questions about my shipping business," Talbot continued. "Not every lady of the *ton* would want to be saddled with a man of business, even if I am well-off. But Lady Juliet is different, like a breath of fresh air."

Victor couldn't agree more, but his heart had started a slow thud when he caught sight of Lady Juliet smiling at

Hudson. They stood apart from the main group on the lawn. Her lips weren't the garish color of Diana's, but a more natural color, which contrasted beautifully with her fair skin and dark lashes. And Victor knew he wasn't the only gentleman in the party studying their hostess.

Lady Juliet laughed at something Hudson had said, and Victor's mood blackened. Here he was, on a lovely summer day at a beautiful estate, and hot anger pulsed through him. Victor exhaled, clapped his hand on Talbot's shoulder, and said, "I think you would be a good match, my friend. I'll be sure to throw a few compliments your way when I'm in conversation with her."

"I would be most grateful," Talbot said.

Victor strode away before the man could continue in his litany of gratitude, because in truth, Victor felt like slamming his fist into something hard. He wished Diana hadn't gone to her room to rest. He could use her by his side to keep his focus where it should be. He'd planned for Lady Diana's presence to act as a continual reminder to Victor of where his priorities were and how he should be focusing on his future.

In fact, to serve as further reminder, he'd kept his father's most recent letter in the inside pocket of his jacket. Victor didn't like to think of the harsh words the missive contained, but he'd forced himself to reread them in the carriage ride to Southill Estate. His father had revised his will so that even if he was dead, Victor would still have to marry Lady Diana in order to inherit the dukedom.

Victor exhaled, his gaze drawn once again to Lady Juliet as he waited for his next turn at bowling. It was two hours into the game, and he had yet to exchange a personal word with her. She was by far the most enchanting woman at the house party, and Victor wasn't basing his opinion on facial features or her figure, but on what Talbot had alluded to. She *was* a breath of fresh air, and the more Victor observed her, the more he was convinced that breathing would always be easier around her.

"How is your father faring?" a voice said, cutting into Victor's thoughts.

Victor looked over at Talbot. "His health has taken a recent decline," Victor said. "He still insisted that I come to the house party." It wasn't exactly true. His father's letter had only insisted that Victor make good on his proposal plans. Weddings took time to plan, especially that of a future duke.

"Ah, Lady Diana is looking very well, I must say," Talbot said with a broad smile.

Victor nodded. "She is indeed. I am a fortunate man, and soon to be more fortunate."

Talbot chuckled and began to speak of one of his ships that was apparently undergoing a renovation, but Victor had noticed that Lady Juliet had separated herself from her group and begun to walk toward the stables. Victor frowned. Where was she going? And why? Surely she didn't mean to brush down the horses? The thought made him smile to himself, and although Talbot was mid-story, Victor interrupted.

"I apologize, but I've just remembered that I need to attend to something," Victor said. "Tell me the rest of your story at dinner."

Talbot gave a good-natured smile, and Victor slipped away. He waited a few minutes before following Lady Juliet so that no one would notice they'd gone to the same place. But when he reached the stables, he didn't see her. A groomsman greeted Victor and asked if he wanted to ride.

"Perhaps I will ride," Victor said, walking by the stalls to find his pair of bays. One was missing.

He turned to face the groomsman. "Do you know where the other bay is?"

The Final Wager

The man paled. "Lady Juliet took it. I hope that is all right."

"Without a riding habit?"

Now the groomsman flushed. "I didn't think it was my place to remind her."

"It's no trouble," Victor said in a casual tone. "Can you saddle up the other bay?"

"Of course, my lord." The groomsman set to work.

Moments later, Victor was riding out into the countryside, leaving his cane behind. His ankle was much better now, but riding a horse for the first time since his injury made him a bit nervous. Instead of thinking how he'd been thrown just a couple of months ago, he focused on how the setting sun had transformed the green of the countryside into a gold orange. The sky's blue had deepened in color, reminding him of the lady he was currently following after. While the heat of the day had faded, there was still plenty of warmth, so Victor appreciated the breeze.

As he rode, he found a path that led through a hedge connecting the estate to what had to be Lord Stratford's place. Victor had met him earlier in the day, and there was no doubt the man had designs on Lady Juliet. She had cited only their age differences in why she wouldn't marry him, but it was clear she wasn't comfortable around him. Victor had plainly seen the man ogling Lady Juliet.

But Victor was willing to count Stratford's proposal as one toward the end goal of three. And with Talbot's interest, Victor had already pinned down two.

He should be pleased with this realization, but it only caused him to urge his bay on, toward the lane that wound past Stratford's place. Up ahead, he saw the form of Lady Juliet upon his other bay. She rode at a canter, and he'd catch up to her soon enough.

It was clear she wanted to be alone, so Victor didn't know how she'd react to seeing him. She disappeared for a moment as she rounded a bend, but when Victor arrived at the same spot, she was even closer. She'd slowed the horse to a walk and removed her hat, and it hung by its ribbons around her neck. She, too, must be enjoying the late afternoon breeze.

Victor slowed his horse as well, since reins were meaningless at this point because the two bays knew each other so well. In fact, he was surprised it took Lady Juliet so long to notice his presence. And when she finally turned, Victor was gratified to see not surprise, but a welcoming smile.

"You've found me." Her voice was like a melody to his ears.

He returned her smile, and soon they rode side by side. "Ditching the party?"

She cast him a sideways glance, and he knew his heart shouldn't quicken, but it did. "I'm not used to conversing with this many people for so long. I can't believe how exhausting it can be."

He smirked. "Socializing is harder than it looks."

She turned her head fully to meet his gaze. With the setting sun splashing its warm colors about, her hair took on the appearance of spun gold, and he could very well imagine her as an artist's model for a storybook painting. He wanted to reach out and run his fingers through the tendrils of her hair to see if her hair felt as soft as it looked.

Instead, he had to settle for riding next to her and keeping his hands to himself. It was better that way; he was nearly an engaged man. "I've been wanting to speak with you since I arrived."

Her lips parted in surprise. "Have you?"

He didn't miss the teasing gleam in her eyes, and he grasped the reins of her horse and drew the bay right next to his so that her skirts brushed against his legs. "Has your brother been behaving himself?"

The amusement faded, and she looked at where his hands held the reins of her horse. "Define *behaving*."

Ten

This man had no business knowing Juliet's personal issues with her brother, yet, if there was anyone who would understand, it was Lord Locken. He had been the one to deliver John on that fateful night three weeks ago. Lord Locken was also the man who'd pulled off this house party. The more Juliet thought about the guest servants, the food, the gazebo renovation, and the new clothing that John sported, the more she knew her brother had made a deal with the devil. Either him or Lord Locken.

And now, she was mere inches away from him, albeit they were riding two bays, but the presence of only the horses, and no other people, made this encounter feel secluded.

"Lady Juliet, surely you must know I am deeply interested in your welfare," Lord Locken said in a low voice, one that filtered through her hesitation. He released the reins of her horse, and the two bays continued side by side along the lane.

"I think you have made that clear." She gave him a half smile. "My brother is behaving himself as far as no gambling. He drinks more than I'd like, and I've heard more than one argument at the door with a creditor. Mostly, he's been moping, although he took great interest in ordering new clothing. I'm not quite sure how he managed to pay for it all."

Lord Locken didn't respond, but Juliet knew he must

have financed the new clothing for her brother. His brown eyes met hers with a steady gaze, and she wanted to lean closer, to be nearer to him.

Instead, she ignored how the setting sun splashed bronze throughout his dark hair and made his olive skin look golden. "How shall I ever thank you for your kindness to my family?"

"You could lose our wager," Lord Locken said, "and let me keep my horses."

She laughed, and he grinned back. "Are we still doing the wager?" she asked. "I wasn't sure."

"We most definitely are."

"There *are* some fine gentlemen on the north lawn," she said.

"Any of them catch your particular attention?" His amusement had fled, and now his gaze was intent on hers as they continued riding their horses at an ambling pace. Was that a mark of a man she could trust? Unlike her brother, who looked everywhere but her, Lord Locken almost challenged her to break her gaze first.

You are the one who's captured my attention, she almost said.

But there could never be anything between them. First of all, her brother was on the cusp of ruin, and even with her dowry, her family's reputation would be an embarrassment. She'd never meet Lord Locken's father's standards.

Besides, Lord Locken had made it clear he was going to propose to Lady Diana Allen. Juliet had no issues with the woman; Diana was a beautiful woman who would no doubt make the perfect duchess. If only Juliet could imagine the two of them together without getting an achy knot in her stomach. Soon, the house party would be over, and everyone would return to their lives. And hopefully by then, Juliet would have a proposal and could start her own future.

"You're doing a lot of thinking," Lord Locken said. "Perhaps there are too many choices in men here?"

"Don't be silly," she said.

"I can assure you," he drawled, "I am never silly." The amusement had returned.

That didn't make her feel more at ease, though. "Yes, there are very real possibilities for a husband at this house party. Although, I think I have a problem discerning flattery from sincerity."

One of his dark brows arched. "How so?"

"Well..." She smoothed back the hair from her forehead as the wind picked up. "It seems that compliments come quite naturally to gentlemen of the *ton*, so how am I to know that a compliment paid to me is not simply a compliment paid to all women?"

"Ah, I see." Lord Locken continued riding for a few more moments. "You are correct in understanding that most men of the *ton* will be generous in their compliments to other women of the *ton*. It is the way of polite society."

"To be insincere?"

"To be *polite*."

"Can that really be a reliable indicator of whether one should accept a marriage proposal?" she asked.

"Of course not," Lord Locken said. "There are plenty of other factors, such as temperaments, compatibility of families, common interests, and perhaps even romance."

Juliet raised her brows. "Do you have all of that with Lady Diana?"

Lord Locken shot a gaze in her direction. "Most."

"Which parts are missing?"

He maneuvered his bay so they were close enough again for him to grasp her reins. Which he did. And he again stopped both of their horses. "You ask a lot of questions," he said as he scanned her face.

The Final Wager

"Only around you, apparently."

A lock of his hair had fallen across his forehead, and like that night he'd slept in the library, she gave into her impulse and reached over to smooth it back. Before she could pull her hand away, he grasped her wrist. And because she wore short gloves, his fingers wrapped around her bare skin.

Juliet had gone too far. She'd allowed her impulses to take over her common sense, and now . . .

"I can assure you, Lady Juliet," he said, still holding her wrist, "that I don't mind your questions."

Lord Locken's hold was loose enough that she knew she could disengage, but she didn't want to. His hand was warm and strong, and the feel of his skin against her wrist sent daggers of heat along her arm.

"Well, then," she said in a quiet voice, "are you going to answer them?"

He turned her wrist over so that her palm was up. Then he leaned over it and pressed a kiss on the inside of her wrist.

Juliet couldn't breathe for a moment, and she was positive her heart had skipped a beat, or two.

Lord Locken lifted his head and met her gaze. In the depths of his eyes, she could see it . . . the same things she felt, the same draw, the same intensity of feelings. Would he tell her he'd changed his mind about Lady Diana and that his father's opinions held no consequence?

No, she thought. He would not. So when he rubbed his thumb lightly over the place on her wrist where he'd kissed, she knew this gesture was his only allowance. Whatever might have been, whatever could have been, was already over.

"Lady Juliet, you can be secure in knowing that any compliments given to you by any of the gentlemen at this house party are indeed sincere." He released her wrist. "Laurence Talbot mentioned how he was impressed with both your intellect and beauty."

Juliet drew her hand away and wished she didn't feel so empty, so bereft. The news Lord Locken had delivered should make her heart soar. Mr. Talbot was a fine man, and he was nice-looking as well. He still had his youth, all his teeth, a full head of hair, wonderful manners, and he didn't smell bad. Juliet didn't know whether to laugh at her inane judgments or cry because the man who made her heart flutter and her dreams sweet had made his intentions clear—for another woman.

"Mr. Talbot *is* a kind gentleman," she said, lifting her gaze.

Lord Locken simply stared at her, neither agreeing nor disagreeing.

"Are you well acquainted with him?" she asked.

He blinked. "With whom?"

"Mr. Talbot."

"Ah, yes." Lord Locken urged his horse forward, and Juliet's moved in accord. "We are distant cousins, on the same side as Lady Diana." They reached a stream, and he let his horse drink, and Juliet's followed suit.

"If you marry Mr. Talbot," he said after a moment, "you and I will likely cross paths in the future. Perhaps at one of our weddings. You might even be cursed with the opportunity to meet my father, should he live that long."

His tone was flat, and she should probably let the subject drop, but she didn't. "Is your father very ill?"

Lord Locken's jaw flexed. "It depends on how you define *ill.* If you define it based on temper and general drunkenness, then he's been ill as long as I can remember. If you define it based on how close a man is to his deathbed, the physician has given him less than a year. Says he will not make it through another wet winter."

Despite the bitter words about his father, Juliet knew

Lord Locken was hurt—she could hear it in his tone of voice. "I'm sorry for his pain *and* your pain."

Lord Locken reached into his jacket and pulled out a folded letter. "Before you feel sorry for my father's slow progress toward death, maybe you should read his latest letter to his only child."

Juliet stared at the letter in his hands. He wanted her to read his personal correspondence? She took the letter and turned it over. Lord Locken's name was scrawled on the front in a spidery handwriting. She felt his gaze upon her as she unfolded the letter. It was a single page, but there were plenty of words in the same spidery writing, filling almost all the space.

She read slowly, digesting each word of the letter. Halfway through, she wished she'd never laid eyes on the thing. The words were cutting, harsh, and insulting. The Duke of Wycliff clearly held the threat of disinheritance over his son's head. But that wasn't the most disturbing thing about the letter. The duke wrote how he wished he'd never had a son and how he should have disposed of him when he was an infant instead of pretending he cared enough to get Lord Locken educated and set up to enjoy a future he didn't deserve. The worst of it was when the duke called his son a murderer.

The words were sickening, and why Lord Locken kept this vile thing on his person was beyond Juliet's comprehension. She blinked back the burning in her eyes, refolded the letter, then said, "I think you should burn this."

His laugh was dry. "It's a good reminder, eh? Keeps me focused on what I must do."

"Marry Lady Diana by the end of the year?"

"You read the edict yourself." His gaze connected with hers, and in his eyes was a fire she hadn't seen before. "My cousin will become the next Duke of Wycliff if I don't comply. It's been drawn up in the will already, so whether my father is alive or dead, the edict still stands."

How could Juliet argue that? Lord Locken was well and truly stuck.

"I have not shared this letter with anyone, nor will I," he said. "And Lady Diana cannot know the contents. She thinks I'm proposing because I want to marry her."

Juliet stared at him. "And you do not."

"I've thought it a duty, one that I could endure, like so many other things associated with my father's dukedom," he said. "It was a bearable fate I had reconciled myself to. Three weeks ago, all of that changed."

Juliet couldn't look away from the intensity in his gaze. She wanted to urge her horse back from the stream and ride away from Lord Locken so she wouldn't have to hear his next words. On the other hand, she had to hear them no matter how much pain resulted.

"What happened three weeks ago?" she whispered.

"I met *you*."

Juliet swallowed and looked away. She didn't know how to respond to him. There was nothing she could say, nothing she could do. His father's edict was clear, and Lord Locken had an entire legacy to uphold.

His horse moved back from the stream, bringing him next to her again.

When his fingers touched her chin and lifted it to meet his gaze, she finally looked at him. The regret in his brown eyes mirrored the regret in her heart. Her heart thumped at his nearness, and her pulse raced to think of what possibilities might have been between them if not for the circumstances.

"Juliet," he said. "Forgive me."

"There's nothing to forgive," she said.

And when he leaned toward her, his gaze on her mouth, she knew she couldn't allow this one, final thing to happen between them. A kiss from him would never be forgotten, and she didn't want to put him into any jeopardy with Lady Diana. Juliet drew away from his touch, and he dropped his hand.

"You'll be a wonderful duke, and a great father and husband," she said in a shaky voice. "I wish you all the best in your life, Lord Locken."

He nodded but said nothing, only continued to gaze at her in a way that made her regret putting him off.

"And I hope you will burn that letter from your father," she continued. "Nothing he says about you is true, and you don't deserve to ever read such vile words again."

He nodded again, saying nothing.

"Please, Victor," she said, placing a hand on top of his.

He looked startled that she'd used his first name, although he'd taken liberty using hers only moments earlier. He looked down at her hand atop of his.

"Burn the letter," she urged. "Forget your father's words. Marry Lady Diana. Begin anew and make your own life with her." Then she released him and took up the reins. She turned the horse toward home and started riding, cantering at first, then breaking into a gallop. She felt Lord Locken's gaze on her, and she hoped that he would get rid of that horrible letter.

As for her heart, she would be strong. For him. He would see her enjoy the house party. He would have the satisfaction that she could have a happy future, and she hoped that would give him the confidence to have the same.

 Eleven

The days passed with unending glimpses of Lady Juliet mingling with the guests, speaking with the gentlemen, laughing with the ladies. And Victor was forced to watch it all. Why he'd decided to come in the first place was beyond him. Oh. Yes. It was to restore her brother's reputation, because then her own reputation would rise in the process. And he'd invited Lady Diana so that he would not be tempted to throw away his own future over a woman he barely knew.

But his heart had other ideas. With every day that the house party progressed, Victor was having a harder time imagining leaving Lady Juliet behind to her brother's care, even if it was temporary.

Southill had confided in Victor a couple of nights ago about how dire his finances truly were. They'd stayed up half the night going over ledgers and debtors' bills. The only solution that Victor could come up with was for Southill to sell some holdings and property. Southill had argued that his sister's dowry would go a long way to resolving the debts, but Victor had stuck to his recommendation of selling the property. He'd left Southill in the library, stewing over his choices.

Victor had little faith in the man, which made it all the more imperative that Lady Juliet marry and leave her brother to his wallowing habits. Unfortunately, whoever married Lady Juliet would also take on Southill as a brother-in-law, but that couldn't be helped.

"You look as if you've the weight of the entire kingdom on your shoulders," Hudson said, joining Victor by the hearth while the gentlemen and ladies had their tête-à-têtes throughout the drawing room. Dinner had been eaten, cigars smoked, port drunk, and the men had rejoined the women.

"I've had a peek into Southill's finances," Victor said.

Hudson scoffed. "Say no more. Do you need a strong drink?"

"Probably," Victor said. "But getting inebriated won't help anything."

Hudson chuckled. "You're a good man, Victor."

Victor nodded. "She told me that too." His gaze landed on Lady Juliet, who was currently in a game of whist with Lady Diana, Lady Penelope, and Mr. Talbot. The latter couldn't take his eyes from Lady Juliet, not that Victor could blame the man. Victor had the same problem. Her pale blue gown brought out the deep blue in her eyes and made her hair a brilliant gold in the candlelight.

Hudson followed Victor's gaze, then cleared his throat. "Uh, look, I know you are doing the honorable thing by bringing us all here to meet Lady Juliet. But, in truth, every man in this room can plainly see how *you* look at her."

Victor's eyes snapped to Hudson's. "What do you mean?"

Hudson lifted his hands. "Don't get upset. You are enamored of our hostess, and none of us blames you. She is lovely and charming and would make any man a fine wife."

"Right." Victor placed a hand on Hudson's shoulder. "And that's why you, my friend, are going to propose to her."

"Our friendship runs deep," Hudson said, "but not that deep. I'll not marry the woman my best friend is in love with."

Victor felt as if he'd been shoved in the chest. "I'm not in love with Lady Juliet."

Hudson didn't even blink.

"I'm proposing to Lady Diana tomorrow afternoon," Victor continued. "I've explained to you, more than once, that my only concern with Lady Juliet is that she leaves Southill Estate. And she needs a husband to do that."

"I understand completely," Hudson said. "But I can't be that husband to her—not when you—"

Victor held up his hand. "We're finished with this conversation."

Hudson clenched his jaw, then nodded and stepped away.

Victor leaned against the edge of the hearth and surveyed the room while trying to keep a more nonchalant expression.

But his gaze landed once again on Lady Juliet at the whist table. She'd bloomed into a confident and gracious hostess in only a few short days, and Lady Diana had told him more than once that this was the most enjoyable house party she'd ever attended.

When those raptures made their way back to London society, Lady Juliet would be flooded with invitations next season.

Tomorrow, he'd determined, he'd do his duty. He'd propose to Lady Diana. A game of shuttlecock was planned for the afternoon, and he would invite her on a walk through the garden. He would get down on bended knee and seal his fate once and for all. Marriage to Lady Diana was the only way he could truly be free. Next time he saw his father, the man's insults would bounce right off because Victor would have won.

At the whist table, Lady Juliet tapped Talbot's arm with one of her cards, then laughed at something.

Victor knew he should be watching Lady Diana, but as long as Lady Juliet was in the same room, that was proving more and more difficult.

"Can you meet me in the library after everyone retires?" someone said close to Victor's ear.

He didn't need to turn to know that it was Southill standing next to him.

Everything inside of Victor wanted to shout *no*. "Of course."

Southill moved away, and Victor was left alone again to contemplate a life that seemed to grow more and more dismal by the moment.

Two hours later, Victor sat across from Southill in the library. Several candles flickered, two had almost guttered out, and the brandy nearly all drunk by Southill. Victor had had half a glass, and even that much had made him queasy, simply because he knew this conversation wasn't going to be a pleasant one.

"I've consulted with another advisor," Southill started out, his blue eyes already unfocused. "He's offered to marry my sister, and he's pledged part of her dowry toward the renovations of my estate. Then we'll combine the fields of our estates and breed horses. The income will eventually pay off my debts."

Victor looked down at the glass in his hand and absently noted how the amber liquid seemed to flash gold in the candlelight. This plan of Southill's could only mean one thing; *Stratford* had made the offer. And Stratford was the one Lady Juliet said she could not imagine marrying—ever.

Victor took a sip of the brandy, wondering how he could put a stop to this match. But who was he kidding? He had no real control over Lady Juliet's future. That detail was in the hands of the man sitting on the other side of the desk.

"What about Laurence Talbot?" Victor said. "The man is growing wealthier by the minute, and you won't have to be under Stratford's thumb."

Southill frowned. "The shipping industry isn't reliable. The man might be making money this year, but what about in ten years?"

Victor leaned back in his chair. "Ten years could bring change for all of us. Perhaps we should embrace it."

Southill scoffed. "Have you spoken to your father lately about embracing change? You and I both are a product of rules, traditions, and more rules." He shrugged and downed another half glass of brandy. "I'd offer you my sister, but you already made your opinion clear when you bashed my face in. Besides, I hear your father's iron grip is going to last far beyond the grave."

Victor set his glass on the desk so he wouldn't accidentally crush it in his hand. "Do you have anything against Lord Hudson?" he asked, trying to keep his voice calm.

Southill barked a laugh. "That old goat? I don't know why he's always hanging around you. Everyone knows his mother's still alive and makes the real decisions in the family. I don't want to wait until the old crony's death before I can talk some sense into Hudson."

Victor exhaled. "Brooks?"

"He's barely out of leading strings," Southill said. "Besides, he's a second son, and we all know nothing ever comes of that. Juliet will spend her life grasping for seconds, and my debts will continue to rise."

Victor leaned forward and rested his elbows on his knees. "It seems Talbot is the best option, and I believe you'll find your sister agreeable, which will make the entire process smooth and quick. She could be married before the leaves change color, and by Christmastide, you'll be a redeemed man."

Southill's lips curled upward, but it wasn't any sort of friendly smile. "You have it all figured out, don't you, Locken? What is Juliet's future to you?"

"Nothing," Victor ground out, but he wasn't fast enough. Southill had seen his hesitation.

Southill shot to his feet, and Victor followed suit.

"Have you compromised my sister?" Southill growled. "Got her with child? Is that why you're trying to marry her off so quickly by throwing money at this house party and covering your tracks?"

Victor didn't move, because if he did, he knew his fist would find its way into Southill's face again.

Southill walked around the desk and approached Victor, stopping right in front of him. So close that Victor could smell the alcohol on the man's breath. The scent made the hairs on the back of Victor's neck rise.

"If I find out that you've even touched my sister," Southill said, "I will, by all that's holy, both above and below ground, cut your throat."

Victor swallowed, but he didn't break his gaze. How he hated this man's face and voice.

Moments ticked by with the two men staring each other down. Victor didn't move a muscle, but he was ready to react in an instant, come what may.

Finally, Southill turned and poured himself another glass of brandy. After downing it, he said in a hoarse voice, "Get out."

Victor wasn't ready to leave, not without getting Southill's agreement about Laurence Talbot. But Southill was on his eighth or ninth glass, and if Victor didn't leave now, nothing about this night would end well.

So Victor left the library, shutting the door behind him, and walked through the dark house. He made his way to the door that led to the garden terrace. He slipped outside to find the air cool and fragrant and the moon high in the sky, casting a cool light over the bushes and trails. It was the balm Victor needed. He crossed the terrace and set off along one of the paths, not paying attention to where he was walking. When he reached the gazebo, he paused, wondering if he should somehow warn Lady Juliet of her brother's decision. He could write a note and have a maid deliver it to her. Or perhaps he could slip it under her door himself.

Or perhaps he should break into her bedchamber, scoop her up, and carry her far away. Frustration pulsed through him, and he turned to the gazebo and slammed his fist into one of the beams.

A small yelp sounded from inside the gazebo, and Victor stilled. *Please be a bird, or a small critter.* But as he rubbed his sore hand and stepped to the entrance, the shadowed form he saw was much too large to be an animal.

The form rose, and the shape was unmistakably a woman's.

"Lord Locken," the woman said in a soft voice.

He'd know her voice anywhere—had listened to it for days, even when he had no part of her conversations.

"Lady Juliet," he began. "My apologies for startling you."

She walked toward the gazebo entrance, and the moonlight skittered across her skin as it filtered through the slatted roof above. She wore the same blue gown from that evening, so it meant she hadn't fully prepared for bed. Apparently she was as restless as he.

She took another step nearer. Her unbound hair tumbled in golden waves about her shoulders, making her look like she'd just walked out of a fairy-tale book. He wanted to reach out and touch her hair, lean in and smell her scent, pull her into his arms and bury his face in her neck. If only once.

"What has you so troubled?" Her voice broke his reverie.

He straightened. "I thought punching a wooden beam would do less damage than what my true desire was."

She took another step so now they were only inches apart. "What are your true desires?"

He could never tell her that, especially here, in the middle of the night in a secluded gazebo. It would be so easy to take her into his arms and kiss her. But he could not do her the disservice. So he contented himself by gazing into the depths of her eyes.

"I've just spoken with your brother." He hated to bring her into this, but it concerned her, after all. "It seems we are at odds with each other once again."

"I know about Stratford," she said in a quiet voice. "When the ladies excused themselves tonight, Stratford asked to have a word with me. He laid out the plan he'd worked on with John." She blinked as a tear stole its way onto her cheek.

Victor had thought he'd been angry when he'd hit the wooden beam, but that was nothing compared to the fury building inside of him as he watched the single tear track down her cheek. He lifted his hand and soaked it up with his thumb. He wore no gloves, and her cheek was cool with the night air. The smoothness of her skin sent a tremor through Victor. He should lower his hand and step away, but he didn't.

Lady Juliet tilted her head so that her cheek rested in his palm. "I will be all right, Lord Locken. Please don't worry yourself on my behalf. Mr. Talbot has made his intentions quite obvious, and my new lady friends believe he will propose soon. I am quite sure that I'll get my brother to agree to the union." She lifted her chin, and another tear brimmed on her eyelash. "As for your wager, I am sure Lord Hudson or Lord Brooks are about to fall into line. Lord Brooks has written me the loveliest poetry. So, you see, you'll more than win the wager. I'll marry... someone... and perhaps our paths will cross in the future." She smiled, but it was a tremulous smile. "We will be happy for each other."

Victor ran his fingers across her cheek, along her jawline, then rested his hand at the base of her neck. The delicate pulse of her heart could be felt there. She didn't seem to mind where his hand was, for she didn't draw away or reprimand him. In fact, she seemed to have inched a bit closer, close enough that her breath brushed against his own neck.

"I don't want to be happy for you," he whispered. "I want to be happy *with* you."

She inhaled, then wrapped her fingers around his wrist, holding his hand in place against her skin. Instead of responding to his declaration, she said, "Did you burn that letter?"

She'd remembered; she'd remembered and worried. He smiled. "I did."

She returned his smile, and he felt his heart crack. Her smile was so pure, her gaze so open, her body so close, that he knew... *knew* she felt the same way about him as he did her.

"I'm glad," she said. "You deserve so much more, Victor Roland."

"You're the only one who thinks so," he murmured. Then he saw something with a square edge sticking out of the lace trim of her bodice. "What's this?"

Before she could move, he'd plucked out what looked like a folded letter.

"Give that to me," she said, grasping for the paper, but he held it out of her reach.

She grabbed his other hand, but he'd already unfolded the letter.

He stared at the words in the moonlight. "It's the note *I* sent you."

"Yes."

He looked down at her. "You keep it in your bodice?"

Her eyelashes fluttered, but she held his gaze. "I don't want it discovered, and I refuse to burn it."

Victor stared at her for a long moment. Then he refolded the letter and ever so gently slipped it back into its place.

"Lady—"

"Call me *Juliet*," she breathed.

"I should go," he said. "I don't trust myself around you right now, Juliet. The moonlight is bewitching my senses, among other things..."

She exhaled. "Tomorrow we will begin our separate lives and fulfill the expectations of our families. But before we say goodbye... please kiss me once."

Victor stared at her, but he knew his ears had not deceived him. She was *asking* him. And he could no longer resist her. He raised his hands and cradled her face, then he pressed his mouth against hers.

She tasted of honey and roses and sweet wine. Her mouth was soft and warm, and when she kissed him back, he thought his body would ignite. Her hands moved up his chest and over his shoulders. Everywhere she touched added new flames to the fire stoked inside of him. Then she slid her hands behind his neck, pulling him closer as their bodies seemed to fit together in perfection. He knew she was an innocent, yet her desire for him felt like the sweetest form of communication he'd ever experienced.

Juliet had no idea what instincts she'd kindled, and Victor had to stop. Even if it was the last thing he wanted to do. He could get lost in her, and he was in danger of completely forgetting all sense and reason.

Twelve

Victor's hands on her face, then her neck, and finally tugging her closer as his mouth explored hers in a warm kiss made Juliet believe that nothing else mattered in her life. Except for *this*. This man. His warmth. His brown eyes. His unruly, dark hair. His heart. His mind. His life. She wanted to be a part of *all* of it. But his world would completely change if that happened. This she knew, yet she still kissed him, because she also knew their time was running out.

He walked her backward, moving deeper into the gazebo so they were in near darkness, and that only made the heat between them flare up more. Juliet supposed she'd imagined how it would feel to be held in his arms, to be pressed against his body, to be kissed by him, but she hadn't expected how completely she would melt into him. And she knew that no matter whom she married, she would never feel this way again.

With only a kiss and embrace, she'd become one with Victor, both in heart and mind. And she didn't know if she could ever let go.

"Juliet," Victor murmured against her lips. And then he trailed kisses along her jaw, down her neck, until he had pulled her close and buried his face in her hair.

Their breathing slowed together, and Juliet knew the seconds were counting down to when he'd release her and step away. She clung to him, all the while dreading their separation, though it was inevitable.

"Juliet," he rumbled again, his breath tickling her neck. "We must stop."

She knew he wasn't seeking a reply.

And so, when he lifted his head and gazed down at her, then slowly traced his fingers over her lips, she felt as if all warmth had fled her body as he released her.

With every step he took across the gazebo, Juliet felt the distance like each step was a league. She remained in place, unmoving, as he finally turned his back and walked slowly down the path, getting farther and farther away. She watched him literally walk out of her life.

Juliet wasn't sure how long she stood in the gazebo, but when she started trembling from the torrent of emotions running through her, she finally made her way back to the house. She didn't want to create a scandal by being discovered sound asleep in the gazebo come morning.

The house was silent when she walked in, and the dark shadows and quiet made her feel like a stranger in her own home. She still trembled, and she wished she'd brought some sort of cloak with her. She climbed the stairs to the second level, then walked silently down the dark hallway. Once in her bedchamber, she undressed, then climbed beneath her covers. She pulled the covers over her head, creating a cocoon of dark warmth in which she could relive the stolen moments of heat with Victor.

Her mind replayed the scene in the gazebo again and again until exhaustion finally took over, and she fell asleep.

When a brisk knock sounded on her door in the morning, Juliet could barely collect her thoughts to call out a coherent, "I am awake."

She peered at the windows. It was nearly midday, which meant she'd slept through the morning meal. Their guests would think she was the worst hostess. She climbed out of bed and groaned at the pounding in her head. Moving to the door of her room, she took a deep breath before opening it.

Eliza, one of the maids, stood there. "Are you ill, my lady?"

"I have a bit of a headache," Juliet said. "But I will dress anyway."

"Very well." Eliza stepped into the room, then paused. "Oh, Lord Locken asked that I deliver this to you as soon as you awoke." She held out a sealed letter.

Juliet stared at it for a moment. A letter from Victor? He'd taken a great risk in writing to her and leaving a letter with a maid. Anyone could have intercepted it. She took the letter, then walked to the window. With her back turned to Eliza and her preparations, Juliet broke the seal.

Just as his first letter, this one was short.

Dear Juliet,

Do not accept any offers. I'm going home to speak with my father. Or, more likely, beg. I hope lady fortune will smile upon us. If my father remains opposed, we will not be bereft, but we will manage our own happiness away from Locken.

Always yours,
—Victor

Juliet reread the letter a second time, then a third. Could this be true? Was Victor really going to throw away a dukedom for her? She pressed the letter against her heart. Her emotions battled against each other—no matter what she felt about him and how much she would love to be his wife, she couldn't allow him to give up so much.

"Eliza," Juliet said, turning to the maid. "Make all haste. I've delayed long enough."

"Yes, my lady."

Less than half an hour later, Juliet was primed and primped—on a smaller scale than she was used to over the past week, but time was of the essence. She had to find Lord Locken and talk him out of his insane notion.

She found the guests on the terrace, visiting with one another as they waited for luncheon to be brought. Before she spoke to anyone, she scanned the group for Lord Locken's dark hair but didn't see him. Next, she looked for her brother. He was absent as well. She hoped that didn't mean the two men were locked in the library in another fierce debate. She finally crossed to Mr. Talbot's side.

"You are feeling better?" he asked immediately.

"I am." She smiled as best as she could manage. "Thank you for asking." She didn't know what rumors had gone around about her health, but she didn't have time to inquire. "Have you seen Lord Locken? My brother was looking for him." It wasn't exactly the truth, but it sounded plausible.

"Locken left early this morning," Mr. Talbot said. "Had an urgent family matter is what we were told. I suspect it's his father's health. I hope he makes it home in time to pay his respects."

Juliet couldn't breathe. Victor had already *left*? "Thank you," she managed to say. "I've got to see to something in the kitchen." Without letting Mr. Talbot question her further, she hurried back inside the house.

Blinking back hot tears, she veered out a side door and headed for the stables. She arrived, out of breath, and found that indeed both of Victor's bays were gone.

The groomsman approached. "Are you going riding again today, my lady?"

"No." She wrapped her arms about her waist, if only to give herself more stability. "When did Lord Locken leave?"

The groomsman scratched at his stubbly chin. "It were still dark out," he said in a thoughtful tone. "Maybe an hour before dawn?"

Victor hadn't slept, then. He'd made the decision after the gazebo ... How could he leave without speaking to her first? She thought they'd agreed to go their separate ways. He was going to marry Diana and keep his dukedom. She would marry Lord Stratford and save Southill Estate.

Now ... Victor would be disinherited. It would be a public humiliation to say the least, and then what? Would she and Victor live at Southill Estate with John, all three of them destitute? Would the two men ever get along? As the years passed, would Victor resent the massive changes and turn to drink like his father had?

"Lady Juliet?" the groomsman said, and Juliet realized she was standing in the middle of the stables, tears dripping down her cheeks.

"I apologize," she whispered, wiping at her tears. Then she hurried out of the stable. She felt heartsick thinking about Victor facing his father with such a request when she knew what a vile man the duke was. She'd do anything to prevent such a scene. But Victor had been gone for hours and had likely reached his family estate by now. She gazed up at the sky, wondering if he was now, at this very moment, speaking with his father.

A rider on horseback caught her attention. The man rode with all haste up the road toward the manor. Juliet raised a hand to her eyes to shield her gaze from the sun's rays to get a better look. It wasn't Victor. This man was thin and smaller in stature, but he rode his horse as if the devil himself were chasing him.

The Final Wager

Juliet picked up her skirts and hurried to the driveway, where her brother John had come out of the house. So, John had seen the rider approach as well. Just as she reached the driveway, the rider reined his horse to a stop and dismounted.

The man had a messenger bag slung over his shoulder, and Juliet realized he was a post deliverer.

"Good day, sir," the messenger said, greeting John. "I've an urgent message for Lord Locken."

John held out his hand. "I will make sure he receives it."

But the man stepped back. "I was told to deliver it in person. No offense, sir."

"Lord Locken is occupied with another matter," John ground out. "I am the master here, and if I say I will deliver it, it shall be done."

The messenger hesitated, his gaze cutting to Juliet. Then, apparently, deciding to be done with his errand, he handed the letter to John, and John gave the messenger a couple of coins.

The moment the messenger had turned his horse and headed down the lane, John broke the seal.

Juliet was about to protest, telling John that the letter was Victor's personal property, but before she could, John had already scanned the words.

He looked up, meeting her gaze. "Roland's father's dead. He probably passed the messenger on his way home." John crumpled the letter in his hand and strode back into the house, the paper still clutched in his hand.

Juliet stared after her brother. Had he just said . . . *No.* This news was even worse than she could have imagined. It meant that Victor's father had passed away before Victor had reached home, or else there would have been no need for a messenger to deliver the news. It also meant that it was too late to change the Duke of Wycliff's will.

Juliet knew as well as Victor did that the contents of the will stated that his father's decision still held after his death. Victor would have to marry Lady Diana by the end of the year in order to take over the dukedom.

"Oh, there you are!" a female voice rang out.

Juliet wiped at her tears and turned to face Lady Diana and Lady Penelope, who'd just come around the house, walking arm in arm.

"Whatever is wrong?" Diana asked.

Juliet had been too slow to hide her distress. She might as well confess, because the news would reach the guests soon enough. "We've just received word," she said in a trembling voice, "Lord Locken's father has passed away."

"Oh." Diana covered her mouth, and Penelope did the same. "Poor man. He must be devastated." She looked at Penelope. "We must prepare to go to Locken. Even if it's not proper for us to attend the funeral, Lord Locken will need the comfort of friends around him."

Juliet stared at the two women. Just like that, they would change their plans. Travel to Locken where they would see Victor, and Victor would certainly know what he must do. There was no other option.

Juliet blinked a few times, determined to keep any new tears at bay. "You are very kind."

Penelope spoke up. "They are nearly betrothed. Of course he would want Diana by his side at a time like this."

"Of course," Juliet said, although her voice sounded faint to her ears. "How may I help you prepare?"

"Send the maids to our rooms," Diana said. "We will leave first thing in the morning."

Thirteen

News of the upcoming funeral for the Duke of Wycliff reached Southill Estate, and everyone made preparations to leave. Juliet didn't think everyone intended to go to the funeral, especially the ladies, since nighttime burials were the custom and the night brought out the ruffians and looting. But once Lady Diana and Lady Penelope announced their intention to leave, the others began to make plans too. And all the while, as Juliet kissed and hugged and bade her guests farewell, she could not forget the words of Victor's letter: *Dear Juliet, Do not accept any offers . . .*

Mr. Talbot had not proposed. His good-bye was charming enough, and Juliet saw the interest in his eyes, but she knew that the momentum of their flirtations would dissipate with his departure. Perhaps he'd heard of Lord Stratford's intentions, or perhaps her brother had warned off Mr. Talbot.

She continued to hold out hope for Victor, although she hated that he'd have to turn his back on his dukedom for her. Yet every night she went to bed, she wondered if a rider would come to Southill Estate and bang on the door. She imagined opening the door to a middle-of-the-night visitor and finding Victor. He'd say he'd come to fetch her, that he'd procured a cottage where they'd live out their days in marital bliss.

But the nights faded to dawn, and dawn gave way to the heat of the summer, and . . . Victor did not come.

Two weeks passed in this manner, then three, and still Juliet held out hope.

That was, until her brother put a stop to it on week six.

He found her in the garden, where she spent an inordinate amount of time in the gazebo reading, or composing letters she promptly ripped up, or simply staring into the garden.

"Lord Stratford will be our guest for dinner tonight," her brother said, stepping into the shade of the gazebo.

Juliet gazed at her brother. New lines pulled at his eyes, and his mouth was a permanent scowl. The sound of his voice grated on her, and she tried not to flinch.

"You have put him off long enough," John continued. "You cannot continue acting in this manner. You are of an age to marry, and we both know we cannot afford a coming out in London."

Juliet exhaled and looked away.

He took another step closer and peered down at her. "You will wear your best dress, you will fashion your hair, and you will treat our guest well."

Juliet could not answer. To do so made it feel like she was giving up all hope. But it had been six long weeks since she last saw Lord Victor Roland. Not a word had been sent her way. There hadn't been an announcement of his marriage, at least not as far as Southill Estate. Her brother didn't pay for the London papers to be brought, so as far as Juliet knew, Victor could already be married to Lady Diana.

"Look at me, Juliet!" her brother barked.

She blinked back the hot tears building in her eyes and lifted her chin to look at her brother.

"You *will* marry Lord Stratford, or you will take on the

post of a governess." He glowered at her. "Is that what you want our family reduced to?"

She shook her head, even though a governess would be a better option than becoming the wife of Lord Stratford.

"Now," John continued in his derisive tone, "Go and make yourself presentable. You have the fate of our family in your hands, and I'll not have you ruin our future with your stubbornness."

Juliet took a deep breath. "*You* could marry, John. There were plenty of heiresses at the house party. Why did you not propose?"

His mouth twisted into a hard smile. "We both know that my reputation has suffered, and your marriage to Lord Stratford will help restore it. Once we are more financially stable, I can court an heiress without the least suspicion."

Juliet hated that her brother was right. The pettiness of the *ton* reached far and wide, and time and money would bring her brother back into favor. The house party had been a large boon toward that, but work was still to be done.

Six weeks. She'd waited long enough. John was right. Marriage to Lord Stratford was her only choice now.

She rose to her feet and walked past her brother. She could do this. She *had* to do this. Something inside her broke when she reached her room, and her hope finally fled. As she prepared for their evening guest, she began the slow and painful process of purging the memories of Victor one by one.

Nine weeks. It had been nine weeks since Juliet had last seen Victor Roland. The banns had been read in the village church for the past three weeks, and now Juliet was to stand before the priest and make marriage vows before God and become Lord Stratford's wife.

"The carriage is ready," her brother said from where he stood at the base of the stairs.

Juliet walked down the stairs, holding one side of her pale lavender wedding gown so that she wouldn't trip. Her brother watched her descend, approval in his eyes. It was the only type of compliment she could ever earn from him.

She picked up the bouquet of wildflowers tied with a lavender ribbon from the hall table. Lord Stratford's daughters had sent them over. They'd now be waiting at the church with their families and the rest of the congregation.

Juliet followed her brother outside, and he handed her up into the carriage lent to them by Lord Stratford. Then they were truly on their way. The early September heat would be merciless by the afternoon, but by then, they should be at the Stratford Estate, where banquet tables would be laden with food and drink. And . . . Juliet would be a married woman.

She tried not to think of how her life would change, of how tonight she'd be sleeping in her new husband's bed since they were foregoing any type of honeymoon, and how in the morning, she'd take on the duties of the mistress of his home. And how her husband and brother would begin their shared business ventures right away while Juliet . . . watched from afar. She would be no more alone than she was now, except for the fact that more would be expected of her. Namely, producing a male heir.

She tried not to think of such details, because then surely the tears would fall, and she feared they'd never stop. The farther the carriage traveled from Southill Estate, the farther her former hopes and dreams seemed to be. She kept her face turned from John, because the last thing she needed was another reprimand.

"Here we are," John said as the carriage pulled up to the church and parked among other carriages, curricles, and wagons.

As John handed her down from the carriage, she gripped the bouquet of flowers while she clutched John's arm with her other hand. He didn't comment on her tight hold, and it was perhaps an allowance on his part. Juliet noticed the garland of flowers and greenery arching across the church's entrance, and she took in their beauty and fragrance. She would have to focus on the good things about her new life and forget the things she'd once hoped for.

All eyes turned on her as she entered the church, and she tried to smile, but it was a rather weak attempt. She also told herself to breathe, in and out, so that she didn't faint in the middle of the aisle.

Up ahead, Lord Stratford waited, standing next to the priest. His oily smile and his searching gaze made Juliet's stomach flip, and not in a good way. She would not become ill. She would keep her chin lifted, her eyes forward, her expression serene. She would save her family's estate, not for her brother, but in honor of her parents and for the children John might have some day.

John released Juliet when she arrived at Lord Stratford's side, and even though she mostly loathed her brother, she didn't want to let go of him, because that meant it was nearly time to say her vows.

"Good morning, dear," Lord Stratford said, his eyes blinking down at her.

Juliet glanced up at him and smiled. At least she tried. She feared the smile was more of a grimace.

"Dearly beloved," the priest began, "we are gathered together here in the sight of God, and in the face of this congregation, to join together this man and this woman in holy matrimony..."

Juliet couldn't concentrate on what the priest was saying. Her mind kept tumbling through scenarios of what her new life would be like. When the priest mentioned children, she felt her headache start.

"Marriage was ordained for the procreation of children, to be brought up in the fear and nurture of the Lord, and to the praise of his holy name," the priest continued. "Therefore if any man can shew any just cause, why they may not lawfully be joined together, let him now speak, or else hereafter forever hold his peace."

The language was standard, but it seemed hope was still a living, breathing thing inside of her, because she imagined the doors of the church flying open and Victor Roland striding through to claim her as his bride. Of course she would have to turn him away, because crying off from Stratford would plunge her brother's reputation deeper into ridicule. And she could not live with herself knowing that Victor had given up his inheritance for her.

But no such thing happened, and the priest continued, looking at Lord Stratford. "Wilt thou have this woman to thy wedded wife, to live together after God's ordinance in the holy estate of matrimony? Wilt thou love her, comfort her, honor, and keep her, in sickness and in health; and, forsaking all other, keep thee only unto her, so long as ye both shall live?"

Juliet heard Lord Stratford's voice in her head before he spoke his vow. It would be the voice she'd listen to for the rest of her life.

But then, before Lord Stratford could reply, the priest said, "What is happening?"

Juliet snapped her head up to look at the priest, not sure what he was asking. Had he been speaking to her? But the man wasn't looking at her or Lord Stratford. The priest's gaze was focused on the church doors—doors that were rattling as if someone was trying to open them.

"Unlock the doors," the priest said in the shocked silence of the congregation. "Who locked them?"

Murmurs arose, and finally a young boy sprang to the doors and lifted the latch that barred whoever was the late comer.

Several men strode inside, dressed in gentlemen's clothing. Juliet didn't recognize any of them and assumed they were friends of Lord Stratford. But when she saw that they carried pistols out in the open, she gasped along with the congregation. Had John's philandering finally caught up with him? Yet, when Juliet looked over at her brother, he appeared as shocked as everyone else.

"Southill, what is going on?" Lord Stratford asked, but her brother merely shook his head, the color of his face nearly white.

Juliet looked again toward the men who circled the congregation as if they were a small army. The women and children shied away from the pistols, and the men appeared ready to bolt out the open doors. "Who are you men?" Lord Stratford called out. "And what are you doing at my wedding?"

"They're my insurance policy that everything runs smoothly," another man's voice answered.

At the same moment Juliet realized she did recognize at least one of the men—Lord Hudson—she saw Victor stride through the now open church doors.

Victor was here. *Here.* In the church. At her wedding.

Juliet couldn't breathe. It seemed that Victor's answer had cast a muteness over the rest of the congregation, because no one spoke as he strode up the aisle. Juliet convinced herself that she was dreaming, yet the man walking toward her was real and solid, with a determination in his eyes that could only belong to Lord Victor Roland.

He no longer had his cane, and the set of his shoulders and steadiness of his stride told her that he was fully recovered from his injury. After all, it had been nine weeks. The only sound in the church was the sound of his footsteps, solid and sure as he walked in boots that looked like he'd encountered a good deal of mud along the way. His boots were black, as were his jacket, vest, and breeches—befitting his state of mourning for his father. Victor neared where Juliet stood with the priest and Lord Stratford, stopping only a couple of feet away. He stood close enough that she could see the perspiration on his forehead and how his hair was windblown from not wearing a hat.

His brown eyes connected with hers as he pulled off his riding gloves. "Tell me, Lady Juliet, have I arrived too late?"

"What is the reason for this rude interruption?" Lord Stratford blustered.

Victor ignored Lord Stratford and scanned Juliet from head to foot.

She was wearing a gown that had been made over from something of her mother's, yes, but she hadn't thought of the full impact that wearing it might have if Victor should see it. Beneath his assessing gaze, her skin flushed warm.

"We have not spoken our vows," Juliet said, surprised she could speak at all.

"Hear, hear," Lord Stratford said, his face growing as red as Juliet's but for a different reason. "You had better not be about to oppose this wedding."

Neither Juliet nor Victor replied to Stratford.

"I am sorry to hear about your father," Juliet said.

"I'm not sorry his misery was put to an end," Victor replied in that frank way of his.

Those in the congregation who sat close enough to hear the quiet conversation gasped at Victor's words.

"Now, listen here, Locken," John said, crossing to the couple.

Juliet noticed that he walked with trepidation, keeping an eye on the other men Victor brought with him.

"Leave my sister in peace," John said. "She's made her decision, and you can keep your dukedom."

Victor turned his gaze upon John. "Who says I can't have both?"

John scoffed. "We all know you reached your father too late." He narrowed his eyes. "The duke was already dead. And my sister will be no mistress of yours."

"My father was dead when I arrived in Locken," Victor said with a nod. "And two weeks later my cousin arrived, ready to take over the estate. I handed him the master's keys and left for London."

"You should have stayed in London, then," John growled. "Southill Estate is no longer your concern."

Victor's mouth lifted into a half smile, and she had to do something soon before these two men brawled in the middle of the church. Victor had come for her, but leaving with him would throw her brother into further scandal. Victor would despise her in the years to come when he realized all he'd given up for her. And as much as she despised many of John's choices and actions, she'd determined to do what was necessary to save Southill Estate.

"Lord Locken," she said in a quiet voice, using his formal title. She stepped forward so she stood between her brother and Victor. "Please forgive me. My brother is right, I have made my choice."

Victor stared at her, and she couldn't quite read his expression. All she knew was that she felt an awful twisting in her stomach. He'd given up Locken for her, but she was unwilling to give up Southill Estate for him. And then it was like her words had finally processed in his mind. His eyes darkened, and a faint flush stole over his cheeks. He opened his mouth, then shut it, his jaw clenched.

Victor nodded to John, then to Lord Stratford, and he said, "I beg your pardon."

With that, Victor turned and slapped his gloves against his thigh, then started the walk back down the church's aisle.

All eyes watched him leave, and just before he reached the church doors, he said, "Men. Let's go." He turned a final time and eyed Juliet from the distance. "I brought the two bays. They are yours now. Won fairly."

He disappeared through the doorway before she could collect her senses.

And when the enormity of what had just happened dawned on her, Juliet wanted to call out after him, to tell him that her heart would always be his, to beg him to return, and tell him that she didn't mind living in the smallest of cottages.

"Well, then," John said, rubbing his hands together. "With that bit of excitement over, we can now proceed."

Juliet swallowed the painful lump in her throat and ignored the tears streaking her cheeks. She turned to Lord Stratford. The man grinned, his eyes focused on her, as if he'd just been awarded a profitable gold mine. Juliet wanted to sink into the earth and never see either of these men again.

"Proceed with the marriage vows." John's blue gaze pierced Juliet as if he'd have no qualms about driving a dagger straight into her heart.

The priest repeated the words. "I require and charge you both, as ye will answer at the dreadful day of judgement, when the secrets of all hearts shall be disclosed, that if either of you know any impediment, why ye may not be lawfully joined together in matrimony, ye do now confess it."

Juliet saw the rest of her life in a single image. Her, sitting alone as an old woman, in the dreary drawing room in the Stratford mansion, her soul wracked with pain because she'd turned down a life of love and happiness. For what? A crumbling manor and a selfish brother?

"I confess," she whispered. "I must confess that I *cannot* marry Lord Stratford," she said louder.

John was by her side in an instant, his fingers grasping her arm. "Juliet," he said through clenched teeth.

She blinked back the tears that had started again and focused on Lord Stratford. "I am truly sorry to have caused you pain and embarrassment, Lord Stratford. But I cannot marry you, *ever*." She would run after Victor and beg for his forgiveness, and if he refused to give it . . . she'd find her own way as a governess.

"Damn you, woman," her brother started, but she cut him off.

"Unhand me now, John," she said in a shaking voice. "You will not dictate my future any longer. You gave up that responsibility when you gambled away your inheritance."

Gasps echoed throughout the church, although Juliet believed that most everyone knew of their ruin.

John's mouth fell open as if she'd slapped him, and it gave her the leverage to wrench away from his grasp. Before he could recover his senses, she picked up her skirts and ran down the aisle. The church doors were still wide open, and she barreled through them. She didn't stop running until she saw that Victor had, indeed, delivered the two bays. Both were saddled, and she made quick work of mounting one, then grabbing the reins of the second. Her dress would likely never recover after the abuse it suffered as she got herself situated and started to ride away from the church.

But she didn't care about her dress or what anyone in all of Southill thought of her. She had a man to catch up to.

Fourteen

Victor should have written Juliet of his coming, but he hadn't trusted that her brother would deliver the letter to her. Besides, he couldn't tell her the truth in the letter. He had to find out if she'd choose *him* over her brother's wishes. She was the type of woman who'd sacrifice her all for another. Was she willing to sacrifice her heart as well?

Apparently, she was.

When he'd heard about the banns posted for Juliet and Lord Stratford, Victor hadn't believed it at first. But upon finding that the marriage was going to happen, he'd wrestled with himself day and night about what to do.

And it wasn't until this morning that everything had become official, and he realized that he could no longer put off his heart. He had to try. So, he came.

A lot of good that had done.

Weeks ago, he'd been willing to live a pauper's life to have Juliet by his side, but she'd made it clear that she wasn't willing to do the same. It was just as well, he supposed, that he discovered it now before he married the woman.

He glanced over at the men he'd rousted on this journey. Surely they thought he was a fool. The only reason Victor wasn't currently ranting and raving himself was because a cold numbness had settled over him. It wouldn't last for long, though. It would soon turn to anger, then grief, then despair. Ironically, this was as close as he'd ever felt to understanding his father, and Juliet was still alive and well.

Victor and his men would all return to London, and as soon as his back was turned, the tales would start. With the exception of Lord Hudson—who was a true friend and would likely wait a few days before he cracked and came up with his own jokes.

"Someone's coming," Hudson said.

Victor said nothing, and he wasn't sure why Hudson was interested in another rider on the road anyway.

"It's Lady Juliet," Hudson added.

Victor froze. Then, slowly, he turned to see a woman on horseback . . . no . . . a woman and two horses. His bays. And she was riding like she was either running from someone or chasing something.

The cold numbness that had surrounded Victor's heart since Juliet had turned him away started to thaw. He blinked once, then twice. No, she wasn't a mirage. She was truly riding his bay in her wedding gown. Since she'd chosen to sit astride the horse, the hem of the dress had risen to mid-calf. Her hair had come out of its pins, and the honey gold streamed behind her. She grasped the reins of both horses so tightly in her hands that her knuckles were white.

Truthfully, she looked like an avenging angel bearing down upon them. Victor was transfixed at the sight as his thudding heart echoed the bays' hoofbeats.

"Do you think she's changed her mind?" Hudson mused.

"Be gone," Victor said in a firm voice. He glanced to the men, who were all gaping at Juliet's approach. "Take yourselves around the bend of the road on the other side of those trees. Give the lady some privacy for what she's come to say."

Hudson smirked, but he and the other men rode on ahead until they'd disappeared around the bend. Not that Victor was exactly watching them, because Juliet had slowed the bays as she neared. Her dark blue eyes were as wild as her appearance, and she reined the horses to a stop, then began to dismount. The dress caught, and Victor hurried to dismount his own horse to help her down.

But he was a moment too late to aid her in a graceful manner, and she nearly tumbled against him as she tried to free her dress from its entanglement. He caught her by the waist, and once she had her balance, he released her and stood back. Holding her in his arms was not the way to keep his mind rational.

What if she were merely demanding that he keep the horses?

She turned to face him, and before he could question her, she sank to her knees.

"Forgive me, Lord Locken," she said. "I have been careless with your heart, and I have hurt my brother and Lord Stratford in the process."

Victor stared down at her, then he grasped her upper arms and drew her to her feet. "Do not kneel before me."

She gazed at him for a moment, her breathing rapid, then she threw her arms about his neck. "I am so sorry," she said into his neck.

He had no choice but to place his hands on her waist, if only to steady himself.

"I don't mind being poor," she said in a breathless voice. "I've grown quite used to it. But I don't want *you* to give up all you have—"

"Juliet," he said, trying to find his sense of reason in all of what she was saying. "What have you done? Why are you here?"

She pulled back so that their gazes met. "I've called off the wedding," she said. "Lord Stratford will now forever hate me. I told him if you will not have me, then I will become a governess. I have never seen my brother so shocked and furious. John will never forgive me, and I'm afraid that I am now without home or family."

"And you mounted the bay and rode after me?" he asked. "Why?"

Her voice fell to a whisper. "Because you came for me." Tears filled her eyes. "And I wanted to tell you that I do choose you. And I love you. Even if we can't marry, you deserve to know that."

Victor wondered if he should laugh at the turn of events or simply kiss her. "There is no reason we cannot marry."

"But—"

He pressed a finger to her lips. "I need to tell you something."

She stilled.

He lowered his finger and rested his hand on her shoulder. "After the funeral, I packed my things in preparation for my cousin's takeover of the dukedom. While sorting through papers in the library, I found a copy of my father's will. Sure enough, he'd revised it to state that I would have to marry Lady Diana by the end of the year in order to keep the dukedom. But something stuck out to me—there was no signature or date. I assumed the signed version was with the solicitor, and I didn't think much about it until I'd returned to London."

"What are you saying, Victor?" Juliet asked.

"I'm saying, my dear, that I looked into the issue," he said. "And I discovered that my father never signed the new will, for whatever reason. I had to go through a mess of litigation with the courts, but as of yesterday, *I* am the rightful Duke of Wycliff."

Her eyes widened. "And you are not married to Lady Diana?"

His smile was slow. "I am not married to Lady Diana. My bride will be of *my* choosing."

"You are free," she whispered, new tears in her eyes. She touched the sides of his face in a caress.

Victor rested his forehead against hers. "I am free to marry you and to love you for the rest of my life."

She moved her hands behind his neck, threading her fingers into his hair. "We will probably need a special license after the scandal I caused in the church."

"No," he said. "We will go to Locken, post the banns there, and then you'll marry me in a wedding ceremony befitting a duchess." He pressed a kiss against the edge of her mouth.

"I will need a new gown," she murmured.

"You shall have one." He kissed the other side of her mouth.

"The bays are still mine, since you're only my second proposal."

He laughed before kissing the edge of her jaw. "You'll need a carriage to go with them. Maybe that can be my wedding gift to you."

She sighed with contentment, and he took the opportunity to trail more kisses down her neck until he reached her collar bone.

"Victor," she said in a quiet voice. "What shall we do about my brother?"

He lifted his head. "We will give him a year to clean up. Then, you'll make the decision whether to help put Southill Estate to rights." He traced her jawline with his fingers while gazing into her blue eyes. "It will be your decision, my dear, solely yours. Because if it were up to me, the outcome would not be sweet."

Her smile was faint, but her eyes were deep pools of gratitude. "You're a good man, Victor Roland."

He grinned at her. "In that case, I must do this properly." He released Juliet and knelt on one knee.

She covered her mouth with one hand, her eyes widening.

"Don't tell me you're surprised," he said. "I mean, I did travel quite a way to crash your wedding."

"You're kneeling in the dirt."

"We'll make a matching pair, then." He winked. "Your dress has half the road on it."

A smile spread across her face.

"Lady Juliet Baldwin," he said, grasping her hand. "Will you do me the honor of becoming my wife?"

She didn't hesitate. Her smile only grew wider as she leaned down and pressed her lips against his.

While her kiss was lovely, she still hadn't answered. "Is that a yes?" he asked after a moment.

She drew back and leveled him with her blue gaze. "It most certainly is, Your Grace."

"Perfect." He rose and pulled her into his arms. "Let's do this properly, then." He kissed her most thoroughly then, as one must do in the middle of a road, after a proposal of marriage is accepted. And as her arms wound around his neck, he inhaled everything that was Juliet—sun, wind, flowers, and promises.

Victor was quite sure they had an audience, and no doubt Hudson and the other men had a good view through the trees. But Victor didn't mind in the least. Juliet was finally his.

And she'd been absolutely right that first night they'd met. Whatever challenges they would face in life as a married couple, if she was his wife, they would find joy.

He would bet on it.

Heather B. Moore is a *USA Today* bestselling author. She writes historical thrillers under the pen name H.B. Moore; her latest are *The Killing Curse* and *Breaking Jess*. Under the name Heather B. Moore, she writes romance and women's fiction; her latest include the Pine Valley Novels. Under pen name Jane Redd, she writes the young adult speculative Solstice series, including her latest release *Mistress Grim*. Heather is represented by Dystel, Goderich & Bourret.

Join Heather's email list: hbmoore.com/contact
Website: HBMoore.com
Facebook: Fans of H. B. Moore
Blog: MyWritersLair.blogspot.com
Twitter: @HeatherBMoore
Instagram: @AuthorHBMoore

An Improbable Wager

-Michele Paige Holmes-

One

SHROPSHIRE, ENGLAND
JUNE 1805

"You're still here?" Sherborne Alexander Rowley III swung a leg over his horse and jumped off, landing crouched in the mud before the animal had come to a full stop.

Young Eli Linfield glanced over his shoulder then resumed his work, knee deep in a posthole. "I am. Though you won't make it to your eleventh birthday, if you keep up stunts like that."

Sherborne grasped the reins and led his horse through the large puddle to the other side. "That was nothing. Last month I jumped from the school roof."

"Mmm," Eli mumbled, both skeptical of Sherborne's bragging and jealous as well. He didn't have a particular desire to jump from a roof, but he thought boarding school sounded exciting—a lot more exciting than preparing posts for a gate in the south pasture. "I wasn't talking about you breaking a leg. It's your boots and breeches that'll be the end of you. Your mum's going to see you thrashed sound for ruining them." Eli knew from sorry experience how averse Sherborne's mother was to any sort of messes or untidiness.

Sherborne shrugged. "I'll just say old Pegasus threw me."

"No, you won't." Eli got a leg up and hoisted himself out of the hole. "Pegasus is old, and you say something like that, they'll get rid of him for sure."

"Then maybe I'd get a better horse to ride." A grin formed across Sherborne's freckled face. "I should definitely say that."

"I'll tell your father you're lying."

"Why should he believe a common farm boy over his son? Why are you still here, anyway? You're not sick anymore."

"Maybe I like it here." Eli looked away, uncomfortable with the turn of the conversation and ruing the day, several months past, when he'd mentioned his private quest to Sherborne. He might have found the answers he'd been searching for since then, as well as a comfortable enough situation, but that didn't mean it couldn't be snatched from him if he didn't keep his part of the bargain.

"You like digging fence holes?" Sherborne laughed out loud as he watched Eli struggle to lift the heavy post into the hole.

"Nothing wrong—with hard work," Eli panted between breaths. *Never be ashamed of who you are.* Times like this it became hard to remember that and to keep the promise he'd made to his mother, that he wouldn't be ashamed. Ever. "Bet you can't lift one of these yourself," he said.

"Course I can." Sherborne took the bait easily, sticking out his chest, blond head held high as he strode toward a second post that lay on the ground.

Eli watched him struggle to right it for at least a full minute or two before walking over to help. "When you're eleven you'll be able to get it by yourself."

"Right." Sherborne nodded. "You're older. That's why you can lift these."

Rather than picking up the post where it was, Eli rolled it closer to the hole, then lifted the far end, using leverage to tip it in. From there it was almost easy to push it upright. "Older and *wiser.*" He dusted his hands on the front of his trousers.

"Not that much older," Sherborne grumbled. "You're not thirteen yet."

"Next month I am." Eli picked up the spade and began shoveling dirt into the hole around the post. "But you're not eleven until the fall."

Sherborne shrugged. "So? The oldest doesn't win anything."

Not this time. "You're right." Eli forced a smile. He wasn't going to allow this encounter—or any other—to upset him. Sherborne didn't deserve that kind of power. "You'll never be older." *I'll never have a father the way you do.* "But you might be stronger someday. If you want a chance at that, you ought to try working once in a while." He pushed the handle of the spade toward Sherborne.

Sherborne caught it easily and began shoveling dirt into the posthole that would brace the new gate. "When I left for school after the holiday, I didn't think I'd see you again. You seemed well."

"I was." Eli wondered uneasily if Sherborne would complain to his father about him. They'd gotten on well enough over the winter holiday, when the weather had been too wet for Sher to go outside much. He'd seemed to enjoy Eli's company then, grateful for someone to play chess or read with to pass time on the long, dreary days.

"Your father allowed me to stay here."

Sherborne frowned. "But weren't you going to find *your* father? So you wouldn't have to work anymore?"

Eli stooped to pack the dirt tight around the post. "That was foolish. My mum was right. Better to let well enough be."

"I'm sorry," Sherborne said, sounding like he meant it and perhaps even regretting his earlier taunts. "I would've liked to have you at school. We had a jolly time together over the holidays."

"We did." Eli's mouth lifted in a smile once more. "We can enjoy your summer holiday as well. Once I'm done with my tasks for the day, I'm free to do as I please."

"What pleases you? What do you do around here?" Sherborne had stopped working after only a few shovelfuls of dirt.

Eli moved to his hole and took over the task that was apparently below the Earl of Shrewbury's heir. "I go swimming." He turned toward the small pile of dirt as a distant flash of color caught his eye. Mid-scoop he stopped and looked up, following the bob of pale blue as it crossed the green meadow. "*That* pleases me."

"Where do you go?" Sherborne asked.

"Same place nearly every day." Eli continued following the blue rider, noting, as she grew closer, that today her rich brown hair—not dissimilar to the chestnuts he loved to collect and roast each fall—was unbound and bounced along with her, shimmering and pretty down her back and around her face. "She never rides on Sunday, of course. And not when her family is away. But the past month I've seen her almost every day, riding the same path around their property."

"What?" Sherborne sounded perplexed. "What are you talking about?" He walked over to Eli and passed a hand in front of his face. "I was talking about swimming, but you're talking about and looking at—a girl?"

"Not just any girl," Eli said. "That's Baron Montgomery's youngest daughter. Emily." He added the last softly, then lifted his hand at the exact second she raised hers, and each waved vigorously.

Sherborne squinted his eyes in the direction Eli was staring. "How can you be sure? Aren't there a lot of Montgomery girls? *All* girls and no boys, I think Father said once."

"There are two," Eli said. He knew all about the Montgomerys, as well as the other families nearby. Eating with the servants below stairs had its benefits. "Emily rides more than her sister." Eli sighed inwardly as Emily reached the point on the trail where it turned away from him and headed north. "I'm going to marry her someday."

Sherborne choked out a laugh. "No, you're not. You can't."

"Can too," Eli said, horrified that he'd inadvertently spoken the thought he'd harbored for months. Once said, there was nothing to do but defend it. "I can marry who I want. My father did."

Sherborne's brows rose. "Fat lot of good that did you. He left you and your mum."

Eli's fingers clenched around the spade handle. "Never mind my father. I'm not him. I can marry who I want, and I'll stay with her, too."

Sherborne shook his head as he stepped in front of Eli so they were facing one another. "You *can't* marry a Montgomery, *because* she's a Montgomery. Her father's a baron, so she'll have to marry a gentleman—someone titled. Like me." Sherborne glanced over his shoulder as he added the last, as if he wished to look at Emily himself now that the possibility of their eventual marriage had occurred to him.

"You're not titled." Eli gripped the handle harder.

"Someday I will be, and that's all that matters."

"You're wrong," Eli said. "Who a person is inside is more important than any title." His mother had been telling him that since before he could walk. "I'm a good person. Emily will see that, and she'll want to marry me."

"I bet she doesn't even know your name." Sherborne stooped to pick up a rock. He tossed it into the mud puddle he'd landed in earlier.

"Not yet," Eli admitted. "But she will."

"Maybe." Sherborne seemed inclined to let the matter drop. He walked to the old stone fence and leaned against it.

Eli breathed an inward sigh of relief, told himself to take more care with his words, and returned to the task of filling the hole.

"What say you to a wager about it?"

Oh no. Eli glanced at Sherborne—boots crossed, arms folded, smug expression.

Eli shook his head. "I don't have anything to wager."

"Not now." Sherborne picked up another rock. "But when you're older you will."

Eli frowned. No good could come of this. Sherborne was nothing if not tricky. Eli had seen him in action over the winter holiday—always managing to come up with this or that item that had belonged to someone else. No doubt he'd been honing his swindling skills these past months at school.

"We'll call it…the wedding wager." Sherborne pushed himself onto the wall then swung his legs up and jumped to a standing position. "Be it known that Mr. Eli—" He paused, then glanced down at Eli. "What is your surname?"

"Linfield." Eli dumped the dirt in the hole, then leaned into the shovel for another scoop. "Eli Alex—Linfield."

"We have almost the same middle name." A grin spread across Sherborne's face.

"Almost."

"Mr. Eli *Alex* Linfield has proclaimed his intention to someday marry Miss Emily Montgomery, daughter of—"

"Quiet!" Eli threw down the spade and marched over to the wall. "I don't want anyone to know."

"I doubt Pegasus will tell." Sherborne jumped down a second before Eli reached him.

"I shouldn't have told you. Forget I said anything." Eli followed Sherborne, half-expecting him to go running off, shouting his secret to the world.

Sherborne stopped suddenly and wheeled about, facing Eli. He stuck a hand out. "I, Sherborne Alexander Rowley, do hereby make a wedding wager with you, Eli Alex Linfield. *If,* when you are both grown up, you marry Miss Emily Montgomery I will give to you…" Sherborne's mouth twisted. "What do you want? My flint-lock?"

Eli shook his head. "It'll be old by then. There will be better rifles probably."

"How about if I just say I'll give you my best weapon?"

"No." Eli saw the loophole in that right away. There was no qualifier for what was "best," and no doubt Sherborne would judge that himself and in fact give the poorest of the lot to Eli. "I don't want a rifle or any other weapon."

"Suit yourself. Hard to hunt without them, though."

As if I have time for hunting. He never would so long as he had to continue working like this. And Sherborne was right, though Eli hated to admit it. Emily would never marry him, not so long as he continued to be the boy who dug posts and shoveled horse dung and did every other menial and unpleasant task—all for very little pay. He needed what Sherborne had. Not his title, or even the grand income that would be left to him. *I need an education—and property.*

Claymere.

"Say that you'll give me Claymere if I marry Emily, and I will wager."

Sherborne's hand dropped and he backed away. "You're mad if you think I'd agree to that. That's father's favorite place in the world. I've heard him say so more than once—as must you have to know of it."

Why is it his favorite? "Why doesn't he ever go there?" Eli challenged.

"I don't know. It's far, I guess. And Mother doesn't like the country."

Eli laughed. "We're in the country now."

"I *won't* wager that property." Sherborne folded his arms across his chest. "What if you married Miss Montgomery and Father was still alive. What would I tell him?"

"I'd go with you to speak with him," Eli promised. "We would tell him together." He imagined the satisfaction such a conversation would bring.

"Perhaps it can't be wagered at all—even if I wanted to offer it up."

"I heard your father speaking to his steward. Claymere is freehold, and he wishes to keep it that way. It will be yours someday, so wager it if you want. Unless… you're worried you'll lose."

"I'm not," Sherborne said a little too quickly. "It's impossible for you to marry a Montgomery, so I shouldn't be worried at all."

"Not at all." Eli wiped his hands on his pants again, this time in preparation for the deal that was about to be struck.

"Still, if I'm going to offer something so valuable, you ought to do the same."

Eli realized he hadn't been as clever as he'd thought. He should have known better. Sherborne lived for winning, whether he really wanted what the other person had or not.

"But you don't own any property."

Of consequence. Eli didn't say anything. He'd not be swindled out of the one home he might someday return to.

"What *do* you have?" Sherborne asked, sounding exasperated.

"Just myself." Eli held out his hands. "No weapons. No

horse. No money." The last wasn't entirely true. He had a bit. Enough to live on—barely—if it came to that.

"That's our wager, then," Sherborne said, smug as he stuck out his hand once more. "If you do not succeed in marrying Emily Montgomery, then you must work for me, with no income paid, for a period of ten years."

"Ten! Now you think I'm mad."

"Claymere has been in the Rowley family for generations. I'm not about to wager that against nothing."

Ten years of my life. Eli swallowed uneasily. What were the odds that he would actually be able to marry Emily Montgomery? He had no doubt his feelings toward her would remain the same. They might never have spoken, but he knew that, like him, she loved horses and the out of doors. And she was friendly, the way she always waved to him each time she passed. He could tell, even from afar, that she was beautiful, too. Years from now he would still *want* to marry her, but would he actually be able to?

"I knew it," Sherborne said. "You were just bluffing."

"I wasn't," Eli said. "And I'm willing to bet ten years of my life on it." *Nearly as long as I've lived.* He reached for Sherborne's hand and clasped it firmly in his before either could change their mind.

Two

FOURTEEN YEARS LATER

Sherborne leaned a shoulder against the timbers framing the entrance to the stable, eyes narrowing as he watched the approaching rider. The man sat tall and proud, cutting a fine figure. There was something familiar about his posture and bearing, almost suggesting he belonged on the grand horse—or felt he did. Sherborne frowned, his irritation growing. His steward had told him the man was a groom of the Montgomerys. *Who'd no business taking out* my *horse.*

"Want to tell me what the deuce you think you're doing?" Sherborne demanded a minute later when man and beast came galloping into the yard.

"Exercising your horse, since you don't." The groom, who could best be described as broad shouldered and scruffy, with a beard of outrageous proportion covering much of his face, dismounted, then gave the mare an affectionate pat. "Good girl." He began guiding the horse away just as Sherborne strode forward to take the reins.

"Stop this moment," he ordered. "Who gave you leave to ride this animal? You don't work for me."

"Thank the heavens," the insufferable bearded man said and continued on his way, the mare obediently following.

"Sage may be your horse, but she needs to be ridden far more than the half dozen weeks a year you deign to be home. I've been riding her as a favor for your estate manager, who at present seems somewhat overburdened and understaffed."

"He has plenty of staff," Sherborne grumbled, recalling Hawkins' incessant badgering of late, requesting additional funds for the management of affairs here.

He'll have them soon enough. Sherborne glanced in the direction of Baron Montgomery's estate.

The groom stopped at the watering trough, then released the reins so Sage could drink freely. "What brings you home this time, Sher? Slow season at the London gaming tables?"

Sher. Sherborne stiffened. Only one person had ever called him that. *One friend, long ago.* He narrowed his eyes, trying to see beyond the overgrowth of facial hair—a difficult feat, as the man was taller than he. If the man would but speak again, or turn and face him instead of continuing to lavish attention on the horse.

"You may go now," Sherborne said authoritatively, deciding that even if the interloper was his old friend, it would not do to allow him to address a member of the peerage in such a manner.

"Not until she's cooled down and I've groomed her—or did you want to do that? You know, actually take care of your own animal?" The man walked past a speechless Sherborne and entered the stables. Sherborne started to go after him, then decided he'd deal with the man later—perhaps he could bring this poor behavior up with Baron Montgomery this afternoon. In the meantime, he was already close to being late.

Sherborne reached Sage's side just as the groom returned, a curry comb and hoof pick in his outstretched hands.

Sherborne shook his head. "I ride. You groom."

"I supposed as much." The groom started to remove Sage's bridle.

"Leave it," Sherborne said. "I'll be taking her."

"Not now, you won't," the beard said. "She needs to cool off. She's been out nearly two hours. Had I known you were coming, I would not have ridden her. No need to punish the horse for it, though."

Sherborne opened his mouth to argue, but managed to hold his tongue. He didn't care for this dressing down but realized it would be foolish to mistreat the animal. He could ill afford another right now. He swallowed his pride and sucked in a breath. "Eli?"

"Mmmhmm." The bridle was off now, set aside as his old friend started to unfasten the saddle.

"It really is you." Though the statement came out sounding more like a question, Sherborne wondered suddenly how he hadn't noticed at once. The mere way Eli answered him, in clipped sentences and a tone suggesting he was an equal and not a servant, all the while he continued his work, should have identified him right away.

Anyone else of this station Sherborne would have taken to task for speaking to him so, but Eli was no longer his father's servant, and he was—or had at one time been—a friend.

Sherborne turned from Eli and walked the few dozen steps to the stablehand himself. "Raymond, I'll need the Golden saddled. Be quick about it. I'm already late."

"The Golden has been gone since last fall," Eli called. "I believe you authorized such—as payment for a debt."

"Devil take it," Sherborne muttered. He'd forgotten about that. His best stallion. "Another one then, Raymond," Sherborne said, hoping he'd something left other than the old bone-setters his father kept.

This was not a good way to begin, being late and making a poor impression upon his hopefully, soon-to-be father-in-law. Baron Montgomery and his wife had invited Sherborne to stop by for tea, the perfect opportunity for him to become reacquainted with them and their daughter, Emily. Rumor had it that her dowry was substantial and her father was looking to improve their family's status through her marriage.

Enter the earl, Sherborne thought smugly as he retraced his steps toward Eli. Really, the situation could not be any easier. He and Emily were practically betrothed already. They'd been neighbors their entire lives, and everyone knew that the earl's title had once come through a Montgomery. Theirs was a match that had been hinted at by both sets of parents since they were children.

He'd heard Emily'd had a brief season in London, but her more reserved personality had not been a good fit with the ton, and she'd returned home early. That was five years ago, and there probably hadn't been anyone at all interested in asking for her hand since.

Sherborne's gaze slid suddenly to Eli. *Anyone suitable.*

"You want to help, you can put this away." Eli thrust the saddle squarely at Sherborne's chest.

Unprepared, Sherborne staggered backward, nearly falling in the muck of the yard.

"We are no longer children, Eli." Sherborne righted himself with as much dignity as possible—not much at all, considering the saddle was still slipping and he was being pulled forward with it to keep it from falling in the spring mud. "You—can—not—treat—me like this." He clutched the blasted contraption to his chest and noted its foul smell of sweaty horse. *Fiend seize it!* He'd have to change before going over to the Montgomerys. If he wasn't going to be quite late before, he definitely would be now.

"I was only trying to include you," Eli said, a definite twitch to his mouth, barely visible behind the beard. "I seem to recall you always found great interest in whatever I was doing."

"As did you, in what *I* was doing," Sherborne huffed, recalling the long summer afternoons of being badgered about everything to do with boarding school. "The truth was, then and now, that I could not be you, and you could not be me." Sherborne said this with honest regret. Of all his friends, Eli had been the one he could most be himself around. He'd wished, more than once, that circumstances were different, that Eli's father hadn't disappeared before Eli was even born, or that he would reappear now—a member of the ton—and claim Eli as his own. It would have been good to be able to consider him an equal. But that was not to be.

"Our differences have never been more apparent or true than now. Look at you—" Sherborne waved a hand at Eli. "Have you made use of a razor even once in the past six months? I've never seen such a face."

"Oh, I think you probably have," Eli said, a slight curve to his lips this time, as if something Sherborne had said amused him.

The response only annoyed Sherborne. "Don't you understand? I am Sherborne Alexander Rowley III, the Earl of Shrewsbury, whereas you are merely Eli Alex Linfield—"

"—The *first*," Eli said. "Believe me, I've never forgotten. You are an earl. I am a stable master. It's quite clear. Common I may be, but simpleminded I am not."

Stable *master?* If that was true, Eli had moved up in the ranks considerably. Sherborne balanced the saddle on top of the fence. "Why are you here, Eli?"

"To exercise and care for your horse." Eli turned his back on Sherborne and took up the curry comb. "I thought we'd established that."

"I mean *here*." Sherborne shifted his gaze toward the Montgomery land once more. "I know you work for the Montgomerys."

There was a visible stiffening in Eli's posture. His neck tensed first, then his back, noticeable beneath the sweat-soaked shirt in the straightening of every notch of his spine. After a moment, during which Sherborne guessed his old friend was struggling with something, Eli turned to face him.

"I've worked for Baron Montgomery the past five years. He treats me fairly, and in return I meet or exceed his expectations—so much so that he has allowed me to come see to your horses several times a week. Baron Montgomery and I have a good working relationship. That is all."

"And his daughter, Emily?" Sherborne asked, deciding there was no point in hinting at the topic when he needed to hurry and Eli was a potential flaw in his plan. "What is your relationship with her?"

Eli's eyes narrowed as he took a step forward. His knuckles whitened with his grip on the comb.

"*Miss* Montgomery and I do not have a relationship. The only interaction I have with all three ladies of the household, Lady Montgomery, Miss Montgomery, and her older sister, Lady Grayson, are limited to their requests regarding their horses. If you should so much as insinuate otherwise—ever again—I shall be forced to call you out for it."

Sherborne barked out a laugh filled with both relief and amusement. *She is untarnished. She can still be mine.* The baron was not looking to marry his daughter off for other reasons. "You would call me out like any gentleman?" It seemed the audacity of Eli's youth had only grown more profound with age.

"Like any gentleman." Eli gave a curt nod. "I have answered your question, but you have not answered mine.

Why are *you* here? Have you come home to court Miss Montgomery?"

"I have," Sherborne answered, though this entire conversation was beneath him. The word *court* was also somewhat disturbing. He hadn't thought much on that, but likely both Miss Montgomery and her parents would expect some sort of effort from him in that respect. He supposed at least a few months of carriage rides, socials, and the like awaited him.

"When is the last time you saw her?" Eli asked in a tone far too demanding for Sherborne's liking.

"I am uncertain," he admitted. "Perhaps three or four years ago. I cannot recall. I met her sister a few months past at an event in London, and she apprised me of Emily's—of Miss Montgomery's—" he hastily amended at Eli's fierce look, "availability. Since then I have been corresponding with her father, who is in favor of the match, particularly since the Earl of Shrewsbury's title originally came through—"

"—a Montgomery." Eli waved his hand dismissively. "I am familiar with the family history."

"Just so long as you are not familiar with the lady."

"I warned you." Eli's fist sprang forward, catching the side of Sherborne's nose as he turned away.

Sherborne feinted to the side but in the same motion swung back, arm out, fist formed, and landed a solid punch to Eli's middle. He'd learned a few tricks himself over the years, particularly those spent at school among other frustrated young men like himself. If ever anyone had deserved to have the wind knocked out of him, it was Eli today. Sherborne felt he'd shown as much patience as he was capable of. Old friend or not, Eli had just crossed the line.

But Eli did not appear either wounded or discouraged. "If there is a next time it will be pistols."

Sherborne shook his head. "You fool. I've come home to

marry Emily Montgomery, so if you're still harboring that boyhood fantasy about having her yourself, you'd best forget it. She may know your name now, but you need to know your place. As for our wager, long ago, I'd have been inclined to forget that as well, but given your actions this afternoon, I've changed my mind. I suggest you give your notice to the Baron sooner rather than later. But don't worry. You'll not work here. Once Emily and I are married I'll send you to Claymere. You can exercise and groom my horses all day long there, and I won't even care if you pretend they're yours."

Definitely late for his appointment now, Sherborne took a step toward the house. "Put the saddle away and finish grooming Sage before you go."

"Do it yourself." Eli tossed the curry brush at Sherborne, who fumbled with it a second before clasping it tightly.

His anger erupted in full blown force. "How dare you tell me what to do. I pay your wage for services here."

"I receive no wage," Eli said in a tone that indicated his own temper was just barely in check. "I came here to help out of respect for the late Earl. But no more."

"You—are not paid?" Sherborne felt his mouth hanging open and snapped it shut. *Impossible.*

"If you don't believe me, confirm it with your steward. I am here out of a sense of loyalty and long-remembered friendship. I did not wish your father's estate to go entirely to ruin."

"How dare you suggest—It's not—" *Entirely.* Sherborne glanced about, noting the neglect he'd tried to ignore. The front garden looked decent enough, if not as glorious as when his parents had lived here, but the grounds in general were overgrown and neglected. The fence needed mending, the stables a fresh coat or two of paint.

Inside the house his personal rooms were clean, but the remainder had the appearance of being left alone far too long.

"Since Father's passing, my mother prefers London. There has been no reason—until now—to concern myself overly with affairs here."

"I hope you do now." Eli walked toward another horse, presumably his own, grazing nearby. "I hope you take greater care here in all your doings, from the upkeep of the house to the care and courting of your bride."

Three

"Wear your hair high with the silver, jeweled combs tonight. They suit you." Lady Sophia Grayson sashayed into her sister's bedroom, pausing to admire her own reflection in the full-length mirror.

"They make my head ache so," Emily complained, looking up from her book and watching her sister pose in front of the glass.

"That's right, see how it's done." Sophia exaggerated the swing of her hips as she crossed behind Emily. "If you want a man to notice you, you have to give him something *to* notice."

"A head full of heavy jewelry?" Emily made a face.

"No, silly. The way you walk. Like this." Sophia paraded past Emily once more.

No, thank you. Emily would die before she'd strut around like that in front of anyone, especially Lord Rowley.

"You want the earl to take interest in you, don't you?"

Emily did not answer immediately. *Do I?* It was what her father wanted, certainly, but she wasn't yet sure she felt the same. Her life here was comfortable. She was content. She didn't need a beau, or especially a husband.

"*Em-ily.*" Sophia dropped down beside her, nudging Emily practically off the chair. "Do you even realize how lucky you are? The earl is near our age. He is handsome, reputable, charming. Would that papa had chosen a gentleman like that for me."

"You were happily married," Emily said, aghast at her sister's suggestion that she had not favored her late husband.

"Henry and I managed well enough, but he was fourteen years my senior and not particularly attractive. His title and money were very admirable, though." Sophia burst into a fit of giggles entirely inappropriate for one her age and in her circumstance.

Emily frowned, recalling how immensely pleased their father had been when the duke offered for Sophia. Their father seemed no less pleased when the earl had called on them two weeks ago and then invited Emily for a drive a day later. They had gone driving again since and ridden together the day before. Tonight's ball was to be the real test.

Will the earl and I suit? Somehow Emily felt certain she would know when they danced. She would feel it when he took her hand and during those times they brushed shoulders as they passed each other and turned round. She would know when they stood across from each other and looked into one another's eyes. She would feel—*something*.

She did not expect excitement or a swoony feeling of romance, but hoped she might feel comfortable, as if she and Lord Rowley might be friends. She had never witnessed that in her parents' relationship but, if she must be married, longed for it in hers.

That wasn't too much to ask, was it?

Sherborne resisted the urge to take out his watch and check the time. He thought it had to be nearing two in the morning. Surely a country ball like this would not carry on into the hour before dawn as those in London frequently did. He'd been Miss Montgomery's partner for the supper dance some hours ago and found her agreeable enough, if not on the quiet side.

During the meal her sister, Lady Grayson, had also been seated nearby and had entertained both her partner and the others around her. Sherborne had requested a dance with her shortly after and now wished—as he watched her holding her gown and turning about prettily—that he might request another. But of course that would send the entirely wrong message. Sherborne's quest here wasn't about finding the woman who most intrigued him, it was about securing the one with the largest dowry. The Collingwood manor and estate needed it. Quickly.

With that to motivate him, Sherborne played the part of the charming guest and danced three times more, doing his best to seek out those he felt had probably danced the least. He soon realized why they were not dancing. If their looks were little to recommend them, their wit held even less. Talk of the weather and fashions and their mad king were boring him to tears. At least the Montgomery sisters were both more interesting than that. Emily enjoyed riding and the countryside, and they had discussed horses and their adjoining property at length. Sophia had had him laughing out loud as she described the idiosyncrasies of each of their neighbors.

At half past three, Sherborne not only checked his watch but deemed it the appropriate time to request a second dance with Emily. She consented with that same demure expression she'd presented to him earlier, and he found himself wondering what it would take to coax her from her shyness. They had spoken somewhat comfortably on their drives the past week. He wasn't certain what had changed this evening.

Perhaps it was that she'd been taught that reserved

females were preferable. He hadn't time for that or any other courting games. They both knew what this dance was about, and he saw no reason for pretense of any sort.

"Miss Montgomery?"

"Yes." Her eyes fully met his for the first time all evening.

She was tired, fighting a yawn this very second, and Sherborne found himself wondering what it would be like to see her sleep. His mind wandered dangerously, imagining a wedding night when they might share a bed.

"I have enjoyed your company tonight," he said truthfully. *As much or more than anyone else here.*

"I have enjoyed yours as well." She smiled, just for him, and Sherborne felt a sudden peculiarity. She wasn't like the other girls he had spent time with. He'd not seen the appeal of marrying someone unaccustomed to the society he relished being a part of, but he suddenly saw possibility there as well— for all the things she might experience with him for the first time. They changed partners once more but passed each other, their shoulders brushing. Such an inconsequential touch compared to those he'd enjoyed from females before, and yet...

She smiled at him again when the cotillion ended. Sherborne took her hand, bent over it, and allowed his lips to linger over her soft skin. "May I call on you again the day after tomorrow?" he asked boldly.

Miss Montgomery nodded, and Sherborne felt the weight of his financial burdens lift a little more.

Four

"It's true! Fortune is going to have her foal tonight?" Emily peeked into the stall, her gloved hands wrapped around the upper bars.

"Let's hope it is tonight." Eli's gaze slid from the mare to Miss Montgomery before he turned away quickly, berating himself for looking at all. One glance had been enough to note her flushed cheeks, upturned lips, and the sparkle in her eyes. *Lord, those eyes.* They were going to haunt him the rest of his life.

"How perfectly vexing." She sighed dramatically.

"More vexing for Fortune than for you, I should think," Eli said.

Miss Montgomery's laugh echoed through the stable. "Oh, Mr. Linfield. You are so amusing. I am going to miss you."

And I you. With a pang of regret Eli realized this might very well be the last time he saw her. He had promised to stay until Miss Montgomery's horse was safely delivered of her foal, but no longer, preferring not to witness Emily's developing affection for Sherborne.

Eli had not shared with the baron or his family the particulars of his new *position,* only that he must take it to honor a promise made long ago. Sherborne and he were the only two privy to the particulars of their arrangement.

An Improbable Wager

The wedding wager, Eli thought bitterly. What a foolish child he'd been when he'd both boasted of marrying Miss Montgomery and then wagered ten years of his life on it.

Though the prospect of never seeing her again was painful, it was best. It had been difficult enough watching Sherborne court her the past month. Living nearby and seeing them together as a married couple would be far worse.

"I meant no ill wishes toward Fortune and would very much like to be by her side, if I might." Emily cast a glance toward the open double doors. "But the earl is on his way, even now, to take me for a drive."

Now that *is vexing.* Eli continued scrubbing down the far wall, making every surface Fortune or her foal might come in contact with as sanitary as possible to avoid the possibility of infection. He'd never lost a foal or its mother on his watch, and he intended to keep it that way.

"I'm sure you'll have an enjoyable time," Eli managed to say with a neutral, if not entirely cordial, tone. "I promise to watch out for your horse. She'll manage quite well and be fit for riding again soon enough."

"Thank you, Mr. Linfield. I don't know what we'll do without you. I wish you didn't have to leave."

"That's kind of you." Eli didn't delude himself that she'd meant it in any reference other than his work here. *But if she had...* It was all too easy to imagine a different scenario. And all the more reason it was time to move on. Even without the wager to fulfill, he would still be leaving. He'd known that for the past five years, when he'd decided to work for the Montgomerys. It had always been a temporary post. Just until Emily married and was settled.

"No need to be late for your drive," Eli said, noting Emily hadn't budged at all during his musings. "Lord Rowley's not a man who likes to be kept waiting—I hear," he amended quickly, lest she wonder how he knew of Sherborne's temperament.

"I suppose not," Emily said quietly. Her hands slid from the bars, but she made no further move to go. "I imagine it comes from the pace of life in London. He quite likes it there and has numerous tales of his adventures."

Instead of sounding impressed or excited, she sounded melancholy.

"This concerns you?" Eli said quietly. He left the wall and walked carefully around Fortune to stand on the opposite side of the stall gate, facing Emily through the bars. *A fitting metaphor.* Just as in life, he was separated from her, perpetually on the wrong side.

She shrugged. "I am not certain the earl and I suit, but Father wants this match. He feared I'd become an old maid, so now to have Lord Rowley express interest…"

"An old maid?" Eli scoffed. "You are all of—twenty-two." He pretended his uncertainty, though there was none. He was more than aware of her age, having noted her birthday each year for many years now.

"My coming out was five years ago. I am *definitely* an old maid—and quite content with my lot."

"Content is good." Eli chose his words carefully, wanting very much to lift her spirits. "But what if there is something beyond that waiting for you? What if marriage will bring you a happiness you've not yet known, or even imagined?"

Emily lifted her face so their eyes met. "I do not think that is possible with the earl. I do not doubt he is a good man, but I fear I will not be able to keep pace with him. London society and I did not complement each other, and it seems Lord Rowley is all for returning to London as soon as possible, both to be nearer his mother and because he is most comfortable in the city."

That was all true. Sherborne had found little to satisfy his interest the two summers he'd spent at Collingwood, so after his thirteenth year, he had not been required to return. Instead, his family had moved their primary residence to London. Only the late earl had returned here somewhat frequently, and only Eli knew the reason he had.

"Perhaps London will surprise you the next time," he said, wondering at his encouragement of this match. But Emily loved her parents, particularly her father, and when it came down to the question of whether or not she would marry Sherborne, Eli felt little doubt that she would agree, for the sake of pleasing them. "The theater is splendid—I've heard. And Hyde Park is a pleasant place to ride. I am certain the earl would not object to Fortune accompanying you to London." No doubt Sherborne would be grateful to add Fortune *and* her foal to his possessions, his own stock having been depleted rather severely over the past few years.

"Thank you, Mr. Linfield. I appreciate your kindness. Thank you for taking the time to listen to the concerns of a silly girl."

"You are not a silly girl." He started to raise his hand, as if to reach through the bars and touch her, but remembered himself in time.

Emily appeared not to have noticed as she stepped back, her gaze on the stable entrance once more. "I believe I just saw the earl's carriage pass. I had best go."

Don't. Don't marry him. There is another option. Eli nodded, his throat thick with the words he could never say.

She turned from him and began walking toward the doors, a ray of afternoon sun guiding her way and shining upon her as if she was an angel descended from Heaven itself.

Eli pressed a hand to his heart, as if doing so might somehow keep it from breaking. All these years it had belonged to Emily, and she would never know.

She stopped suddenly, turning within that shaft of light to face him once more.

"Truly you shall be missed, Mr. Linfield. More than you may know. Father says you're the best worker he's ever had."

Eli forced a smile and gave a curt nod as she once more turned away and retreated down the wide walkway between the stalls.

The best worker, but not nearly good enough for his daughter.

Five

Fortune's bandaged tail switched with agitation as the mare struggled to her feet once more.

"Easy, girl," Eli said in hushed tones. In the low lantern light, he watched Fortune carefully for signs of stress as she labored. "It shouldn't be long now." *It had better not be.* He was prepared—arm scrubbed, sleeve rolled up to nearly his shoulder—to help her if need be, but pulling a foal from within a mare was not his preference. It was always better when nature worked as it should and the mother took care of things herself.

A door creaked behind him, startling both Eli and the mare, who tossed her head and whinnied pitifully. Eli glanced over his shoulder, then gave a start himself at the white figure moving toward them.

"Is she delivered yet?" Miss Montgomery held a lantern in her hand, its light reflecting against her long, white dressing gown, making her appear even more angelic than she had earlier.

Eli shook his head and brought a finger to his lips. "Put out your lantern," he whispered.

She obeyed and slowed her steps toward them.

Another contraction seized Fortune, and Eli's attention

was all for the mare, particularly her straining hind quarters. She was tiring quickly. It had been almost thirty minutes of hard labor. She needed to birth the foal soon, else they both would be in danger.

"Is she all right?" Miss Montgomery stood at the gate again, much as she had earlier. "I couldn't sleep, for thinking of Fortune and her baby. Shouldn't he be here by now?"

"Soon," Eli whispered. "We must be very careful not to spook her. She'd prefer to be alone, though I've need to watch her in case."

"In case?" Miss Montgomery worried her lip, momentarily distracting Eli.

"Sometimes a foal is not in the correct position and needs help to be born." He waited, then watched as another pain gripped Fortune. *Something's not right.* She was pushing, but no forelegs had appeared.

"You shouldn't be here, Miss Montgomery." Carefully he moved nearer the laboring horse.

"Please," her voice wavered. "I can see she's in terrible pain. Is there anything I can do to help?"

"She'll be all right," Eli said, as much to comfort the horse as to reassure its owner. "Run along to bed, and you can come see the new foal in the morning."

"You speak to me as if I'm a child." Miss Montgomery's voice rose slightly, and the mare nickered her complaint.

"Sorry," she whispered, sounding contrite. "*Please,* let me stay."

Eli shook his head. "It's not proper. You're not even dressed, and what if you faint? I'd not be able to care for both you and your horse. Birthing is a bloody mess." He was in position now, awaiting Fortune's next contraction.

"You've no need to worry over me," Miss Montgomery said. "I've a strong constitution. No one need find out I've been here, and no matter if they did. You are leaving by the week's end, your new position already secured. And just today the earl offered for me. We are each secure in our futures, regardless of anything that might happen tonight."

Anything that might happen. Eli did not like the sound of that or what it so readily conjured in his mind. Nor did he miss the tone of Miss Montgomery's voice. She did not sound like a woman who had just been proposed to ought—happy and giddy, or at least pleased.

But he had no more thought for Miss Montgomery, or what was proper, as Fortune's body convulsed with another pain. With tender care, Eli pushed his hand inside the birth canal, reaching for her foal. He found one leg easily. It was right there, ready to make its escape from the womb. But the other he could not locate and spent several frantic seconds searching for it, while his other hand held Fortune's bound and twitching tail out of the way.

Where are you? Come on! Fortune's contraction ended, and Eli still hadn't located the foal's other foreleg.

He withdrew his hand and used his other to swipe at the sweat dripping into his eyes.

"Try again. You can do this." Miss Montgomery had entered the stall and stood beside him. She took Fortune's tail and moved it out of his way, standing on tip toe to keep it from his face.

"Thank you." Eli worked his hand inside once more, as gently as possible, and began his search again, higher this time. He felt the foal's nose, then an ear and then—*hoof!* He grabbed it and pulled, lowering the limb over the foal's face, then forward until it was parallel with the other. He hooked his hand over both and tugged, just a little, then withdrew and stepped back quickly as Fortune and nature took care of the rest.

"Oh!" Emily exclaimed softly as she watched the foal appear between them.

Eli knelt to catch it, helping it safely to the waiting bed of straw.

"Let go of her tail now," Eli instructed, and Emily, as if just realizing her hand was still aloft, released Fortune's tail and moved back into the far corner of the stall.

The mare turned, so her head was nearer her baby, then lay down beside the awkward bundle struggling to free itself entirely from the sac.

"Good girl," Eli whispered affectionately as he rose and backed into the corner opposite Miss Montgomery.

"Are you talking to me or Fortune?"

"Both." Eli grinned, feeling extraordinarily happy, overcome once more with the miracle of life. He glanced over at Miss Montgomery, realizing she was on the wrong side of the mare—effectively trapped until Fortune either decided to get up or change positions again.

"Are you all right?" he asked with concern, guessing that most well-bred young ladies would never experience something so raw as a horse birthing.

"I am wonderful." She returned his smile, and their eyes met over mother and baby, hers moist and shining. "That was—astounding. *Beautiful.*"

You are beautiful. "It is the same every time. I am glad you were able to experience it."

"As am I. Thank you, Mr. Linfield."

"Eli," he corrected, meeting her gaze once more. He'd be gone in a few days. There seemed no harm in being more personable until then, or tonight at least, when they'd just been bystanders, if not complete participants, in one of the most intimate acts of life.

"Thank you, Eli," she said, smiling warmly.

"You're most welcome—Emily."

She might have blushed at his forwardness, but he couldn't be certain, as her face was partly in shadow. In either case, he looked away, somewhat abashed at his own behavior. He'd taken Sherborne to task for speaking of her casually. *Yet here I am, calling her by name as we're alone, in the dead of night, and her not even dressed properly.* Eli realized it was a very good thing he was leaving soon. He wasn't quite sure he'd ever be the same after tonight.

Forcing his attention back to Fortune and her new colt, he began carefully pulling the dirty straw back and replacing it with clean. After several minutes, Fortune, who appeared to have been taking a well-deserved nap, stood, severing the umbilical cord at the same time the afterbirth was delivered.

As she began cleaning her colt, Eli maneuvered around her to gather the rest of the mess. He made his way to the side, glanced at Emily once more, and noted all signs of her blushing had gone. Her face had turned a ghostly white, and she held one hand to her stomach.

"Miss Montgomery, are you we—"

She went down, falling almost gracefully into the straw. Eli jumped over the back of the colt, muttering an apology as Fortune nipped at him.

"Miss Montgomery." He lifted her head, checking for injury, finding none, and thanking the heavens he'd spread the straw extra deep.

Not so immune after all. He might tease her about this later—or he would have if he was going to be around longer than the end of the week.

Emily's breathing was even, so he laid her out comfortably, there not being much else he could do. Smelling salts weren't to be found in the stable, and he didn't think she would want him to alert someone at the house.

He knelt beside her, waiting for her to come to. Speaking each other's names had seemed intimate, but this seemed even more so. He'd never been this close to her before and took the opportunity to touch her cheek once again.

Her skin was as soft as he'd imagined, as was her hair. He touched that next, with the excuse to himself that he ought to lay it over her shoulder to keep the straw from it as much as possible. Emily's lashes were long and still, dark in contrast to her pale skin. Yet she didn't appear fragile, but simply serene. She might have fainted at the last, but she'd witnessed the birth and found wonder in it instead of being repulsed.

The stable door squeaked for the second time that night. Instead of jumping to his feet, Eli froze, tension flooding his body at the sound of voices. The higher, female one he recognized at once.

Lady Grayson. She'd been in here a time or two before with various companions. Once, Eli had avoided being seen. The second time he had discreetly looked away and said not a word about it. She was a young widow. He would not fault her. No doubt loneliness and missing her husband had driven her to such behavior. Regardless, it was not his to judge. With any luck, she and her companion would not be here long, and no one would be any the wiser of his—or Emily's—presence.

"The stable? Really, Lady Grayson, you surprise me. I would think a tussle in the hay far below your standards."

Sherborne! Eli's fists clenched.

Sherborne's words were slightly slurred, as if he was foxed.

"Oh, don't be such a bore," Lady Grayson said. "I'm only speaking of a midnight ride to the pond. It's so refreshing to swim after a hot day like today."

"As refreshing as it sounds, I have just this day offered for your sister. I do not think—"

"Precisely," Lady Grayson said. "*Don't* think. Just feel. Soon enough you'll be a tenant for life, and I promise Emily will never be one for doing anything adventurous at midnight."

How little you know. Eli glanced at Emily, her dressing gown spread out around her, except for the one slightly bunched corner revealing an ankle. He quickly pulled it down.

"I do feel—you are a tempting armful." Sloppy kissing sounds followed Sherborne's equally sloppy sentence.

How dare he. If not for Emily's presence, Eli would have put an immediate end to all Sherborne was feeling.

"Lady Grayson—perhaps—we ought not—there is your father to consider," Sherborne managed.

Her father? What about Emily? Foxed or not, Sherborne had no excuse for such deplorable behavior.

Emily's head moved slightly. She was still unaware of the drama around her, but probably not for much longer.

Eli gathered handfuls of the straw and tossed it over Emily, covering all but her nose and mouth. Then, grabbing the pitchfork, he stood and cleared his throat loudly, unwilling and unable to let Sherborne dally with his future wife's sister.

"Quiet, if you please," Eli said, his back to the front of the stable and their voices. "Miss Montgomery's horse has just given birth and should not be disturbed."

"Oooh. I want to see."

Eli cringed, cursing silently. He ought to have realized his warning would have the opposite effect on the curious Lady Grayson.

"It's not safe yet," he called, his voice rising oddly as the straw at his feet shifted. "It was a difficult birth, and Fortune is not yet herself."

"Just a small peek." Lady Grayson's voice grew closer.

"Need to clean up the afterbirth. No place for a lady," Eli said as Emily's hand emerged from the straw.

"You heard the man," Sherborne said, his voice deeper as if he was attempting to disguise it. "Let's be off now."

Yes. Be off. The straw shifted once more, this time accompanied by a low moan.

"Is everything all right?" Lady Grayson called.

"It is now," Eli replied. "Colt had a bit of a hard time. One of its legs was trapped. Fortune will take care of him, though. You can see them tomorrow."

The stable door hinges squeaked a third time, followed by a loud gasp and the door slamming shut. Had Sherborne left? If Lady Grayson alone discovered Emily, her presence might be explained away. Lady Grayson, of all people, should know better than to cast judgment.

Eli's hope was short-lived as both Lady Grayson's and Sherborne's heads appeared outside the stall.

"Oh, look at—" Lady Grayson stopped midsentence, her mouth open, even as Sherborne's pressed into a serious line.

Eli glanced behind him as Emily sat up, straw falling away, one hand held to her head. She glanced at her legs, still buried in straw, then up at him, her brow wrinkled with confusion.

"What on earth—Eli?"

Six

"Emily? *Eli?*" Sophia's voice and the earl's echoed over one another in the cavernous stable.

Still feeling dazed, Emily looked to Mr. Linfield for some sort of explanation. Eli, he had asked her to call him, and she had been happy to do so, having tried out his name in her mind dozens of times before.

"Let me help you," he said, reaching a hand down, pulling her from the straw. His other hand went to her arm, steadying her until she caught her balance. "You fainted," he explained.

"And then—"

"What is the meaning of this, Eli? What are you doing here with my fiancée?" Mottled with anger, Lord Rowley's face appeared outside the stall gate.

"Seeing to her horse's well-being, as I've already explained," Mr. Linfield responded with a calm that belied the situation. He released Emily and stepped away. "What are *you* doing here, with Miss Montgomery's sister?"

"Don't take that tone with me." The earl opened the gate and stepped into the stall. "Not when—"

"Sherborne, please." Sophia put a hand on the earl's arm. "We mustn't disturb—oh—ooh." Her hand flew to her mouth, and she backed up, away from Fortune and the palpable effects of birth.

Emily glanced down at her mare, careful to keep her own eyes averted from anything other than her horse's face. The birth had all been so perfect, so completely amazing, until the last. She remembered feeling ill, and then the next thing she knew she'd awoken covered in straw. Perhaps Eli had covered her because he believed she was cold?

"I must admit to severe disappointment, Miss Montgomery." Lord Rowley frowned at her, causing a stir of unease in her middle, not dissimilar to that she'd felt moments ago.

"I believed we had an agreement, and as such, you would not dare to even consider compromising your reputation like this."

Emily opened her mouth to refute his horrible insinuations, but before she could speak, Eli stepped in front of her and hit the earl square in the mouth.

Sophia screamed and jumped back as the earl staggered, then fell at her feet.

Fortune whinnied and nipped at Eli's leg.

"I warned you to never again speak ill of Miss Montgomery." Eli shook out his hand as if it hurt.

The earl has spoken ill of me before? They *have spoken of me?*

"Look at what you've done! Oh, my poor Sherborne." Sophia dropped to his side.

"Your *poor Sherborne?*" Emily's voice shook. Gingerly she made her way around the edge of the stall to stand beside Eli. "What do you mean by this, sister?"

Instead of answering, Sophia reached for the earl, her fingers just brushing his arm as he struggled to his feet. Head forward, as a bull ready to charge, he came at Eli, who swung the gate the opposite direction, directly into the earl's lowered head.

It struck with a clang. The earl cursed savagely. Emily

gasped at such language from him, while Sophia rushed to his side, seemingly only more encouraged to tend him.

Let her have him. Tears smarted in Emily's eyes, and she wasn't certain why. She hadn't loved the earl and had only agreed to his offer to please her father, so why should she care if Sophia had stolen him? *Why should I care that he played me false scarcely a day into our betrothal?* No doubt he would do the same once they were married and living in London and he discovered that she did not care for the parties and goings on he had described.

"I will not marry you," Emily said, finding her voice. She stepped past Eli, out of the stall to face Sherborne. "Whatever it is you think I've been doing is nothing compared to what you and Sophia *were* doing." Emily cast a pained glance at Sophia before returning her attention to the earl. "At the least, it is obvious that you and I do not suit, so I believe it best that the arrangement we came to earlier this evening is now broken."

"You've the gall to accuse me?" Sherborne grabbed her arm when she made to leave. "I suppose you'll marry him, then." Sherborne glared past her at Eli.

"I shall not marry anyone," Emily said. Had their situations been different she felt she might have enjoyed being courted by the kind and gentle Eli, but of course that was not possible. "If you would please remove your hand from my arm, I would like to return to bed."

"You shall not return anywhere until we—"

"Why have I been summoned from my bed at this hour?" The barn door crashed open, and her father's girth filled the empty space. He paused, taking in all of them. "What is the meaning of all this?" His deep voice boomed through the stable, eliciting a rather menacing sound from Fortune.

Emily glanced at her horse and saw Eli exiting the stall, carefully closing the gate behind him.

She faced forward again. Sherborne's hand dropped from her arm as her father strode toward them. He seemed to have eyes only for her, and they narrowed as he approached, his gaze traveling from the top of her tousled head down the length of her dressing gown to her feet peeking out below.

Accusation in his eyes, his head swung sharply toward Sherborne, standing sandwiched between Emily and Sophia.

Emily wasted no time in launching into her explanation. "I couldn't sleep for worrying about Fortune and her baby, so I came to the stable to check on her. I arrived just in time to watch the birth."

"Which explains the straw in your hair and your mussed clothes," Sherborne muttered.

"And how do you explain *your* presence here—with my sister?" Emily's voice rose shrilly.

"Is this true?" Father's gaze, growing more severe by the minute, settled on Sophia.

"We were going to go for a ride, is all," she said.

"And a moonlit swim," Eli added.

Sherborne swung toward him, fist raised. "How dare—"

Eli caught his arm, as if he'd been expecting the move. Looking beyond Sherborne, he said, "I am only repeating what I heard said by you and Lady Grayson."

"Go to the house, Sophia. We will discuss this later. And don't you dare wake your mother. This would gravely upset her." Father raised his face to the ceiling as if in supplication for guidance, or perhaps patience. "Just when we'd believed we finally had your sister's future settled."

"It is *still* settled." Sherborne, having jerked his arm from Eli's grasp, turned and straightened himself before her father, smoothing the front of his coat, as if that somehow corrected all that had gone wrong here. "In spite of the implications against her, I will still marry your daughter—the younger one, that is." His words, while not as slurred as before, were not crisp, and he moved as if half-sprung.

Sophia turned down her lips, and her eyes filled with tears. "You played me false, Sherborne."

"To the house," Father roared, then took Sophia by the arm, pulling her forward and propelling her toward the stable doors.

"You might want to reconsider my sister," Emily said. "Because I will *not* marry *you.*" It was a rare occasion that she stood up to anyone, but the misgivings she'd felt about the earl before had multiplied exponentially in the last quarter of an hour. To her father, she spoke again. "The earl does not care for me, as evidenced by his dalliance with Sophia the very night of our betrothal."

"She approached me," Sherborne cried. "If your daughters were not such light skirts—"

"How dare you!" Father thrust a chubby finger into the earl's chest.

"I most certainly dare," Lord Rowley said, turning upon Emily quite suddenly. "Your daughter, my betrothed, is the one who has made a cake of herself—and me as well—standing before us, clad in her nightclothes, the irrefutable evidence of a midnight tryst in her hair." He snatched a piece of hay from Emily's head and held it up victoriously.

"The one you *were* betrothed to," Emily said. Then to her father, "I'll not marry him."

"Miss Montgomery fainted," Mr. Linfield said, his calm tone still in place. "As most well-bred young ladies would likely do, were they to witness a birth."

"When she arrived, why did you not send her back to her room at once?" Father demanded.

"Because he was trying to help Fortune," Emily said, not about to let Mr. Linfield be blamed for any of this. "He had his arm up inside of her and—"

"Pray do not speak of such things," Sophia cried. Her progress toward the house had stopped short of the stable doors and seemed inclined to stay there, unless further force from their father was applied.

"Which brings us back to Em—Miss Montgomery," Sherborne said. His tone was somehow authoritative now, as if he had assessed the situation and taken charge. "Whether or not her intentions were pure, she has placed herself in a compromising situation this night. No doubt the servant who alerted you is already spreading the tale far and wide. By this time tomorrow half of Shrewsbury—not to mention all the guests still in residence from the ball—will know your daughter is ruined." He paused, as if to allow the horror of such a statement to sink in. "However, I am still willing to marry her in spite of that. The sooner the better, given the circumstances."

Tears in her eyes, Emily folded her arms across her middle and turned away, noting Sophia in much the same position. Emily could not fault Sophia entirely. She was lonely, and it did seem—on the occasions he had visited—that she and the earl had quickly been at ease with one another.

"Emily?" Her father's hand on her shoulder was gentle.

"Yes, Father."

"You have heard Lord Rowley's proposal. What say you to a special license and marrying quickly? It is quite possibly the only way to avoid scandal—or most of it, anyway."

The tears that had been hovering spilled over. "I *cannot* marry him. Not now. Please don't force me to it."

"Given the circumstances, I've little choice." Father came around to stand before her. "He is correct that your reputation is ruined. Only a quick marriage can possibly salvage it now. If not... think of what the gossip will do to your mother."

Emily squeezed her eyes shut, wishing she might wake in

her own bed, and this entire night—from when Lord Rowley first offered for her until now—might be only a nightmare. "What of Sophia? What about *her* reputation?"

"I will deal with Sophia later." Father's gentle voice tensed once more. "Her situation is somewhat less—delicate—than yours, as she was married previously."

So unfair. Sophia *had* done something wrong—or intended to, at least. *Whereas I merely wished to ascertain my horse's well being.*

"Emily?" Father asked once more, sounding less patient than a moment ago.

Only marriage can salvage it... Only marriage...

Lord Rowley stared, awaiting her response while Mr. Linfield watched him, as if wary the earl would lash out again. It was odd how they had gone at one another so quickly. Lord Rowley's earlier words rang through her mind.

I suppose you'll marry him then... A terrible, brilliant idea struck.

"I will marry *him*." She grasped Eli's arm and looked up hopefully. "I will marry Mr. Linfield. Lord Rowley can have Sophia."

Seven

For several, long seconds no one spoke. Eli supposed the Baron and Sherborne were too stunned by Emily's refusal and alternate suggestion to muster words. He felt overcome as well—with disbelief and a tentative, cautious joy at such an unexpected suggestion. He dare not let that show. *Keep your wits about you,* his mother would have said.

Play your cards carefully, his father would have agreed.

Eli intended to, now that Fortune had literally thrust his fondest desire within his grasp. He glanced over the stall at the horse and her colt. The colt was nursing, but Fortune seemed agitated and pinned Eli with a look that spoke of betrayal.

Right. You've just given birth. Some privacy is in order.

"May I suggest we move our discussion outside, or nearer the doors at least. We are disturbing Fortune and her colt, who have both had a very long night."

"Not as long as I've had." Sherborne held a hand to his forehead.

"There is nothing to discuss," the baron said. With a swish of his dressing gown he shifted his girth and strode toward the stable doors.

"But there is, Papa," Sophia exclaimed, stepping in front of him before he could exit. "Emily's idea is splendid. The earl and I can marry, and the Montgomery connection will be in place once more, just as you wanted."

"And you would have your sister wed a groomsman?" The baron's tone indicated something deeper than anger.

Regret, perhaps? Eli did not believe it was resignation—not yet. He brought up the rear of the party, following Sherborne and Emily, whose hand had slid from his arm. They clustered around the baron, awaiting his next move.

It was to Emily that he spoke at last. "You like horses so much, you would marry a man who takes care of them all day, someone far beneath your touch?"

"It isn't about horses, or titles, or anything else," Emily said. "It is about marrying someone who will be kind to me."

"I'm kind," Sherborne exclaimed, the truthfulness of his statement brought into immediate question by the loud belch that followed. Hand to his mouth, he turned away.

Kind of foxed, you mean. Eli kept the thought to himself.

"It's more than that," Emily continued, neither protesting nor agreeing with Sherborne. "We have little in common. You planned to return to London once we were wed, to continue a life filled with parties and social engagements." She paused, turning her attention from Sherborne back to the baron. "You know as well as anyone, Father, how ill-suited I am for such a lifestyle."

"I never said you had to go," Sherborne said. "You can live at my estate here."

"While you gad about London, enjoying free rein with mistresses?" Eli could keep his peace no longer. "Miss Montgomery deserves better than that."

"Exactly," Sherborne spat. "She deserves a fine house to live in and someone who can pass a title down to her son."

"If she marries me, she will have more than a title to pass down." Eli addressed his words to the baron now. "I have a family home near Aylesbury. It is modest, but it is comfortable. In addition, I have a yearly income as well as a savings of the entirety of the wages I have earned over the past decade. Our children will be able to attend Eton, if they wish."

"Your boys, you mean," Sophia said with a pout.

"It will take more than the income of a groomsman to pay for that," Sherborne scoffed.

"It is not my income that would pay for their education, but the same trust, provided by my father, that paid for mine." Eli kept his eyes on the baron's, watching for the slightest change in his granite composure. "I would no longer work as a groomsman if Emily and I marry, but concentrate on maintaining the property left to me. With a little care, I am confident it may shortly produce a profit each year."

"If you're a landowner and you've an education, why have you been working *here*?" Sophia asked.

Eli chose his next words carefully. "I returned to the area out of loyalty to the late earl. It was he who first employed me and provided many opportunities. By working here, I was able to help during the present earl's frequent and extended absences."

"Come now, that isn't the *only* reason you've worked here." Sherborne's eyes narrowed shrewdly. "Tell them how you set your cap for Miss—"

"Loyalty to the earl is *not* the only reason," Eli said, knowing he must speak before Sherborne. "There are friendships here that I value greatly, including yours, Baron Montgomery, along with your family's. I came with the hope of enjoying those a while longer. Never once, however, did I believe I would have the opportunity to marry Miss Montgomery. But now that it has been presented, I would be most honored and pleased to marry her—to marry you," he amended, turning to face Emily, who had not spoken to him once since her suggestion.

"Of course you'd be pleased," Sherborne said. "Her dowry would be a fortune to someone like you."

"There will be no dowry if you marry Mr. Linfield," the baron said to Emily. Then to Sherborne, "And don't think you'll be getting one with Sophia either. She's had hers already." He leveled a heavy gaze on Sherborne, then Eli, then back again. "Neither of you are getting one cent. What you can have is a taste of what I've dealt with all these years, in a household of females."

"That does not change my position on the matter," Eli said. What did he want with money when he might have Emily?

The baron sighed, almost as if he had expected such an answer. "As much as I like you, Mr. Linfield, I cannot condone your lower social standing. As the daughter of a baron, Emily has certain expectations regarding marriage."

"I expected to be happy about it," Emily said. "To feel as if the one I was marrying was my friend."

Sherborne stepped forward. "I'm your—"

"A friend does not do what you were about tonight." Emily fixed Sherborne with a look Eli had never seen from her before. Though her voice remained calm, it was apparent she felt anything but.

"If Miss Montgomery and I marry, it would not be for hope of any dowry," Eli reiterated. "I have no expectation of financial support of any kind. I would ask only that you attend our wedding. Beyond that, your correspondence with her will be entirely at your—and her—disposal. You would always be welcome to visit at our home, and I would hope that your daughter would always be welcome in yours. It would be understandable if I am not, but I would certainly never prohibit her from visiting."

"Well said, Mr. Linfield." Sophia clapped her hands. "It's

a perfectly marvelous solution, Papa. Both of your daughters will be wed and past your concern within a fortnight."

"That would require a special license," Sherborne reminded her. "Those are expensive."

The baron shook his head. "And the alternative—posting banns, announcing that our daughter is to marry a groomsman—would kill your mother. She'd never be able to go out again."

Her choice, Eli thought with little sympathy. But he would do anything he could to make this happen. It was an opportunity he'd never thought to have, and he wasn't about to let Emily slip through his fingers.

"I will pay for the license. I'll go the day after tomorrow, after I'm assured Fortune and her colt are both well. It would not be a very fitting wedding gift to my wife to allow her horse to fall ill." He looked down at Emily, still pale, her eyes wide and stricken by the night's events.

"*You* cannot obtain a special license," Sherborne said. "Even had you the £5. Only a member of the peerage is able to meet with the Archbishop."

"Let me worry about that," Eli said. Then ignoring the others, he took Emily's hand and led her a short distance away.

"Is this truly what you want?" he asked.

"Yes," she whispered, not meeting his gaze. "I wanted to remain at home, unwed, but if I now must marry…" Her voice trailed off just as her tears began to fall. "I'm so sorry." She looked up at him. "It was selfish of me to drag you into this. You don't have to do this. I'm—"

"Don't be sorry." Eli brought her hand to his lips and placed a gentle kiss over the finger that would soon wear his ring. "Don't be sorry," he whispered again. "I'm not."

Eight

Eli raised his hand and, for the first time ever, lifted one of the brass door knockers on Baron Montgomery's front double doors. Three times he let it fall, the heavy metal thuds coinciding with the hammering of his heart.

Lowering his hand, Eli glanced down, checking his attire once more—clean, white muslin shirt, smartly tied cravat, trousers that were not buckskin, a newer pair of suspenders, and a borrowed waist coat. He had no jacket, or one he wished to wear anyway, in this heat. *Comfort over propriety.* His boots were scuffed, but also clean, having taken him a good hour to get that way, sitting on an overturned bucket in the stable and scrubbing with the stiffest brush he could find. His responsibilities were not kind to his footwear.

No doubt the Lady Montgomery—if she saw him today—would take notice of that and his simple clothing. He would remedy his shortcomings there before the wedding but had no time for that now. He intended to be off this morning to obtain a license to marry. While he was confident that the Archbishop would meet with him, locating the man could take days.

After what seemed an inordinate amount of time, the door was opened by the baron's capable butler, Benson. Eli had taken dinner with him a time or two below stairs and also at the local pub.

"Good day, Benson." Eli paused, discomfited by the unusual circumstance before him. Servants did not call at their employer's front door—ever. *Nor do they marry their employer's daughter.* He ignored the disapproval in Benson's knowing eyes and downturned mouth, and plunged ahead. "Is Miss Montgomery at home? I am here to see her briefly about a matter of importance."

Benson said nothing but stepped back into the foyer, pulling one of the massive doors with him so that Eli might follow.

"Wait here." Benson left Eli to take in the foyer with its circular staircase, immense portraits, polished floors, and vases of fresh flowers.

I cannot give Emily anything this grand. Eli studied the painting closest to him, a Montgomery ancestor looking down upon him with a severe expression. Instead of feeling disturbed or discouraged by the wealth surrounding him, Eli felt a thrill of excitement at the challenge ahead. He could not give Emily any*thing* this fine, but he could give her much more of importance and show her how freeing and grand life could truly be.

"Mr. Linfield." The female voice did not belong to Emily, but her mother, who had always been polite, if not quite cordial, to him before.

"Lady Montgomery." Eli gave a slight bow.

"Emily is presently being fitted for her wedding gown. Is there something I can help you with?"

Lady Montgomery spoke almost as if Emily was to be married to someone other than himself.

"I came to inquire of her the date and time she wishes to wed. I intend to stop at the church on my way to obtain the license."

Lady Montogmery's lips pressed into a thin line. "You intend to go through with this, then?"

Eli nodded. "Unless or until the time your daughter tells me she does not wish to."

"If you care for Emily at all—and it appears you must somewhat, as my husband has made it clear there will be no financial gain for you, should you marry—then it would seem in her best interest for you to bow out and leave her to restore her engagement to the Earl of Shrewsbury."

"I do not wish to restore that engagement, Mother." Emily descended from the top stair, her pale pink gown trailing behind.

Eli had hardly ever seen her dressed in anything other than a riding habit, and this morning found she took his breath away, with her curls bouncing and the feminine drape of her gown.

Her mother moved toward the stairway, as if to intercept Emily before she could reach her destination. "We have discussed—"

"—Even if Mr. Linfield has come to tell me he has changed his mind, I will not marry the earl." Emily sidestepped her mother, then slowed her steps until she stood before Eli. "*Have* you come to withdraw your offer?"

He smiled. "I believe you were the one who offered for me, but no. I have not changed my mind about accepting."

As Eli wondered at his audacity to tease her, the color in her cheeks rose, surpassing the pink of her gown while still complimenting it nicely.

"Have *you* second thoughts, Miss Montgomery?"

She shook her head and met his gaze only briefly.

"In that case, there are a few matters of business we must attend to. I shall be leaving today to obtain our license to marry. Is Saturday next at ten o'clock in the morning agreeable to you?"

"Saturday next," Lady Montgomery exclaimed. "It is preposterous to think of planning a wedding so quickly."

"Make that two weddings, Mother." Lady Grayson entered the room from a side door. "Sherborne has already left to obtain our license. We are to be married on Friday." She sashayed past her mother and gave Emily a quick hug. "Isn't it splendid, sister?"

Emily nodded but did not say anything.

"I've also brought a bit of string—" Eli felt his own face warm as they stared at him. He wished he was out of this house, away from so many females, or away from two of them, at least. Emily did not seem like her mother and sister. "—to measure your finger for a ring. May I?"

Emily hesitated, glanced at her mother and received a disapproving frown, then held her hand out to him anyway. With great care he wound the string once around the third finger of her left hand, holding the measured piece between his thumb and forefinger when done. Emily lowered her hand, and he pulled out a knife and cut the string where he held it, then tucked the piece carefully into his pocket.

Too late he realized this was probably not how this process was done. Lady Montgomery's eyes had gone wide, and her mouth pinched so severely Eli wondered if perhaps it might become stuck that way. Lady Grayson hid her face behind her hand, in a poor attempt at hiding a fit of giggles.

"Thank you," Emily said. "That was very thoughtful. I had not expected a ring."

No doubt she did not expect much at all of their marriage, save for a way to escape the gossips, the earl, and her father's wrath. Eli could not fault her for this. This union was the fulfilling of *his* wildest dream, not hers. But he could not let himself worry that he would disappoint either Emily or her parents. He had a few surprises—for all of them.

"Until Saturday next." He bowed slightly, first at Emily and then her mother and sister.

"Thank you," Emily said once more. Their gazes touched briefly before he turned away, and the look of vulnerability in hers was such that he wished he could whisk her away this very moment, or at the least convince her that all would be well.

Emily Montgomery and the baron and his family would not be the source of fevered gossip in the months to come. Or, if they were, it would be with a sense of wonder at the baron's cleverness in marrying his youngest daughter off as he had. It was with great difficulty that Eli held his tongue.

Nine

"Are you still terribly angry with me, Em?" Sophia adjusted the circlet of flowers on Emily's head. "You've hardly spoken a word to me the past two weeks."

"Not angry, but I am hurt—that you would so completely disregard my feelings in your quest to steal the earl from me."

"One cannot steal from someone who does not have." Sophia rose up on her tiptoes, adjusting the fragrant petals this way and that. "You, my dear sister, never had Lord Rowley—at least, not in the way that matters."

Emily sighed and looked at both their reflections in the long mirror. She ought to be further hurt by such a statement, but there was truth in it, and she could not feel bad about her loss. The earl had not loved her and she had not loved him. Likely, Sophia had just saved them both from a lifetime of misery.

Sophia met her eye in the glass. She nodded slowly. "I see you have come to the same conclusion."

"If only you had asked me if you might have him," Emily said. "I would have given him willingly. What hurts is that you went about it behind my back. And now look what has become of me."

"What has become of you!" Sophia exclaimed. Grasping

Emily's shoulders, she turned her around so they were facing one another. "You are about to be married to a man who adores you, who will worship the ground you tread upon all your days. He will make you happy, Em. Just wait and see."

"But Father and Mother are both so terribly *un*happy with my choice."

"Bah." Sophia swatted the air. "Who cares what they think. We are grown women now and must make our own decisions."

It was a terribly forward way of thinking, but then Sophia had always been terribly forward. Emily admired that about her, wished for at least some of that bravery herself. Perhaps she had found the one shred she possessed, that night in the stables when she had declared she would wed Mr. Linfield.

"Do you love Lord Rowley, then, and does he love you?" Emily asked. Though she'd not voiced her concerns, she was fearful for Sophia. The earl had not procured the license as promised. Yesterday, the day they were to wed, had come and gone, with no sign of him.

"I don't know that love is the way of things between us as yet, but I've no doubt it will come." Sophia did not sound concerned in the least. "We have a jolly good time together. He makes me laugh, and I amuse him, and that is far more than I had with my first husband."

"Do you think—will he return with your license today, or will banns be posted?"

"I received word late last night that he was home." Sophia's dreamy sigh turned to one of resignation. "He will have the license now. I had to give him the money for it. Alas, he is somewhat cleaned out at present." She smiled suddenly. "But not for long. My inheritance was generous, and I am happy to share it with him."

"It will be more than sharing, if you wed," Emily said soberly. "It will be his."

Sophia shrugged, then smiled coyly—a gesture Emily knew all too well.

"What are you up to, sister?"

"Up to?" Sophia's brows rose as if surprised, while her wide eyes and parted lips portrayed a near-convincing look of innocence.

Emily wondered how long it would be before the earl could decipher such looks. "Well?"

"*I* am up to nothing," Sophia insisted. "My fortune, however, has recently been up and away, disbursed in various locations, so that the earl's acquisitions upon our marriage are not the entirety of my monies. I am well aware of his gambling habits, and until I've cured him of them—have provided other amusements to occupy his time and attention and am assured they will continue to do so—he shall have no idea of the true wealth he has married into."

Emily frowned. "That sounds a dangerous game. Men are so particular about money."

"Most men, you mean." Sophia turned away with a swish of skirts. "Your Mr. Linfield does not seem to value it overmuch. I thought I should die of laughter at Mother's look of horror when we saw him hold your bare hand and wrap that bit of string around your finger."

"How else was he to measure for a ring?" Emily asked, indignant on Eli's behalf. She had found it a sweet gesture. "That he thought of a ring at all, after the money he had to spend for the license..." Her voice trailed off as the secret worry she'd harbored the past week returned. In spite of Eli's promise that he could provide for her, she felt misgivings, knowing nothing of where or how they would live.

"Do not be surprised or dismayed if the one he gives you today is little better than the string—pinchbeck at best." Sophia paused in front of the dressing table to check her reflection. "He does love you, Em. I can see it in his eyes. But all love comes at a cost. Yours is giving up this." She swept her hand across the room, indicating the grandeur they had grown up in.

"You might have thought of that before your dalliance." Emily twisted her hands in agitation.

"Don't muss your gown." Sophia pulled Emily's hands away from the layers of satin stitching. "You do realize I did not intend to involve *you* in my affairs that night—other than to free you from a betrothal you didn't want in the first place?" Sophia held up a hand when Emily would have spoken. "When I passed by your door earlier that night I heard you, crying your heart out. And don't tell me it was with concern for your horse. You were weeping with dread over your impending marriage to the earl. I set out to free us both from situations we did not wish. That you happened to be at the stable was your own doing."

"You *meant* to be found out," Emily said, only now realizing the depth of her sister's deception and planning.

"I did." Sophia raised her chin, showing absolutely no regret. "I told my maid when to check the stable and when to fetch Father, so he would discover us. Only he discovered more than I had bargained for."

It was Emily's turn to sigh. Because of that night she was about to pledge herself to a man for the rest of her life. She would be leaving everything and everyone she knew. *Except Eli.* That thought was both terrifying and hopeful.

Sophia grabbed her hand and pulled her toward the door. "It is time, sister. Do not make your bridegroom wait."

Emily allowed herself to be pulled from the room. The time for regrets or second guessing was over.

Ten

The groom would not look at her. Emily walked up the aisle on her father's arm, conscious of the stares from those few persons seated in the pews on either side, but even more conscious of the fact that her intended stood stiffly at the front of the chapel—facing away from her.

She'd attended enough weddings in the past to recognize that this was not a good sign. At her friends' weddings, the bridegrooms had always stood facing the back of the church, or at least sideways, where they might turn their heads to see the bride approaching.

Perhaps Mr. Linfield has never attended a wedding. Perhaps he does not realize...

If so, this would be only the first of many social faux pas he was likely to commit. Her mother had feared it would be so and had tried time and again to dissuade Emily from her decision. But Emily would not budge. Her reputation in tatters, she must do what she could to salvage it. She didn't care how many mistakes Mr. Linfield made or if he embarrassed them all. He was kind and would be true to her, and at this point that was all she might hope for from marriage.

As they reached the front of the church and Mr. Linfield's side, Emily slid her hand from her father's arm. She leaned forward to kiss his cheek and glimpsed the sorrow in his eyes. He had not wanted her to marry this man, under these—or any other—circumstances. But he had not forced her to wed the earl, and for that she felt grateful.

With a pang of regret that she had disappointed her father again and that this could not be a happier day for him, Emily took her place beside Mr. Linfield. A hush fell over the already near-silent gathering.

"Dearly beloved—"

Mr. Linfield's arm brushed against hers. A second later his hand followed, moving around a bit until his pinky finger laced with hers. Emily's heart pounded, and she felt her face heat. *Such intimacy!* And in front of her mother. Emily didn't need to be told this was scandalous. But she found comfort and courage from his touch, convinced now that he had not been unwilling to look at her, simply that he had not known to do so. Just as he did not realize it was not proper to be touching during the ceremony for all to see.

"We have come together in the presence of God to witness and bless the joining together of this man and this woman in Holy Matrimony."

Her mother sniffled loudly, making it difficult for Emily to concentrate on the words being spoken. Or perhaps it was the sensations going from her finger to her hand, up her arm, to her pounding heart. Save for a few dances during her coming-out season and at last month's ball, and those occasions she had been helped in and out of a carriage or upon a horse, no man had ever touched her. She'd never stood so close to one, either, with her arm brushing against Mr. Linfield's as it was.

"The union of husband and wife in heart, body, and mind is intended by God for their mutual joy—"

Joy—or a chance at something like it. That was why she

was doing this. Over the years she and Mr. Linfield had become friends. They'd never had opportunity to develop that friendship, but Emily believed they could. *Far more than the earl and I ever could have.* It was not a romantic notion so much as a practical one. If nothing else, she knew that their mutual love of horses afforded them some commonality.

"—for the help and comfort given one another in prosperity and adversity."

Her mother's sniffles grew louder, and Emily felt a pinch of unease. *It does not matter if we are prosperous or not. It does not matter...*

At the priest's cue, she turned to face Mr. Linfield. Her eyes traveled from the shoulder

of his crisp, new tailcoat to his pale, *beardless* face—a face she had not seen without hair for many, many years, not since they were scarcely older than children.

Eli? Her lips parted, but no words came. A sort of strangled cry sounded from the pews behind them, but Emily had no concern for whomever might be upset. She felt overcome herself, staring up at the stranger before her, a handsome man with a strong jaw and a dimple on one side when he smiled.

Emily's gaze left his upturned mouth as she sought his eyes. Relief flooded her as she recognized the familiar, warm brown tones. Eli's smile had reached them as well.

The priest finished speaking, his voice rising in question. Emily had no idea what he'd just said but, when he looked at her, remembered enough to answer, "I will."

He turned promptly and began speaking to Eli. "Eli Alexander Linfield Ro—"

An outright cry came from the congregation, and Emily took her eyes off Eli long enough to shoot her mother a dark look. But it wasn't her mother who appeared to be protesting, but her father, who had risen from his seat, face purple, eyes popping, mouth open as if he was about to interrupt.

"How is this—" Her father's strangled mutterings competed with the priest's calm, methodical words.

"—love her, comfort her, honor and keep her, in sickness and in health; and, forsaking all others, be faithful to her as long as you both shall live?"

Emily looked at Eli again and just in time.

Still smiling, he spoke his promise loud and clear. "I will."

Perhaps this at last resigned her father to their marriage, for he sat down hard, the pew creaking beneath his weight. But the others in attendance were far from quiet.

Urgent whispers between the earl and Sophia flew back and forth. Emily didn't bother attempting to reprimand her sister. Sophia had always had a mind and will of her own and never hesitated to kick up a lark wherever she went. Perhaps she and the earl, taken with one another as they were, could not keep their peace even a half hour.

Emily felt slightly infatuated herself, unable to cease staring at Mr. Linfield. *Eli.* He made a striking figure in his new dark coat and trousers. She had never seen Eli in anything but work clothes before. *And his face—*she'd been attracted to his kindness, but the face he'd been hiding behind his beard truly surprised her. One might have called it aristocratic, had they not known he was of the working class. Being so, he was not above smiling and looking extraordinarily, unabashedly happy.

She couldn't stop the fluttery feeling erupting inside of her, an unexpected hope that this was all going to turn out so much better than she had dared imagine.

At the priest's cue, Eli took her right hand in his and began to speak once more.

"I, Eli Alexander Linfield Rowley, take thee—"

Rowley? Emily's eyes snapped from their joined hands to his face. Surely she'd misheard.

"—Emily Montgomery, to be my wedded wife, to have and to hold from this day forward, for better for worse, for richer for poorer, in sickness and in health, to love and to cherish, till death us do part, according to God's holy ordinance; and thereto I plight thee my troth."

Her head was spinning. As if he realized this, Eli tightened his hand around hers.

"I, Emily Montgomery, take thee, Eli Alexander Linfield—"

"Rowley," he whispered.

"Absurd! Cease at once." The earl's angry voice carried to the front. Everyone turned to look at him, including the priest.

Sophia held onto one of his arms, trying, to no avail, to pull him back down again.

"This marriage will not be legal. He is using a false name." The earl attempted to push past Sophia, but she stood, blocking his way.

"Sit down at once, or I will leave this place—and you."

The priest exchanged a knowing look with Eli, as if they had both expected this. "I assure you, *all* is in order. Now please, allow us to continue."

The priest's gentle words, combined with Sophia's threat, must have reached Lord Rowley, as he sat down hard, much as Father had a few moments before.

Voice shaking and head still spinning, Emily finished her vows. *Rowley—how? What else don't I know? He is a stranger.*

The ring came next, and when she thought she could handle no more surprises, Mr. Linfield—*Mr. Rowley—Eli—* slipped the most exquisite ring she'd ever seen on her finger.

Emily gave an audible gasp. This was no pinchbeck but a brilliant gold band with a rose-cut diamond at the center, positioned between two smaller rubies. She lifted her astonished gaze to his.

He merely smiled and kept her hand, stepping closer as he spoke. "With this ring I thee wed; with my body I thee worship." His thumb moved in slow circles over the back of her hand. "All my worldly goods I thee endow."

She glanced at the beautiful ring once more and felt her earlier concerns slip away.

Eli kissed the back of her hand over the ring, allowing his lips to linger, then tucked her hand through his arm as they turned to face the priest.

Silence reigned at last, along with the most curious feelings Emily had ever known. She felt her heart might burst and was not surprised when the tears flooding her eyes began to spill from them. She glanced up at Eli and smiled to let him know she was all right. *Better than all right.* In that moment she was happy.

Eleven

Lady Montgomery was sniffling again, though Eli felt it might be for different reasons than she had at the beginning of the ceremony. His bride was crying, too, silent tears sliding down her cheeks, but she had smiled at him, as if to assure him all was well. It was, but he suspected she was only just realizing that herself. She'd married him with no guarantee—other than his word—that she would be provided for.

He loved Emily for it all the more and felt grateful that, today at least, he'd been able to spoil her with his mother's ring. There wouldn't be many times in their future when he could lavish his wife with jewels, but she would always have a wedding ring she could be proud of.

The priest finished his prayer over them and pronounced them husband and wife. Emily looked at him long enough to offer a shy smile. It was all Eli could do not to pick her up and carry her out of the church and into his new carriage. But first, there were the marriage lines to be entered into the parish register.

With some reluctance he stepped aside, allowing her hand to slide from his arm so she might pen the necessary signature. He added his beside and felt another surge of joy at seeing their names together. He had really married Emily Montgomery. He felt as if his life was beginning this very moment. All that had come before had been in preparation, and now he could truly begin to live.

"Shall we receive our congratulations?" he whispered, bracing himself for what was to come and offering his arm once more.

"If we must." She, too, sounded as if she would have been happy to escape to his carriage.

Her response elicited a chuckle. "I do so enjoy your company, Mrs. Rowley," he admitted. "And you are so beautiful—the most beautiful bride I have ever seen."

"Have you seen many?" Her brows drew together quizzically.

"No," he admitted with a short bark of laughter, which he tried to disguise as a cough. "I haven't seen any brides before. Nonetheless, you are beautiful. Today and always you will shine everyone else down—regardless of the number of weddings we attend."

With her hand on his arm, he turned her toward the witnesses and well-wishers—and Sherborne's fist, which only narrowly missed his face and only then because Lady Grayson lunged forward and grabbed his arm at the last second.

Emily and her mother screamed. The baron swore and moved his large frame up the aisle faster than Eli would have believed possible, putting himself between his daughters and Sherborne, knocking the latter to the ground as he did.

"What is the meaning of this?" the baron demanded, reminding Eli of that fateful night in the stables.

"Why don't you ask him?" Sherborne pointed a finger at Eli as he rose. "What do you mean by using my name, and looking like—" He stared hard at Eli. "And that ring—"

Sherborne's gaze shifted to Emily's hand. "It was my grandmother's. If you don't believe me, come look in the portrait hall at Collingwood."

The baron shifted his focus from Sherborne to Eli. "You've definitely some explaining to do. Thought I was seeing a ghost when you turned around. No doubt you're a Rowley, but how?"

Eli wrapped a protective arm around Emily and pulled her farther away, well out of Sherborne's reach. "The same way the earl is. The ring belonged to *our* grandmother. Years ago she gave it to our father, who gave it to his wife, my mother, on their wedding day."

The wedding breakfast was to have been a simple affair, held at the house and for the family only, as there was no joy in their daughter's hasty marriage to a common man. But the table remained empty, the food long since cold, before Emily or anyone else was able to enjoy it.

Unexpected circumstances being what they were, Father was in no mood to eat—a rarity—and had instead ordered his new son-in-law and Lord Rowley into his study when they arrived. For the past three quarters of an hour they had been in there, arguing heatedly, given the volume of their voices carrying through to the other side of the door where Sophia stood, her ear pressed to the wood.

Every few minutes she would tiptoe across the foyer to the sitting room and relay to Emily and their mother exactly what was being said. Thus far she had discerned that the main argument centered around how Emily was to be addressed from now on. Their father said that, as she had married an earl after all, she must be reintroduced to society as Lady Rowley. Likewise Eli, as well, should be presented as the heir he was.

Eli, however, disagreed rather vehemently with her father, and he, along with the earl—no longer entitled to be called such—did not wish anything to be different than it had been before this morning. But now that the proper documents, evidence of Lord Rowley's first marriage, had been produced there were bound to be repercussions.

Sophia was at the door again now, looking both resplendent in her pale-green gown and delighted with whatever she was hearing.

Emily watched her sister through the open sitting room doors. *She has always been one for drama and excitement.* This morning they had both in spades.

Sophia left her post and practically skipped back to them. "The earl—*my* earl," she clarified, "has just said that he will see your earl in court before he forfeits his title or property. Your earl—" Sophia looked at Emily, "—said he has no interest in either the title or property. He said he would never have revealed himself as Lord Rowley's son, had there not been need for it in order to meet with the Archbishop to get the license to marry you."

"His face alone revealed his parentage," Mother said. "When he turned at the church, so that we saw his profile—it was as if we were seeing Lord Rowley some twenty years ago. Such a shock to your poor father."

"Poor father?" Sophia said. "And what of Sherborne? How do you think he felt?"

"Rather terrible," Emily said, actually feeling sorry for him. How devastating it must be to know that everything one had, from his title to his property, might be swept away.

"I don't see what all the fuss is about." Their mother stood and looked out the window, checking, as she had repeatedly since their return, to see that no one was coming up the drive to witness the catastrophe that was her daughter's wedding day. "Emily's husband was never acknowledged as legitimate, so it matters not who his father was or that he was born first."

"It should always matter who one's father is—titled or not," Emily said. Her emotions were still jumbled, and likely would be for some time, but the thought of what Eli had been through these many years was enough to elicit a well of compassion that swelled her heart toward him even more.

"It did not matter enough, nor, apparently, did your husband's mother to Lord Rowley. By the time her baby arrived, he had wed another."

"That's just it, Mother!" Sophia jumped onto the sofa, landed on her knees, and clutched a pillow to her chest. "The new earl insists—"

"—*Sophia,*" Mother exclaimed in a harsh whisper. "For heaven's sake act your age and like a lady. Jumping on the furniture..." She brought a hand to her head as if it pained her.

"Ladies my age are boring." Sophia leaned forward, apparently eager to share what she had overheard. "Emily's husband insists that his father *never* divorced his mother. So it is Sherborne who is illegitimate."

Mother's mouth opened and closed repeatedly for several seconds, bringing to mind a guppy.

"If that is true," she said at last. "This is an even worse scandal. I cannot see why you, of all people, Sophia, should be excited by this. After all, you were set to marry the man."

"We shall still marry, regardless, Mother. We are happy together. I have had my titled husband and paid for it dearly with several years of loneliness and boredom."

"Marriage is not about happiness," Mother snapped.

"For Emily and I, it is—or so I hope it to be." Eli stood in the doorway, looking somewhat disheveled, his tailcoat long since abandoned, his waistcoat unbuttoned, shirt partly untucked, and his cravat loosened to a slouchy mess about his neck.

Emily wondered how he felt about all these fancy clothes. While he looked exceptionally fine in them, she sensed his discomfort—with the clothing and all else that came with the life of an earl. She felt no desire to force it upon him.

Emily's mother crossed the room to stand before Eli. "Tell me of your mother."

"Her name was Margaret Linfield." A sad, fleeting smile curved his lips. "She died when I was eleven. I loved her very much. Ours was a happy home."

Simple statements, yet Emily felt a depth in them that had been lacking in her own upbringing. She knew her parents loved her, of course, but there were expectations tied to that love—expectations that, since her failure of a season years earlier, she had not met.

"But *who* was she," Mother persisted. "Who were her parents?"

Eli smiled. "My grandfather was the gardener at Claymere."

"This changes nothing, then," Mother exclaimed. "Your father did what Emily has just done and married far below his station."

"My father married for love," Eli said. "He just did not have the courage to stay for it.

But you are correct; this changes nothing." Eli looked past her mother to catch Emily's gaze. "I am still Eli Linfield—a common man, my *own* man. I prefer it that way—independent of any title or inheritance for either my well-being, sustenance, *or* happiness."

"Oh, well said, well said." Sophia rose to her knees once more on the sofa and clapped enthusiastically. "If you had not married him already, Emily, I might have."

Emily cast her sister a dark look of warning. Sophia had stolen the earl from her, but she could not have Eli.

Sophia laughed. "Not to worry, sister. I shall let you keep this one. I can see that you want him."

"Enough!" Mother whirled from Eli and marched toward Sophia. "You are the one who sounds as if she was raised a heathen. Have you no mind for what is proper conversation?"

"I have had my fill of proper, Mother. Let me be." Sophia jumped up from the couch and headed toward the door, pausing to give Emily a hug. "Be happy," she whispered. "You don't know how lucky you are."

Twelve

Eli dismissed the footman with a brief nod, then held his own hand out for Emily to clasp as she climbed into the carriage. He cared not that it was considered uncouth. *Why allow another to take my wife's hand, when I might assist her myself?* He climbed into the carriage behind her, and the step was put up shortly and the door closed.

Holding in a sigh of relief as they started down the drive, Eli glanced at his bride, seated across from him, and searched for any signs of anxiety or sorrow as she left her home to journey to his.

He noted no tears, and her hands lay placidly in her lap. *Not too nervous, then.* That was good. He'd enough nerves for both of them. It had been one thing to speak his mind to the baron, but it was another entirely to figure out how to please his new wife. Fortune and her colt could not travel yet, so she would miss her horse, at least. He hoped the pair he had purchased would do decently for riding until such time as she and Fortune might be reacquainted.

"Penny for your thoughts," he said when another minute had passed in which neither had spoken.

"I am indeed thinking of pennies—and pounds. I was wondering how much this fine carriage has set you back, on top of the license, your clothing—and all other expenses you've incurred on my behalf in the past two weeks."

"Ah… Money worries already." Eli settled into the seat more comfortably, stretching his legs out to the side of hers. "The carriage is used, and I obtained it at a fair price. You should know I'm a shrewd bargainer." He winked. "I considered borrowing or renting one, but I wish you to be able to return home to visit your family whenever you like."

"That is very thoughtful of you."

"I am nothing, if not thoughtful." Eli grinned. "On top of being shrewd, that is."

"Humble too, I see." Emily returned his smile.

"What else are you wondering about?" Eli asked, grateful for her teasing that had lessened the awkwardness between them. Conversing with Emily had always been easy, and he did not wish that to change now. Though their previous encounters had been brief, and he had kept strictly to the rules, regarding her as his employer, she had often chatted with him as he readied her horse, inquiring about the animals he cared for and even about himself at times.

"I am curious who my new husband really is," she confessed. "Since the moment you turned to face me in the church, I have wondered where the gentle, bearded giant who cares for our horses has gone. I believed I was marrying Eli Linfield, head groomsman, and instead I am discovering you are much more."

"Having a title makes me more?" he asked warily. *Gentle, bearded giant?*

She shook her head. "That is not what I meant. You have been without home or family since you were *eleven*. You've lost both parents and had to fend for yourself from a young age. Your father would not acknowledge you—in society, anyway. You—"

"Wait." Eli held up a hand. "Let me address those points you have made already, before you bring up any more."

"Of course." Emily looked away, as if abashed.

He nudged her foot with his own. "There is nothing you cannot ask me. It is all right to be curious. You need not feel embarrassed about anything. We are husband and wife."

This speech brought a return of the pink he so loved to her cheeks.

To set her at ease, Eli began the story of his parents' courtship, as told him by his mother. It had seemed a fairytale to him as a boy, the story of two children growing up together in the splendid gardens of Claymere. They had run and played and laughed, and, as they grew older, read and talked and walked together on the vast estate. Then one day something both frightening and magical had happened. The boy had kissed the girl and asked her to wait for him while he was several years away at school.

She did, never marrying another, never even allowing herself to be courted by any of the boys in the village, though she was very beautiful. They wrote letters secretly. His family would not approve.

Her father grew ill and died unexpectedly.

"And when he received her letter telling of the tragedy, *my* father came home as quickly as he could," Eli said, wistful at this part of the story as he always was, regretting that he had never had the opportunity to know his grandfather.

"Did she find your father much changed?" Emily asked. Her blushes had long since passed, her attention rapt throughout his tale.

"Not as much as one might believe," Eli said. "He was similar to you—having lived in the world of the spoiled without becoming spoiled himself."

"He still loved her?" Emily seemed almost breathless as she asked the question.

"Yes." Eli imagined his father had felt very much like he did at this moment, looking at Emily, knowing she was truly his—in name, at least. Now he must win her heart. "My father was to stay at Claymere for the summer, learning to manage affairs there. Though the gardens and grounds are magnificent, the manor is considerably smaller than Collingwood. His parents would never have allowed him to be there, had they any inkling that what they had perceived to be the infatuation of his childhood was actually the love of his life.

"The weekend after the funeral, he and my mother eloped to Gretna Green. They returned home married, no one the wiser. She continued to live in the gardener's cottage. He stayed at the manor, but they spent time together every day, and he came to the cottage as often as he might."

"How long was it before they were found out?" Emily, on the edge of her seat now, leaned forward eagerly.

Eli wondered how many months it might be before she leaned toward him like that for another reason, or if she might ever look at him as she was, anticipating a kiss instead of a story.

"Both my mother and father told me it was a wonderful, glorious summer—the happiest of their lives."

"Just one summer? How sad." Emily fell back against her seat.

"It is," Eli agreed. Feeling bold, he moved to her side of the carriage and sat beside her. "I want our story to be different."

"It is already," Emily said. "We did not share our childhood as your parents did."

"Perhaps not," Eli said. "But I remember watching for and then waving to you daily, for many months, summer after summer, a girl in blue out riding her father's property. You may not have realized it, but seeing you was often the best part of my day."

"I *so* wanted to ride over to meet the boy who always greeted me." Emily smiled warmly. "I was afraid to disobey my father and leave our property, but I wish now that I had. We might have made acquaintance so much earlier."

"A wish for what is past is no good," Eli said. "A wish for the future is what matters."

"Let us make one, then," Emily suggested.

"All right. What shall we wish for?" He angled his body on the seat so that he was facing her.

"We should wish for *many* wonderful, glorious summers."

"And winters, too," Eli added.

"Autumns and springs as well. Those are some of my favorite times of year."

"Mine too," he said. "How about simply wishing for years—a great many of them, spent together happily."

"Yes." She gave a resolute nod. "That is a good wish."

"Then it shall be ours, and much more than a wish. It will be the beginning of a beautiful life together." He pounded on the roof.

The carriage began to slow almost at once, and when it had stopped completely, Eli rose from his seat and opened the door. Without waiting for the step he jumped down and held his hands out for Emily.

She leaned forward and he caught her around the waist, lowering her carefully to the ground.

"Still a gentle giant, I see." She smiled up at him.

"You make me sound like some monstrosity." He stuck his lip out, pretending hurt.

"Not at all." Emily leaned back, over exaggerating her need to tilt her head to look up at him. "It is just that for as long as I can remember you have been so much taller than me. You were always able to help me up on a horse with little effort, yet you never boasted of your strength as some of the other stable hands did."

"Because my strength is naught compared to your beauty." He took her hand and pulled her from the road, into the field beyond, searching until he found what he was looking for. Bending low, he snapped a dandelion from the ground and held it between them. "We can make our wish with this."

Emily looked up at him through her eyelashes, a speculative expression in her gaze. "Mr. Linfield, how do *you* know about wishing on dandelions?"

"I may have seen a certain young lady do it once or twice before."

"Did you used to spy on me?" Emily's free hand went to her hip.

"I wouldn't call it spying, but more watching out for your safety every now and again. I was never close enough to hear anything you said. I haven't any idea whom those wishes were for. Though I do admit to being curious. It is believed, is it not, that if all the seeds blow away your love returns your affection."

"I suppose." Emily shrugged and tried to turn away, but Eli held her hand fast.

"Who was it?" he asked. "Sherborne? Or the vicar's son? I remember when he used to come around to see you."

"Neither," she said. "Shall we make our wish?"

"Are you attempting to change the subject in the middle of a serious discussion?"

"Serious?" She laughed. "There is nothing serious about wishing on a dandelion. It is the stuff of myths and fairytales."

"If it is not real, then you should tell me whose affection you were seeking with all those wishes."

"All?" She gasped. "You said you saw me once or twice. This is getting worse by the minute. Why, you're no better than Sophia. I've married a spy."

"If you won't tell me I may die of curiosity, and then this wish for years of happiness will be in vain."

Emily rolled her eyes. "You'd laugh."

He pouted, but she shook her head, refusing to give in. Eli let the subject go for now, but intended to ask later, some future day when they knew each other much better.

Facing one another they held the dandelion between them and spoke their wish at the same time. Then they each blew, successfully sending all the seeds flying—into each other's faces.

"Oh!" Emily exclaimed just before she began sneezing.

Eli dared not laugh at her; he was fairly certain one of the seeds had gone up into his nose.

"Come here," he said, when she was finally still after four sneezes in a row. "You've one in your eyebrow."

Emily tilted her head up obediently, and with great care Eli leaned close and brushed the piece of fluff away. "All gone." His fingers lingered, then slowly made their way down the side of her face, tracing the curve of her cheekbone. "I fear I must be dreaming, and I will wake up and find you are not mine after all."

"There is nothing to fear," she said quietly. "We are really here, and I will not abandon you as your father did your mother."

Eli's chest tightened at the mention of his greatest fear. To have no hope of Emily had been bearable. But to have her and then lose her…

As if she sensed his worry, Emily spoke again. "You needn't fear that my earlier wishes were for another man. My heart's desire was that Fortune would love me as much as I loved her."

Eli stared for several seconds, uncertain he had heard her correctly. "Your wishes were for—your horse?"

Color flooded Emily's cheeks once more. "It is silly, I know, but Sophia also wanted Fortune to be hers, and Father had said the horse would choose its owner and—"

"Your horse!" Eli threw his head back and laughed, a great rumble from his middle that soon had him near doubling over.

"It isn't *that* amusing." Emily tugged her hand from his and crossed her arms in front of her. "See if I ever tell you anything again." Her toe tapped the ground.

Eli wiped his eyes. "I'm sorry. I just—I knew you loved your horse, but that is *real* love." He paused, considering. "Your first love was a large, hairy beast. And then you voluntarily wed a gentle, bearded giant. I believe I'm seeing the connection now. I am not quite as good as a horse, but perhaps passable." He grinned. "I suppose you'll want me to grow that obnoxious beard again."

"No. I do not."

She met his eye, and Eli could see she was having difficulty containing a smile.

"I find your face quite handsome without it."

His smile widened. "Considering your first love was a horse, I am not at all certain that is a compliment."

They picnicked later that afternoon, enjoying the delicacies provided in the basket from the baron's cook. It was then Eli cautiously presented some of the realities of their new life.

"I have not hired any servants yet, but we have enough presently to hire one or two of your choosing."

"Presently?"

He heard it there, the subtle undertone of worry in her voice. Coming from the life she had—never wanting for anything—the idea of going without must be frightening. It was something he would have to be aware of. He'd started with so little that what he had now seemed more than enough, but she very well might not feel that way.

"With our current income," he explained. "In the future, we may be able to afford more."

She nodded.

"I would suggest perhaps that we first set about employing a cook—unless you are inclined to that task yourself."

"Me—cook?" Her eyes grew wide and terrified. "If we are dependent upon my skills in the kitchen, I fear that in very short order we shall starve."

"We cannot have that, not after I assured your father I could provide for you." Eli smiled to let her know he was neither surprised nor upset. "A cook we shall have, along with a housekeeper once or twice a week. I'm afraid the rest we'll have to manage ourselves."

"I suppose that how properly a bed is made—or not made—will not affect our health too badly." She returned his smile, but it was a little too wide, her effort at trying to be cheerful and positive somewhat obvious.

He tried to see her side of things, to imagine if the tables were turned and he was forced to step into the role of the Earl of Shrewsbury. He would not have liked it one bit, yet he would have done it—for Emily. *If it comes down to it, I shall do it for her.* But it was not his first choice. Aside from the harm it would cause Sherborne and the uproar and scandal that would ripple through the peerage, the life of an earl wasn't a life he wanted to have.

His father had lived in a prison of privilege and luxury his entire life, never free to be with the woman he loved or to have the life he wanted. Eli had seen two different homes, and he knew the kind he wished to have.

The one we will *have.* He would simply have to love Emily so much that it made up for all she'd left behind.

Their talk turned to other things. She shared tales of Sophia and all the mischief she used to cause and the fun they used to have, in spite of their age and personality differences.

Eli told of his father and the winter storm that had brought him to his doorstep.

"He did not know who I was at first, and I was too ill to tell him, to realize that the man I had been searching for was the one who had found me and brought me to his home, literally saving my life. Later my father said it was my mother's presence that guided him to me that night. She appeared in his mind, and it was almost as if they were having a conversation. She told him where to find me."

"And he listened?" Emily leaned forward, again paying rapt attention.

"He did." Noting the late hour, Eli began returning things to the basket. Emily joined him, and their hands bumped as they both reached for the same item.

"I'm sorry." They each spoke at once.

Eli leaned back, allowing her to pick up the bottle and place it in the basket. "You can bump into me any time."

"How is it that all these years we've known each other, I never realized you are such a tease? And I never would have dreamed so many fascinating stories of your past. It is most disturbing to think that I never took the time to learn this of you."

"You could not," Eli said. "Neither could I suggest such a thing. As an employee of your father, it would never have been right."

"Marrying me was right?" Eyes filled with worry lifted to meet his.

You suggested it. He kept the flippant remark to himself.

He had used that once already, and perhaps it had been mildly amusing then. He doubted she would find it so a second time. Besides, she might have been the one to voice the idea out loud, but he was the one who had harbored secret affection for her these many years.

"I can think of nothing more right," he said. "Give me a chance, Emily. Give *us* a chance. We can be happy together. I promise."

Thirteen

They arrived well after midnight. Emily had long since fallen asleep, her head against his shoulder. Eli's mind had been so filled with the day's events and the wonder of having Emily beside him that sleep would not come, likely not anytime tonight.

When the carriage stopped before the house and the step let down and the door opened, he nudged her carefully from his shoulder, propping her head up with his hand as he maneuvered from the seat.

"We're here," he said quietly. "Let me help you out."

"Thank you, Mr. Linfield." She gave him a sleepy smile, and with both hands he reached for her, helping her from the carriage and lifting her in his arms without banging either of their heads on the door frame. *Quite a feat.*

"I can walk," Emily said, even as she turned her face into his chest and her eyes closed again.

He chuckled and felt his heart swell as he looked down on her. "I'm sure you can."

After giving brief instructions to the driver, Eli made his way up the familiar path, trimmed and tidied by himself in the past week, then turned sideways and fitted the key to the gardener's cottage, fetched from his pocket as he'd exited the carriage, into the door.

He paused before opening it and crossing the threshold with his bride in his arms. Some twenty-seven years ago, also at the beginning of summer, his father had carried his mother through this same doorway. What had he been thinking in that moment?

Did he believe the obstacles before them would simply disappear? That their two, vastly different worlds would somehow blend seamlessly? Eli could not deny similar hopes this night. He'd done the difficult thing and had managed—by some miracle of fate—to marry the woman he loved. *But will she stay? Will she be able to live a simple, humble life?*

His father could have if it came down to it. He loved Claymere and had hoped to be able to move his bride from the gardener's residence to the manor here; but if that was not possible, he had found contentment and happiness within the stone walls that made up the cottage.

It was his father's parents who could not abide his choice. They had forced him to choose—not between the life of an earl or his wife, but between his *family* and his wife. He would have been abandoned not only in fortune but in name as well, never welcome evermore in the home of his childhood.

Eli could not fault his father his choice. Neither had his mother faulted him, though she had never stopped loving him—and hoping.

Emily does not face that same ultimatum. Surely that improved their odds.

He pushed the door open and stepped inside. Emily stirred in his arms, snuggling her face deeper into his chest. For a moment he considered spending the rest of the night on the sofa, holding her thus, but he wasn't certain how she would feel upon awaking to that in the morning.

Instead, he continued on through the main room to the first of two bedrooms, the larger one, likely still small by any standard she was used to. He placed Emily carefully on the bed and removed the slippers from her feet, then took a quilt from the end of the bed and tucked her in. Before leaving the room, he watched her a minute, still in awe of his good fortune. *The luckiest man alive.* He bent to kiss her forehead, then walked quietly from the room. Morning would be upon them soon enough, and with it the first tests of their marriage.

Emily awoke feeling positively ravenous. The smell of bacon wafting from some other part of the house set her stomach to growling and made her decision not to linger abed any longer an easy one.

A wardrobe stood on the opposite wall. Intending to dress, Emily arose and walked across the bare floor. The doors stuck a bit at first, but she managed to open them, only to discover the piece entirely empty.

Of course. She felt suddenly foolish. Eli had told her no servants were in place yet, and even when the two they could employ did arrive, it was not as if she would have anyone to tend to her clothing or help her dress.

No matter. She might not know how to cook, but she was certainly capable of dressing herself. Emily turned a slow circle about the room, noting the simple white curtains, blank walls, and Spartan furnishings. There was nothing frilly or fancy about the space. Her mother would have been horrified, but Emily found the plainness did not bother her. The room was clean and had everything she might need, if not want. She had imagined far less when thinking of the sort of home that awaited her.

She spied her trunk near the door and upon opening it discovered her favorite dress at the top. The gossamer fabric and lace edging the pale blue bodice and sleeves seemed a stark contrast to the humble room. How long would such a gown last, if she was to be expected to work in it? A pang of homesickness struck, and Emily longed for the kind, thoughtful maid who had attended her. No doubt she had been thinking of Emily when she packed, guessing, perhaps, that a favorite dress would be much needed today.

Telling herself to cease being so mawkish, Emily replaced yesterday's white gown, crumpled from travel and sleep, with the blue dress.

Once dressed, she realized she could not wash—there was no water in the basin, and no rope to pull or servant to summon to bring any. Instead, she sat at the small dressing table and decided she must do something about her hair. The floral circlet her sister had arranged so carefully was now a matted mess of wilted blooms. Emily removed the pins holding it in place and tore it from her hair, inadvertently pulling several strands loose from their arrangement at the same time. The resulting style was a sagging chignon with long, wild spikes spiraling out in every direction.

"Like Medusa," she muttered crossly, then took the remaining pins from her hair, until the tangled mass descended well past her shoulders.

Leaving the dressing table, Emily returned to her trunk to locate her brush. After digging through the entire contents, she gave up finding it without removing everything. She gathered an armful of clothing, carried it to the unmade bed, and tossed the load upon it. This she searched through and, not finding the brush, repeated the process again until her trunk was emptied and the bed piled high with shoes, gowns, shawls, bonnets, petticoats, and chemises all strewn about wildly, as if an animal or a very small child had been amongst them.

And still no brush.

Her stomach growling with hunger, Emily returned to the dressing table and used her fingers to comb through her tangles as best she could. Gathering her hair was another matter, one she found exceedingly difficult without a brush. Three times she tried pulling the masses back and twisting them into a simple knot, only to have more pieces escape than stay.

Her arms ached and drooped. On her fourth attempt she stabbed the back of her head with a pin, cried out, let go of her half-done hair, and burst into tears.

It was thus that Eli found her, head buried in her arms, sobbing at the dressing table.

"Forgive me entering," he said. "I knocked, and there was no answer, but I could hear you were in distress."

Emily cried louder, embarrassed, and angry with herself at her inability to do such a simple task. She felt frightened at being so far from home, pledged to a life with a man she knew so little of and who could not give her the things she was used to.

There it was again. That snobbishness she so loathed in others. She did not wish to be notoriously picksome as her mother, but feared she was. *I am just as bad. I am spoiled and utterly wretched.*

"What is it, Emily? What is so terrible this morning? I haven't shaved yet, if it will make you feel any better. Perhaps I look a little more like my old, hairy self."

She raised her head to look at him through the glass but saw only her own, splotchy face, puffy eyes, and disastrous hair. "*I* do not look like myself," she cried, then buried her head again. "Please go away, Mr. Linfield."

"Eli," he corrected. "Please," he added more kindly. "And that is the one thing I will not do. I will not go away and leave you in distress. Besides, our breakfast is growing cold. So please tell me what is troubling you and let me do what I can to help, so we can begin our day together."

"You can't help." She shook her head and did not look up.

"You don't know that unless you ask." He placed a gentle hand upon her shoulder. It was warm and comforting and somehow made her feel the tiniest bit better. This was Mr. Linfield, the groomsman. He would not judge her for how she looked. Yet, she found that she cared a great deal about how he saw her. She wanted to be beautiful for him. Beautiful and capable. *I don't want to let him down.*

Swallowing her pride—if she'd any left—and mustering her courage, Emily lifted her head and met his gaze in the mirror. "I am pathetic," she whispered. "I cannot even arrange my own hair." She swallowed, awaiting his disappointment or perhaps laughter.

"I am quite certain you can," he said easily. "It will take some practice, is all. Would you like me to help you today—not that I'll be much better at it. But perhaps, between the two of us..."

She nodded, relieved at his answer and grateful he had not judged her, not aloud at least.

"All right." He took a deep breath and looked down on her head, as if preparing for an invasion of some sort. "Hand me your brush. You must tell me if I am not using it correctly or hurting you. After all, I've only experience with horses."

"I can't *find* my brush." Her voice sounded small and forlorn, as if she was five years old instead of a grown woman. *I have been acting like I am five.* For the moment, with her emotions so on edge, she couldn't seem to help herself. Emily turned in the chair and inclined her head toward the mess of clothing and shoes haphazardly strewn across the bed. "I've made a mull of everything."

"Not everything." Eli's brows arched as he looked at the pile. "Though near everything does seem to be on your bed. No wonder your trunk was so heavy. I did not realize it held so much. Was the brush not in your valise either?"

Emily brought a hand to her mouth and then her head as she bent forward, feeling like an even bigger fool. "I forgot about the valise," she admitted.

"I set it right here last night, on the floor beside the bed." Eli reached for it, just an arm's length away. "I wanted you to see it as soon as you arose, guessing that whatever you might need most was inside." He held it out to her.

"That was a good guess." Emily took the bag, opened it, and saw her brush at once. "I'm so embarrassed. So sorry." She met his eyes once more, apology in hers.

"Don't be. You are in a new circumstance, and that will take some getting used to." He held his hand out for the brush. "May I?"

Though she felt perfectly capable of taming her hair now that she had a brush, she handed it to him.

Eli began at the back of her head, starting at the top and gently pulling the brush down through her hair. After a minute of watching him in the mirror, Emily allowed her eyes to close and her shoulders to relax. He was careful, as he'd always been. Gentle. *Tender.* She no longer felt embarrassed that she had been unable to find her brush; she felt grateful. Because his touch was... *heaven.*

He continued several minutes, during which she felt first her worries and then her defenses melting away as some other foreign and delicious sensations moved in to take their place.

"What do you think?" Eli ceased brushing, and Emily held back a sigh of disappointment.

"I think I shall require your help every day." *Not having a lady's maid may have its advantages.*

He laughed. "You haven't even looked yet. Open your eyes."

She did and saw that he had indeed tamed her tangled mass. It fell sleek and shiny, down her back and over her shoulders.

"I much prefer brushing your hair to brushing Fortune's," he said jovially.

"Thank you—I think?" She felt grateful the reflection in the mirror now looked more like her old self. "I suppose I should put it up."

"Only if you want to," Eli said. "There is no one here to judge you for it either way."

"In that case, I shall leave my hair down for now. I should like to investigate this breakfast you mentioned."

"Right this way." He set the brush on the table, then pulled her chair out for her.

Emily stood and turned, and found her nose nearly touching his chest. Her heartbeat quickened, and the same giddiness she'd felt at their wedding returned. She lifted her head to look at him.

"Thank you for trusting me," he said. "I know this—" he indicated the sparse room, "—is different from what you are accustomed to, but if you will be patient with me, and yourself, I believe you can be happy here."

"I am already." It was true. Had she not spent yesterday laughing and talking more comfortably than she ever had with anyone? When he drew near, did Eli not make her heart pound with excitement? Was he not every bit as kind and gentle as she had always known him to be? Pieces of her fear slipped away at these realizations and the comfort that *he* would be patient with her. So long as she kept trying, Eli would not give up on her.

These thoughts struck her core, and with them came the

understanding that her greatest fear was not about living with less or having to learn to do things for herself, or what the neighbors might think. It was about failing. She was afraid she would fail at this endeavor, at her marriage to Eli, and it was that possibility she found terrifying.

Because I care for him a great deal already. From those summers as children when they had waved to one another, to the years she had known him while he worked for her father, Emily had admired Eli from afar, and she had secretly wished for a man like him to come into her life. *Not a man* like *him. I was waiting for* him. *For Eli.* Their marriage had not been mere happenstance. "I did not suggest it randomly," she murmured, shocked at this discovery.

"What was not random?" Eli's brow wrinkled, anxious concern in his gaze.

"I—" It was one thing to admit her feelings to herself, but what would he think to know she had—perhaps subconsciously—wanted to marry him? And, when the opportunity came to have him, she had leapt. *Be honest. You must tell him.*

"The night in the stables, I didn't just come to check on Fortune, I came to talk with you. I was troubled and knew you would listen to my concerns about marrying Lord Rowley. And later, when I suggested *we* marry, it was not just to salvage my reputation or that I wished to be free of the earl. It was because—I *wanted* to marry you."

"As I wanted to marry you," Eli said kindly, still with that look of concern in his eyes. "You're a little pale. Are you feeling well?" He held onto her arm, as if worried she might faint. "Perhaps we should go into breakfast. Once you've eaten you may feel better."

"I feel perfectly marvelous." If she was a little lightheaded… well, that was his fault for standing so near to her. Since his hand had first found hers during the wedding ceremony yesterday, she had not seemed able to control her body's reactions to him. Not that she wanted to. This kind of lightheadedness she found rather enjoyable.

Chunks of her fear were shattering all around them now, breaking into pieces, turning into dust. She wasn't afraid of him or his touch; she enjoyed it. With Eli she could speak her mind. She could be herself. It had always been that way. *It was always* him.

Acknowledging this, and finally being allowed to let those feelings, her heart's desire, surface sent her spirits soaring. It was all she could do not to behave like Sophia and run and jump on the bed, then fly about the room. For the first time that Emily could remember, she was not afraid of anything. She smiled up at him, wondering at this miracle and the joy and freedom in her pounding heart. "I think I am in love with you."

He searched her eyes, the initial concern in his changing to shock, then disbelief, and then, at last, cautious hope. His lips rose slowly as his hands came up to touch her face. "I *know* I am in love with you, Emily. For me there has never been another." He bent his head to hers, and their lips touched briefly, then he crushed her to him in a not-so-gentle hug.

Fourteen

"Chocolate?" Emily's eyes lit up, and she smiled before tipping the cup to her lips a second time.

"I promised that you would be well taken care of," Eli said, pleased to have surprised her. "I believe that includes indulging in a daily cup of chocolate as part of your morning routine."

"You knew?" There was no accusation in her voice, only happy astonishment.

"I am a spy, remember?"

She laughed. "I believe you must be."

The morning had not quite gone as he had envisioned, but he hoped—after taming her hair and hearing her sudden, unexpected confession that she cared for him—that they were back on track. He wasn't certain what to make of his wife's wildly swinging emotions thus far, but he supposed they were warranted, given the extreme changes to her life.

He wanted to believe that she did love him—a little, at least. But it was too soon for that. She had allowed him to kiss her, though, and that fleeting second, followed by the longer seconds when he had held her tightly to him, had been the best of his life.

The rest of their breakfast was perhaps not as fine as she

was used to, but it was all he could manage until they hired someone to cook. When Emily discovered it was he who had prepared everything, she praised every bite.

"You were here last week, getting all of this ready?"

"Well, not the food," he said. "Would have been a bit moldy by now, don't you think?" He loved teasing her. "But I did arrange for the delivery of some basic items, and I cleaned and aired the cottage. Would you like to see the rest of it?"

"Oh, yes." She dabbed the side of her mouth with her napkin, then placed it upon the small, round table that filled a good portion of the tiny kitchen.

Eli pulled out her chair for her and showed her around the rest of the cottage—all two rooms of it. "This is the sitting room." He led her to the main, rectangular room at the front of the house. A large stone fireplace and shelves covered one wall, with a well-worn sofa, a few chairs, and a rug his mother had made finishing out the room. It was not large by any means, but room enough for the two of them—and any children that came along eventually.

"It's so cozy," Emily exclaimed. "I can imagine curling up in here before the fire with a good book. I think this shall be my favorite room."

He hoped not, but did not voice that thought just yet. He showed her the other bedroom next. "This is my room, same as it was when I was a child."

Emily peered in at the room smaller than her own, and he wondered what she was thinking. Feeling sorry for him? Wondering how he survived with so few material possessions?

"How marvelous that it is so close to your mother's room. She must have always come when you had nightmares."

Again, her reaction surprised him. Eli could not remember ever calling for his mother at night, but he sensed a topic for exploration. "Did you have many nightmares as a child?"

Emily nodded. "My parents could never hear my cries. Our rooms were too distant from one another. It was always a nanny who came—if anyone."

"Well, if you have a nightmare now, I shall hear you, and I shall come at once," he promised.

Her smile seemed somehow wistful. "Thank you, Eli." She glanced down the portrait-less hall. "I think I shall enjoy it here very much."

Chapter Fifteen

Emily bent to inhale the sweet scent of a rose. "I have found a new love, aside from horses."

"Of course you have—me." Eli looked up long enough to wink at her, then returned to his work, clearing underbrush and spreading manure beneath the roses along the north walk.

"Well, yes, there is that—I mean you," Emily said. "But I also meant these flowers and gardening. I've never seen such beautiful grounds in all my life."

"Wait until we have returned them to their former glory." He wondered, as he had a dozen times in the first two weeks of their marriage, when and if her feelings for him might surface again. They had not, since that first morning here, and he fervently wished they would, along with an opportunity to kiss her again.

"It would seem the restoring might be more quickly accomplished if you allowed me to help." She frowned at him.

"Perhaps sometime," he said, giving her the same vague answer he had before. "I don't want to overwhelm you with all that needs to be done around here." He had already shown her the field that was theirs, and they had discussed at length what might do well planted there. They had talked about the possibility of selling some of their garden flowers to local estates, as well as taking the apples from their small orchard to market. Though the parcel of land that went with the cottage was not large, Eli believed that, if tended carefully, it could turn a profit. Enough, with his small income, to keep them at least as comfortable as they were now.

"Stop working a minute and take a drink." Emily appeared at his side, a dipper in her hand, and the bucket he had felt too heavy for her to carry.

He accepted the dipper, gulping the water too quickly, so that some trickled down the sides of his mouth. Emily touched one of the squiggles of water making its way down his chin. "What am I to do with you, Mr. Linfield?"

"What do you *want* to do with me?" he asked, brows rising up and down as he flirted shamelessly.

She laughed. "Everything. But you won't let me. I *can* work, if you'll only teach me how. I know I was horrid that first day, with my missing brush and my clothes thrown about, but have you seen my room since? And do I not look presentable?" She turned her head, showing off the simple knot at the back of her head.

"You look more than presentable," he said, eyeing her bare neck. He took another drink to cool himself, then licked his lips, wishing he might lick hers instead. "And I have seen your room. That you managed to contain all your numerous articles of clothes within that one, narrow wardrobe is a feat indeed." He had stood in her doorway for a moment every night, checking to see that she was well and that nothing troubled her. Though it was wrong, he almost wished she'd have a nightmare so he would have an excuse to come into her room and comfort her in bed. *Patience,* he reminded himself. *All in good time.* The sweet torture of wanting her was not entirely unpleasant.

"I am glad one of us is looking well." Emily's nose wrinkled as she stared at him. "But you, good sir, are not. You've more dirt on you than the plants you've been digging about. I believe you shall require a bath before dinner. I shall help."

A surge of cool well water caught him square in the chest and across his face. He sputtered and blinked as the bucket clattered to the ground and Emily ran away shrieking. Feeling as shocked as he had the morning she'd told him she thought she loved him, Eli started after her, tossing the dipper aside.

He caught her easily, her slippers being no match for his boots and the longer strides he could take on the cobbled path. He grasped her from behind, lifted her around her middle, and swung her once around.

"Eli," she shrieked. "What will the neighbors think?"

He laughed. "We have no neighbors, remember? Claymere has not been inhabited for many years, and I doubt it will be for some time to come." He set her down and turned her in his arms to face him. "Thanks to you, milady, I am quite wet. And we are quite alone."

They had been behaving thus the past several days, dancing around one another, hinting at things to come, and at their feelings for one another, sometimes getting close to crossing that line into intimacy, but always she had withdrawn before he might explore those avenues.

No more. "Do you realize that tomorrow we have been married for two weeks?"

"The best weeks of my life." She placed one hand on his shirt sleeve and the other on his soaked shirt front, over his rapidly beating heart.

"Do you mean that?"

She nodded vigorously. "I do. I feel—different here. Free. Happy. Accepted."

Loved? "Excellent. All that chocolate is working."

She laughed, a sound he heard frequently and never tired of. "It is."

"And yet… you repay me with a bucket of water to the face."

"It was for your own good. You were beginning to smell like the manure you spread."

"I shall keep that in mind for future reference." He would. He would bathe every night if that was what it took to be close to her.

"May I ask how *your* first weeks of marriage have been?" Her eyes flickered to his, and he glimpsed the vulnerability he had seen before. He understood it better now. *She is worried about pleasing me.*

"Aside from the forced bathing, it has been—wanting." Eli took a chance, hoping his gamble was not too great.

Hurt widened and filled her eyes. "How—"

He could not bear her stricken expression and rushed to explain. "I want more time with you. The days are not long enough. I want more laughter, more time before the fire at night reading stories, more hours to ride and walk and dine together. More kisses. I want to hold you close as you sleep and see your face first thing when I awake."

"Oh."

He watched her swallow and waited for the blush he was sure to follow. It didn't.

Instead her hands fidgeted on his shirt. "I have been wanting those things, too. Only I did not know if it was proper for a wife to feel that way."

She too… His heart pounded beneath his wet shirt. "We do not concern ourselves with what is proper in this household. We concern ourselves with what is *right.* Do you feel it is right for a husband to want, very badly, to kiss his wife?"

She nodded.

"I, likewise, feel it absolutely correct for a wife to want to kiss her husband. I feel I have let you down." Eli hung his head as if shamed. "I promised you would want for nothing, and here you are, practically starving for affection. We shall have to remedy the situation at once."

Instead of laughing at his silliness, her look turned more serious. "Please, Eli," she whispered. "Don't tease about this. Of all the things I fear I shall make a mull of, it is this. What it is between us is most of all what I am frightened of—of losing."

"What is between us is only going to grow." He took her face in his hands as he had that morning in her room, and bent to kiss her. This time his lips lingered, exploring the softness and shape of hers and feeling his heart soar when she kissed him back.

Slowly, tentatively, her hands slid up his arm and chest to wrap around the base of his neck. Eli felt himself pulled closer, his wet shirt pressed against her bodice. Their kiss grew fiercer, full of need and desire and passion. The wick had finally caught fire.

But he intended it to be a slow burn. Like a precious candle, he intended to savor every drip of their ardor and stretch out the moments before them. They were in no hurry. They belonged to one another and had a lifetime together to look forward to.

With a last, playful nibble to Emily's bottom lip, he pulled back a little, allowing them to catch their breaths and him to regain his sanity. *Restraint.* If he was not careful he might make love to her right here amongst the roses, and that was no way to treat his wife—at least at first.

"You realize we are kissing one another out in the open, in the middle of the garden, in the daylight hours."

"We *were* kissing," Emily corrected. "*You* stopped." The pout she gave him could only have been learned from her sister.

"I need a bath, remember?" Eli said. "And we need to pay the cook. It is Friday. She will not come tomorrow."

"Yes. Of course. You bathe. I'll pay Mrs. Judd. I'll prepare the table for dinner. I'll—" Emily pulled him close once more, as their mouths found one another again.

"You are not as shy as I had supposed," Eli said, breathing heavily when at last they broke apart again.

"Neither are you as gentle as I had believed."

I will be.

They smiled at one another, both unwilling to move from their embrace until Eli finally, regretfully stepped back. "A half hour," he promised. "I'll bathe at the pond."

"I'll pay Mrs. Judd and prepare the table."

He wished she wouldn't. He wasn't hungering for food at the moment. "I love you, Emily."

She smiled in return. "Perhaps almost as much as I love you."

Sixteen

Emily, wearing a long white apron over her pastel gown, hummed to herself as she laid out the plates and silverware. Noting that the cloth covering the table was fraying, she decided she would begin embroidering a new one. She adored the cottage as it was, but had begun to see small improvements she might make here or there, which would make it even cozier.

When she had finished the tasks indoors and Eli still had not returned, she left the kitchen and walked along the tidy rows of the vegetable garden, stooping now and again to snap beans from the vine. It was one of the few outdoor tasks Eli had allowed her to help with thus far.

When her apron pockets were full, she wandered from the garden, past the roses he had tended earlier, and the bucket and dipper still lying on the ground where they had fallen. Emily touched her lips, remembering Eli's kisses and yearning for another. Any minute now he should be coming up the path; she decided to walk toward the pond and meet him along the way.

Her light steps had not carried her far when voices—Eli's and one other—stopped her. Emily paused, undecided if she should return or continue on.

"You know this is not why I married her."

Eli's words persuaded her to the latter.

"Nevertheless, Claymere is yours—if not by rights of our wager, by right as the firstborn and legitimate heir."

Lord Rowley? Wager? Emily left the path to hide behind a tree where she might listen but not be seen.

"My mind has not changed," Eli said. "I want no part of the earldom. I wish to be left in peace with my wife."

"You call this peace?" Lord Rowley sounded incredulous. "I saw you earlier—laboring in the dirt then getting a face full of water."

"Ah, but did you see what followed? I assure you Emily's warm affection counteracted any ill effect of the cold water. And laboring on her behalf, for her support, does not seem a labor at all."

She heard the smile in Eli's voice and hoped Lord Rowley had not witnessed their kissing by the roses, though could not exactly fault him for spying when she was doing the same.

Eli continued. "There is a great satisfaction to be found in living this way, truly earning one's bread or growing the food brought to one's table."

Fingers curling around the beans in her pocket, Emily silently agreed. After only a short while here she was beginning to understand what he meant. *To have purpose, to be useful... To be thankful for what one has.*

"Madness," Lord Rowley muttered. "As would be your refusal of Claymere. I intended to hold you to your bargain and would have made you work without wages the ten years. Take now what is yours."

Emily flattened herself against the tree as they passed. *Ten years.* Was that the new position Eli had alluded to before it was decided they would marry?

"Had you lost our wager," Lord Rowley suggested, "I doubt you would find digging in the dirt as satisfying."

"I would not," Eli agreed soberly.

Peeking from behind the trunk, she saw that he walked with his hands clasped behind his back, as if he did not wish any chance of receiving the scroll Lord Rowley held clutched in his fist. Eli's hair was still wet from the pond, and he had changed from the clothes he wore earlier.

"I would have been pleased to work at Claymere—under any circumstance—but I would have mourned your victory and my loss greatly. I love Emily. Already she has brought more joy to my life than I had imagined possible."

Not wishing to diminish that joy by eavesdropping further, Emily stepped out from her hiding place.

"I wish you the same happiness with Lady Grayson," Eli said.

"Then I beg you to accept this deed." Lord Rowley stopped walking and extended his hand with the papers. "You are aware of my selfish nature. On my own I should have been extremely reluctant to part with this property. Sophia insists I must, or she will withdraw from our agreement—a most awkward situation as the banns have been posted two weeks already. If nothing else, her mother will have my head if the wedding is off."

"Why banns? I thought you'd obtained a license." Eli stopped as well, turning toward Lord Rowley and catching sight of Emily hurrying to catch up with them.

"Yes, well… I'd hoped to make better use of the £5 Sophia gave to purchase the license. I gambled it—and lost. Seems to be rather the way of my luck lately." Lord Rowley gave a short cough. "Ah, here is your lovely wife now."

"Lord Rowley." Emily curtsied and allowed him to take her hand and kiss it, feeling somewhat awkward as only a month earlier he had been courting her.

His eyes lingered on them as she stepped closer to Eli and

he put his arm around her. "Marriage suits you both, it seems. You are looking very well, Lady Rowley."

"Thank you." She found she did not care for that title anymore than Eli would likely enjoy being called the earl. "I regret that I cannot say the same of you." Lord Rowley's trousers and boots were dusty, his face drawn, eyes bloodshot. "Were your travels overly tiresome?" Selfishly she hoped he would not ask to stay with them tonight.

Lord Rowley's mouth turned up curiously. "I do not believe I have ever heard you speak your mind like that. I must say it is a vast improvement over your previous reserve. And yes, my travel was tiresome. I came by horse, as quickly as I might. Perhaps you can talk some sense into your husband. If I cannot persuade him to my way of thinking, I am in danger of losing your sister, and I have grown to care for her a great deal."

"Her? Or her money?" Emily asked, concerned as she had been before, for Sophia.

"Both, if I am being honest. Though I do not believe I shall have much control over the latter. Sophia is rather put out with my gambling at present. I shall have to toe the mark if I am to win her affection as it appears Eli has so readily won yours."

Lord Rowley held out the scroll. "I have here the deed to all of Claymere. It is Eli's for the taking."

"By right of birth—and wager," Emily added, her eyes shifting from one man to another. "You made a bet who would be the one to marry me?"

"When I was twelve, Sherborne ten." Eli's hand tightened at her waist as if he was afraid she might flee. "I was lovestruck—even then—and foolishly let my desire to make you mine be known."

"I forced him to the wager, believing it impossible that he

could win," Lord Rowley admitted. "Eli was to have all of Claymere if he married you. If he did not, if he lost, he was to work for me, ten years without wage."

"My time and labor was the only thing of value I had to offer," Eli said quietly. "And it had to be a great deal of both, if Sherborne was to risk Claymere."

Emily's lips pressed into a thin line until she remembered the way her mother appeared when wearing such an expression.

"But I don't want Claymere anymore." Eli turned her toward him, taking both of her hands in his. "I was a boy then, one who had just found his father only to learn that he had another son—a brother I could not claim—and that boy was to have it all. Sherborne asked what I wished if I won, and I named the place that had been dear to my parents." Eli caught her eyes, his own pleading. "All I really wanted was what they had shared together—a tremendous love, to be happy here and never alone. I have found that in you."

"Yet you would have left Shrewsbury, would have allowed me to marry another, without even attempting to win my hand? When all you had to do to ask for it yourself was to reveal your true identity?" Emily's head was spinning, questions, accusation, and hurt firing through her mind at rapid speed.

Eli's face crumpled with distress. "Until that night in the stable, I believed I had no hope of winning your hand *or* heart. I thought you content being courted by Sherborne, and I knew such pleased your father—and that you would wish to please him. As soon as I realized you were not happy, I did what I must to marry you. Have you any idea how difficult it was for me to go before the Archbishop? I didn't want what came with my parentage. I'd had the education I yearned for years before, and had known since then—after seeing the expectations and restrictions placed upon those who are titled—that I did not wish for that life."

"Yet you risked that, to be with her?" Lord Rowley sounded perplexed.

"I would risk far more," Eli said. "I will be the earl if that is what you wish, Emily."

Both men stared at her, and she read equal trepidation in their expressions. Lord Rowley did not wish to lose his privileged life, while Eli did not wish to take it upon him.

She was still not pleased at having been the subject of their wager. But it had been so long ago. *Eli has cared for me for so long. He truly did wish to marry me.* She had not quite believed that until now, thinking he had only gone along with her proposal that fateful night, out of the goodness of his heart.

His love for her was not new, as was hers for him, but had been growing these many years. Thinking back on those years now, and their many interactions, she felt a sort of dizzy panic. What if she had not come to the stable that night? What if Sophia had not come as well and brought Lord Rowley with her?

What if I had missed the opportunity to be Eli's wife? Knowing this and feeling as she did for him, she could not ask him to assume a position he did not want. She would not force the life of an earl upon him. Yet… could not Claymere still be his?

Tugging her hand free of Eli's, Emily turned slightly toward Lord Rowley and took the scroll from him. Facing Eli once more she placed it in his hand.

"Your father wanted this. He wished to live at Claymere with your mother—wherever they pleased upon the estate. We shall do that for them, but no more. Lord Rowley will continue on as the earl."

Seventeen

Eli stared at the scroll in his hand then slowly allowed his fingers to close around it. *Claymere.* He thought not of the grand house at the top of the hill, but the whole of the glorious gardens, the fields that produced already, the tenants who lived upon the land. Though long neglected, Eli knew that, if managed correctly, the estate could turn a handsome profit. He and Emily would never want for anything.

We do not want for anything now. He pulled his gaze from the papers to his wife, her eyes anxious as she looked at him.

"Eli?"

Just hearing her say his name was heaven. He leaned forward and kissed her softly, answering the question in her voice with a token of love followed by his own smile.

Eli turned to Sherborne. "Thank you—brother."

Sherborne's reaction appeared mixed. For a fleeting second a pout appeared, as if he was offended, but then the corners of his mouth turned up.

"I should have known long ago that you were my brother. You were always a pain."

"Likewise." Grinning, Eli held his hand out. Sherborne took it at once in a tight clasp of brotherhood, and Eli felt a new kind of joy and hope. In the future, family might come to mean more than Emily and their children. Perhaps those children would grow up having an aunt and uncle and cousins.

As if she had read his mind, Emily spoke. "You must come visit us here, and bring Sophia."

"And we request your presence at our wedding, Saturday next," Sherborne said. "Providing I can keep myself out of trouble between now and then."

Eli caught Emily's eye. "A man can do a lot of things for love."

Moonlight shone through the bedroom window and the open curtains flapped gently in the breeze as Eli looked down on his wife. With care he brushed the strands of hair from her face then leaned over and whispered, "Emily."

She stirred at once, responding to him in sleep much as she had when awake. He marveled to think of it, how in the two weeks of their marriage she had been both trusting of him and giving of herself, stepping willingly into this new life. She was everything he had imagined her to be and more.

Her hand came up to touch his cheek. "Are you having a nightmare?"

His heart squeezed then expanded at her concern, and he recognized the feeling. His love for her had grown a little more.

"Quite the opposite." He took Emily's hand from his face and pressed his lips to her wrist then proceeded to work his kisses up her arm to the bend of her elbow.

She giggled. "Oh. I see."

"Not yet, you haven't." He flung the covers away from both of them then jumped from the bed and held a hand out to her. "Come on."

"Where are we going?" She rose, and he helped her into the same dressing gown she'd worn that night in the stables. It seemed very fitting to him that she should be wearing the same garment tonight that she had when hope of a future with her had first presented itself.

"To see Claymere. It is most glorious in full moonlight."

He pulled her from the room and they left the cottage, starting up the same path they'd traversed a few times already today. A short ways down it they encountered the dipper and pail still on the ground where they had been tossed aside. Eli thought he might leave them there permanently, as a reminder of a particularly sweet memory.

They left the roses and the confines of the property that adjoined the gardener's cottage and wandered up the hill toward Claymere Manor. Though steps carved into the hillside made the climbing easier, it was still steep, and by the time they reached the top Emily was breathing heavily.

"All right?" he asked, stopping so she might catch her breath.

She nodded. Her face was flushed, but they'd just a little farther to go, so he continued on, following an overgrown pathway until they reached a terrace garden.

"This is as far as we'll go," Eli said as Emily collapsed on a bench. From this vantage point, about two-thirds of the distance to the manor, they could see in all directions. Behind them, at the top of another, smaller hill, overlooking all, stood the house, a grand building with a pillared front and circular drive. Eli had pointed out the front of it to her before, from the road below, which had a more gradual slope on which teams and carriages might travel.

"We've come up the foot path, the back way." He sat beside her.

"The way your father snuck down to see your mother?" Emily asked as she snuggled into the crook of his arm.

"Yes. How did you know?"

"It would take true love to traverse those steps often."

He laughed, pulled her closer, and kissed the top of her head. "No sneaking for us."

Eli shifted his gaze down the hill, to the stone cottage, so covered with ivy it blended almost seamlessly into the surrounding garden. "The cottage will always be ours—whether we live there or not. We'll keep it as our special place, somewhere we can escape to whenever we wish."

"I like that idea." Emily sat up and turned to him. "We don't have to live in the manor, Eli. It just—seemed right that you should have all this. It was your parents' place and their dream."

"I am no longer concerned with their dream, but mine, right here." He took Emily's face in his hands and kissed her, long and slow. Moonlight spilled over the garden, seeming to rest just over them, over her, illuminating all that was good and beautiful within.

"I think," he said, quite seriously, "that I would wager my entire life to have had this night with you."

"Fortunately." She kissed him once more. "You don't have to."

Michele Paige Holmes spent her childhood and youth in Arizona and northern California, often curled up with a good book instead of out enjoying the sunshine. She graduated from Brigham Young University with a degree in elementary education and found it an excellent major with which to indulge her love of children's literature.

Her first novel, *Counting Stars*, won the 2007 Whitney Award for Best Romance. Its companion novel, a romantic suspense titled *All the Stars in Heaven*, was a Whitney Award finalist, as was her first historical romance, *Captive Heart*. *My Lucky Stars* completed the Stars series.

In 2014 Michele launched the Hearthfire Historical Romance line, with the debut title, *Saving Grace*. *Loving Helen* is the companion novel, with a third, *Marrying Christopher*, followed by the companion novella *Twelve Days in December*.

When not reading or writing romance, Michele is busy with her full-time job as a wife and mother. She and her husband live in Utah with their five high-maintenance children, and a Shitzu that resembles a teddy bear, in a house with a wonderful view of the mountains.

You can find Michele on the web:
MichelePaigeHolmes.com
Facebook: Michele Holmes
Twitter: @MichelePHolmes

www.ingramcontent.com/pod-product-compliance
Lightning Source LLC
LaVergne TN
LVHW021756060526
838201LV00058B/3116